SUSAN EDMONSTONE FERRIER

(1782-1854) was born in Edinburgh, the youngest of the ten children of a respectable Clerk of Sessions, James Ferrier. The family lived at Lady Stair's Close, moving in 1784 to George Street, and Susan attended James Stalker's Academy there, where Henry Brougham was also a pupil. Her father was a close friend of the Duke of Argyll and Susan accompanied him on visits to Inverary and Rosneath, becoming a good friend of the Duke's niece, Charlotte Clavering. They corresponded frequently and developed the idea of collaborating on a novel. But Charlotte favoured a Gothic style which Susan resisted and so she contributed to only a very early part of the work which was to become *Marriage*.

After her mother's death in 1797 Susan, who remained the only unmarried daughter, kept house for her father, dividing her time between George Street and East Morningside House, their summer residence. She read to her father the novel she was working on, initially hiding its authorship from him. Written in 1810 and published anonymously eight years later, *Marriage* attracted a wide readership, not least because its characters were based on real people. Her second novel *The Inheritance* followed in 1824. Sir Walter Scott, a friend of the family, was a great admirer of Susan Ferrier, seeing her work as a continuation of the Scottish tradition he established in his *Waverley* novels. He helped her to change publisher for her third novel *Destiny* (1831) which she dedicated to him. Susan Ferrier was by now earning a substantial amount from her writing, but her eyesight was failing and she disliked the publicity and notoriety which accompanied publication. In addition, her growing interest in religion culminated in her conversion to Evangelicalism and she published no further novels. Susan Ferrier's only other works were narratives of visits to Ashestiel and Abbotsford, where she visited Scott during his last illness. After joining the Free Church she retired completely from the literary scene, devoting her time to charity, temperance, missions and the abolition of slavery.

Susan Ferrier's complete works were published posthumously in 1892 and her letters in 1898, testifying to the sharp eye and wry wit so evident in her novels. Admirers of her work included Joanna Baillie, Sydney Smith, Macaulay, Sir James Mackintosh, Curran and Mrs Piozzi.

MARRIAGE

SUSAN FERRIER

With a New Introduction by
ROSEMARY ASHTON

PENGUIN BOOKS – VIRAGO PRESS

PENGUIN BOOKS
Viking Penguin Inc., 40 West 23rd Street,
New York, New York 10010, U.S.A.
Penguin Books Ltd, Harmondsworth,
Middlesex, England
Penguin Books Australia Ltd, Ringwood,
Victoria, Australia
Penguin Books Canada Limited, 2801 John Street,
Markham, Ontario, Canada L3R 1B4
Penguin Books (N.Z.) Ltd, 182-190 Wairau Road,
Auckland 10, New Zealand

First published in Great Britain by Wm. Blackwood 1818
First published in the United States of America by
A. T. Goodrich & Co. 1818

This edition first published in Great Britain by
Virago Press Limited 1986
Published in Penguin Books 1986

Introduction copyright © Rosemary Ashton, 1986
All rights reserved

Printed in Finland by
Werner Söderström, a member of Finnprint

INTRODUCTION

Many a nineteenth-century novel, from those of Maria
Edgeworth and Jane Austen at the beginning of the century
to those of George Eliot and Meredith towards the end of it,
could have been entitled "Marriage". The relations
between men and women, with all the rites of preparation,
courtship, the wedding ceremony, and, increasingly, the
married state itself, were almost invariably the stuff of the
novel, or romance, as the genre was also called at the
beginning of the period. In fact, the novel had evolved
during the eighteenth century as an extension of the
medieval "romance", which was typically a story of
adventure and chivalry. But, except in the Gothic novels of
the late eighteenth century, with their gloomy and sublime
landscapes, medieval castles, gory plots and exploitation of
the supernatural, the new genre was a far more
sophisticated thing than its ancestor. For one thing, it
aspired to realism, both historical and psychological. For
another, its practitioners usually professed a desire to
instruct their readers as well as to entertain them. The most
common theme was the education of the individual, most
often a girl, for adult life. As most girls could expect to find
scope for adult experience only in marriage, their education
was largely, in novels as in life, a preparation for that
blessed state.

The novel which actually was entitled *Marriage* was the
first of three to be written by an Edinburgh woman in her
thirties, Susan Ferrier. It began as a collaborative venture
with Charlotte Clavering, niece of the Duke of Argyll, in
1809 or 1810, but Susan Ferrier persevered alone after
Charlotte dropped out and published the work,
anonymously, in 1818. Letters between the two friends
show that Charlotte was an adherent of the Gothic school;
her idea was to have plenty of murder, mystery and suicide.
But the robust Miss Ferrier scotched the plan as early as

February 1810, when she wrote, "Now, I'll groan for you till the very blood shall curdle in my veins, or I'll shriek and stare till my own eyes start out of their sockets with surprise—but as to writing with you, in truth it would be as easy to compound a new element out of fire and water, as that we two should jointly write a book!" In short, "I *will not* enter into any of your raw head and bloody bones schemes." And so Charlotte bowed out, leaving marks of her co-authorship only in the lifeless, unconvincing, conventional but mercifully short "History of Mrs Douglas" early in the book.

If Susan Ferrier was adamant that there should be no ghosts and no suicides, she was less sure about what her novel should include. On the one hand, she expressed her aversion to the overt moralising of Maria Edgeworth in her "Fashionable Tales". "It is high time all *good ladies* and *grateful little girls* should be returned to their gilt boards," she declared in 1809. And on reading the same author's novel *Patronage* (1814), Susan thought it "the greatest lump of cold Lead I ever attempted to swallow". Works of fiction, she was sure, should amuse rather than instruct, and though Maria Edgeworth offered "Truth, Nature, Life, and Sense" in abundance, she lacked "imagination, taste, wit, or sensibility". On the other hand, when Susan read Charlotte's outlandish suggestions for their joint venture, her chief objection was that Charlotte's plot lacked "a *moral*". "The only good purpose of a book is to inculcate morality, and convey some lesson of instruction as well as delight." The apprentice authoress was finding out how difficult it was to achieve a balance between those two desiderata for literature enunciated in classical times and restated time and again since—namely, that it should please and instruct.

Susan Ferrier was torn between the two aims at the outset. The novel itself betrays some indecisiveness in places, though at its best it is the vehicle for a complex tension between the two. As contemporary reviewers pointed out, there are passages of authorial moralising which are merely sententious; more often, though, passages of dialogue wittily express the writer's sharp social observation, raising, in the fashion of Jane Austen, moral questions indirectly and by means of comic pleasure. The last paragraph of the book, appropriately enough, describes a wedding. The author pronounces piously:

Colonel and Mrs Lennox . . . found as much happiness as earth's pilgrims ever possess, whose greatest felicity must spring from a higher source. The extensive influence which generally attends upon virtue joined to prosperity, was used by them for its best purposes. It was not confined either to rich or to poor, to caste or sect—but all shared in their benevolence whom that benevolence could benefit. And the poor, the sick, and the desolate united in blessing what Heaven had already blessed—this happy Marriage.

Fortunately, there is relatively little of this kind of inert generalising in the novel. Contrast the racy beginning, in which Lady Juliana's irascible and authoritarian father, a descendant in some respects of Fielding's Squire Western in *Tom Jones*, heartlessly announces that she is to marry a hunchbacked duke of fifty with a squint and red hair. To his daughter's "romantic" plea to be allowed to marry "the choice of one's heart", he replies, "The choice of a fiddlestick!"

The theme is thus sounded. Lady Juliana is for romance on a shoestring; her father stands for the old view that "persons of rank must be guided entirely by family considerations in the connexions they form" and "must marry for the still greater aggrandisement of their family". Lady Juliana's notion of marrying for love reflects the change in sensibility and the concomitant change in ideas about marriage among the upper and middle classes which had come about over the preceding two centuries. As Lawrence Stone has argued in *The Family, Sex, and Marriage in England 1500-1800* (1977), a combination of social, cultural and political factors brought about a revolutionary change—none the less startling for having been gradually prepared for—in ideas about marriage in the late eighteenth century, the age variously, and tellingly, described as that of Reason, or Sensibility, or Enlightenment.

During the Renaissance, when it was still possible to believe in the divine right of a king to rule and when a strictly hierarchical view of society endorsed the rights of the few and the unquestioned duties of the many, a patriarchal attitude to marriage prevailed, at least among the nobility and the gentry. A father thus had the right, even the duty, to direct his sons and daughters to marry in the interest, financial, political or social, of the family. His children had the duty to obey, and no right to refuse on grounds of personal preference. With the political revolution of the seventeenth century, and the elaboration by John Locke and other philosophers of a contractual view of the state by which kings were answerable to Parliament and people as well as vice versa, it became correspondingly harder to insist upon the unilateral right of the father to expect filial obedience in the matter of marriage. Add to this the Puritans' insistence on both the exercise of individual conscience and the holiness of marriage, and one can see why stress began to be placed on marriage as a sacrament based on mutual affection rather than family interest.

The growth of the novel was itself a symptom of these and other changes in society. Examples of the new genre abounded in the later eighteenth century, filling the greatly expanded book market created by increased literacy and leisure—particularly among middle-class women—and by improved and cheaper techniques of printing. As a narrative form the novel characteristically reflected the changed and changing view of marriage. Naturally enough, however, much confusion and tension surrounded the topic. Many a patrician father stuck to the criterion of marrying his children into other well-born families, or, in cases of financial need, into respectable families of the rising mercantile and industrial class. The children, products of an age in which Locke, Rousseau and later Wordsworth insisted on the primacy of individual experience and on the importance of nurturing, rather than repressing, emotions, often clashed with their parents. Runaway marriages in Gretna Green became common enough in reality and were soon obligatory events in romantic novels. There is one such marriage, "at the altar of Vulcan", in chapter one of *Marriage*.

But the clash between family interest and individual affection was far from being a simple one. In an age when society was still grounded in the rights of property, the former could be seen as both prudent and for the general good of family and class, rather than as mere paternal selfishness. And the question of personal affection was even more complex. How was an impressionable, inexperienced young person, particularly a sheltered daughter, to be trusted to place her affections in a worthy object? Was it not the duty of a parent to protect children from making dreadful mistakes? Though Pope might write in his most optimistic moments that "REASON, PASSION, answer one great aim", the two faculties were much more likely to be perceived as oppositional. Hence the prevalence, in both autobiographical and fictional writing of the time, of the vocabulary of "reason" and "sense" versus "romance" and "sensibility". Jane Austen, whom Susan Ferrier admired, addressed herself to these issues, and seemed to favour the reconciliation of the apparent opposites by means of what Maria Edgeworth, in her treatise *Practical Education* (1798), had called "the education of the heart". Inclination and emotion were the true guide towards a happy marriage, but they must be aided by prudent education, so that it might be possible for a choice to be both spontaneous and wise.

Susan Ferrier adds her contribution to the question in the present novel, in which marriage is the chief topic of interest and conversation, and in which the author fixes her sharp eye on a number of characteristically failed marriages. Marriages, here, may fail because they have been contracted entirely on passionate grounds; hence Susan Ferrier's explanation to her friend that "the moral to be deduced" from the comic opening concerning Lady Juliana is *not* that irascible fathers must be rebelled against in the name of love, but rather that "all young ladies" must be warned against "runaway matches". On this account, a contemporary reviewer described Miss Ferrier's turn of mind as "the very reverse of *romantic*". On the other hand, a marriage of convenience, such as that entered into by one of Lady Juliana's twin daughters, is described with a negative economy not unlike that of Jane Austen:

The die was cast. Amidst pomp and magnificence, elate with pride, and sparkling with jewels, Adelaide Douglas reversed the fate of her mother; and while her affections were bestowed on another, she vowed, in the face of Heaven, to belong only to the Duke of Altamont!

The answer to the riddle of reconciling inclination to judgement is education. Thus the other twin, Mary, is brought up by a wise aunt who teaches her niece by her own example, so that

while she was almost unconsciously practising the quiet virtues of patience and fortitude, and self-denial, and unostentatiously sacrificing her own wishes to promote the comfort of others—her example, like a kindly dew, was shedding its silent influence on the embryo blossoms of her pupil's heart.

The result is a happy marriage in Mary herself of sense and sensibility, of a "well-regulated mind" and "the best affections of her heart". However, lest we should find this success too cloying, particularly at the point where Mary declaims on the desirability of a wife's feeling deference towards her future husband, Susan Ferrier gives Mary a conversational sparring partner of more spirit and independence. Her cousin, Lady Emily, is an embryonic feminist who undermines such a view with the assertion that "my husband and I shall have a more equitable division; for, though a man is a reasonable being, he shall know that a woman is so too—sometimes." Lady Emily is altogether a more interesting figure—though unfortunately we hear nothing about *her* education—than is the ostensible heroine, Mary.

The kind of education for women which Susan Ferrier advocates is not that of a bluestocking. She shows up the artificiality of ladies' literary circles in a chapter near the end of the book in which Mrs Bluemits presides over an assembly of ladies who converse almost entirely in quotations from favourite poets of the age, from the melancholy Young to Byron, Scott and Thomas Campbell. Though literature is clearly, for Susan Ferrier herself, of great educational importance—she might even be accused of quoting from contemporary authors rather too often in the narrative—what is more important is the influence of a good teacher. Moreover, there is a suggestion, not fully developed, that natural environment also plays an influential part in the education of the individual. She adapts Wordsworth's belief in the "influence of natural objects" and the educational function of the Lake District scenery on his own youth to the possibility that Mary's upbringing in the Highlands of Scotland has something to do with the success of her education. Mary's twin sister Adelaide, by contrast, is brought up not only by a selfish, fashionable mother, but also in that well-known graveyard of morality, London. This is, however, a feature of the novel which remains latent, and I think there are two main reasons for this.

Firstly, Susan Ferrier was herself an Edinburgh girl, youngest child of a respectable Clerk of Session. Her father was a friend and colleague of Walter Scott, and the family was acquainted with most of the important literary and intellectual celebrities of the "Athens of the North". Henry Mackenzie, author of the successful and lachrymose novel,

The Man of Feeling (1771), Francis Jeffrey, Henry Brougham
and other stars of the influential *Edinburgh Review*, as well as
Scott and the younger set of Edinburgh lawyers who
contributed to *Blackwood's Magazine*, were her intimates.
Her attitude to the wild Highland scenery in which her
noble friend Charlotte Clavering lived was thus rather
superior, though pleasantly tongue-in-cheek. She accosted
her friend in a letter of 1809:

How could you compare the savage enjoyments to be found
amongst your misty mountains to the elegant seclusion and
refined pleasures to be met with in this queen of cities? *There* you
behold nothing but decaying nature, such as dropping leaves,
fading flowers, drooping trees. *Here* I contemplate the progress of
the Arts in streets building, houses repairing, shops painting.
There no sound salutes your ear save the monotonous din of some
tinkling rill or tumbling cascade. *Here* I am regaled from morning
till night with an enchanting variety, from the majestic rumble of
a Hackney coach to the elegant trot of a post-chaise.

Though Susan was clearly attracted to the Highland
scenery with its ruggedness and "romantic" associations,
she was a well-bred inhabitant of a sophisticated modern
city who could not be expected to admire equally the
rugged customs of the Highlanders. No doubt she knew
Samuel Johnson's not unkind comment about Scotland,
and particularly the Highlands, having risen only recently
out of barbarity. Moreover, if social intercourse was to be
shown as an important factor in a young girl's education,
the still patriarchal society of the lairds and chieftains could
hardly contribute significantly to it. Romantic waterfalls
and deserted mountains might serve a positive purpose, but
living amongst "Hottentots", or "Oaten-toads", as Lady
Juliana's English maid calls the inhabitants of Glenfern
Castle in *Marriage*, could scarcely do so.

Secondly, the setting of the early part of the novel in the
sublime but gloomy Highlands was undertaken primarily
for comic purposes. This, too, would have made a serious
insistence on natural influences awkward. Susan Ferrier

rightly thought that some fine social comedy could be achieved by describing "the sudden transition of a high-bred English beauty, who thinks she can sacrifice all for love, to an uncomfortable solitary Highland dwelling among tall red-haired sisters and grim-faced aunts". The confrontation between Lady Juliana and the garrulous aunts Miss Jacky, Miss Nicky and Miss Grizzy, is richly comic, as is the shock to the romantic ideas of Lady Juliana of her first sight of Glenfern Castle with its "sullen-looking lake", its "rugged cloud-capped hills" and its "few dingy turnip fields", approached by a wretched road and in drizzling rain. The larger part of the satire is directed against the snobbish English girl, but the Highlanders are a set of comic rustics, by no means idealised. In the second part of the novel, Aunt Grizzy ventures south to visit Mary in fashionable Bath, where she cuts a crude, provincial figure. (When asked by the bluestockings at Mrs Bluemits' house if she knows the great Thomas Campbell, Grizzy launches into a catalogue of all the Campbells she knows in the vicinity of Glenfern Castle.) Susan Ferrier's talent, in short, is for social comedy produced by misunderstandings which are themselves the product of social and national differences.

No doubt Scott's Scottish novels, beginning with *Waverley* (1814), provided an example for Susan Ferrier. He, too, exploited misunderstandings owing to local customs and dialect, and he and she shared a sophisticated Edinburgh superiority which co-existed happily with some sympathy and admiration for the simple downrightness of their provincial country-people. Thus, while we may disapprove of the laird of Glenfern's old-fashioned view of what should constitute the education of a young lady, we sympathise with his contemptuous dismissal of Lady Juliana's education for idleness:

'Edication! what has her edication been, to mak her different frae other women? If a woman can nurse her bairns, mak their claes, and manage her house, what mair need she do? If she can play a tune on a spinnet, and dance a reel, and play a rubber at whist—no doubt these are accomplishments, but they're soon learnt. Edication! pooh!'

Susan Ferrier's use of dialect in *Marriage* is skilful. There is so much regional speech in the novels of the later nineteenth century—those of Dickens, George Eliot and Hardy, for example—that we are apt to think of it as the norm. But Maria Edgeworth had been the first to write a regional novel, using dialect in her Irish novel, *Castle Rackrent* (1800). And Scott, in his scrupulous and generous way, announced in the postscript to *Waverley* that his intention had been "in some distant degree to emulate the admirable Irish portraits drawn by Miss Edgeworth". Susan Ferrier had only these two major examples before her, and she created robust and comic characters which may have been on the verge of caricature, as George Moir complained in his *Edinburgh Review* survey of her novels in 1841, but which were clearly based on close observation. Not only did Susan's Edinburgh friends chatter about cousins and aunts who may have unconsciously sat for their literary portraits as the Scottish characters in *Marriage*. We also have the testimony of two observers about a particular type of old lady to be found in Scotland. Dr Johnson wrote to his friend Mrs Thrale from Edinburgh on the eve of his departure for the Highlands and islands in August 1773, "At dinner on Monday were the Duchess of Douglas, an old Lady who talks broad Scotch with a paralytick voice, and is scarce understood by her own countrymen . . ." And Lord Cockburn, the greatest of Edinburgh lawyers in Susan Ferrier's own day, remembered in *Memorials of his Time* "a singular race of excellent Scotch old ladies" who were "indifferent about the modes and habits of the modern world; and adhering to their own ways, so as to stand out, like primitive rocks, above ordinary society." Such women, placed in the rugged setting of Glenfern Castle and with their eccentricities magnified, are the aunts in *Marriage*.

Scott himself gave credit to Susan Ferrier's gift for social observation. In a postscript to the last of his *Tales of my Landlord* in 1819, he wrote (prematurely), "I retire from the field, conscious that there remains behind not only a large harvest, but labourers capable of gathering it in." Moreover, he added:

More than one writer has of late displayed talents of this description; and if the present author, himself a phantom, may be permitted to distinguish a brother, or perhaps a sister shadow, he would mention, in particular, the author of a very lively work entitled *Marriage*.

A few years later, in 1826, he confided to his journal the difficulty he experienced, and observed others to experience, in describing "the actual current of society; whose colours are so evanescent that it is difficult to fix them on the canvas". "The women", he concluded, "do this better—Edgeworth, Ferrier, Austen have all had their portraits of real society far superior to anything Man vain Man has produced of the like nature."

Susan Ferrier's first novel certainly compares favourably with those of Maria Edgeworth, and at its best it has something akin to Jane Austen's wit. Her later efforts, *Inheritance* (1824) and *Destiny* (1831), contain more moralising and less comic originality. *Marriage* has the distinction of having attacked head-on one of the vital questions of contemporary society: what should marriage be and how should women be educated for it? Finally, one contemplates with pleasure the irony of a family friend, Matthew ("Monk") Lewis, author of the Gothic novel, *The Monk* (1796), remarking in 1818:

I hear it rumoured that Miss F----r doth write novels, or is about writing one. I wish she would let such idle nonsense alone . . . as a rule I have an aversion, a pity, a contempt for all female scribblers. The needle, not the pen, is the instrument they should handle, and the only one they ever use dexterously.

As Lewis died in 1818, we do not know what his opinion of the finished novel would have been. Nor how he would have viewed the wielding of the pen by such women among the next generation of novelists as the Brontës, Mrs Gaskell and George Eliot.

Rosemary Ashton, London, 1985

MARRIAGE.

————✳————

Chapter I.

Love!—A word by superstition thought a god; by use
turned to an humour; by self-will made a flattering madness.
—*Alexander and Campaspe*

"COME hither, child," said the old Earl of Courtland to his daughter, as, in obedience to his
summons, she entered his study: "come
hither, I say; I wish to have some serious conversation
with you: so dismiss your dogs, shut the door, and sit
down here."

Lady Juliana rang for the footman to take Venus;
bade Pluto be quiet, like a darling, under the sofa; and,
taking Cupid in her arms, assured his lordship he need
fear no disturbance from the sweet creatures, and that
she would be all attention to his commands—kissing
her cherished pug as she spoke.

"You are now, I think, seventeen, Juliana," said his
lordship, in a solemn important tone.

"And a half, papa."

"It is therefore time you should be thinking of
establishing yourself in the world. Have you ever
turned your thoughts that way?"

" N—no, papa, not exactly in the way of establishing myself," replied the lady, hesitatingly.

" That is well; you have left that for me to do, like a good, wise little girl, as you are.   Is it not so, my pretty Jule?"

" Perhaps, papa; but I—I don't know "——She stopped in evident embarrassment.

" It is right you should know, however," said the Earl, knitting his brow, " that I can give you no fortune."

" Oh, I don't in the least care about fortune, papa," eagerly interrupted his daughter, who knew about as much of arithmetic as of alchymy.

" Don't interrupt me, and don't talk nonsense, child," said Lord Courtland, peevishly.   " As I can give you no fortune, you have, perhaps, no greater right than many other pretty portionless girls to expect a very brilliant establishment."

This was *said*, but not *thought* either by the father or daughter.

" At any rate, I don't in the least care about that sort of thing," said the lady, disdainfully; " else, if I chose—— but I assure you, papa, I don't at all care about what is called a brilliant establishment."

" Indeed! and pray what *do* you care for, then?" inquired the earl, opening his eyes to their utmost extent.

" Why, I shouldn't at all mind being poor," said Lady Juliana, assuming a most heroic air.

" You shouldn't at all mind being poor!" repeated his lordship, in utter amazement.   " You shouldn't at all mind being poor!   Do you know what you are saying, child?   Do you know what it is to be poor?"

" *Perfectly*, papa," was pronounced by her ladyship, in a tone of the most high-flown emphasis.

" You do?   You have tried it, then?"

" No, papa ; but I can easily imagine what it is."

Lord Courtland hemmed. " Then I suppose I am to understand that you prefer the single state and poverty ? "

" Dear papa ! you quite misunderstand me ; I only meant that—that it was nothing to be poor when—when"——

" When what ? " demanded the earl, angrily.

" When united to the choice of one's heart," answered the lady, in a very romantic key.

" The choice of a fiddlestick ! " exclaimed Lord Courtland, in a rage. " What have you to do with a heart ? what has any body to do with a heart when their establishment in life is at stake ? Keep your heart for your romances, child, and don't bring such nonsense into real life—heart, indeed ! "

Lady Juliana felt she was now in the true position of a heroine : a handsome lover—an ambitious father—cruel fortune—unshaken constancy. She sighed deeply—even dropped a tear, and preserved a mournful silence.

The father proceeded in a solemn tone : " You ought to be aware by this time, Julia, that persons of rank must be guided entirely by family considerations in the connexions they form."

" Of course, papa, one wouldn't marry any but a person of good family, and tolerable fortune, and in the best society "——

" Pooh ! these are nothing," cried the earl, contemptuously ; " people of birth must marry for the still greater aggrandisement of their family—for the extending of their political influence—for "——

" I don't in the least care about politics, papa ; and I am determined I never will marry anybody who talks politics to me—I hate politics ! "

" You are a little fool, and don't know what you will

do, or what you are talking about. What does your
wise head or heart know about these things? What
do you know of the importance of political family
connexions?"

"O, thank heaven! I know nothing about the
matter," replied Lady Julia, in a peevish tone. "Have
done, Cupid!"

"I thought not; so you have only to be guided by
those who do know—that's all, my dear!"

"Have done, Cupid!" cried the lady, still more
fretfully, to her favourite pug, who was amusing himself
by tearing the beautiful veil that partly shaded the head
of his fair mistress.

The earl tried to be facetious. "And pray, my
pretty Julia, can this same wonderful wise little head of
yours tell you who is the happy man with whom I am
about to form an alliance for you?"

"For me, papa!" exclaimed Lady Juliana, in a
flutter of surprise; "surely you are not serious?"

"Perfectly so—come, guess."

Had Lady Juliana dared to utter the wishes of that
heart, she would have been at no loss for a reply; but
she saw the necessity for dissimulation; and, after
naming such of her admirers as were most indifferent
to her, she declared herself quite at a loss, and begged
her father to put an end to her suspense.

"Now, what would you think of the Duke of
L——?" asked the earl, in a voice of half-smothered
exultation and delight.

"The Duke of L——!" repeated Lady Juliana,
with a scream of horror and surprise; "surely, papa,
you cannot be serious: why, he is red-haired and
squints, and he's as old as you, and"——

"If he were as old as sin, and as ugly too," interrupted the enraged earl, "he should be your husband;
and with my consent you never shall have any other!"

The youthful beauty burst into tears, while her father traversed the apartment with an inflamed and wrathful visage.

" If it had been any body but that odious duke ! " sobbed the lovely Juliana.

" If it had been any body but that odious duke," repeated the earl, mimicking her, "they should not have had you. It has been my sole study, ever since I saw your brother settled, to bring about this alliance ; and, when this is accomplished, my utmost ambition will be satisfied. So, no more whining—the affair is settled ; and all that remains for you to do, is to study to make yourself agreeable to his grace, and to sign the settlements. No such mighty sacrifice, when repaid with a ducal coronet, the most splendid jewels, the finest equipages, the most magnificent house, the most princely establishment, and the largest jointure, of any woman in England."

Lady Juliana raised her head, and wiped her eyes. Lord Courtland perceived the effect his eloquence had produced upon the childish fancy of his daughter, and continued to expatiate upon the splendid joys that awaited her, in an union with a nobleman of the duke's rank and fortune ; till at length, dazzled, if not convinced, she declared herself " satisfied that it was her duty to marry whoever papa pleased ; but "—and a sigh escaped her, as she contrasted her noble suitor with her gay handsome lover—the admired of all admirers,—" but if I should marry him, papa, I am sure I shall never be able to love him."

The earl smiled at her childish simplicity, as he assured her that was not at all necessary ; that love was now entirely confined to the lower orders : that it was very well for ploughmen and dairy-maids, and such *canaille*, to marry for love ; but for a young woman of rank to think of such a thing, was plebeian in the extreme !

Lady Juliana did not entirely subscribe to the arguments of her father; but the gay and glorious vision that floated in her brain stifled for a while the pleadings of her heart; and with a sparkling eye, and an elastic step, she hastened to prepare for the reception of the duke.

For a few weeks the delusion lasted. Lady Juliana was flattered with the homage she received as a future duchess; she was delighted with the eclat that attended her, and charmed with the daily presents showered upon her by her noble suitor.

"Well, really, Favolle," said she to her maid, one day, as she clasped on her beautiful arm a resplendent bracelet, "it must be owned the duke has a most exquisite taste in trinkets; don't you think so? And, do you know, I don't think him so very—*very* ugly. When we are married, I mean to make him get a Brutus, cork his eyebrows, and have a set of teeth." But just then, the blue eyes, curling hair, and fine-formed person of a certain captivating Scotsman, rose to view in her mind's eye; and, with a peevish "pshaw!" she threw the bauble aside.

Educated for the sole purpose of forming a brilliant establishment, of catching the eye, and captivating the senses, the cultivation of her mind, or the correction of her temper, had formed no part of the system by which that aim was to be accomplished. Under the auspices of a fashionable mother, and an obsequious governess, the froward petulance of childhood, fostered and strengthened by indulgence and submission, had gradually ripened into that selfishness and caprice which now, in youth, formed the prominent features of her character. The earl was too much engrossed by affairs of importance, to pay much attention to any thing so perfectly insignificant as the mind of his daughter. Her *person* he had predetermined should be entirely at his disposal, and he therefore contemplated with delight the uncommon beauty which already distinguished it; not with the fond partiality of parental love, but with the heartless satisfaction of a crafty politician.

The mind of Lady Juliana was consequently the sport of every passion that by turns assailed it. Now swayed by ambition, and now softened by love: the struggle was violent, but it was short. A few days before the one which was to seal her fate, she granted an interview to her lover, who, young, thoughtless, and enamoured as herself, easily succeeded in persuading her to elope with him to Scotland. There, at the altar of Vulcan, the beautiful daughter of the Earl of Courtland gave her hand to her handsome but penniless lover; and there vowed to immolate every ambitious desire, every sentiment of vanity and high-born pride. Yet a sigh arose as she looked on the sordid room, uncouth priest, and ragged witnesses; and thought of the special licence, splendid saloon, and bridal pomp that would have attended her union with the duke. But the rapturous expressions which burst from the impassioned Douglas made her forget the gaudy pleasures of pomp and fashion. Amid the sylvan scenes of the neighbouring lakes, the lovers sought a shelter; and, mutually charmed with each other, time flew for a while on downy pinions.

At the end of a few months, however, the enamoured husband began to suspect that the lips of his " angel Julia " could utter very silly things;—while the fond bride, on her part, discovered that, though her " adored Henry's " eyes were perfectly beautiful, yet sometimes she thought they wanted expression; and though his figure was symmetry itself, yet it certainly was deficient in a certain air—a *je ne sais quoi*—that marks the man of fashion.

"How I wish I had my pretty Cupid here!" said her ladyship with a sigh one day as she lolled on a sofa:

"he had so many pretty tricks, he would have helped
to amuse us, and make the time pass; for really this
place grows very stupid and tiresome; don't you think
so, love?"

"Most exceedingly so, my darling," replied her
husband, yawning sympathetically as he spoke.

"Then suppose I make one more attempt to soften
papa, and be received into favour again?"

"With all my heart."

"Shall I say I'm very sorry for what I have done?"
asked her ladyship with a sigh: "you know I did not
say that in my first letter."

"Ay, do; and, if it will serve any purpose, you may
say that I am no less so."

In a few days the letter was returned, in a blank
cover; and, by the same post, Douglas saw himself
superseded in the *Gazette*, being absent without leave!

There now remained but one course to pursue; and
that was to seek refuge at his father's, in the Highlands
of Scotland. At the first mention of it, Lady Juliana
was transported with joy; and begged that a letter
might be instantly despatched, containing the offer of a
visit. She had heard the Duchess of M—— declare
nothing could be so delightful as the style of living in
Scotland: the people were so frank and gay, and the
manners so easy and engaging: oh! it was delightful!
And then Lady G—— and Lady Mary L——, and a
thousand other lords and ladies she knew, were all *so*
charmed with the country, and all *so* sorry to leave it.
Then dear Henry's family must be *so* charming! An
old castle, too, was her delight—she should feel quite
at home while wandering through its long galleries; and
she quite loved old pictures, and armour, and tapestry—
and then her thoughts reverted to her father's magnificent
mansion in D——shire.

At length an answer arrived, containing a cordial

invitation from the old laird to spend the winter with them at Glenfern Castle.

All impatience to quit the scenes of their short-lived felicity, they bade a hasty adieu to the now fading beauties of Windermere ; and, full of hope and expectation, eagerly turned towards the bleak hills of Scotland. They stopped for a short time at Edinburgh, to provide themselves with a carriage and some other necessaries. There, too, they fortunately met with an English Abigail and footman, who, for double wages, were prevailed upon to attend them to the Highlands ; which, with the addition of two dogs, a tame squirrel, and mackaw, completed the establishment.

———o———

Chapter ij.

What transport to retrace our early plays,
Our early bliss, when each thing joy supplied ;
The woods, the mountains, and the warbling maze
Of the wild brooks.   THOMSON.

MANY were the dreary muirs, and rugged mountains, her ladyship had to encounter in her progress to Glenfern Castle ; and, but for the hope of the new world that awaited her beyond those formidable barriers, her delicate frame, and still more sensitive feelings, must have sunk beneath the horrors of such a journey. But she remembered the duchess had said the inns and roads were execrable ; and the face of the country, as well as the lower orders of people, frightful : but what signified those things ? There were balls, and rowing matches, and sailing parties, and shooting parties, and fishing parties, and parties of every description : and the certainty of being recompensed by the festivities of

Glenfern Castle reconciled her to the ruggedness of the
approach.

Douglas had left his paternal home and native hills
when only eight years of age. A rich relation of his
mother's, happening to visit them at that time, took a
fancy to the boy; and, under promise of making him
his heir, had prevailed on his parents to part with him.
At a proper age he was placed in the Guards, and had continued to maintain himself in the favour of his benefactor
until his imprudent marriage, which had irritated the old
bachelor so much, that he instantly disinherited him, and
refused to listen to any terms of reconciliation. The
impressions which the scenes of his infancy had left upon
the mind of the young Scotsman, it may easily be supposed, were of a pleasing description. He spoke of his
own family with all the warmth of early recollection.
His father was quite the *beau idéal* of a Highland
gentleman of the old school—frank, high-minded, and
warm-hearted; his aunts so kind, simple, and affectionate; his brother so gay, handsome, and good-humoured;
his five lovely sisters, Elizabeth, Rebecca, Barbara,
Isabella, and Robina,—how charming they must be if
they had fulfilled their early promises of youthful and
infant beauty!—how his dear Juliana would love them,
and how they would love his dear Juliana! Then he
would expatiate on the wild but august scenery that
surrounded his father's castle, and associate with the
idea the boyish exploits which, though faintly remembered, still served to endear them to his heart. He
spoke of the time when he used to make one of a
numerous party on the lake, and, when tired of sailing
on its glassy surface, to the sound of soft music, they
would land at some lovely spot; and, after partaking of
their banquet beneath a spreading tree, conclude the day
by a dance on the grass.

Lady Juliana would exclaim, "How delightful!

I dote upon pic-nics and dancing! — *à-propos,*
Henry, there will surely be a ball to welcome our
arrival?"

The conversation was interrupted; for just at that
moment they had gained the summit of a very high hill,
and the post-boy, stopping to give his horses breath,
turned round to the carriage, pointing, at the same
time, with a significant gesture, to a tall, thin, grey
house, something resembling a tower, that stood in the
vale beneath. A small sullen-looking lake was in
front, on whose banks grew neither tree nor shrub.
Behind, rose a chain of rugged cloud-capped hills, on
the declivities of which were some faint attempts at
young plantations; and the only level ground consisted
of a few dingy turnip fields, enclosed with rude stone
walls, or dikes, as the post-boy called them. It was
now November; the day was raw and cold, and a
thick drizzling rain was beginning to fall. A dreary
stillness reigned all around, broken only at intervals by
the screams of the sea-fowl that hovered over the lake;
on whose dark and troubled waters was dimly descried
a little boat, plied by one solitary being.

"What a scene!" at length Lady Juliana exclaimed, shuddering as she spoke. "What a scene!
how I pity the unhappy wretches who are doomed to
dwell in such a place! And yonder hideous grim
house; it makes me sick to look at it. Do bid him
drive on!" Another significant look from the driver
made the colour mount to Douglas's cheek, as he
stammered out, "Surely it can't be; yet somehow I
don't know. Pray, my lad," letting down one of the
glasses, and addressing the post-boy, "what is the name
of that house?"

"Hooss!" repeated the driver; "ca' ye thon a
hooss? Yon's gude Glenfern Castle."

Lady Juliana, not understanding a word he said, sat

silently, wondering at her husband's curiosity respecting such a wretched-looking place.

"Impossible! you must be mistaken, my lad: why, what's become of all the fine wood that used to surround it?"

"Gin you mean a wheen auld firs, there's some o' them to the fore yet," pointing to two or three tall, bare, scathed Scotch firs, that scarcely bent their heads to the wind that now began to howl around them.

"I insist upon it that you are mistaken; you must have wandered from the right road," cried the now alarmed Douglas in a loud voice, which vainly attempted to conceal his agitation.

"We'll shune see that," replied the phlegmatic Scot, who, having rested his horses, and affixed a drag to the wheel, was about to proceed; when Lady Juliana, who now began to have some vague suspicion of the truth, called to him to stop, and, almost breathless with alarm, inquired of her husband the meaning of what had passed.

He tried to force a smile as he said, "It seems our journey is nearly ended; that fellow persists in asserting that that is Glenfern, though I can scarcely think it. If it is, it is strangely altered since I left it twelve years ago."

For a moment Lady Juliana was too much alarmed to make a reply: pale and speechless, she sank back in the carriage; but the motion of it, as it began to proceed, roused her to a sense of her situation, and she burst into tears and exclamations.

The driver, who attributed it all to fears at descending the hill, assured her she "needna be the least feared, for there were na twa cannier beasts atween that and Johnny Groat's Hooss; and that they wad hae her at the castle door in a crack, gin they were ance down the brae."

Douglas's attempts to soothe his high-born bride were not more successful than those of the driver: in vain he made use of every endearing epithet and tender expression, and recalled the time when she used to declare that she could dwell with him in a desert; her only replies were bitter reproaches and upbraidings for his treachery and deceit, mingled with floods of tears, and interrupted by hysterical sobs. Provoked at her folly, yet softened by her extreme distress, Douglas was in the utmost state of perplexity,—now ready to give way to a paroxysm of rage,—then melting into pity, he sought to soothe her into composure; and, at length, with much difficulty, succeeded in changing her passionate indignation into silent dejection.

That no fresh objects of horror or disgust might appear to disturb this calm, the blinds were pulled down, and in this state they reached Glenfern Castle. But there the friendly veil was necessarily withdrawn; and the first object that presented itself to the high-bred Englishwoman was an old man, clad in a short tartan coat and striped woollen nightcap, with blear eyes and shaking hands, who vainly strove to open the carriage door.

Douglas soon extricated himself, and assisted his lady to alight; then accosting the venerable domestic as "Old Donald," asked him if he recollected him?

"Weel that, weel that, Maister Harry, and ye're welcome hame; and ye tu, bonny sir" * (addressing Lady Juliana, who was calling to her footman to follow her with the mackaw); then, tottering before them, he led the way, while her ladyship followed, leaning on her husband, her squirrel on her other arm, preceded by her dogs, barking with all their might, and

* The Highlanders use this term of respect indifferently to both sexes.

attended by the mackaw, screaming with all his strength :
and in this state was the Lady Juliana ushered into the
drawing-room of Glenfern Castle !

———o———

Chapter iij.

What can be worse
Than to dwell here ?

Paradise Lost.

IT was a long, narrow, low-roofed room, with a
number of small windows, that admitted feeble
lights in every possible direction. The scanty
furniture bore every appearance of having been constructed at the same time as the edifice ; and the friendship thus early formed still seemed to subsist, as the
high-backed worked chairs adhered most pertinaciously to the grey walls, on which hung, in narrow black
frames, some of the venerable ancestors of the Douglas
family. A fire, which appeared to have been newly
kindled, was beginning to burn, but, previous to showing itself in flame, had chosen to vent itself in smoke,
with which the room was completely filled, and the
open windows seemed to produce no other effect than
that of admitting the wind and rain.

At the entrance of the strangers, a flock of females
rushed forward to meet them. Douglas good-humouredly submitted to be hugged by three long-chinned
spinsters, whom he recognised as his aunts, and warmly
saluted five awkward purple girls he guessed to be his
sisters : while Lady Juliana stood the image of despair,
and, scarcely conscious, admitted in silence the civilities
of her new relations ; till, at length, sinking into a
chair, she endeavoured to conceal her agitation by
calling to the dogs, and caressing her mackaw.

The laird, who had been hastily summoned from his farming operations, now entered. He was a good-looking old man, with something of the air of a gentleman, in spite of the inelegance of his dress, his rough manner, and provincial accent. After warmly welcoming his son, he advanced to his beautiful daughter-in-law, and, taking her in his arms, bestowed a loud and hearty kiss on each cheek ; then, observing the paleness of her complexion, and the tears that swam in her eyes, "What! not frightened for our Highland hills, my leddy? Come, cheer up—trust me, ye'll find as warm hearts among them as ony ye hae left in your fine English *policies* "—shaking her delicate fingers in his hard muscular gripe, as he spoke.

The tears, which had with difficulty been hitherto suppressed, now burst in torrents from the eyes of the high-bred beauty, as she leant her cheek against the back of a chair, and gave way to the anguish which mocked control.

To the loud, anxious inquiries, and oppressive kindness of her homely relatives, she made no reply ; but, stretching out her hands to her husband, sobbed, " Take, oh ! take me from this place ! "

Mortified, ashamed, and provoked, at a behaviour so childish and absurd, Douglas could only stammer out something about Lady Juliana having been frightened and fatigued ; and, requesting to be shown to their apartment, he supported her almost lifeless to it, while his aunts followed, all three prescribing different remedies in a breath.

" Oh, take them from me ! " faintly articulated Lady Juliana, as she shrank from the many hands that were alternately applied to her pulse and forehead.

After repeated entreaties and plausible excuses from Douglas, his aunts at length consented to withdraw ; and he then exerted all the rhetoric he was master of, to reconcile his bride to the situation love and necessity had thrown her into. But in vain he employed reasoning, caresses, and threats ; the only answers he could extort were tears and entreaties to be taken from a place where she declared she felt it impossible to exist.

" If you wish my death, Harry," said she, in a voice almost inarticulate from excess of weeping, " oh ! kill me quickly, and do not leave me to linger out my days, and perish at last with misery here ! "

" Only tell me what you would have me to do," said her husband, softened to pity by her extreme distress, " and, if possible, I will comply with your wishes."

" Oh ! then, stop the horses, and let us return immediately—do fly, dearest Harry, else they will be gone, and we shall never get away from this odious place ! "

" Where would you go ? " asked he, with affected calmness.

" Oh, any where—no matter where, so as we do but get away from hence—we can be at no loss."

" None in the world," interrupted Douglas, with a bitter smile, " as long as there is a prison to receive us. See," continued he, throwing a few shillings down on the table, " there is every sixpence I possess in the world."

Lady Juliana stood aghast.

At that instant, the English Abigail burst into the room ; and, in a voice choking with passion, she requested her discharge, that she might return with the driver who had brought them there.

" A pretty way of travelling, to be sure, it will be," continued she, " to go bumping behind a dirty chaise-driver ; but better to be shook to a jelly altogether, than stay amongst such a set of *Oaten-toads.*" *

* Hottentots

" What do you mean ? " inquired Douglas, as soon as the voluble Abigail allowed him an opportunity of asking.

" Why, my meaning, sir, is to leave this here place immediately. Not that I have any objections either to my lady, or you, sir ; but, to be sure, it was a sad day for me that I engaged myself to her ladyship. Little did I think that a lady of distinction would be coming to such a poor pitiful place as this. I am sure I thought I should ha' swooned when I was showed the hole where I was to sleep."

At the bare idea of this indignity to her person, the fury of the incensed fair one blazed forth with such strength as to choke her utterance.

Amazement had hitherto kept Lady Juliana silent ; for to such scenes she was a stranger. Born in an elevated rank—reared in state—accustomed to the most obsequious attention—and never approached but with the respect due rather to a divinity than to a mortal,— the strain of vulgar insolence that now assailed her was no less new to her ears than shocking to her feelings. With a voice and look that awed the woman into obedience, she commanded her to quit her presence for ever ; and then, no longer able to suppress the emotions of insulted pride, wounded vanity, and indignant disappointment, she gave way to a violent fit of hysterics.

In the utmost perplexity, the unfortunate husband, by turns, cursed the hour that had given him such a wife ; now tried to soothe her into composure ; but at length, seriously alarmed at the increasing attack, he called loudly for assistance.

In a moment, the three aunts and the five sisters all rushed together into the room, full of wonder, exclamation, and inquiry. Many were the remedies that were tried, and the experiments that were suggested ; till, at length, the violence of passion exhausted itself, and a faint sob, or deep sigh, succeeded the hysteric scream.

Douglas now attempted to account for the behaviour of his noble spouse, by ascribing it to the fatigue she had lately undergone, joined to distress of mind at her father's unrelenting severity towards her.

" O the amiable creature ! " interrupted the unsuspecting spinsters, almost stifling her with their caresses as they spoke. " Welcome, a thousand times welcome, to Glenfern Castle ! " said Miss Jacky, who was esteemed by much the most sensible woman, as well as the greatest orator, in the whole parish. " Nothing shall be wanting, dearest Lady Juliana, to compensate for a parent's rigour, and make you happy and comfortable. Consider this as your future home. My sisters and myself will be as mothers to you : and see these charming young creatures," dragging forward two tall, frightened girls, with sandy hair and great purple arms ; " thank Providence for having blest you with such sisters ! "

" Don't speak too much, Jacky, to our dear niece at present," said Miss Grizzy ; " I think one of Lady Maclaughlan's composing draughts would be the best thing for her—there can be no doubt about that."

" Composing draughts at this time of day ! " cried Miss Nicky ; " I should think a little good broth a much wiser thing. There are some excellent family broth making below, and I'll desire Tibby to bring a few."

" Will you take a little soup, love ? " asked Douglas. His lady assented ; and Miss Nicky vanished, but quickly re-entered, followed by Tibby, carrying a huge bowl of coarse Scotch broth, swimming with leeks, greens, and grease. Lady Juliana attempted to taste it, but her delicate palate revolted at the homely fare ; and she gave up the attempt, in spite of Miss Nicky's earnest entreaties to take a few more of these excellent family broth.

"I should think," said Henry, as he vainly attempted to stir it round, "that a little wine would be more to the purpose than this stuff."

The aunts looked at each other; and, withdrawing to a corner, a whispering consultation took place, in which "Lady Maclaughlan's opinion, birch, balm, currant, heating, cooling, running risks," &c., &c., transpired. At length the question was carried; and some tolerable sherry, and a piece of very substantial *short-bread*, were produced.

It was now voted by Miss Jacky, and carried *nem. con.*, that her ladyship ought to take a little repose till the hour of dinner.

"And don't trouble to dress," continued the considerate aunt, "for we are not very dressy here: and we are to be quite a charming family party, nobody but ourselves, and," turning to her nephew, "your brother and his wife. She is a most superior woman, though she has rather too many of her English prejudices yet to be all we could wish; but I have no doubt, when she has lived a little longer amongst us, she will just become one of ourselves."

"I forget who she was?" said Douglas.

"A grand-daughter of Sir Duncan Malcolm's, a very old family of the —— blood, and nearly allied to the present earl. And here they come," exclaimed she, on hearing the sound of a carriage; and all rushed out to receive them.

"Let us have a glimpse of this scion from a noble stock," said Lady Juliana, mimicking the accent of the poor spinsters, as she rose and ran to the window.

"Oh, Henry! do come and behold this equipage!" and she laughed with childish glee, as she pointed to a plain old-fashioned gig, with a large top. A tall handsome young man now alighted, and lifted out a female figure, so enveloped in a cloak, that eyes less penetrating

than Lady Juliana's could not, at a single glance, have
discovered her to be a "frightful quiz."

"Only conceive the effect of this dashing equipage
in Bond Street!" continued she, redoubling her mirth
at the bright idea: then suddenly stopping, and sighing,
"Ah, my pretty *vis-à-vis!* I remember the first time
I saw you, Henry, I was in it at a review;" and she
sighed still deeper.

"True; I was then aide-de-camp to your handsome
lover, the Duke of L——."

"Perhaps I might think him handsome now. People's
taste alter according to circumstances."

"Yours must have undergone a wonderful revolution,
if you can find charms in a hunchback of fifty-three."

"He is not a hunchback," returned her ladyship
warmly; "only a little high-shouldered: but, at any
rate, he has the most beautiful place and the finest house
in England."

Douglas saw the storm gathering on the brow of his
capricious wife, and, clasping her in his arms, "Are
you indeed so changed, my Julia, that you have forgot
the time when you used to declare you would prefer a
desert with your Henry, to a throne with another?"

"No, certainly, not changed; but—I—I did not
very well know then what a desert was; or, at least, I
had formed rather a different idea of it."

"What was your idea of a desert?" said her husband, laughing; "do tell me, love?"

"Oh! I had fancied it a beautiful place, full of
roses and myrtles, and smooth green turf, and murmuring rivulets, and, though very retired, not absolutely
out of the world; where one could occasionally see
one's friends, and give *déjeûnés et fêtes champêtres.*"

"Well, perhaps the time may come, Juliana, when
we may realise your Elysian deserts; but, at present,
you know, I am wholly dependent on my father. I

hope to prevail on him to do something for me; and that our stay here will be short; as, you may be sure, the moment I can I will take you hence. I am sensible it is not a situation for you; but for my sake, dearest Juliana, bear with it for a while, without betraying your disgust. Will you do this, darling?" and he kissed away the sullen tear that hung on her cheek.

"You know, love, there's nothing in the world I wouldn't do for you," replied she, as she played with her squirrel; "and, as you promise our stay shall be short, if I don't die of the horrors I shall certainly try to make the agreeable. O my cherub!" flying to her pug, who came barking into the room, "where have you been, and where's my darling Psyche, and sweet mackaw? Do, Harry, go and see after the darlings."

"I must go and see my brother and his wife first. Will you come, love?"

"Oh, not now; I don't feel equal to the encounter: besides, I must dress. But what shall I do, since that vile woman's gone? I can't dress myself. I never did such a thing in my life; and I am sure it's impossible that I can," almost weeping at the hardships she was doomed to experience in making her own toilette.

"Shall I be your Abigail?" asked her husband, smiling at the distress; "methinks it would be no difficult task to deck my Julia."

"Dear Harry, will you really dress me? Oh, that will be delightful! I shall die with laughing at your awkwardness;" and her beautiful eyes sparkled with childish delight at the idea.

"In the mean time," said Douglas, "I'll send some one to unpack your things; and after I have shook hands with Archie, and been introduced to my new sister, I shall enter on my office."

" Now do, pray, make haste ; for I die to see your
great hands tying strings, and sticking pins."

Delighted with her gaiety and good humour, he
left her caressing her favourites ; and, finding rather a
scarcity of female attendance, he despatched two of
his sisters to assist his helpless beauty in her arrangements.

———o———

Chapter ib.

And ever against eating cares,
Lap me in soft Lydian airs.   *L'Allegro.*

Such solace as the bagpipe can give, they have long enjoyed.
—Dr JOHNSON's *Journey to the Western Isles.*

WHEN Douglas returned, he found the floor
strewed with dresses of every description ;
his sisters on their knees before a great trunk
they were busied in unpacking, and his lady in her
wrapper, with her hair about her ears, still amusing
herself with her pets.

" See, how good your sisters are," said she, pointing
to the poor girls, whose inflamed faces bore testimony
to their labours.   " I declare, I am quite sorry to see
them take so much trouble," yawning as she leant back
in her chair ; " is it not quite shocking, Tommy ? "
kissing her squirrel.   " Oh, pray, Henry, do tell me
what I am to put on ; for I protest I don't know.
Favolle always used to choose for me ; and so did that
odious Martin, for she had an exquisite taste."

" Not so exquisite as your own, I am sure ; so, for
once, choose for yourself." replied the good-humoured
husband ; " and pray make haste, for my father waits
dinner."

Betwixt scolding, laughing, and blundering, the dress
was at length completed ; and Lady Juliana, in all the

pomp of dress and pride of beauty, descended, leaning on her husband's arm.

On entering the drawing-room, which was now in a more comfortable state, Douglas led her to a lady who was sitting by the fire; and, placing her hand within that of the stranger, " Juliana, my love," said he, " this is a sister whom you have not yet seen, and with whom I am sure you will gladly make acquaintance."

The stranger received her noble sister with graceful ease; and, with a sweet smile and pleasing accent, expressed herself happy in the introduction. Lady Juliana was surprised, and somewhat disconcerted. She had arranged her plans, and made up her mind to be *condescending;* she had resolved to enchant by her sweetness, dazzle by her brilliancy, and overpower by her affability. But there was a simple dignity in the air and address of the lady, before which even high-bred affectation sunk abashed. Before she found a reply to the courteous yet respectful salutation of her sister-in-law, Douglas introduced his brother; and the old gentleman, impatient at any farther delay, taking Lady Juliana by the hand, pulled rather than led her into the dining-room.

Even Lady Juliana contrived to make a meal of the roast mutton and muirfowl; for the laird piqued himself on the breed of his sheep, and his son was too good a sportsman to allow his friends to want for game.

" I think my darling Tommy would relish this grouse very much," observed Lady Juliana, as she secured the last remaining wing for her favourite; " bring him here!" turning to the tall, dashing lacquey who stood behind her chair, and whose handsome livery and well-dressed hair formed a striking contrast to old Donald's tartan jacket and bob-wig.

" Come hither, my sweetest cherubs!" extending her arms towards the charming *trio,* as they entered,

barking, and chattering, and flying to their mistress. A
scene of noise and nonsense ensued.

Douglas remained silent, mortified and provoked at
the weakness of his wife, which not even the silver
tones of her voice, or the elegance of her manners,
could longer conceal from him. But still there was a
charm in her very folly, to the eye of love, which had
not yet wholly lost its power.

After the table was cleared, observing that he was
still silent and abstracted, Lady Juliana turned to her
husband ; and, laying her hand on his shoulder, " You
are not well, love ! " said she, looking up in his face,
and shaking back the redundant ringlets that shaded her
own.

" Perfectly so," replied her husband, with a sigh.

" What, dull ? then I must sing to enliven you."
And, leaning her head on his shoulder, she warbled a
verse of the beautiful little Venetian air *La Biondina in
Gondoletta.* Then suddenly stopping, and fixing her
eyes on Mrs Douglas, " I beg pardon, perhaps you
don't like music ; perhaps my singing's a bore ? "

" You pay us a bad compliment in supposing so,"
said her sister-in-law, smiling ; " and the only atonement you can make for such an injurious doubt is to
proceed."

" Does any body sing here ? " asked she, without
noticing this request. " Do, somebody, sing me a
song."

" O ! we all sing, and dance too," said one of the
old young ladies ; " and after tea we will show you
some of our Scotch steps ; but, in the mean time, Mrs
Douglas will favour us with her song."

Mrs Douglas assented good-humouredly, though
aware that it would be rather a nice point to please
all parties in the choice of a song. The laird reckoned
all foreign music, *i.e.*, everything that was not Scotch,

an outrage upon his ears; and Mrs Douglas had too
much taste to murder Scotch songs with her English
accent. She therefore compromised the matter as well
as she could, by selecting a Highland ditty clothed in
her own native tongue; and began to sing, with much
pathos and simplicity, a verse or two of the lamented
Leyden's " Fall of Macgregor."

" In the vale of Glenorchy the night breeze was sighing
    O'er the tomb where the ancient Macgregors are lying;
    Green are their graves by their soft murmuring river,
    But the name of Macgregor has perish'd for ever.

' On a red stream of light, by his grey mountains glancing,
    Soon I beheld a dim spirit advancing;
    Slow o'er the heath of the dead was its motion,
    Like the shadow of mist o'er the foam of the ocean.

" Like the sound of a stream through the still evening dying,—
    Stranger! who treads where Macgregor is lying?
    Darest thou to walk, unappall'd and firm-hearted,
    'Mid the shadowy steps of the mighty departed?

" See! round thee the caves of the dead are disclosing
    The shades that have long been in silence reposing;
    Thro' their forms dimly twinkles the moonbeam descending,
    As upon thee their red eyes of wrath they are bending.

" Our grey stones of fame through the heath-blossom cover,
    Round the fields of our battles our spirits still hover;
    Where we oft saw the streams running red from the
        mountains;
    But dark are our forms by our blue native fountains.

" For our fame melts away like the foam of the river,
    Like the last yellow leaves on the oak-boughs that shiver:
    The name is unknown of our fathers so gallant;
    And our blood beats no more in the breasts of the valiant.

" The hunter of red deer now ceases to number
    The lonely grey stones on the field of our slumber.—
    Fly, stranger! and let not thine eye be reverted;
    Why should'st thou see that our fame is departed? "

"Pray, do you play on the harp?" asked the volatile lady, scarcely waiting till the first stanza was ended; "and, *à-propos*, have you a good harp here?"

"We've neither gude nor bad," said the old gentleman gruffly : "the lassies hae something else to do than to be strumming upon harps."

"We have a very sweet spinnet," said Miss Jacky, "which, in my opinion, is a far superior instrument; and Bella will give us a tune upon it. Bella, my dear, let Lady Juliana hear how well you can play."

Bella, blushing like a peony rose, retired to a corner of the room, where stood the spinnet ; and, with great, heavy, trembling hands, began to belabour the unfortunate instrument, while the aunts beat time, and encouraged her to proceed with exclamations of admiration and applause.

"You have done very well, Bella," said Mrs Douglas, seeing her preparing to *execute* another piece, and pitying the poor girl, as well as her auditors. Then whispering Miss Jacky that Lady Juliana looked fatigued, they arose to quit the room.

"Give me your arm, love, to the drawing-room," said her ladyship, languidly. "And now, pray, don't be long away," continued she, as he placed her on the sofa, and returned to the gentlemen.

————o————

Chapter 6.

You have displac'd the mirth, broke the good meeting
With most admir'd disorder.   *Macbeth.*

THE interval, which seemed of endless duration to the hapless Lady Juliana, was passed by the aunts in giving sage counsel as to the course of life to be pursued by married ladies. Worsted stockings and quilted petticoats were insisted upon as indispensable articles of dress; while it was plainly insinuated, that it was utterly impossible any child could be healthy, whose mother had not confined her wishes to barley broth and oatmeal porridge.

"Only look at these young lambs," said Miss Grizzy, pointing to the five great girls; "see what pictures of health they are! I'm sure I hope, my dear niece, your children will be just the same—only boys, for we are sadly in want of boys. It's melancholy to think we have not a boy among us, and that a fine auntient race like ours should be dying away for want of male heirs." And the tears streamed down the cheeks of the good spinster as she spoke.

The entrance of the gentlemen put a stop to the conversation.

Flying to her husband, Lady Juliana began to whisper, in very audible tones, her inquiries, whether he had yet got any money—when they were to go away, &c., &c.

"Does your ladyship choose any tea?" asked Miss Nicky, as she disseminated the little cups of coarse black liquid.

"Tea! oh no, I never drink tea—I'll take coffee; but Psyche loves tea." And she tendered the beverage, that had been intended for herself, to her favourite.

"Here's no coffee," said Douglas, surveying the tea-table; "but I will ring for some," as he pulled the bell.

Old Donald answered the summons.

"Where's the coffee?" demanded Miss Nicky.

"The coffee!" repeated the Highlander; "troth, Miss Nicky, an' it's been clean forgot. An' 'deed it's nae wonder, considering the confusion that has been in this hooss this day!" And he held up his hands, as if to bear testimony to what his tongue was unable to declare.

"Well, but you can get it yet?" said Douglas.

" 'Deed, Maister Harry, the night's ower far gane for't noo ; for the fire's a' ta'en up, ye see," reckoning with his fingers, as he proceeded ; " there's parritch makin' for oor supper ; and there's patatees boiling for the beasts ; and "——

" I'll see about it myself," said Miss Nicky, leaving the room, with old Donald at her back, muttering all the way.

The old laird, all this while, had been enjoying his evening nap ; but, that now ended, and the tea equipage being dismissed, starting up, he asked what they were about, that the dancing was not begun.

" Come, my leddy, we'll set the example," snapping his fingers, and singing, in a hoarse voice,

> " The mouse is a merry beastie,
>   And the moudiwort wants the een ;
>   But folk sall ne'er get wit,—
>   Sae merry as we twa hae been."

" But whar's the girlies ? " cried he. " Ho ! Belle, Becky, Betty, Baby, Beeny—to your posts ! "

The young ladies, eager for the delights of music and dancing, now entered, followed by Coil, the piper, dressed in the native garb, with cheeks seemingly ready blown for the occasion. After a little strutting and puffing, the pipes were fairly set agoing in Coil's most spirited manner. But vain would be the attempt to describe Lady Juliana's horror and amazement at the hideous sounds that for the first time assailed her ear. Tearing herself from the grasp of the old gentleman, who was just setting off in the reel, she flew shrieking to her husband, and threw herself trembling into his arms, while he called loudly to the self-delighted Coil to stop.

" What's the matter—what's the matter ? " cried the whole family, gathering round.

" Matter ! " repeated Douglas warmly, " you have frightened Lady Juliana to death ;—what did you mean," turning fiercely to the astonished piper, " by blowing that abominable bladder ? "

Poor Coil gaped with astonishment ; for never before had his performance on the bagpipe been heard but with admiration and applause.

" A bonny bargain, indeed, that canna stand the pipes," said the old gentleman, as he went puffing up and down the room : " she's no the wife for a Heeland-man ;—abominable blather, indeed !   By my troth, ye're no blate ! "

" I declare it's the most distressing thing I ever met with," sighed Miss Grizzy ; " I wonder whether it could be the sight or the sound of the bagpipe that frightened our dear niece.   I wish to goodness Lady Maclaughlan was here ! "

" It's impossible the bagpipe could frighten anybody," said Miss Jacky, in a high key ; " nobody with common sense could be frightened at a bagpipe."

Mrs Douglas here mildly interposed, and soothed down the offended pride of the Highlanders, by attri-buting Lady Juliana's agitation entirely to *surprise.* The word operated like a charm ; all were ready to admit, that it was a surprising thing when heard for the first time.   Miss Jacky remarked, that we are all liable to be surprised ; and the still more sapient Grizzy said, that indeed it was most surprising the effect that surprise had upon some people.   For her own part, she could not deny but that she was very often frightened when she was surprised, and very often surprised at having been frightened.

Douglas, meanwhile, was employed in soothing the terrors, real or affected, of his delicate bride ; who declared herself so exhausted with the fatigue she had undergone, and the sufferings she had endured, that she

must retire for the night.   Henry, eager to escape from
the questions and remarks of his family, gladly availed
himself of the same excuse ; and, to the infinite mortification of both aunts and nieces, the ball was broke up.

———o———

Chapter VI.

What choice to choose for delicacy best.

MILTON.

OF what nature were the remarks passed in the
parlour upon the young couple, has not
reached the writer of these memoirs with as
much exactness as the foregoing circumstances ; but
they may in part be imagined from the sketch already
given of the characters which formed the Glenfern
party.   The conciliatory indulgence of Mrs Douglas,
when aided by the good natured Miss Grizzy, doubtless had a favourable effect on the irritated pride, but
short-lived acrimony, of the old gentleman.   Certain
it is, that before the evening concluded they appeared all
restored to harmony, and retired to their respective chambers in hopes of beholding a more propitious morrow.

Who has not perused sonnets, odes, and speeches, in
praise of that balmy blessing, sleep ; from the divine
effusions of Shakspeare down to the drowsy notes of
newspaper poets?

Yet cannot too much be said in its commendation.
Sweet is its influence on the care-worn eyes, to tears
accustomed !   In its arms the statesman forgets his
harassed thoughts ; the weary and the poor are blessed
by its influence ; and conscience—even conscience—is
sometimes soothed into silence while the sufferer sleeps.
But no where, perhaps, is its influence more happily
felt, than in the heart oppressed by the harassing accu-

mulation of petty ills : like a troop of locusts, making up by their number and their stings what they want in magnitude.

Mortified pride in discovering the fallacy of our own judgment,—to be ashamed of what we love, yet still to love,—are feelings most unpleasant ; and, though they assume not the dignity of deep distress, yet philosophy has scarce any power to soothe their worrying, incessant annoyance. Douglas was glad to forget himself in sleep. He had thought a vast deal that day, and, of unpleasant subjects, more than the whole of his foregoing life would have produced. If he did not execrate the fair object of his imprudence, he at least execrated his own folly and himself ; and these were his last waking thoughts.

But Douglas could not repose as long as the seven sleepers ; and, in consequence of having retired sooner to bed than he was accustomed to do, he waked at an early hour in the morning.

The wonderful activity which people sometimes feel when they have little to do with their bodies, and less with their minds, caused him to rise hastily and dress, hoping to pick up a new set of ideas by virtue of his locomotive powers.

On descending to the dining parlour, he found his father seated at the window, carefully perusing a pamphlet, written to illustrate the principle, *Let nothing be lost,* and containing many sage and erudite directions for the composition and dimensions of that ornament to a gentleman's farm-yard, and a cottager's front door, yclept, in the language of the country, a *midden*—with the signification of which we would not, for the world, shock the more refined feelings of our southern readers.

Many were the inquiries about dear Lady Juliana : hoped she had rested well : hoped they found the bed comfortable, not too many blankets, nor too few pillows,

&c., &c. These inquiries were interrupted by the laird, who requested his son to take a turn with him while breakfast was getting ready, that they might talk over past events, and new plans; that he might see the plantation on the hill; the draining of the great moss; with other agricultural concerns which we shall omit, not having the same power of commanding attention from our readers, as the laird had from his hearers.

After repeated summonses, and many inquiries from the impatient party already assembled round the break-fast table, Lady Juliana made her appearance, accompanied by her favourites, whom no persuasions of her husband could prevail upon her to leave behind.

As she entered the room, her olfactory nerves were smote with gales, not of "Araby the blest," but of old cheese and herrings, with which the hospitable board was amply provided.

The ladies having severally exchanged the salutations of the morning, Miss Nicky commenced the operation of pouring out tea, while the laird laid a large piece of herring on her ladyship's plate.

"What am I to do with this?" exclaimed she: "do take it away, or I shall faint!"

"Brother, brother!" cried Miss Grizzy, in a tone of alarm, "I beg you won't place any unpleasant object before the eyes of our dear niece. I declare!— Pray, was it the sight or the smell of the beast * that shocked you so much, my dear Lady Juliana? I'm sure, I wish to goodness Lady Maclaughlan was come!"

Mr Douglas, or the major, as he was styled, immediately rose, and pulled the bell.

"Desire my gig to be got ready immediately after breakfast!" said he.

* In Scotland, everything that flies and swims ranks in the bestial tribe.

The aunts drew up stiffly, and looked at each other, without speaking; but the old gentleman expressed his surprise that his son should think of leaving them so soon.

"May we inquire the reason of this sudden resolution?" at length said Miss Jacky, in a tone of stifled indignation.

"Certainly, if you are disposed to hear it. It is because I find there is company expected."

The three ladies turned up their hands and eyes in speechless horror.

"Is it that virtuous woman, Lady Maclaughlan, you would shun, nephew?" demanded Miss Jacky.

"It is that insufferable pest I would shun," replied her nephew, with a heightened colour, and a violence very unusual with him.

The good Miss Grizzy drew out her pocket handkerchief; while Mrs Douglas vainly endeavoured to silence her husband, and avert the rising storm.

"Dear Douglas!" whispered she, in a tone of reproach.

"Oh, pray let him go on," said Miss Jacky, almost choking under the effort she made to appear calm. "Let him go on. Lady Maclaughlan's character, luckily, is far above the reach of calumny; nothing that Major Archibald Douglas can say will have power to change our opinions, or, I hope, to prejudice his brother and Lady Juliana against this most exemplary, virtuous woman—a woman of family, although English—of fortune—of talents—of accomplishments!—a woman of unblemished reputation! of the strictest morals! sweetest temper! charming heart! delightful spirits!—so charitable! every year gives fifty flannel petticoats to the old people of the parish "——

"Then such a wife as she is!" sobbed out Miss Grizzy. "And no wonder, considering that she has

been twice married ; and she has discovered I can't tell
you how many most invaluable medicines for his complaint, and makes a point of his taking some of them
every day : but for her, I'm sure he would have been
in his grave long ago—there can be no doubt about
that."

"She is doing all she can to send him there, as she
has done many a poor wretch already, with her vile
compositions," said Mr Douglas.

Here Miss Grizzy sunk back in her chair, overcome
with horror ; and Miss Nicky let fall the tea-pot, the
scalding contents of which discharged themselves upon
the unfortunate Psyche, whose yells, mingling with the
screams of its fair mistress, for a while drowned even
Miss Jacky's oratory.

"Oh ! what shall I do ? " cried Lady Juliana, as she
bent over her favourite. "Do send for a surgeon ; pray
do fetch one directly, or she will die ; and it would quite
kill me to lose my darling. Do fly, dearest Harry ! "

"My dear Julia, how can you be so absurd ? there is
no surgeon within twenty miles of this."

"No surgeon within twenty miles ! " exclaimed she,
starting up. "How could you bring me to such a place !
Those dear creatures may die—I may die myself before
I can get any assistance ! "

"Don't be frightened, my dear niece," said the good
Miss Grizzy in a soothing accent. "I assure you you
are perfectly safe here, for we are all doctors, and have
plenty of every kind of medicine you can think of in
the house—our excellent friend Lady Maclaughlan takes
good care of that ; and I'm sure if it hadn't been for
her we might all have been dead twenty times over ;
but she is perfect mistress of every disease that ever was
heard of,—there's no doubt about that ! "

"Put a cauld patatee to the beast's paw," said the
laird gruffly.

"Animals must learn patience as well as others," said Miss Jacky.

"We are never too old to learn," said Miss Nicky.

"I'm sure that's true—nobody can dispute that," said Miss Grizzy, "but at the same time I declare I think we ought to try that new box of scald ointment of Lady Maclaughlan's; I'm certain she would think it well bestowed."

"If it don't cure, it will kill," said Mr Douglas, with a smile.

"Brother!" said Miss Jacky, rising with dignity from her chair, and waving her hand as she spoke—"Brother! I appeal to you, to protect the character of this most amiable, virtuous, respectable matron from the insults and calumny your son thinks proper to load it with. The daughter of Sir Hildebrand Dak—the great-grand-daughter of our common ancestress Lady Janet Campbell—the widow of Colonel Lawless—the wife of Sir Sampson Maclaughlan—to be thus blackened and wounded by your son! Brother! Sir Sampson Maclaughlan is your friend; and it therefore becomes your duty to defend his wife to your latest breath!"

"Troth, but I'll hae enough to do, if I am to stand up for a' my friends' wives," said the old gentleman. "But, however, Archie, you are to blame: Leddy Maclaughlan is a very respectable woman; at least, as far as I ken, though she is a little free in the gab; and, out of respect to my auld friend Mr Sampson, it is my desire that you should remain here to receive him, and that you treat both him and his leddy discreetly."

This was said in too serious a tone to be disputed; and his son was obliged to submit.

The ointment meanwhile having been applied to Psyche's paw, peace was restored, and breakfast recommenced.

"I declare our dear niece has not tasted a morsel," observed Miss Nicky.

"Bless me, here's charming barley-meal scones," cried one, thrusting a plateful of them before her.—"Here's tempting pease-bannocks," interposed another, "and oat cakes! I'm sure your ladyship never saw such cakes."

"I can't eat any of those things," said their delicate niece, with an air of disgust. "I should like some muffin and chocolate."

"You forget you are not in London, my love," said her husband, reproachfully.

"No, indeed I do not forget it. Well, then, give me some toast," with an air of languid condescension.

"Unfortunately, we happen to be quite out of loaf bread at present," said Miss Nicky; "but we've sent to Drymsine for some. They bake excellent bread at Drymsine."

"Is there nothing within the bounds of possibility you could fancy, Julia?" asked Douglas. "Do think, love."

"I think I should like some grouse, or a beef steak, if it was very nicely done," returned her ladyship in a languishing tone.

"Beef steak!" repeated Miss Grizzy.

"Beef steak!" responded Miss Jacky.

"Beef steak!" reverberated Miss Nicky.

After much deliberation and consultation amongst the three spinsters, it was at length unanimously carried that the lady's whim should be indulged.

"Only think, sisters," observed Miss Grizzy in an undertone, "what reflections we should have to make upon ourselves, if any of our descendants were to resemble a moor-fowl!"

"Or have a face like a raw beef steak!" said Miss Nicky.

These arguments were unanswerable; and a smoking

steak and plump moor-fowl were quickly produced; of which Lady Juliana partook, in company with her four-footed favourites.

————o————

Chapter vij.

When winter soaks the fields, and female feet—
Too weak to struggle with tenacious clay,
Or ford the rivulets—are best at home.
The Task.

THE meal being at length concluded, Glenfern desired Henry to attend him on a walk, as he wished to have a little more private conversation with him. Lady Juliana was beginning a remonstrance against the cruelty of taking Harry away from her; when her husband whispering her, that he hoped to make something of the old gentleman, and that he should soon be back, she suffered him to depart in silence.

Old Donald having at length succeeded in clearing the table of its heterogeneous banquet, it was quickly covered with the young ladies' work.

Miss Nicky withdrew to her household affairs. Miss Jacky sat with one eye upon Lady Juliana, the other upon her five nieces. Miss Grizzy seated herself by her ladyship, holding a spread letter of Lady Maclaughlan's before her as a screen.

While the young ladies busily plied their needles, the elder ones left no means untried to entertain their listless niece, whose only replies were exclamations of weariness, or expressions of affection bestowed upon her favourites.

At length even Miss Jacky's sense, and Miss Grizzy's good-nature, were *at fault;* when a ray of

sunshine darting into the room suggested the idea of a
walk. The proposal was made, and assented to by her
ladyship, in the twofold hope of meeting her husband
and pleasing her dogs, whose whining and scratching
had for some time testified their desire of a change.
The ladies therefore separated to prepare for their *sortie*,
after many recommendations from the aunts to be sure
to *hap* * well; but, as if distrusting her powers in that
way, they speedily equipped themselves, and repaired to
her chamber, arrayed *cap-à-pié* in the walking costume
of Glenfern Castle. And, indeed, it must be owned
their style of dress was infinitely more judicious than
that of their fashionable niece; and it was not surprising that they, in their shrunk duffle great-coats, vast
poke-bonnets, red worsted neckcloths, and pattens,
should gaze with horror at her lace cap, lilac satin
pelisse, and silk shoes. Ruin to the whole race of
Glenfern, present and future, seemed inevitable from
such a display of extravagance and imprudence. Having surmounted the first shock, Miss Jacky made a
violent effort to subdue her rising wrath; and, with a
sort of convulsive smile, addressed Lady Juliana:
" Your ladyship, I perceive, is not of the opinion of
our inimitable bard, who, in his charming poem ' The
Seasons,' says, ' Beauty needs not the foreign aid of
ornament; but is, when unadorned, adorned the
most.' That is a truth that ought to be impressed on
every young woman's mind."

Lady Juliana only stared. She was as little accustomed to be advised as she was to hear Thomson's
Seasons quoted.

" I declare that's all quite true," said the more tem-
porising Grizzy; "and certainly our girls are not in
the least taken up about their dress, poor things!
which is a great comfort. At the same time, I'm sure

* Wrap

it's no wonder your ladyship should be taken up about yours, for certainly that pelisse is most beautiful,—nobody can deny that; and I dare say it is the very newest fashion. At the same time, I'm just afraid that it's rather too delicate, and that it might perhaps get a little dirty on our roads; for although, in general, our roads are quite remarkable for being always dry, which is a great comfort in the country, yet, you know, the very best roads of course must be wet sometimes. And there's a very bad step just at the door almost, which Glenfern has been always speaking about getting mended. But, to be sure, he has so many things to think about, that it's no wonder he forgets sometimes; but I dare say he will get it done very soon now."

The prospect of the road being mended produced no better effect than the quotation from Thomson's Seasons. It was now Miss Nicky's turn.

" I'm afraid your ladyship will frighten our stirks and stots with your finery. I assure you, they are not accustomed to see such fine figures; and," putting her hand out at the window, "I think it's spitting already." *

All three now joined in the chorus, beseeching Lady Juliana to put on something warmer and more wise-like.

" I positively have nothing," cried she, wearied with their importunities, "and I shan't get any winter things now till I return to town. My *roquelaire* does very well for the carriage."

The acknowledgment at the beginning of this speech was enough. All three instantly disappeared, like the genii of Aladdin's lamp, and, like that same person, presently returned, loaded with what, in their eyes, were precious as the gold of Arabia. One displayed a hard worsted shawl, with a flower-pot at each corner; another held up a tartan cloak, with a hood; and a

* A common expression in Scotland to signify slight rain.

third thrust forward a dark cloth joseph, lined with
flannel ; while one and all showered down a variety of
old bonnets, fur tippets, hair soles, clogs, pattens, and
endless *et ceteras.* Lady Juliana shrank with disgust
from these "delightful haps," and resisted all attempts
to have them forced upon her, declaring, in a manner
which showed her determined to have her own way,
that she would either go out as she was, or not go out
at all. The aunts were therefore obliged to submit, and
the party proceeded to what was termed the high road,
though a stranger would have sought in vain for its
pretensions to that title. Far as the eye could reach,
and that was far enough, not a single vehicle could be
descried on it, though its deep ruts showed that it was
well frequented by carts. The scenery might have
had charms for Ossian, but it had none for Lady
Juliana ; who would rather have been entangled in a
string of Bond Street equipages, than traversing "the
lonely heath, with the stream murmuring hoarsely ; the
old trees groaning in the wind ; the troubled lake," and
the still more troubled sisters. As may be supposed,
she very soon grew weary of the walk. The bleak
wind pierced her to the soul ; her silk slippers and lace
flounces became undistinguishable masses of mud ; her
dogs chased the sheep, and were, in their turn, pursued
by the "nowts," as the ladies termed the steers. One
sister expatiated on the great blessing of having a peat
moss at their door ; another was at pains to point out
the purposed site of a set of new offices ; and the third
lamented that her ladyship had not on thicker shoes,
that she might have gone and seen the garden. More
than ever disgusted and wretched, the hapless Lady
Juliana returned to the house, to fret away the time till
her husband's return.

————o————

Chapter viij.

—— On se rend insupportable dans la société par des
défauts légers, mais qui se font sentir à tout moment.——
VOLTAIRE.

THE family of Glenfern have already said so much
for themselves, that it seems as if little remained
to be told by their biographer. Mrs Douglas
was the only member of the community who was at all
conscious of the unfortunate association of characters and
habits that had just taken place. She was a stranger to
Lady Juliana; but she was interested by her youth,
beauty, and elegance, and felt for the sacrifice she had
made,—a sacrifice so much greater than it was possible
she ever could have conceived or anticipated. She
could in some degree enter into the nature of her feelings
towards the old ladies; for she, too, had felt how disagreeable people might contrive to render themselves,
without being guilty of any particular fault; and how
much more difficult it is to bear with the weaknesses
than the vices of our neighbours. Had these ladies'
failings been greater in a moral point of view, it might not
have been so arduous a task to put up with them. But
to love such a set of little, trifling, tormenting foibles, all
dignified with the name of virtues, required, from her
elegant mind, an exertion of its highest principles; a
continual remembrance of that difficult Christian precept,
" to bear with one another." A person of less sense
than Mrs Douglas would have endeavoured to open the
eyes of their understandings, on what appeared to be
the folly and narrow-mindedness of their ways; but
she refrained from the attempt, not from want of
benevolent exertion, but from an innate conviction that
their foibles all originated in what was now incurable;
viz., the natural weakness of their minds, together

with their ignorance of the world, and the illiberality
and prejudices of a vulgar education. "These poor
women," reasoned the charitable Mrs Douglas, "are,
perhaps, after all, better characters in the sight of God
than I am. He who has endowed us all as his wisdom
has seen fit, and has placed me amongst them,—Oh!
may he teach me to remember, that we are all his
children, and enable me to bear with their faults, while
I study to correct my own."

Thus did this amiable woman contrive, not only to
live in peace, but, without sacrificing her own liberal
ideas, to be actually beloved by those amongst whom
her lot had been cast, however dissimilar to herself.
But for that Christian spirit, (in which must ever be
included a liberal mind and gentle temper), she must
have felt towards her connexions a still stronger repugnance than was even manifested by Lady Juliana;
for Lady Juliana's superiority over them was merely that
of refined habits and elegant manners; whereas Mrs
Douglas's was the superiority of a noble and highly
gifted mind, which could hold no intercourse with theirs,
except by stooping to the level of their low capacities.
But, that the merit of her conduct may be duly
appreciated, I shall endeavour to give a slight sketch
of the female *dramatis personæ* of Glenfern Castle.

Miss Jacky, the senior of the trio, was what is
reckoned a very sensible woman—which generally
means, a very disagreeable, obstinate, illiberal director
of all men, women, and children—a sort of super-
intendent of all actions, time, and place—with unquestioned authority to arraign, judge, and condemn,
upon the statutes of her own supposed sense. Most
country parishes have their sensible woman, who lays
down the law on all affairs spiritual and temporal.
Miss Jacky stood unrivalled as the sensible woman
of Glenfern. She had attained this eminence, partly

from having a little more understanding than her
sisters, but principally from her dictatorial manner,
and the pompous, decisive tone, in which she delivered
the most common-place truths. At home, her
supremacy in all matters of sense was perfectly established; and thence the infection, like other super-
stitions, had spread over the whole neighbourhood.
As a sensible woman, she regulated the family, which
she took care to let everybody see; she was con-
ductor of her nieces' education, which she took care
to let every body hear; she was a sort of postmistress-
general—a detector of all abuses and impositions;
and deemed it her prerogative to be consulted about
all the useful and useless things, which every body
else could have done as well. She was liberal of
her advice to the poor, always enforcing upon them
the iniquity of idleness, but doing nothing for them
in the way of employment—strict economy being
one of the many points in which she was particularly
sensible. The consequence was, while she was lecturing half the poor women in the parish for their
idleness, the bread was kept out of their mouths, by
the incessant shaping, and sewing, and marking, and
marring, and putting in, and picking out, and carding
of wool and knitting of stockings, and spinning, and
reeling, and winding, and pirning, that went on
amongst the ladies themselves. And, by the bye, Miss
Jacky is not the only sensible woman who thinks
she is acting a meritorious part, when she converts what
ought to be the portion of the poor into the employment
of the affluent.

In short, Miss Jacky was all over sense. A skilful
physiognomist would, at a single glance, have detected
the sensible woman, in the erect head, the compressed
lips, square elbows, and firm judicious step. Even her
very garments seemed to partake of the prevailing char-

acter of their mistress: her ruff always looked more sensible than any other body's; her shawl sat more sensibly on her shoulders; her walking shoes were acknowledged to be very sensible; and she drew on her gloves with an air of sense, as if the one arm had been Seneca, the other Socrates. From what has been said, it may easily be inferred that Miss Jacky was, in fact, any thing but a sensible woman; as indeed no one can be, who bears such visible outward marks of what is in reality the most quiet and unostentatious of all good qualities. But there is a spurious sense, which passes equally well with the multitude: it is easily assumed, and still easier maintained; common truths, and a grave, dictatorial air, being all that is necessary for its support.

Miss Grizzy's character will not admit of as long a commentary as that of her sister: she was merely distinguishable from nothing by her simple good nature, the inextricable entanglement of her thoughts, which she always sought to adjust by an emphatic asseveration, her love of letter-writing, and her friendship with Lady Maclaughlan. Miss Nicky had about as much sense as Miss Jacky; but, as no kingdom can maintain two kings, so no family can admit of two sensible women; and Nicky was, therefore, obliged to confine hers to the narrowest possible channels of housekeeping, mantua-making, &c., and to sit down for life (or at least till Miss Jacky should be married) with the dubious character of " not wanting for sense either." With all these little peccadilloes, the sisters possessed some good properties: they were well-meaning, kind-hearted, and, upon the whole, good-tempered; they loved one another, revered their brother, doated upon their nephews and nieces, took a lively interest in the poorest of their poor cousins a hundred degrees removed, and had a firm conviction of the perfectibility of human nature, as exemplified in the persons of all their own friends. " Even their failings leaned to virtue's side;" for whatever they did was with the intention of doing good, though the means they made use of generally produced an opposite effect. In short, they were not of the M'Larty, or "*canna be fashed*," school; for their life was one continued *fash* about every thing or nothing. But there are so many Miss Douglases in the world, that doubtless every one of my readers is as well acquainted with them as I am myself. I shall, therefore, leave them to finish the picture according to their own ideas, while I return to the parlour, where the worthy spinsters are seated in expectation of the arrival of their friend.

———o———

Chapter ix.

Though both
Not equal, as their sex not equal seemed—
For contemplation he, and valour formed;
For softness she, and sweet attractive grace.

MILTON.

"WHAT *can* have come over Lady Maclaughlan?" said Miss Grizzy, as she sat at the window in a dejected attitude.

"I think I hear a carriage at last," cried Miss Jacky, turning up her ear: "Wisht! let us listen."

"It's only the wind," sighed Miss Grizzy.

"It's the cart with the bread," said Miss Nicky.

"It's Lady Maclaughlan, I assure you," pronounced Miss Jacky.

The heavy rumble of a ponderous vehicle now proclaimed the approach of the expected visitor; which pleasing anticipation was soon changed into blissful certainty, by the approach of a high-roofed, square-bottomed, pea-green chariot, drawn by two **long-tailed**

white horses, and followed by a lacquey in the Highland garb.   Out of this equipage issued a figure clothed
in a light coloured, large flowered chintz raiment, carefully drawn through the pocket holes, either for its own
preservation, or the more disinterested purpose of displaying a dark short stuff petticoat, which, with the
same liberality, afforded ample scope for the survey of
a pair of delicately formed feet and ankles, clad in
worsted stockings and black leather shoes something
resembling buckets.   A faded red cloth jacket, which
bore evident marks of having been severed from its
native skirts, now acted in the capacity of a spencer.
On the head rose a stupendous fabric, in the form of a
cap, on the summit of which was placed a black beaver
hat, tied *à la poissarde.*   A small black satin muff in
one hand, and a gold-headed walking-stick in the
other, completed the dress and decoration of this
personage.

The lacquey, meanwhile, advanced to the carriage ;
and putting in both his hands, as if to catch something,
he pulled forth a small bundle, enveloped in a military
cloak, the contents of which would have baffled conjecture, but for the large cocked hat, and little booted
leg, which protruded at opposite extremities.

A loud, but slow and well modulated, voice now
resounded through the narrow stone passage that conducted to the drawing-room.

" Bring him in—bring him in, Philistine !   I always
call my man Philistine, because he has Sampson in his
hands. Set him down there," pointing to an easy chair,
as the group now entered, headed by Lady Maclaughlan.

" Well, girls ! " addressing the venerable spinsters,
as they severally exchanged a tender salute : so you're
all alive, I see :—humph ! "

" Dear Lady Maclaughlan, allow me to introduce
our beloved niece, Lady Juliana Douglas," said Miss

Grizzy, leading her up, and bridling as she spoke, with ill suppressed exultation.

"So—you're very pretty—yes, you are very pretty!" kissing the forehead, cheeks, and chin of the youthful beauty, between every pause. Then, holding her at arm's length, she surveyed her from head to foot, with elevated brows, and a broad fixed stare.

"Pray sit down, Lady Maclaughlan," cried her three friends all at once, each tendering a chair.

"Sit down!" repeated she; "why, what should I sit down for? I choose to stand—I don't like to sit —I never sit at home—Do I, Sir Sampson?" turning to the little warrior, who, having been seized with a violent fit of coughing on his entrance, had now sunk back, seemingly quite exhausted, while the *Philistine* was endeavouring to disencumber him of his military accoutrements.

"How very distressing Sir Sampson's cough is!" said the sympathising Miss Grizzy.

"Distressing, child! No—it's not the least distressing. How can a thing be distressing that does no harm? He's much the better of it—it's the only exercise he gets."

"Oh! well, indeed, if that's the case, it would be a thousand pities to stop it," replied the accommodating spinster.

"No, it wouldn't be the least pity to stop it!" returned Lady Maclaughlan, in her loud authoritative tone; "because, though it's not distressing, it's very disagreeable. But it cannot be stopped—you might as well talk of stopping the wind — it is a cradle cough."

"My dear Lady Maclaughlan!" screamed Sir Sampson, in a shrill pipe, as he made an effort to raise himself, and rescue his cough from this aspersion; "how can you persist in saying so, when I have told you so often it proceeds entirely from a cold caught a few years ago, when I attended his Majesty at " —— Here a violent relapse carried the conclusion of the sentence along with it.

"Let him alone—don't meddle with him," called his lady to the assiduous nymphs who were bustling around him—"leave him to Philistine; he's in very good hands when he is in Philistine's." Then, resting her chin upon the head of her stick, she resumed her scrutiny of Lady Juliana.

"You really are a pretty creature! You've got a very handsome nose, and your mouth's very well, but I don't quite like your eyes, they're too large and too light; they're saucer eyes, and I don't like saucer eyes. Why ha'nt you black eyes? you're not a bit like your father—I knew him very well. Your mother was an heiress, your father married her for her money, and she married him to be a countess, and so that's the history of their marriage—humph."

This well-bred harangue was delivered in an unvarying tone, and with unmoved muscles; for though the lady seldom failed of calling forth some conspicuous emotion, either of shame, mirth, or anger, on the countenances of her hearers, she had never been known to betray any correspondent feelings on her own. Yet her features were finely formed, marked, and expressive; and, in spite of her ridiculous dress and rude eccentric manners, an air of aristocracy, and even of dignity, was diffused over her whole person, that screened her from the ridicule or insult to which she must otherwise have been exposed. For amazement at the uncouth garb and singular address of Lady Maclaughlan, was seldom unmixed with terror at the stern imperious manner that accompanied all her words and actions. Such were the feelings of Lady Juliana, as she remained subjected to her rude gaze, and impertinent remarks.

" My lady ! " squeaked Sir Sampson from forth his easy chair.

" My love ? " interrogated his lady, as she leaned upon her stick.

" I want to be introduced to my Lady Juliana Douglas ; so give me your hand," attempting, at the same time, to emerge from the huge leathern receptacle into which he had been plunged by the care of the kind sisters.

" Oh, pray sit still, dear Sir Sampson," cried they as usual all at once ; " our sweet niece will come to you ; don't take the trouble to rise, pray don't," each putting a hand on this man of might, as he was half risen, and pushing him down.

" Ay, come here, my dear," said Lady Maclaughlan ; " you're abler to walk to Sir Sampson than he to you," pulling Lady Juliana in front of the easy chair ; " there —that's her ; you see she is very pretty."

" Zounds, what is the meaning of all this ! " screamed the enraged baronet. " My Lady Juliana Douglas, I am shocked beyond expression at this freedom of my lady's. I beg your ladyship ten thousand pardons ; pray be seated. I'm shocked—I am ready to faint at the impropriety of this introduction, so contrary to all rules of etiquette. How *could* you behave in such a manner, my Lady Maclaughlan ? "

" Why, you know, my dear, your legs may be very good legs, but they can't walk," replied she, with her usual *sang froid*.

" My Lady Maclaughlan, you perfectly confound me ! " stuttering with rage. " My Lady Juliana Douglas, see here," stretching out a meagre shank, to which not even the military boot and large spur could give a respectable appearance. " You see that leg strong and straight," stroking it down ; " now, behold the fate of war ! " dragging forward the other, which was shrunk and shrivelled to almost one half its original dimensions. "These legs were once the same; but I repine not—I sacrificed it in a noble cause—to that leg my sovereign owes his life!"

"Well, I declare, I had no idea; I thought always it had been rheumatism," burst from the lips of the astonished spinsters, as they crowded round the illustrious limb, and regarded it with looks of veneration.

"Humph!" emphatically uttered his lady.

"The story's a simple one, ladies, and soon told: I happened to be attending his majesty at a review; I was then aide-de-camp to Lord ——. His horse took fright, I— I— I,"—here, in spite of all the efforts that could be made to suppress it, the *royal cough* burst forth with a violence that threatened to silence its brave owner for ever.

"It's very strange you will talk, my love," said his sympathising lady, as she supported him; "talking never did and never will agree with you; it's very strange what pleasure people take in talking—humph!"

"Is there any thing dear Sir Sampson could take?" asked Miss Grizzy.

"*Could* take? I don't know what you mean by *could* take. He couldn't take the moon, if you mean that; but he must take what I give him; so call Philistine, he knows where my cough tincture is."

"Oh, we have plenty of it in this press," said Miss Grizzy, flying to a cupboard; and, drawing forth a bottle, she poured out a bumper, and presented it to Sir Sampson.

"I'm poisoned!" gasped he, feebly; "that's not my lady's cough-tincture."

"Not cough-tincture!" repeated the horror-struck doctress, as for the first time she examined the label; "O! I declare, neither it is—its my own stomach lotion. Bless me, what will be done!" and she wrung her hands in despair. "Oh, Murdoch," flying to the *Philistine*, as he entered with the real cough-tincture, "I've given Sir Sampson a dose of my own stomach lotion by mistake, and I am terrified for the consequences!"

"Oo, but hur needna be feared, hur will no be a hair the war o't; for hur wadna tak' the stuff that the leddie ordered hur yesterday."

"Well, I declare things are wisely ordered," observed Miss Grizzy; "in that case, it may do dear Sir Sampson a great deal of good."

Just as this pleasing idea was suggested, Douglas and his father entered, and the ceremony of presenting her nephew to her friend was performed by Miss Grizzy in her most conciliating manner.

"Dear Lady Maclaughlan, this is your nephew Henry, who, I know, has the highest veneration for Sir Sampson and you. Henry, I assure you, Lady Maclaughlan takes the greatest interest in everything that concerns Lady Juliana and you."

"Humph!" rejoined her ladyship, as she surveyed him from head to foot: "so your wife fell in love with you, it seems: well, the more fool she; I never knew any good come of love marriages;—my first marriage was a love match—humph! my second was —— humph!"

Douglas coloured, while he affected to laugh at this extraordinary address, and, withdrawing himself from her scrutiny, resumed his station by the side of his Juliana.

"Now, girls, I must go to my toilette; which of you am I to have for my handmaid?"

"Oh, we'll all go!" eagerly exclaimed the three nymphs; "our dear niece will excuse us for a little; young people are never at a loss to amuse one another."

"Venus and the Graces!" exclaimed Sir Sampson,

bowing with an air of gallantry; "and now I must go
and adonise a little myself."

The company then separated, to perform the important
offices of the toilet.

————o————

Chapter X.

Nature here
Wanton'd as in her prime, and played at will
Her virgin fancies.

MILTON.

THE gentlemen were already assembled round the
drawing-room fire, impatiently waiting the hour
of dinner, when Lady Maclaughlan and her three
friends entered.   The masculine habiliments of the morning had been exchanged for a more feminine costume.
She was now arrayed in a pompadour satin négligée, and
petticoat trimmed with Brussels lace.   A high starched
handkerchief formed a complete breastwork, on which,
amidst a large bouquet of truly artificial roses, reposed a
miniature of Sir Sampson, *à la militaire*.   A small fly
cap of antique lace was scarcely perceptible on the
summit of a stupendous frizzled toupee, hemmed in on
each side by large curls.   The muff and stick had been
relinquished for a large fan, something resembling an
Indian skreen, which she waved to and fro in one hand,
while a vast brocaded work-bag was suspended from the
other.

"So, Major Douglas, your servant," said she, in
answer to the constrained formal bow with which he
saluted her on her entrance—"why, it's so long since
I've seen you, that you may be a grandfather for aught
I know."

The poor awkward Misses at that moment came
sneaking into the room: "As for you, girls, you'll

never be grandmothers ; you'll never be married, unless
to wild men of the woods. I suppose you'd like that ;
it would save you the trouble of combing your hair, and
tying your shoes, for then you could go without clothes
altogether—humph ! you'd be much better without
clothes than to put them on as you do," seizing upon
the luckless Miss Baby, as she endeavoured to steal
behind backs.

And here, in justice to the lady, it must be owned,
that, for once, she had some grounds for animadversion
in the dress and appearance of the Misses Douglas.

They had staid out, running races, and riding on a
pony, until near the dinner hour ; and, dreading their
father's displeasure should they be too late, they had,
with the utmost haste, exchanged their thick morning
dresses for thin muslin gowns, made, by a mantua-
maker of the neighbourhood, in the extreme of a two-
year-old fashion, when waists *were not.*

But as dame Nature had been particularly lavish in
the length of theirs, and the staymaker had, according
to their aunt's direction, given them *full measure* of
their new dark stays, there existed a visible breach between the waists of their gowns and the bands of their
petticoats, which they had vainly sought to adjust by a
meeting. Their hair had been curled, but not combed ;
and dark gloves had been hastily drawn on to hide red
arms.

" I suppose," continued the stern Lady Maclaughlan, as she twirled her victim round and round ; " I
suppose you think yourself vastly smart and well
dressed. Yes, you are very neat, very neat indeed :
one would suppose Ben Jonson had you in his eye
when he composed that song " : Then in a voice like
thunder, she chanted forth—

> " Give me a look, give me a face
> That makes simplicity a grace ;

Robes loosely flowing, hair as free,
Such sweet neglect more taketh me," &c., &c.

Miss Grizzy was in the utmost perplexity, between
her inclination to urge something in extenuation for
the poor girls, and her fear of dissenting from Lady
Maclaughlan, or rather of not immediately agreeing
with her; she, therefore, steered, as usual, the middle
course, and kept saying, " Well, children, really what
Lady Maclaughlan says, is all very true; at the same
time," turning to her friend,—" I declare it's not much
to be wondered at; young people are so thoughtless,
poor lambs ! "

" Thoughtless ! " in a tone that struck a panic into
poor Miss Grizzy's gentle breast. " Thoughtless !
why, what have these girls to think about but lacing
their stays and combing their hair ? It don't signify
what you wear," continued she, addressing the culprits,
as they sat in a corner, in all the various postures which
awkwardness suggests—" I say, it don't signify what
you wear, so as it's clean and well put on ;—you would
be more respectable figures in your father's nightcaps
than with these mops."

" What's a' this wark aboot ? " said the old gentleman, angrily ; " the girlies are weel eneugh ; I see
naething the matter wi' them—they're no dressed like
auld queens, or stage-actresses " ; and he glanced his
eye from Lady Maclaughlan to his elegant daughter-
in-law, who just then entered, hanging, according to
custom, on her husband, and preceded by Cupid ; Mrs
Douglas followed, and the sound of the dinner-bell put
a stop to the dispute.

" Come, my leddy, we'll see how the dinner's
dressed," said the laird, as he seized Lady Maclaughlan
by the tip of the finger, and, holding it up aloft, they
marched into the dining-room.

" Permit me, my Lady Juliana Douglas," said the

little baronet, with much difficulty hobbling towards her, and attempting to take her hand—" Come, Harry, love; here Cupid," cried she; and, without noticing the enraged Sir Sampson, she passed on humming a tune, and leaning upon her husband.

"Astonishing! perfectly astonishing!" exclaimed the baronet; "how a young woman of Lady Juliana's rank and fashion should be guilty of such a solecism in good breeding.

" She is very young," said Mrs Douglas, smiling, as he limped along with her, "and you must make allowances for her; but, indeed, I think her beauty must ever be a sufficient excuse for any little errors she may commit, with a person of such taste and gallantry as Sir Sampson Maclaughlan."

The little baronet smiled, pressed the hand he held; and, soothed by the well-timed compliment, he seated himself next to Lady Juliana with some complacency. As she insisted on having her husband on the other side, Mr Douglas was condemned to take his station by the hated Lady Maclaughlan, who, for the first time, observing Mrs Douglas, called to her,—

"Come here, my love; I hav'n't seen you these hundred years"; then, seizing her face between her hands, she saluted her in the usual style: "There," at length releasing Mrs Douglas from her gripe—"there's for you; I love you very much; you're neither a fool nor a hoyden; you're a fine intelligent being."

Having carefully rolled up and deposited her gloves in her pocket, she pulled out a pincushion, and calling Miss Bella, desired her to pin her napkin over her shoulder; which done, she began to eat her soup in silence.

Peace was, however, of short duration. Old Donald, on removing a dish of whipt cream, unfortunately over-turned one upon Lady Maclaughlan's pompadour satin petticoat; the only part of her dress that was unprotected.

"Do you see what you have done, you old Donald!" cried she, seizing the culprit by the sleeve; "why, you've got St Vitus's dance—a fit hand to carry whipt cream, to be sure! why, I could as well carry a custard on the point of a bayonet—humph!"

"Dear me, Donald, how could you be so senseless!" cried Miss Jacky.

"Preserve me, Donald, I thought you had more sense!" squeaked Miss Nicky.

"I am sure, Donald, that was not like you!" said Miss Grizzy, as the friends all flocked around the petticoat, each suggesting a different remedy.

"It's all of you, girls, that this has happened: why can't you have a larger table-cloth upon your table?—and that old man has the palsy; why don't you electrify him?" in a tone admirably calculated to have that effect.

"I declare it's all very true," observed Miss Grizzy; "the table-cloth *is* very small, and Donald certainly *does* shake,—that cannot be denied;" but, lowering her voice, "he is so obstinate, we really don't know what to do with him; my sisters and I attempted to use the flesh-brush with him."

"Oh, and an excellent thing it is; I make Philistine rub Sir Sampson every morning and night. If it was not for that and his cough, nobody would know whether he were dead or alive; I don't believe he would know himself—humph!"

Sir Sampson's lemon face assumed an orange hue, as he overheard this domestic detail; but, not daring to contradict the facts, he prudently turned a deaf ear to them, and attempted to carry on a flirtation with Lady Juliana, through the medium of Cupid, whom he had coaxed upon his knee.

Dinner being at length ended, toasts succeeded; and each of the ladies having given her favourite laird, the signal of retreat was given, and a general movement took place.

Lady Juliana, throwing herself upon a sofa, with her pugs, called Mrs Douglas to her: "Do sit down here, and talk with me," yawned she.

Her sister-in-law, with great good humour, fetched her work, and seated herself by the spoilt child.

"What strange thing is that you are making?" asked she, as Mrs Douglas pulled out her knitting.

"A child's stocking," replied her sister-in-law.

"A child's stocking! Oh, by the bye, have you a great many children?"

"I have none," answered Mrs Douglas, with a half-stifled sigh.

"None at all!" repeated Lady Juliana, with surprise; "then why do you make children's stockings?"

"I make them for those whose parents cannot afford to purchase them."

"La! what poor wretches they must be that can't afford to buy stockings," rejoined Lady Juliana with a yawn; "its monstrous good of you to make them, to be sure; but it must be a shocking bore! and such a trouble!" and another long yawn succeeded.

"Not half such a bore to me as to sit idle," returned Mrs Douglas, with a smile; "nor nearly so much trouble as you undergo with your favourites."

Lady Juliana made no reply, but, turning from her sister-in-law, soon was, or affected to be, sound asleep, from which she was only roused by the entrance of the gentlemen.

"A rubber or a reel, my leddy?" asked the laird, going up to his daughter-in-law.

"Julia, love," said her husband, "my father asks you if you choose cards or dancing"

"There's nobody to dance with," said she, casting a languid glance around; "I'll play at cards."

"Not whist, surely!" said Henry.

"Whist! oh, no."

"Weel, weel, you youngsters will get a round game; come, my Leddy Maclaughlan, Grizzy, Mrs Douglas, hey for the odd trick and the honours!"

"What would your ladyship choose to play at?" asked Miss Jacky, advancing with a pack of cards in one hand, and a box of counters in the other.

"Oh, any thing; I like loo very well, or quadrille, or—I really don't care what."

The Misses, who had gathered round, and were standing gaping in joyful expectation of Pope Joan, or a pool at commerce, here exchanged sorrowful glances.

"I am afraid the young people don't play at these games," replied Miss Jacky; "but we've counters enough," shaking her little box, "for Pope Joan, and we all know that."

"Pope Joan! I never heard of such a game," replied Lady Juliana.

"Oh, we can soon learn you," said Miss Nicky, who, having spread the green cloth on the tea-table, now advanced to join the consultation.

"I hate to be taught," said Lady Juliana with a yawn; "besides, I am sure it must be something very stupid."

"Ask if she plays commerce," whispered Miss Bella to Miss Baby.

The question was put, but with no better success, and the young ladies' faces again bespoke their disappointment; which their brother observing, he good-naturedly declared his perfect knowledge of commerce; "and I must insist upon teaching you, Juliana," gently dragging her to the table.

" What's the pool to be ? " asked one of the young ladies.

" I'm sure I don't know," said the aunts, looking to each other.

" I suppose we must make it sixpence," said Miss Jacky, after a whispering consultation with her sister.

" In that case we can afford nothing to the best hand," observed Miss Nicky. " And we ought to have seven lives and grace," added one of the nieces.

These points having been conceded, the preliminaries were at length settled. The cards were slowly *doled* out by Miss Jacky; and Lady Juliana was carefully instructed in the rules of the game, and strongly recommended always to try for a sequence, or pairs, &c. " And if you win," rejoined Miss Nicky, shaking the snuffer-stand in which was deposited the sixpences, " you get all this."

As may be conjectured, Lady Juliana's patience could not survive more than one life : she had no notion of playing for sixpences, and could not be at the trouble to attend to any instructions ; she therefore quickly retired in disgust, leaving the aunts and nieces to struggle for the glorious prize.

" My dear child, you played that last stroke like a perfect natural," cried Lady Maclaughlan to Miss Grizzy, as, the rubber ended, they arose from the table.

" Indeed, I declare, I dare say I did," replied her friend, in a deprecating tone.

" Dare say you did! I know you did—humph! I knew the ace lay with you ; I knew that as well as if I had seen it. I suppose you have eyes—but I don't know ; if you have, didn't you see Glenfern turn up the king, and yet you returned his lead—returned your adversary's lead in the face of his king. I've been telling you these twenty years not to return your adversary's lead; nothing can be more despicable; nothing can be a greater proof of imbecility of mind—humph!" Then, seating herself, she began to exercise her fan with considerable activity. "This has been the most disagreeable day I ever spent in this house, girls. I don't know what's come over you, but you are all wrong! my petticoat's ruined; my pocket's picked at cards;—it won't do, girls—it won't do—humph!"

"I am sure, I can't understand it," said Miss Grizzy, in a rueful accent; "there really appears to have been some fatality "——

"Fatality!—humph! I wish you would give every thing its right name. What do you mean by fatality?"

"I declare—I am sure—I—I really don't know," stammered the unfortunate Grizzy.

"Do you mean that the spilling of the custard was the work of an angel?" demanded her unrelenting friend.

"Oh, certainly not."

"Or that it was an evil one tempted you to throw away your ace there? I suppose there's a fatality in our going to supper just now," continued she, as her deep-toned voice resounded through the passage that conducted to the dining-room; "and I suppose it will be called a fatality if that old Fate," pointing to Donald, "scalds me to death with that mess of porridge he's going to put on the table—humph!"

No such fatality, however, occurred; and the rest of the evening passed off in as much harmony as could be expected from the very heterogeneous parts of which the society was formed.

——o——

Chapter xj.

O thoughtless mortals, ever blind to fate,
Too soon dejected, and too soon elate,
Sudden these honours shall be snatch'd away!

POPE.

What virgins these in speechless woe
That bend to earth their solemn brow?

GRAY.

THE family group had already assembled round the breakfast table, with the exception of Lady Juliana, who chose to take that meal in bed: but, contrary to her usual custom, no Lady Maclaughlan had yet made her appearance. All was busy speculation and surmise as to the *could-be* cause of this lapse of time on the part of that hitherto most perfect of morning chronometers. Scouts had been sent ever and anon to spy, to peep, to listen; but nothing was brought back but idle guesses and shallow conjectures. It had, however, been clearly ascertained that Sir Sampson had been heard to cough and find fault with Murdoch in the dressing-room, and Lady Maclaughlan to humph! in her sternial tone, as she walked to and fro in her chamber. So far all was well. But for Lady Maclaughlan still to be in her chamber twenty minutes after the breakfast-bell had rung—'twas strange—'twas passing strange!

" The scones will be like leather," said Miss Grizzy, in her most doleful accent, as she wrapped another napkin round them.

" The eggs will be like snow-balls," cried Miss Jacky, warmly, popping them into the slop-basin.

" The tea will be like brandy," observed Miss Nicky, sharply, as she poured more water to the three tea spoonfuls she had infused.

" I wish we saw our breakfast," said the laird, as he finished the newspapers, and deposited his spectacles in his pocket.

" It *is* rather hard to be kept starving all day for that——," said Mr Douglas, as he swallowed a slice of cold beef, that carried the conclusion of the sentence along with it.

At that moment the door opened, and the person in question entered in her travelling dress, followed by Sir Sampson ; Philistine bringing up the rear, with a large green bag and a little band-box under his arm.

" Good morning, dear Lady Maclaughlan ! Good morning, dear Sir Sampson ! We are all delighted to see you—we were beginning to get a little uneasy, for you are always so punctual !—but you are in charming time—neither too soon nor too late," immediately burst as if from a thousand voices, while the sisters officiously fluttered round their friend.

" Humph ; " quoth the lady.

" I hope your bed was warm and comfortable ? "

" I hope you rested well ? "

" I hope Sir Sampson had a good night ? " immediately burst as from a thousand voices.

" I rested very ill ; my bed was very uncomfortable ; and Sir Sampson's as yellow as a duck's foot—humph ! "

Three disconsolate " Bless me's ! " here burst forth.

" Perhaps your bed was too hard ? " said Miss Grizzy.

" Or too soft ? " suggested Miss Jacky.

" Or too hot ? " added Miss Nicky.

" It was neither too hard, nor too soft, nor too hot, nor too cold," thundered the lady, as she seated herself at the table ; " but it was all of them."

" I declare, that's most distressing," said Miss Grizzy, in a tone of sorrowful amazement. " Was your head high enough, dear Lady Maclaughlan ? "

" Perhaps it was too high," said Miss Jacky.

" I know nothing more disagreeable than a high head," remarked Miss Nicky.

" Except a fool's head—humph!

> " Now my weary lips I close;
> Leave me, leave me to repose."

And she betook herself to the business of the morning with the air of one who was determined to utter no more till that was despatched. There was something so portentous in the tone and responses of their oracle, that, inquisitive as the sisters were, still they were not so pertinacious in their curiosity as King Odin: for once on a time, therefore, all three were silenced in a breath, and a pause of mute consternation ensued.

Soon, however, the sound of a carriage broke the solemn stillness, and set all ears on full stretch, when presently the well-known pea-green drew up.

" Dear me! Bless me! Goodness me!" shrieked the three ladies at once. " Surely, Lady Maclaughlan, you can't—you don't—you won't—this must be a mistake?"

" There's no mistake in the matter, girls," replied their friend, with her accustomed *sang froid*. " I'm going home; so I ordered the carriage; that's all— humph!"

" Going home!" faintly murmured the disconsolate spinisters.

" What! I suppose you think I ought to stay here and have another petticoat spoiled; or lose another half-crown at cards; or have the finishing stroke put to Sir Sampson; or see you all turned into Bedlamites— humph!"

" Oh, Lady Maclaughlan!" was three times uttered in reproachful accents.

" I don't know what else I should stay for: you are

not yourselves, girls; you've all turned topsy-turvy. I've visited here these twenty years, and I never saw things in the state they are now—humph?"

"I declare it's very true," sighed Miss Grizzy; "we certainly are a little in confusion,—that can't be denied."

"Denied! why, you might as well deny that you ever were born!"

"Oh, Lady Maclaughlan!" exclaimed Grizzy, in great trepidation; "I'm sure nobody would ever deny that!"

"Can you deny that my petticoat has been ruined?"

"It will dye," said Nicky.

"So will you," thundered the lady, proceeding in her interrogatories. "Can you deny that my pocket has been picked of half-a-crown? Can you deny that Sir Sampson has been half poisoned? Can you deny that you have all been very disagreeable?"

"My Lady Maclaughlan!" gasped Sir Sampson, who had hitherto been choking under the affront put upon his complexion,—"I—I—I—am surprised—I am shocked—I won't suffer this—I can't stand such" ——and pushing away his tea-cup, he rose, and limped to the window. Murdoch now entered to inform his mistress that "every thing was ready."——"Steady, boys, steady! _I_ always am ready," responded the lady in a tone adapted to the song. "Now I am ready—say nothing, girls—you know my rules.—Here, Philistine, wrap up Sir Sampson, and put him in.—Get along, my love.—Good bye, girls; and I hope you will all be restored to your right senses soon."

"Oh, Lady Maclaughlan!" whined the weeping Grizzy, as she embraced her friend, who, somewhat melted at the signs of her distress, bawled out from the carriage, as the door was shut, "Well, good bye, dear girls, and may ye all become what ye have been; and

you must some of you come to Loch Marlie soon, and
bring your pretty niece and your five senses along with
you : now no more at present from your affectionate
friend."

The carriage then drove off, and the three disconsolate sisters returned to the parlour, to hold a cabinet
council as to the causes of the late disasters.

———o———

Chapter xij.

If there be cure or charm
To respite or relieve, or slack the pain
Of this ill mansion.

MILTON.

TIME, which generally alleviates ordinary distresses, served only to augment the severity
of Lady Juliana's, as day after day rolled
heavily on, and found her still an inmate of Glenfern
Castle. Destitute of every resource in herself, she yet
turned with contempt from the scanty sources of occupation or amusement that were suggested by others ; and
Mrs Douglas's attempts to teach her to play at chess
and read Shakspeare were as unsuccessful as the endeavours of the good aunts to persuade her to study
Fordyce's Sermons and make baby-linen.

In languid dejection, or fretful repinings, did the
unhappy beauty therefore consume the tedious hours,
while her husband sought alternately to soothe with
fondness he no longer felt, or flatter with hopes which
he knew to be groundless. To his father alone he
could now look for any assistance, and from him he was
not likely to obtain it in the form he desired ; as the
old gentleman repeatedly declared his utter inability to
advance him any ready money, or to allow him more

than a hundred a year, moreover to be paid quarterly;
a sum which could not defray their expenses to
London.

Such was the state of affairs, when the laird one
morning entered the dining-room with a face of much
importance, and addressed his son with—"Weel, Harry,
you're a lucky man; and it's an ill wind that blaws
naebody gude: here's poor Macglashan gone like snow
off a dike."

"Macglashan gone!" exclaimed Miss Grizzy. "Impossible, brother; it was only yesterday I sent him a
large blister for his back!"

"And I," said Miss Jacky, "talked to him for
upwards of two hours last night, on the impropriety
of his allowing his daughter to wear white gowns on
Sunday."

"By my troth, an' that was eneugh to kill ony man,"
muttered the laird.

"How I am to derive any benefit from this important
demise is more than I can perceive," said Henry, in a
somewhat contemptuous tone.

"You see," replied his father, "that, by our agree-
ment, his farm falls vacant in consequence."

"And I hope I am to succeed to it?" replied the
son, with a smile of derision.

"Exactly. By my troth, but you have a bein down-
set. There's three thousand and seventy-five acres of
as good sheep-walk as any in the whole country-side;
and I shall advance you stocking and stedding, and
every thing complete, to your very peat-stacks. What
think ye of that?" slapping his son's shoulder, and
rubbing his own hands with delight as he spoke.

Horror-struck at a scheme which appeared to him a
thousand times worse than any thing his imagination
had ever painted, poor Henry stood in speechless consternation; while "charming! excellent! delightful!"

was echoed by the aunts, as they crowded round, wishing him joy, and applauding their brother's generosity.

"What will our sweet niece say to this, I wonder," said the innocent Grizzy, who in truth wondered none. "I would like to see her face when she hears it;" and her own was puckered into various shapes of delight.

"I have no doubt but her good sense will teach her to appreciate properly the blessings of her lot," observed the more reflecting Jacky.

"She has had her own good luck," quoth the sententious Nicky, "to find such a down-set all cut and dry."

At that instant the door opened, and the favoured individual in question entered. In vain Douglas strove to impose silence on his father and aunts. The latter sat, bursting with impatience to break out into exclamation; while the former, advancing to his fair daughter-in-law, saluted her as "Lady Clachandow!" Then the torrent burst forth; and, stupefied with surprise, Lady Juliana suffered herself to be kissed and hugged by the whole host of aunts and nieces; while the very walls seemed to reverberate the shouts; and the pugs and mackaw, who never failed to take part in every commotion, began to bark and scream in chorus.

The old gentleman, clapping his hands to his ears, rushed out of the room. His son, execrating his aunts, and every thing around him, kicked Cupid, and gave the mackaw a box on the ear, as he also quitted the apartment, with more appearance of anger than he had ever yet betrayed.

The tumult at length began to subside. The mackaw's screams gave place to a low quivering croak; and the insulted pug's yells yielded to a gentle whine. The aunts' obstreperous joy began to be chastened with fear for the consequences that might follow an abrupt disclosure; and, while Lady Juliana condoled with her favourites, it was concerted between the prudent aunts that the joyful news should be broke to their niece in the most cautious manner possible. For that purpose, Misses Grizzy and Jacky seated themselves on each side of her; and, after duly preparing their voices by sundry small hems, Miss Grizzy thus began :—

" I'm sure—I declare—I dare say, my dear Lady Juliana, you must think we are all distracted."

Her auditor made no attempt to contradict the supposition.

" We certainly ought, to be sure, to have been more cautious; but the joy—though, indeed, it seems cruel to say so,—and I am sure you will sympathise, my dear niece, in the cause, when you hear that it is occasioned by poor Macglashan's death, which, I'm sure, was quite unexpected. Indeed, I declare I can't conceive how it came about; for Lady Maclaughlan, who is an excellent judge of these things, thought he was really a remarkable stout-looking man for his time of life; and indeed, except occasional colds, which you know we are all subject to, I really never knew him complain. At the same time there can be no doubt "——

" I don't think, sister, you are taking the right method of communicating the intelligence to our niece," said Miss Jacky.

" You cannot communicate any thing that would give me the least pleasure, unless you could tell me that I was going to leave this place," cried Lady Juliana, in a voice of deep despondency.

" Indeed! if it can afford your ladyship so much pleasure to be at liberty to quit the hospitable mansion of your amiable husband's respectable father," said Miss Jacky, with an inflamed visage and outspread hands, " you are at perfect liberty to depart when you think proper. The generosity, I may say the munificence, of my excellent brother, has now put it in your power to do as you please, and to form your own plans.''

" Oh, delightful ! '' exclaimed Lady Juliana, starting up; "now I shall be quite happy. Where's Harry? Does he know?—is he gone to order the carriage?—can we get away to-day?'' And she was flying out of the room, when Miss Jacky caught her by one hand, while Miss Grizzy secured the other.

" Oh, pray don't detain me! I must find Harry; and I have all my things to put up," struggling to release herself from the gripe of the sisters; when the door opened, and Harry entered, eager, yet dreading, to know the effects of the *eclaircissement*. His surprise was extreme at beholding his wife, with her eyes sparkling, her cheeks glowing, and her whole countenance expressing extreme pleasure. Darting from her keepers, she bounded towards him with the wildest ejaculations of delight; while he stood alternately gazing at her and his aunts, seeking, by his eyes, the explanation he feared to demand.

" My dearest Juliana, what is the meaning of all this?'' he at length articulated.

" Oh, you cunning thing! So you think I don't know that your father has given you a great—great quantity of money, and that we may go away whenever we please, and do just as we like, and live in London, and—and—Oh, delightful!'' And she bounded and skipped before the eyes of the petrified spinsters.

" What does all this mean?'' asked Henry, addressing his aunts, who, for the first time in their lives, were struck dumb by astonishment. But Miss Jacky, at length recollecting herself, turned to Lady Juliana, who was still testifying her delight by a variety of childish but graceful movements, and thus addressed her:—

" Permit me to put a few questions to your ladyship,

in presence of those who were witnesses of what has already passed."

"Oh, I can't endure to be asked questions; besides, I have no time to answer them."

"Your ladyship must excuse me; but I can't permit you to leave this room under the influence of an error. Have the goodness to answer me the following questions, and you will then be at liberty to depart:—Did I inform your ladyship that my brother had given my nephew a great quantity of money?"

"Oh, yes—a great, great deal—I don't know how much, though"——

"Did I?" returned her interrogator.

"Come, come, have done with all this nonsense!" exclaimed Henry passionately. "Do you imagine I will allow Lady Juliana to stand here all day, to answer all the absurd questions that come into the heads of three old women? You stupefy and bewilder her with your eternal tattling and round-about harangues." And he paced the room in a paroxysm of rage, whilst his wife suspended her dancing, and stood in breathless amazement.

"I declare—I'm sure—it's a thousand pities that there should have been any mistake made, and I can't conceive how it has happened," whined poor Miss Grizzy.

"The only remedy is to explain the matter quickly," observed Miss Nicky; "better late than never."

"I have done," said Miss Jacky, seating herself with much dignity.

"The short and the long of it is this," said Miss Nicky: "my brother has not made Henry a present of money. I assure you, money is not so rife; but he has done what is much better for you both,—he has made over to him that fine thriving farm of poor Macglashan's."

" No money!" repeated Lady Juliana, in a disconsolate tone : then quickly brightening up, " It would have been better, to be sure, to have had the money directly ; but you know we can easily sell the estate. How long will it take ?—a week ? "

" Sell Clachandown!" exclaimed the three horror-struck daughters of the house of Douglas. " Sell Clachandown! Oh! Oh! Oh!"

" What else could we do with it?" inquired her ladyship.

" Live at it, to be sure," cried all three.

" Live at it!" repeated she, with a shriek of horror that vied with that of the spinsters—" Live at it! Live on a thriving farm! Live all my life in such a place as this! Oh! the very thought is enough to kill me! "

" There is no occasion to think or say any more about it," interrupted Henry, in a calmer tone; and, glancing round on his aunts, " I therefore desire no more may be said on the subject."

" And is this really all ? And have you got no money? And are we not going away?" gasped the disappointed Lady Juliana, as she gave way to a violent burst of tears, that terminated in a fit of hysterics ; at sight of which, the good spinsters entirely forgot their wrath ; and, while one burnt feathers under her nose, and another held her hands, a third drenched her in floods of Lady Maclaughlan's hysteric water. After going through the regular routine, the lady's paroxysm subsided ; and, being carried to bed, she soon sobbed herself into a feverish slumber ; in which state the harassed husband left her, to attend a summons from his father.

———o———

Chapter xiij.

Haply this life is best,
Sweetest to you, well corresponding
With your stiff age ; but unto us it is
A cell of ignorance, a prison for a debtor.   *Cymbeline.*

HE found the old gentleman in no very complaisant humour, from the disturbances that had taken place, but the chief cause of which he was still in ignorance of. He therefore accosted his son with—

"What was the meaning o' a' that skirling and squeeling I heard a while ago? By my troth, there's no bearing this din ! Thae beasts o' your wife's are enough to drive a man out of his senses. But she maun gie up thae maggots when she becomes a farmer's wife. She maun get stirks and stots to make pets o', if she maun hae *four-footed* favourites ; but, to my mind, it would set her better to be carrying a wise-like wean in her arms, than trailing aboot wi' senseless dougs an' paurits."

Henry coloured, bit his lips, but made no reply to this elegant address of his father's; who continued, " I sent for you, sir, to have some conversation about this farm of Macglashan's ; so sit down there, till I show you the plans."

Hardly conscious of what he was doing, poor Henry gazed in silent confusion, as his father pointed out the various properties of this his future possession. Wholly occupied in debating within himself how he was to decline the offer, without a downright quarrel, he heard, without understanding a word, all the old gentleman's plans and proposals for building dikes, draining moss, &c. ; and, perfectly unconscious of what he was doing, yielded a ready assent to all the improvements that were suggested.

"Then as for the house and offices—let me see," continued the laird, as he rolled up the plans of the farm, and pulled forth that of the dwelling-house, from a bundle of papers: "Ay, here it is. By my troth, ye'll be weel lodged here. The house is in a manner quite new, for it has never had a brush upon it yet. And there's a byre—fient a bit, if I would mean the best man i' the country to sleep there himsel."

A pause followed, during which Glenfern was busily employed in poring over his parchment; then taking off his spectacles, and surveying his son, "And now, sir, that you've heard a' the outs and ins of the business, what think you your farm should bring you at the year's end?"

"I — I — I'm sure — I — I don't know," stammered poor Henry, awakening from his reverie.

"Come, come, gie a guess."

"I really — I cannot — I haven't the least idea."

"I desire, sir, ye'll say something directly, that I may judge whether or no ye have common sense," cried the old gentleman angrily.

"I should suppose — I imagine — I don't suppose it will exceed seven or eight hundred a year," said his son, in the greatest trepidation at this trial of his intellect.

"Seven or eight hunder a year!" cried the incensed laird, starting up and pushing his papers from him; "by my troth, I believe ye're a born idiot! Seven or eight hunder a year!" repeated he, at least a dozen times, as he whisked up and down the little apartment with extraordinary velocity, while poor Henry affected to be busily employed in gathering up the parchments with which the floor was strewed.

"I'll tell you what, sir," continued he, stopping; "you're no fit to manage a farm; you're as ignorant as yon cow, an' as senseless as its calf. Wi' gude management, Clachandow should produce you twa hunder and

odd pounds yearly, wi' a free house, and plenty of peats,
mutton, and patatees into the bargain ; but, in your
guiding, I doubt if it will yield the half of what it
should do. However, tak it or want it, mind me, sir,
that it's a' ye hae to trust to in my lifetime ; so ye may
mak the maist o't."

Various and painful were the emotions that struggled
in Henry's breast at this declaration. Shame, regret,
indignation, all burned within him ; but the fear he entertained of his father, and the consciousness of his
absolute dependence, chained his tongue, while the bitter
emotions that agitated him painted themselves legibly in
his countenance. His father observed his agitation ;
and, mistaking the cause, felt somewhat softened at what
he conceived his son's shame and penitence for his folly :
he therefore extended his hand towards him, saying,
" Weel, weel, nae mair aboot it ; Clachandow's yours,
as soon as I can put you in possession : in the mean
time, stay still here, and welcome."

" I — am much obliged to you for the offer, sir ; I
— feel very grateful for your kindness," at length
articulated his son ; " but — I — am, as you observe,
so perfectly ignorant of country matters, that I — I —
in short, I am afraid I should make a bad hand of the
business."

" Nae doot, nae doot ye would, if ye was left to your
ain discretion ; but ye'll get mair sense, and I shall put
ye upon a method, and provide ye wi' a grieve ; an' if
you are active, and your wife managing, there's nae fear
o' you."

" But Lady Juliana, sir, has never been accustomed "—

" Let her serve an apprenticeship to your aunts ; she
cou'dna be in a better school."

" But her education, sir, has been so different from
what would be required in that station," resumed her

husband, choking with vexation at the idea of his beauteous high-born bride being doomed to the drudgery of household cares.

" Edication! what has her edication been, to mak her different frae other women? If a woman can nurse her bairns, mak their claes, and manage her house, what mair need she do? If she can play a tune on the spinnet, and dance a reel, and play a rubber at whist— no doubt these are accomplishments, but they're soon learnt. Edication! pooh!—I'll be bound Leddy Jully Anie will mak as gude a figure by and bye as the best edicated woman in the country."

" But she dislikes the country, and "——

" She'll soon come to like it. Wait a wee till she has a wheen bairns, an' a house o' her ain, an' I'll be bound she'll be as happy as the day's lang."

" But the climate does not agree with her," continued the tender husband, almost driven to extremities by the persevering simplicity of his father.

" Stay a wee till she gets to Clachandow! There's no a finer, freer-aired situation in a' Scotland: the air's sharpish, to be sure, but fine and bracing; and you have a braw peat moss at your back to keep you warm."

Finding it in vain to attempt *insinuating* his objections to a pastoral life, poor Henry was at length reduced to the necessity of coming to the point with the old gentleman, and telling him plainly, that it was not at all suited to his inclinations, or Lady Juliana's rank and beauty.

Vain would be the attempt to paint the fiery wrath and indignation of the ancient Highlander, as the naked truth stood revealed before him :—that his son despised the occupation of his fathers, even the feeding of sheep, and the breeding of black cattle; and that his high-born spouse was above fulfilling those duties which

he had ever considered the chief end for which woman
was created. He swore, stamped, screamed, and even
skipped with rage, and, in short, went through all
the evolutions, as usually performed by testy old gentlemen on first discovering that they have disobedient
sons and undutiful daughters. Henry, who, though
uncommonly good tempered, inherited a portion of his
father's warmth, became at length irritated at the invectives that were so liberally bestowed on him, and
replied in language less respectful than the old laird was
accustomed to hear; and the altercation became so
violent, that they parted in mutual anger; Henry returning to his wife's apartment in a state of the greatest
disquietude he had ever known. To her childish
questions and tiresome complaints he no longer vouchsafed to reply, but paced the chamber with a disordered
mien, in sullen silence; till at length, distracted by her
reproaches, and disgusted with her selfishness, he rushed
from the apartment, and quitted the house.

Chapter xib.

Never talk to me; I *will* weep.
As You Like It.

TWICE had the dinner-bell been loudly sounded
by old Donald, and the family of Glenfern
were all assembled, yet their fashionable guests
had not appeared. Impatient of delay, Miss Jacky
hastened to ascertain the cause. Presently she returned in the utmost perturbation, and announced, that
Lady Juliana was in bed in a high fever, and Henry
nowhere to be found. Thereupon the whole eight
rushed upstairs to ascertain the fact, leaving the old
gentleman much discomposed at this unseasonable delay.

Some time elapsed ere they again returned, which they did with lengthened faces, and in extreme perturbation. They had found their noble niece, according to Miss Jacky's report, in bed—according to Miss Grizzy's opinion, in a brain fever; as she no sooner perceived them enter, than she covered her head with the bed-clothes, and continued screaming for them to be gone, till they had actually quitted the apartment.

"And what proves, beyond a doubt, that our sweet niece is not herself," continued poor Miss Grizzy, in a lamentable tone, "is, that we appeared to her in every form but our own! She sometimes took us for cats; then thought we were ghosts haunting her; and, in short, it is impossible to tell all the things she called us; and she screams so for Harry to come and take her away, that I am sure—I declare—I don't know what's come over her!"

Mrs Douglas could scarcely suppress a smile at the simplicity of the good spinsters. Her husband and she had gone out, immediately after breakfast, to pay a visit a few miles off, and did not return till near the dinner hour. They were therefore ignorant of all that had been acted during their absence; but, as she suspected something was amiss, she requested the rest of the company would proceed to dinner, and leave her to ascertain the nature of Lady Juliana's disorder.

"Don't come near me!" shrieked her ladyship, on hearing the door open: "send Henry to take me away —I don't want any body but Henry!"—and a torrent of tears, sobs, and exclamations followed.

"My dear Lady Juliana," said Mrs Douglas, softly approaching the bed, "compose yourself; and if my presence is disagreeable to you, I will immediately withdraw."

"Oh, is it you?" cried her sister-in-law, uncovering her face at the sound of her voice: "I thought it had been those frightful old women come to torment me; and I shall die—I know I shall—if ever I look at them again.   But I don't dislike *you ;* so you may stay if you choose,—though I don't want any body but Harry, to come and take me away."

A fresh fit of sobbing here impeded her utterance; and Mrs Douglas, compassionating her distress, while she despised her folly, seated herself by the bedside, and, taking her hand, in the sweetest tone of sympathy attempted to soothe her into composure.   But it was long ere the words of wisdom and kindness could win their way into ears closed against all but her own passionate exclamations and incoherent expressions of grief, anger, disappointment, and injury.   From these, any one ignorant of the real state of the case might reasonably have inferred that she was an unhappy lady who had been basely trepanned from her beloved home, and taken captive to a barbarous country, where she was undergoing every species of cruelty and oppression her inhuman persecutors could invent or inflict.   Having at length exhausted herself in the detail of her wrongs and sufferings, Mrs Douglas spoke a few words of consolation, which were received with tolerable composure. She then proceeded, in her own mild accents, to use such reasonable arguments as she thought adapted even to the weak capacity she was endeavouring to enlighten.

" The only way in which you can be less miserable, is to support your present situation with patience, which you may do by looking forward to brighter prospects. It is *possible* that your stay here may be short; and it is *certain* that it is in your own power to render your life more agreeable, by endeavouring to accommodate yourself to the peculiarities of your husband's family. No doubt, they are often tiresome and ridiculous; but they are always kind and well-meaning."

" You may say what you please, but I think them all

odious creatures; and I won't live here with patience; and I shan't be agreeable to them; and all the talking in the world won't make me less miserable. If you were me, you would be just the same; but you have never been in London—that's the reason."

"Pardon me," replied her sister-in-law, "I spent many years of my life there."

"You lived in London!" repeated Lady Juliana, in astonishment. "And how then can you contrive to exist here?"

"I not only contrive to exist, but to be extremely contented with existence," said Mrs Douglas, with a smile. Then assuming a more serious air, "I possess health, peace of mind, and the affections of a worthy husband; and I should be very undeserving of these blessings, were I to give way to useless regrets, or indulge in impious repinings, because my happiness might once have been more perfect, and still admits of improvement."

"I don't understand you," said Lady Juliana, with a peevish yawn. "Who did you live with in London?"

"With my aunt, Lady Audley."

"With Lady Audley!" repeated her sister-in-law, in accents of astonishment. "Why, I have heard of her; she lived quite in the world, and gave balls and assemblies; so that's the reason you are not so disagreeable as the rest of them. Why did you not remain with her, or marry an Englishman?—but I suppose, like me, you didn't know what Scotland was!"

Happy to have excited an interest, even through the medium of childish curiosity, in the bosom of her fashionable relative, Mrs Douglas briefly related such circumstances of her past life as she judged proper to communicate; but as she sought rather to amuse than instruct by her simple narrative, we shall allow her to pursue her charitable intentions, while we do more justice to her character by introducing her regularly to the acquaintance of our readers.

HISTORY OF MRS DOUGLAS.

" The selfish heart deserves the pang it feels ;
  More generous sorrow, while it sinks, exalts,
  And conscious virtue mitigates the pang."   Young.

Mrs Douglas was, on the maternal side, related to an English family. Her mother had died in giving birth to her ; and her father, shortly after, falling in the service of his country, she had been consigned in infancy to the care of her aunt. Lady Audley had taken charge of her, on condition that she should never be claimed by her Scottish relations, for whom that lady entertained as much aversion as contempt. A latent feeling of affection for her departed sister, and a large portion of family pride, had prompted her wish of becoming the protectress of her orphan niece ; and, possessed of a high sense of rectitude and honour, she fulfilled the duty, thus voluntarily imposed, in a manner that secured the unshaken gratitude of the virtuous Alicia.

Lady Audley was a character more esteemed and feared than loved, even by those with whom she was most intimate. Firm, upright, and rigid, she exacted from others those inflexible virtues which in herself she found no obstacle to performing. Neglecting the softer attractions which shed their benign influence over the commerce of social life, she was content to enjoy the extorted esteem of her associates ; for friends she had none. She sought in the world for objects to fill up the void which her heart could not supply. She loved *eclat*, and had succeeded in creating herself an existence of importance in the circles of high life, which she considered more as due to her consequence than essential to her enjoyment. She had early in life been left a widow, with the sole tutelage and management of an only son ; whose large estate she regulated with the most admirable prudence and judgment.

Alicia Malcolm was put under the care of her aunt at two years of age. A governess had been procured for her, whose character was such as not to impair the promising dispositions of her pupil. Alicia was gifted by nature with a warm affectionate heart, and a calm imagination attempered its influence. Her governess, a woman of a strong understanding and enlarged mind, early instilled into her a deep and strong sense of religion ; and to it she owed the support which had safely guided her through the most trying vicissitudes.

When at the age of seventeen, Alicia Malcolm was produced in the world. She was a rational, cheerful, and sweet-tempered girl, with a fine-formed person, and a countenance in which was so clearly painted the sunshine of her breast, that it attracted the *bienveillance* even of those who had not taste or judgment to define the charm. Her open natural manner, blending the frankness of the Scotch with the polished reserve of the English woman, her total exemption from vanity, were calculated alike to please others, and maintain her own cheerfulness undimmed by a single cloud.

Lady Audley felt for her niece a sentiment which she mistook for affection ; her self-approbation was gratified at the contemplation of a being who owed every advantage to her, and whom she had rescued from the coarseness and vulgarity which she deemed inseparable from the manners of every Scotch woman.

If Lady Audley really loved any human being, it was her son. In him were centred her dearest interests ; on his aggrandisement and future importance hung her most sanguine hopes. She had acted con-

trary to the advice of her male relations, and followed
her own judgment, by giving her son a private education. He was brought up under her own eye, by a
tutor of deep erudition, but who was totally unfitted
for forming the mind and compensating for those advantages which may be derived from a public education.
The circumstances of his education, therefore, combined rather to stifle the exposure than to destroy the
existence of some very dangerous qualities, that seemed
inherent in Sir Edmund's nature. He was ardent,
impetuous, and passionate, though these propensities
were cloaked by a reserve, partly natural, and partly
arising from the repelling manners of his mother and
tutor.

His was not the effervescence of character which
bursts forth on every trivial occasion; but when any
powerful cause awakened the slumbering inmates of his
breast, they blazed with an uncontrolled fury, that
defied all opposition, and overleaped all bounds of reason
and decorum.

Experience often shows us, that minds formed of
the most opposite attributes more forcibly attract each
other than those which appear cast in the same mould.
The source of this fascination is difficult to trace: it
possesses not reason for its basis, yet it is perhaps the
more tyrannical in its influence from that very cause.
The weakness of our nature occasionally makes us feel
a potent charm in " errors of a noble mind."

Sir Edmund Audley and Alicia Malcolm proved
examples of this observation. The affection of childhood had so gradually ripened into a warmer sentiment,
that neither were conscious of the nature of that sentiment till after it had attained strength to cast a material
influence on their after-lives. The familiarity of near
relatives, associating constantly together, produced a
warm sentiment of affection, cemented by similarity of

pursuits, and enlivened by diversity of character; while the perfect tranquillity of their lives afforded no event that could withdraw the veil of ignorance from their eyes.

Could a woman of Lady Audley's discernment, it may be asked, place two young persons in such a situation, and doubt the consequences? Those who are no longer young are liable to forget that love is a plant of early growth, and that the individuals that they have but a short time before beheld placing their supreme felicity on a rattle and a go-cart, can so soon be actuated by the strongest passions of the human breast.

Sir Edmund completed his nineteenth year, and Alicia entered her eighteenth, when this happy state of unconscious security was destroyed by a circumstance which rent the veil from her eyes, and disclosed his sentiments in all their energy and warmth. This circumstance was no other than a proposal of marriage to Alicia, from a gentleman of large fortune and brilliant connexions, who resided in their neighbourhood. His character was as little calculated as his appearance to engage the affections of a young woman of delicacy and good sense. But he was a man of consequence; heir to an earldom; member for the county: and Lady Audley, rejoicing at what she termed Alicia's good fortune, determined that she should become his wife.

With mild firmness she rejected the honour intended her; but it was with difficulty that Lady Audley's mind could adopt or understand the idea of an opposition to her wishes. She could not seriously embrace the conviction, that Alicia was determined to disobey her; and, in order to bring her to a right understanding, she underwent a system of persecution that tended naturally to increase the antipathy her suitor had inspired. Lady Audley, with the undiscriminating zeal of prejudiced and overbearing persons, strove to recommend

him to her niece by all those attributes which were of
value in her own eyes ; making allowance for a certain
degree of indecision in her niece, but never admitting a
doubt that in due time her will should be obeyed, as it
had always hitherto been.

At this juncture, Sir Edmund returned from a short
excursion, and was struck by the altered looks and
pensive manners of his once cheerful cousin. About a
week after his arrival, he found Alicia one morning in
tears, after a long conversation with Lady Audley. Sir
Edmund tenderly soothed her, and entreated to be
made acquainted with the cause of her distress. She
was so habituated to impart every thought to her cousin,
the intimacy and sympathy of their souls was so entire,
that she would not have concealed the late occurrence
from him, had she not been withheld by the natural
timidity and delicacy a young woman feels in making
her own conquests the subject of conversation. But
now, so pathetically and irresistibly persuaded by Sir
Edmund, and sensible that every distress of hers wounded
his heart, Alicia candidly related to him the pursuit of
her disagreeable suitor, and the importunities of Lady
Audley in his favour. Every word she had spoken had
more and more dispelled the mist that had so long hung
over Sir Edmund's inclinations. At the first mention
of a suitor, he had felt that to be hers was a happiness
that comprised all others ; and that the idea of losing
her made the whole of existence appear a frightful blank.
These feelings were no sooner known to himself, than
spontaneously poured into her delighted ears ; while she
felt that every sentiment met a kindred one in her breast.
Alicia sought not a moment to disguise those feelings
which she now, for the first time, became aware of ; they
were known to the object of her innocent affection as
soon as to herself, and both were convinced, that, though
not conscious before of the nature of their sentiments,

friendship had long been mistaken for love in their hearts.

But this state of blissful serenity did not last long. On the evening of the following day, Lady Audley sent for her to her dressing-room. On entering, Alicia was panic-struck at her aunt's pale countenance, fiery eyes, and frame convulsed with passion. With difficulty, Lady Audley, struggling for calmness, demanded an instant and decided reply to the proposals of Mr Compton, the gentleman who had solicited her hand. Alicia entreated her aunt to waive the subject, as she found it impossible ever to consent to such an union.

Scarcely was her answer uttered, when Lady Audley's anger burst forth uncontrollably, and Alicia gathered from it that her rage had its source in a declaration her son had made to her of his affection for his cousin, and his resolution of marrying her as soon as he was of age : which open avowal of his sentiments had followed Lady Audley's injunctions to him to forward the suit of Mr Compton.

That her son, for whom she had in view one of the first matches in the kingdom, should dare to choose for himself, and, above all, to choose one whom she considered as much his inferior in birth as she was in fortune, was a circumstance quite insupportable to her feelings.

Of the existence of love, Lady Audley had little conception ; and she attributed her son's conduct to wilful disobedience and obstinacy. In proportion as she had hitherto found him complying and gentle, her wrath had kindled at his present firmness and inflexibility. So bitter were her reflections on his conduct, so severe her animadversions on the being he loved, that Sir Edmund, fired with resentment, expressed his resolution of acting according to the dictates of his own will ; and expressed his contempt for her authority, in terms the most unequivocal. Lady Audley, ignorant of the arts of persuasion, by every word she uttered more and more widened the breach her imperiousness had occasioned, until Sir Edmund, feeling himself no longer master of his temper, announced his intention of leaving the house, to allow his mother time to reconcile herself to the inevitable misfortune of beholding him the husband of Alicia Malcolm.

He instantly ordered his horses and departed, leaving the following letter for his cousin :—

" I have been compelled, by motives of prudence, of which you are the sole object, to depart without seeing you. My absence became necessary from the unexpected conduct of Lady Audley, which has led me so near to forgetting that she was my mother, that I dared not remain, and subject myself to excesses of temper which I might afterwards repent. Two years must elapse before I can become legally my own master ; and, should Lady Audley so far depart from the dictates of cool judgment as still to oppose what she knows to be inevitable, I fear that we cannot meet till then. My heart is well known to you ; therefore I need not enlarge on the pain I feel at this unlooked-for separation. At the same time, I am cheered with the prospect of the unspeakable happiness that awaits me—the possession of your hand ; and the confidence I feel in your constancy is in proportion to the certainty I experience in my own : I cannot therefore fear that any of the means which may be put in practice to disunite us will have more effect on you than on me.

" Looking forward to the moment that shall make you mine for ever, I remain, with steady confidence and unspeakable affection, your

" EDMUND AUDLEY."

With a trembling frame, Alicia handed the note to Lady Audley, and begged leave to retire for a short time; expressing her willingness to reply at another moment to any question her aunt might choose to put to her with regard to her engagement with Sir Edmund.

In the solitude of her own chamber, Alicia gave way to those feelings of wretchedness which she had with difficulty stifled in the presence of Lady Audley, and bitterly wept over the extinction of her bright and newly-formed visions of felicity. To yield to un-merited ill-usage, or to crouch beneath imperious and self-arrogated power, was not in the nature of Alicia; and, had Lady Audley been a stranger to her, the path of duty would have been less intricate. However much her own pride might have been wounded by entering into a family which considered her as an intruding beggar, never would she have consented to sacrifice the virtuous inclinations of the man she loved to the will of an arrogant and imperious mother. But, alas! the case was far different. The recent ill-treatment she had experienced from Lady Audley could not efface from her noble mind the recollection of benefits con-ferred from the earliest period of her life, and of un-varying attention to her welfare. To her aunt she owed all but existence: she had wholly supported her—had bestowed on her the most liberal education; and from Lady Audley sprung every comfort and pleasure she had hitherto enjoyed.

Had she been brought up by her paternal relations, she would in all probability never have beheld her cousin; and the mother and son might have lived in uninterrupted concord. Could she be the person to inflict on Lady Audley the severest disappointment she could experience? The thought was too dread-ful to bear; and, knowing that procrastination could but increase her misery, no sooner had she felt con-vinced of the true nature of her duty, than she made a

steady resolution to perform and to adhere to it.   Lady
Audley had *vowed, that, while she had life, she would
never give her consent to her son's marriage ;* and Alicia
was too well acquainted with her disposition to have
the faintest expectation she would relent.

But to remain any longer under her protection was
impossible ; and she resolved to anticipate any proposal
of that sort from her protectress.

When Lady Audley's passion had somewhat cooled,
she again sent for Alicia.   She began by repeating her
invincible enmity to the marriage, in a manner the most
impressive, and rendered still more decisive by the cool
collectedness of her manner.   She then desired to hear
what Alicia had to say in exculpation of her conduct.

The profound sorrow which filled the heart of Alicia
left no room for timidity or indecision.   She answered
without hesitation or embarrassment, and asserted her
innocence of all deceit, in such a manner as to leave no
doubt at least of honourable proceeding.   In a few
words she expressed her gratitude for the benefits her
aunt had through life conferred upon her ; and, while
she openly professed to think herself, in the present
instance, deeply wronged, she declared her determination of never uniting herself to her cousin without the
consent of his mother.

She then proceeded to ask, where her aunt deemed
it most advisable for her to reside in future.

Lady Audley, convinced that moderate measures
would be most likely to insure a continuance of Alicia's
obedience, expressed herself grieved at the necessity
of parting with her, and pleased that she should have
the good sense to perceive the propriety of such a
separation.

Sir Duncan Malcolm, the grandfather of Alicia, had,
in the few communications that had passed between
Lady Audley and him, always expressed a wish to

see his granddaughter before he died. Her ladyship's
antipathy to Scotland, however, was such, that she
would have deemed it absolute contamination for her
niece to have entered the country; and she had, therefore, always eluded the request.

It was now, of all plans, the most eligible; and she
graciously offered to convey her niece as far as Edinburgh. The journey was immediately settled; and,
before Alicia left her aunt's presence, the promise was
exacted with unfeeling tenacity, and given with melancholy firmness, never to unite herself to Sir Edmund
unsanctioned by his mother.

Alas! how imperfect is human wisdom! Even in
seeking to do right, how many are the errors we commit! Alicia judged wrong in thus sacrificing the
happiness of Sir Edmund to the pride and injustice of
his mother;—but her error was that of a noble, self-
denying spirit, entitled to respect, even though it cannot
claim approbation. The honourable open conduct of
her niece had so far gained upon Lady Audley, that
she did not object to her writing to Sir Edmund, which
she did as follows:—

"DEAR SIR EDMUND,
"A painful line of conduct is pointed out to me by
duty; yet, of all the regrets I feel, not one is so
poignant as the consciousness of that which you will
feel at learning that I have for ever resigned the claims
you so lately gave me to your heart and hand. It was
not weakness—it could not be inconstancy—that produced the painful sacrifice of a distinction still more
gratifying to my heart than flattering to my pride.

"Need I remind you, that to your mother I owe
every benefit in life? nothing can release me from the
tribute of gratitude, which would be ill repaid by
braving her authority and despising her will. Should

I give her reason to regret the hour she received me
under her roof, to repent of every benefit she has
hitherto bestowed on me,—should I draw down a
mother's displeasure, what reasonable hopes could we
entertain of solid peace through life? I am not in a
situation which entitles me to question the justice of
Lady Audley's will; and that will has pronounced
that I shall never be Sir Edmund's wife.

"Your first impulse may perhaps be, to accuse me of
coldness and ingratitude, in quitting the place and
country you inhabit, and resigning you back to yourself,
without personally taking leave of you; but I trust that
you will, on reflection, absolve me from the charge.

"Could I have had any grounds to suppose that a
personal interview would be productive of comfort to
you, I would have joyfully supported the sufferings it
would have inflicted on myself. But, question your
own heart as to the use you would have made of such
a meeting; bear in mind, that Lady Audley has my
solemn promise never to be yours without her consent—
a promise not lightly given—then imagine what must
have been an interview between us under such circumstances.

"In proof of an affection which I can have no
reason to doubt, I conjure you to listen to the last
request I shall ever make to my dear cousin. Give
me the heart-felt satisfaction to know that my departure
has put an end to those disagreements between mother
and son of which I have been the innocent cause.

"Farewell, dear Edmund! May every happiness
attend your future life!   A. M."

To say that no tears were shed during the composition
of this letter, would be to overstrain fortitude beyond
natural bounds. With difficulty Alicia checked the
effusions of her pen: she wished to have said much

more, and to have soothed the agony of renunciation
by painting with warmth her tenderness and her regret;
but reason urged, that, in exciting his feelings and displaying her own, she would defeat the chief purpose of
her letter: she hastily closed and directed it, with a
feeling almost akin to despair.

The necessaay arrangements for the journey having
been hastily made, the ladies set out two days after Sir
Edmund had so hastily quitted them. The uncomplaining Alicia buried her woes in her own bosom;
and neither murmurs on the one hand, nor reproaches
on the other, were heard.

At the end of four days, the travellers entered Scotland; and, when they stopped for the night, Alicia,
fatigued and dispirited, retired immediately to her
apartment.

She had been there but a few minutes, when the
chambermaid knocked at the door, and informed her
that she was wanted below.

Supposing that Lady Audley had sent for her, she
followed the girl without observing that she was conducted in an opposite direction; when, upon entering
an apartment, what was her astonishment at finding
herself, not in the presence of Lady Audley, but in the
arms of Sir Edmund! In the utmost agitation, she
sought to disengage herself from his almost frantic embrace; while he poured forth a torrent of rapturous
exclamations, and swore that no human power should
ever divide them again.

"I have followed your steps, dearest Alicia, from
the moment I received your letter. We are now in
Scotland—in this blessed land of liberty. Every thing
is arranged; the clergyman is now in waiting; and, in
five minutes, you shall be my own beyond the power of
fate to sever us."

Too much agitated to reply, Alicia wept in silence;

and, in the delight of once more beholding him she had
thought never more to behold, forgot, for a moment,
the duty she had imposed upon herself.   But the native
energy of her character returned.   She raised her head,
and attempted to withdraw from the encircling arms of
her cousin.

"Never until you have vowed to be mine!   The
clergyman—the carriage—every thing is in readiness "——

At this juncture, the door opened, and, pale with
rage, her eyes flashing fire, Lady Audley stood before
them.   A dreadful scene now ensued.   Sir Edmund
disdained to enter into any justification of his conduct,
or even to reply to the invectives of his mother, but
lavished the most tender assiduities on Alicia; who,
overcome more by the conflicts of her own heart than
with alarm at Lady Audley's violence, sat the pale and
silent image of consternation.

Baffled by her son's indignant disregard, Lady Audley turned all her fury on her niece ; and, in the most
opprobrious terms that rage could invent, upbraided her
with deceit and treachery—accusing her of making her
pretended submission instrumental to the more speedy
accomplishment of her marriage.   Too much incensed
to reply, Sir Edmund seized his cousin's hand, and was
leading her from the room.

"Go, then—go, marry her ; but first hear me swear,
solemnly swear ! "—and she raised her hands and eyes
to heaven—"that my malediction shall be your portion !
Speak but the word, and no power shall make me
withhold it ! "

"Dear Edmund ! " exclaimed Alicia, distractedly,
"never ought I to have allowed time for the terrifying
words that have fallen from Lady Audley's lips: never
for me shall your mother's malediction fall on you.
Farewell for ever ! " and, with the strength of despera-

tion, she rushed past him, and quitted the room. Sir
Edmund madly followed, but in vain. Alicia's feelings
were too highly wrought at that moment to be touched
even by the man she loved ; and, without an additional
pang, she saw him throw himself into the carriage which
he had destined for so different a purpose, and quit for
ever the woman he adored.

It may easily be conceived of how painful a nature
must have been the future intercourse betwixt Lady
Audley and her niece. The former seemed to regard
her victim with that haughty distance which the unrelenting oppressor never fails to entertain towards the
object of his tyranny ; while even the gentle Alicia, on
her part, shrank, with ill-concealed abhorrence, from the
presence of that being whose stern decree had blasted
all the fairest blossoms of her happiness.

Alicia was received with affection by her grandfather ;
and she laboured to drive away the heavy despondency
which pressed on her spirits, by studying his taste and
humours, and striving to contribute to his comfort and
amusement.

Sir Duncan had chosen the time of Alicia's arrival
to transact some business ; and, instead of returning immediately to the Highlands, he determined to remain
some weeks in Edinburgh for her amusement.

But, little attractive as dissipation had ever been, it
was now absolutely repugnant to Alicia. She loathed
the idea of mixing in scenes of amusement with a heart
incapable of joy, a spirit indifferent to every object that
surrounded her ; and in solitude alone she expected
gradually to regain her peace of mind.

In the amusements of the gay season of Edinburgh,
Alicia expected to find all the vanity, emptiness, and
frivolity of London dissipation, without its varied brilliancy and elegant luxury ; yet, so much was it the
habit of her mind to look to the fairest side of things,

and to extract some advantage from every situation in which she was placed, that, pensive and thoughtful as was her disposition, the discriminating only perceived her deep dejection, while all admired her benevolence of manner and unaffected desire to please.

By degrees, Alicia found that, in some points, she had been inaccurate in her idea of the style of living of those who form the best society of Edinburgh. The circle is so confined, that its members are almost universally known to each other; and those various gradations of gentility, from the cit's snug party to the duchess's most crowded assembly, all totally distinct and separate, which are to be met with in London, have no prototype in Edinburgh. There, the ranks and fortunes being more on an equality, no one is able greatly to exceed his neighbour in luxury and extravagance. Great magnificence, and the consequent gratification produced by the envy of others, being out of the question, the object for which a reunion of individuals was originally invented becomes less of a secondary consideration. Private parties for the actual purpose of society and conversation are frequent, and answer the destined end; and in the societies of professed amusement are to be met the learned, the studious, and the rational,—not presented as shows to the company by the host and hostess, but professedly seeking their own gratification.

Still the lack of beauty, fashion, and elegance disappoint the stranger accustomed to their brilliant combination in a London world. But Alicia had long since sickened in the metropolis at the frivolity of beauty, the heartlessness of fashion, and the insipidity of elegance; and it was a relief to her to turn to the variety of character she found beneath the cloak of simple, eccentric, and sometimes coarse manners.

We are never long so totally abstracted by our own

feelings, as to be unconscious of the attempts of others to please us.

Amongst the many who expressed good-will towards Alicia, there were a few whose kindness and real affection failed not to meet with a return from her; and others, whose rich and varied powers of mind, for the first time, afforded her a true specimen of the exalting enjoyment produced by a communion of intellect. She felt the powers of her understanding enlarge in proportion; and, with this mental activity, she sought to solace the languor of her heart, and save it from the listlessness of despair.

Alicia had been about six weeks in Edinburgh, when she received a letter from Lady Audley. No allusions were made to the past; she wrote upon general topics, in the cold manner that might be used to a common acquaintance; and slightly named her son as having set out upon a tour to the Continent.

Alicia's heart was heavy, as she read the heartless letter of the woman whose cruelty had not been able to eradicate wholly from her breast the strong durable affection of early habit.

Sir Duncan and Alicia spent two months in Edinburgh, at the end of which time they went to his country seat in ——shire. The adjacent country was picturesque; and Sir Duncan's residence, though bearing marks of the absence of taste and comfort in its arrangements, possessed much natural beauty.

Two years of tranquil seclusion had passed over her head, when her dormant feelings were all aroused by a letter from Sir Edmund. It informed her that he was now of age; that his affection remained unalterable; that he was newly arrived from abroad; and concluded by declaring his intention of presenting himself at once to Sir Duncan, and soliciting his permission to claim her hand.

Alicia read the letter with grateful affection and poignant regret. Again she shed the bitter tears of disappointment, at the hard task of refusing for a second time so noble and affectionate a heart. But conscience whispered, that to hold a passive line of conduct would be, in some measure, to deceive Lady Audley's expectations; and she felt, with exquisite anguish, that she had no means to put a final stop to Sir Edmund's pursuits, and to her own trials, but by bestowing her hand on another. The first dawning of this idea was accompanied by the most violent burst of anguish; but, far from driving away the painful subject, she strove to render it less appalling by dwelling upon it, and labouring to reconcile herself to what seemed her only plan of conduct. She acknowledged to herself, that, to remain still single, a prey to Sir Edmund's importunities, and the continual temptations of her own heart, was, for the sake of present indulgence, submitting to a fiery ordeal, from which she could not escape unblameable without the most repeated and agonising conflicts.

Three months still remained for her of peace and liberty, after which Sir Duncan would go to Edinburgh. There she would be sure of meeting with the loved companion of her youthful days; and the lurking weakness of her own breast would then be seconded by the passionate eloquence of the being she most loved and admired upon earth.

She wrote to him, repeating her former arguments; declaring that she could never feel herself absolved from the promise she had given Lady Audley, but by that lady herself, and imploring him to abandon a pursuit which would be productive only of lasting pain to both.

Her arguments, her representations, all failed in their effect on Sir Edmund's impetuous character. His answer was short and decided; the purport of it, that

he should see her in Edinburgh the moment she arrived
there.

" My fate then is fixed," thought Alicia, as she read
this letter ; " I must finish the sacrifice."

The more severe had been the struggle between love
and victorious duty, the more firmly was she determined
to maintain this dear-bought victory.

Alicia's resolution of marrying was now decided, and
the opportunity was not wanting. She had become
acquainted, during the preceding winter, in Edinburgh,
with Major Douglas, eldest son of Mr Douglas of
Glenfern. He had then paid her the most marked
attention ; and, since her return to the country, had
been a frequent visitor at Sir Duncan's. At length he
avowed his partiality, which was heard by Sir Duncan
with pleasure, by Alicia with dread and submission.
Yet she felt less repugnance towards him than to any
other of her suitors. He was pleasing in his person,
quiet and simple in his manners, and his character stood
high for integrity, good temper, and plain sense. The
sequel requires little farther detail. Alicia Malcolm
became the wife of Archibald Douglas.

An eternal constancy is a thing so rare to be met
with, that persons who desire that sort of reputation
strive to obtain it by nourishing the ideas that recall the
passion, even though guilt and sorrow should go hand
in hand with it. But Alicia, far from piquing herself
in the love-lorn pensiveness she might have assumed
had she yielded to the impulse of her feelings, diligently
strove, not only to make up her mind to the lot which
had devolved to her, but to bring it to such a frame of
cheerfulness as should enable her to contribute to her
husband's happiness.

When the soul is no longer buffeted by the storms
of hope or fear, when all is fixed unchangeably for life,
sorrow for the past will never long prey on a pious and

well regulated mind. If Alicia lost the buoyant spirit of youth, the bright and quick play of fancy, yet a placid contentment crowned her days; and, at the end of two years, she would have been astonished had any one marked her as an object of compassion.

She scarcely ever heard from Lady Audley; and, in the few letters her aunt had favoured her with, she gave favourable, though vague, accounts of her son. Alicia did not court a more unreserved communication, and had long since taught herself to hope that he was now happy. Soon after their marriage, Major Douglas quitted the army, upon succeeding to a small estate on the banks of Lochmarlie, by the death of an uncle; and there, in the calm seclusion of domestic life, Mrs Douglas found that peace which might have been denied her amid gayer scenes.

———o———

Chapter xb.

And joyous was the scene in early summer.

Madoc.

ON Henry's return from his solitary ramble, Mrs Douglas learnt from him the cause of the mis-understanding that had taken place; and judging that, in the present state of affairs, a temporary separation might be of use to both parties, as they were now about to return home, she proposed to her husband to invite his brother and Lady Juliana to follow and spend a few weeks with them at Lochmarlie Cottage.

The invitation was eagerly accepted; for though Lady Juliana did not anticipate any positive pleasure from the change, still she thought that every place must be more agreeable than her present abode, especially as she stipulated for the utter exclusion of the aunts from the party.

To atone for this mortification, Miss Bella was invited to fill the vacant seat in the carriage ; and, accordingly, with a cargo of strong shoes, great-coats, and a large work-bag well stuffed with white-seam, she took her place at the appointed hour.

The day they had chosen for their expedition was one that " sent a summer feeling to the heart."

The air was soft and genial ; not a cloud stained the bright azure of the heavens ; and the sun shone out in all his splendour, shedding life and beauty even over the desolate heath-clad hills of Glenfern. But, after they had journeyed a few miles, suddenly emerging from the valley, a scene of matchless beauty burst at once upon the eye. Before them lay the dark-blue waters of Lochmarlie, reflecting, as in a mirror, every surrounding object, and bearing on its placid transparent bosom a fleet of herring-boats, the drapery of whose black suspended nets contrasted with picturesque effect the white sails of the larger vessels, which were vainly spread to catch a breeze. All around, rocks, meadows, woods, and hills mingled in wild and lovely irregularity.

On a projecting point of land stood a little fishing village ; its white cottages reflected in the glassy waters that almost surrounded it. On the opposite side of the lake, or rather estuary, embosomed in a wood, rose the lofty turrets of Lochmarlie Castle ; while here and there, perched on some mountain's brow, were to be seen the shepherd's lonely hut, and the heath-covered summer shealing.

Not a breath was stirring, not a sound was heard, save the rushing of a waterfall, the tinkling of some silver rivulet, or the calm rippling of the tranquil lake ; now and then, at intervals, the fisherman's Gaelic ditty, chanted, as he lay stretched on the sand in some sunny nook ; or the shrill distant sound of childish glee. How delicious to the feeling heart to behold so fair a scene of unsophisticated nature, and to listen to her voice alone, breathing the accents of innocence and joy !

But none of the party who now gazed on it had minds capable of being touched with the emotions it was calculated to inspire.

Henry, indeed, was rapturous in his expressions of admiration ; but he concluded his panegyrics by wondering his brother did not keep a cutter, and resolving to pass a night on board one of the herring-boats, that he might eat the fish in perfection.

Lady Juliana thought it might be very pretty, if, instead of those frightful rocks and shabby cottages, there could be villas, and gardens, and lawns, and conservatories, and summer-houses, and statues.

Miss Bella observed, if it was hers, she would cut down the woods, and level the hills, and have races.

The road wound along the sides of the lake, sometimes overhung with banks of natural wood, which, though scarcely budding, grew so thick as to exclude the prospect ; in other places surmounted by large masses of rock, festooned with ivy, and embroidered by mosses of a thousand hues that glittered under the little mountain streamlets. Two miles further on stood the simple mansion of Mr Douglas. It was situated in a wild sequestered nook, formed by a little bay at the further end of the lake. On three sides it was surrounded by wooded hills, that offered a complete shelter from every nipping blast. To the south, the lawn, sprinkled with trees and shrubs, sloped gradually down to the water.

At the door, they were met by Mrs Douglas, who welcomed them with the most affectionate cordiality, and conducted them into the house through a little circular hall, filled with flowering shrubs and foreign plants.

" How delightful ! " exclaimed Lady Juliana, as she stopped to inhale the rich fragrance. " Cape jasmine,

and geraniums! I do delight in them,"—twisting off
the fairest blossoms of each in token of her affection:
"and I quite dote upon heliotrope,"—gathering a hand-
ful of its flowers as she spoke. "What quantities I
used to have from papa's conservatories!"

Mrs Douglas made no reply; but conducted her to
the drawing-room, where her chagrin was dispelled by
the appearance of comfort and even elegance that it
bore. "Now, this is really what I like," cried she,
throwing herself on one of the couches; "a large fire,
open windows, quantities of roses, comfortable ottomans,
and pictures; only what a pity you haven't a larger
mirror."

Mrs Douglas now rang for refreshments, and apologised for the absence of her husband, who, she said, was
so much interested in his ploughing, that he seldom
made his appearance till sent for.

Henry then proposed that they should all go out and
surprise his brother; and though walking in the country
formed no part of Lady Juliana's amusements, yet, as
Mrs Douglas assured her the walks were perfectly dry,
and her husband was so pressing, she consented. The
way lay through a shrubbery, by the side of a brawling
brook, whose banks retained all the wildness of unadorned nature. Moss, and ivy, and fern clothed the
ground; and, under the banks, the young primroses and
violets began to raise their heads; while the red wintry
berry still hung thick on the hollies.

"This is really very pleasant," said Henry, stopping
to contemplate a view of the lake through the branches
of a weeping birch; "the sound of the stream, and the
singing of the birds, and all those wild flowers, make it
appear as if it was summer in this spot: and only look,
Julia, how pretty that wherry looks lying at anchor."
Then whispering to her, "What would you think of
such a desert as this, with the man of your heart?"

Lady Juliana made no reply, but by complaining of the heat of the sun, the hardness of the gravel, and the damp from the water.

Henry, who now began to look upon the condition of a Highland farmer with more complacency than formerly, was confirmed in his favourable sentiments at sight of his brother, following the primitive occupation of the plough, his fine face glowing with health, and lighted up with good humour and happiness. He hastily advanced towards the party, and, shaking his brother and sister-in-law most warmly by the hand, expressed, with all the warmth of a kind heart, the pleasure he had in receiving them at his house : then observing Lady Juliana's languid air, and imputing to fatigue of body what, in fact, was the consequence of mental vacuity, he proposed returning home by a shorter road than that by which they had come. Henry was again in raptures at the new beauties this walk presented, and at the high order and neatness in which the grounds were kept.

" This must be a very expensive place of yours, though," said he, addressing his sister-in-law ; " there is so much garden and shrubbery, and such a number of rustic bridges, bowers, and so forth : it must require half a dozen men to keep it in any order."

" Such an establishment would very ill accord with our moderate means," replied she : " we do not pretend to one regular gardener ; and had our little embellishments been productive of much expense, or tended solely to my gratification, I should never have suggested them. When we first took possession of this spot, it was a perfect wilderness, with a dirty farm-house on it : nothing but mud about the doors, nothing but wood and briers and brambles beyond it ; and the village presented a still more melancholy scene of rank luxuriance, in its swarms of dirty idle girls and mischievous boys. I have generally found, that wherever an evil exists, the remedy is not far off; and in this case it was strikingly obvious. It was only engaging these ill-directed children, by trifling rewards, to apply their lively energies in improving instead of destroying the works of nature, as had formerly been their zealous practice. In a short time, the change on the moral as well as the vegetable part of creation became very perceptible : the children grew industrious and peaceable ; and, instead of destroying trees, robbing nests, and worrying cats, the bigger boys, under Douglas's direction, constructed those wooden bridges and seats, or cut out and gravelled the little winding paths that we had previously marked out. The task of keeping every thing in order is now easy, as you may believe when I tell you the whole of our pleasure-grounds, as you are pleased to term them, receive no other attention than what is bestowed by children under twelve years of age. And now having, I hope, acquitted myself of the charge of extravagance, I ought to beg Lady Juliana's pardon for this long, and, I fear, tiresome detail."

Having now reached the house, Mrs Douglas conducted her guest to the apartment prepared for her; while the brothers pursued their walk.

As long as novelty retained its power, and the comparison between Glenfern and Lochmarlie was fresh in remembrance, Lady Juliana, charmed with every thing, was in high good-humour. But as the horrors of the one were forgotten, and the comforts of the other became familiar, the demon of *ennui* again took possession of her vacant mind ; and she relapsed into all her capricious humours and childish impertinences. The harpsichord, which, on her first arrival, she had pronounced to be excellent, was now declared quite shocking ; so much out of tune, that there was no possibility of playing upon it. The small collection of well-chosen novels she soon exhausted, and then they became "the

stupidest books she had ever read ; " the smell of the
heliotrope now gave her the head-ache ; the sight of
the lake made her sea-sick.

Mrs Douglas heard all these civilities in silence ; and
much more " in sorrow than in anger." In the wayward inclinations, variable temper, and wretched inanity
of this poor victim of indulgence, she beheld the sad
fruits of a fashionable education ; and thought, with
humility, that, under similar circumstances, such might
have been her own character.   .

" Oh, what an awful responsibility do those parents
incur," she would mentally exclaim, " who thus neglect
or corrupt the noble deposit of an immortal soul !
And who, alas ! can tell where the mischief may end ?
This unfortunate will herself become a mother ; yet,
wholly ignorant of the duties, incapable of the self-
denial, of that sacred office, she will bring into the
world creatures to whom she can only transmit her
errors and her weaknesses ! "

These reflections at times deeply affected the generous heart and truly Christian spirit of Mrs Douglas ;
and she sought, by every means in her power, to
restrain those faults which she knew it would be vain to
attempt eradicating.

To diversify the routine of days which grew more
and more tedious to Lady Juliana, the weather being
remarkably fine, many little excursions were made to
the nearest country seats ; which, though they did not
afford her any actual pleasure, answered the purpose of
consuming a considerable portion of her time.

Several weeks passed away, during which little inclination was shown on the part of the guests to quit
their present residence, when Mr and Mrs Douglas
were summoned to attend the sick-bed of Sir Duncan
Malcolm ; and though they pressed their guests to
remain during their absence, yet Henry felt that it

would be highly offensive to his father were they to do so, and therefore resolved immediately to return to Glenfern.

————o————

Chapter xbj.

They steeked doors, they steeked yetts,
 Close to the cheek and chin;
They steeked them a' but a little wicket,
 And Lammikin crap in.

Now quhere's the lady of this castle?
  *   *   *   *
  *   *   *   *
  *   *   *   *

Old Ballad.

THE party were received with the loudest acclamations of joy by the good old ladies; and even the laird seemed to have forgotten that his son refused to breed black cattle, and that his daughter-in-law was above the management of her household.

The usual salutations were scarcely over, when Miss Grizzy, flying to her little writing-box, pulled out a letter, and, with an air of importance, having enjoined silence, she read as follows :—

'Lochmarlie Castle, March 27. 17—

"Dear Child,

"Sir Sampson's stomach has been as bad as it could well be, but not so bad as your roads—he was shook to a jelly. My petticoat will never do. Mrs M'Hall has had a girl. I wonder what makes people have girls; they never come to good: boys may go to the mischief, and be good for something—if girls go, they're good for nothing I know of. I never saw such roads—I suppose Glenfern means to bury you all in the highway—there are holes enough to make you graves,

and stones big enough for coffins.   Colonel G—— is
dead—he was near a hundred ; she is ninety ; so their
loves have not been nipt in the bud.   She is a Portu-
guese—he married her in India for her money.   She
was jealous, and fancied every woman in love wid de
colonel.   Pretty Miss Macdonald staid two days with
them.   When she was going away, Mrs G—— said to
her, ' You will come again when I do ask you; and
dat,' stamping her foot, ' will be—never ! '   Poor
thing ! I went to visit her last week.   She cried like
a baby—she was in weeds, and wore the colonel's long
queue fastened to her widow's cap, and hanging down
her back—a fact which can be attested by living witnesses : it was his own hair.   She said she had sent for
de minister to make her de Protestant, dat she might
go to de same place wid de dear good colonel.   She is
an oddity ;—beware of becoming oddities, dear girls,
and hanging *queues* to your widow's caps—if ever you
have any.   I like you all very much, and you must all
come and spend Tuesday here—not all, but some of
you—you, dear child, and your brother, and a sister,
and your pretty niece, and handsome nephew—I love
handsome people.   Miss M'Kraken has bounced away
with her father's footman—I hope he will clean his
knives on her.   Come early, and come dressed, to
your loving friend,

" ISABELLA MACLAUGHLAN."

The letter ended, a volley of applause ensued, which
at length gave place to consultation.   " Of course we
all go—at least as many as the carriage will hold : we
have no engagements, and there can be no objections."

Lady Juliana had already frowned a contemptuous
refusal, but in due time it was changed to a sullen assent,
at the pressing entreaties of her husband, to whom any
place was now preferable to home.   In truth, the men-

tion of a party had more weight with her than either her husband's wishes or her aunt's remonstrances; and they had assured her, that she should meet with a large assemblage of the very first company at Loch-marlie Castle.

The day appointed for the important visit arrived; and it was arranged that two of the elder ladies, and one of the young ones, should accompany Lady Juliana in her barouche, which Henry was to drive.

At peep of dawn the ladies were astir, and at eight o'clock breakfast was hurried over, that they might begin the preparations necessary for appearing with dignity at the shrine of this their patron saint. At eleven they reappeared in all the majesty of sweeping silk trains and well-powdered toupees. In outward show, Miss Bella was not less elaborate. The united strength and skill of her three aunts and four sisters had evidently been exerted in forcing her hair into every position but that for which nature had intended it; curls stood on end around her forehead, and tresses were dragged up from the roots and formed into a club on the crown : her arms had been strapped back till her elbows met; and her respiration seemed suspended by means of a pink riband of no ordinary strength or doubtful hue — what wine-merchants call a "full body."

Three hours were passed in all the anguish of full-dressed impatience, an anguish in which every female breast must be ready to sympathise. But Lady Juliana sympathised in no one's distresses but her own; and the difference of waiting in high dress or in *déshabille* was a distinction to her inconceivable. But those to whom *to be dressed* is an event, will readily enter into the feelings of the ladies in question, as they sat, walked, wondered, exclaimed, opened windows, wrung their hands, adjusted their dress, &c. &c., during the three

tedious hours they were doomed to wait the appearance
of their niece.

Two o'clock came, and with it Lady Juliana, as if
purposely to testify her contempt, in a plain morning
dress and mob cap. The sisters looked blank with
disappointment; for, having made themselves mistresses
of the contents of her ladyship's wardrobe, they had
settled amongst themselves that the most suitable dress
for the occasion would be black velvet, and accordingly many hints had been given the preceding evening
on the virtues of black velvet gowns : they were warm,
and not too warm ; they were dressy, and not too dressy ;
Lady Maclaughlan was a great admirer of black velvet
gowns ; she had one herself with long sleeves, and that
buttoned behind ; black velvet gowns were very much
wore ; they knew several ladies who had them ; and
they were certain there would be nothing else wore
amongst the matrons at Lady Maclaughlan's, &c. &c.

Time was, however, too precious to be given either
to remonstrance or lamentation. Miss Jacky could only
give an angry look, and Miss Grizzy a sorrowful one,
as they hurried away to the carriage, uttering exclamations of despair at the lateness of the hour, and the
impossibility that any body could have time to dress
after getting to Lochmarlie Castle.

The consequence of the delay was, that it was almost
dark by the time they reached the place of destination.
The carriage drove up to the grand entrance ; but
neither lights nor servants greeted their arrival ; and no
answer was returned to the ringing of the bell.

"This is most alarming, I declare ! " cried Miss
Grizzy.

" It is quite incomprehensible ! " observed Miss Jacky.
" We had best get out, and try the back door."

The party alighted, and another attack being made
upon the rear, it met with better success ; for a little

boy now presented himself at a narrow opening of the door, and, in a strong Highland accent, demanded "wha ta war seekin'?"

"Lady Maclaughlan, to be sure, Colin," was the reply.

"Weel, weel," still refusing admitance; "but ta leddie's no to be spoken wi' to-night."

"Not to be spoken with!" exclaimed Miss Grizzy, almost sinking to the ground with apprehension. "Good gracious!—I hope!—I declare!—Sir Sampson!"——

"Oo ay, hur may see Lochmarlie hursel." Then opening the door, he led the way to a small sitting-room, and ushered them into the presence of Sir Sampson, who was reclining in an easy chair, arrayed in a *robe-de-chambre* and night-cap. The opening of the door seemed to have broken his slumber; for, gazing around with a look of stupefaction, he demanded, in a sleepy peevish tone, "who was there?"

"Bless me, Sir Sampson!" exclaimed both spinsters at once, darting forward and seizing a hand; "bless me, don't you know us!—and here is our niece, Lady Juliana."

"My Lady Juliana Douglas!" cried he, with a shriek of horror, sinking again upon his cushions—"I am betrayed—I——Where is my Lady Maclaughlan?—where is Murdoch?—where is—distraction!—this is not to be borne! My Lady Juliana Douglas, the Earl of Courtland's daughter, to be introduced to Lochmarlie Castle in so vile a manner, and myself surprised in so indecorous a situation!" And, his lips quivering with passion, he rang the bell.

The summons was answered by the same attendant that had acted as gentleman usher.

"Where are all my people?" demanded his incensed master.

"Hurs aw awa tull ta Sandy Mor's."

" Where is my lady ? "

" Hurs i' ta teach-tap." *

" Where is Murdoch ? "

" Hurs helpin' ta leddie i' ta teach-tap."

" Oh, we'll all go up-stairs, and see what Lady
Maclaughlan and Murdoch are about in the laboratory,"
said Miss Grizzy.   " So, pray just go on with your nap,
Sir Sampson ; we shall find the way—don't stir : "
and, taking Lady Juliana by the hand, away tripped
the spinsters in search of their friend.   " I cannot
conceive the meaning of all this," whispered Miss
Grizzy to her sister as they went along.   " Something
must be wrong ; but I said nothing to dear Sir Sampson,
his nerves are so easily agitated.   But what can be
the meaning of all this ?   I declare it's quite a mystery ! "

After ascending several long dark stairs, and following
divers windings and turnings, the party at length reached
the door of the *sanctum sanctorum ;* and having gently
tapped, the voice of the priestess was heard, in no very
encouraging accents, demanding " who was there ? "

" It's only us," replied her trembling friend.

" Only us ! humph ! I wonder what fool is called
' *only us !* '   Open the door, Philistine, and see what
' *only us* ' wants."

The door was opened, and the party entered.   The
day was closing in, but, by the faint twilight that
mingled with the gleams from a smoky smouldering
fire, Lady Maclaughlan was dimly discernible, as she
stood upon the hearth, watching the contents of an
enormous kettle, that emitted both steam and odour.
She turned round on the entrance of the party, and
regarded the invaders with her usual marble aspect, but
without moving either joint or muscle as they drew
near.

" I declare—I don't think you know us, Lady
* House-top.

Maclaughlan," said Miss Grizzy, in a tone of affected vivacity, with which she strove to conceal her agitation.

" Know you ! " repeated her friend—" humph ! Who you are, I know very well ; but what brings you here, I do *not* know. Do you know yourselves ? "

" I declare — I can't conceive—" began Miss Grizzy ; but her trepidation arrested her speech, and her sister therefore proceeded—

" Your ladyship's declaration is no less astonishing than incomprehensible. We have waited upon you by your own express invitation on the day appointed by yourself ; and we have been received in a manner, I must say, we did not expect, considering this is the first visit of our niece, Lady Juliana Douglas."

" I'll tell you what, girls," replied their friend, as she still stood with her back to the fire, and her hands behind her ; " I'll tell you what, you are not yourselves —you are all lost—quite mad—that's all—humph ! "

" If that's the case, we cannot be fit company for your ladyship," retorted Miss Jacky, warmly ; " and therefore the best thing we can do is to return the way we came : come, Lady Juliana—come, sister."

" I declare, Jacky, the impetuosity of your temper is —I really cannot stand it"—and the gentle Grizzy gave way to a flood of tears.

" You used to be rational, intelligent creatures," resumed her ladyship ; " but what has come over you I don't know. You come tumbling in here in the middle of the night—and at the top of the house—nobody knows how—when I never was thinking of you ; and because I don't tell a parcel of lies, and pretend I expected you, you are for flying off again—humph ! Is this the behaviour of women in their senses ? But, since you are here, you may as well sit down, and say what brought you. Get down, Gil Blas—go along, Tom Jones ! " addressing two huge cats, who occupied a three-cornered leather chair by the fire-side, and who relinquished it with much reluctance.

"How do you do, pretty creature?" kissing Lady Juliana, as she seated her in this cat's cradle. "Now, girls, sit down, and tell what brought you here to-night—humph!"

"Can your ladyship ask such a question, after having formally invited us?" demanded the wrathful Jacky.

"I'll tell you what, girls; you were just as much invited by me to dine here to-day, as you were appointed to sup with the Grand Seignior—humph!"

"What day of the week does your ladyship call this?" demanded Jacky, with assumed composure.

"I call it Tuesday; but I suppose the Glenfern calendar calls it Thursday: Thursday was the day I invited you to come."

"I'm sure—I'm thankful we've got to the bottom of it at last," cried Miss Grizzy; "I read it, because I am sure I thought you wrote it, Tuesday."

"How could you be such a fool, my love, as to read it any such thing? Even if it had been written Tuesday, you might have had the sense to know it meant Thursday. When did you know me invite anybody for a Tuesday?"

"I declare it's very true;—I certainly ought to have known better. I am quite confounded at my own stupidity; for, as you observe, even though you had said Tuesday, I might have known that you must have meant Thursday—there can be no doubt about that!"

"Well, well, no more about it: since you are here, you must stay here, and you must have something to eat, I suppose. Sir Sampson and I have dined two hours ago; but you shall have your dinner for all that. I must shut shop for this day, it seems, and leave my resuscitating tincture all in the dead-thraw—Methusalem pills quite in their infancy. But there's no help for it: since you are here, you must stay here, and you must be fed and lodged : so get along, girls, get along. Here, Gil Blas—come, Tom Jones." And, preceded by her cats, and followed by her guests, she led the way to the parlour.

———o———

Chapter xvij.

Point de milieu : l'hymen et ses liens
Sont les plus grands ou des maux ou des biens.

L'Enfant Prodigue.

ON returning to the parlour, they found Sir Sampson had, by means of the indefatigable Murdoch, been transported into a suit of regimentals, and well-powdered peruke, which had in some measure restored him to his usual complacency. Henry, who had gone in quest of some person to take charge of the horses, now entered ; and shortly after a tray of provisions was brought, which the half-famished party eagerly attacked, regardless of their hostess's admonitions to eat sparingly, as nothing was so dangerous as eating heartily when people were hungry.

The repast being at length concluded, Lady Maclaughlan led her guests into the saloon. They passed through an antechamber, which seemed, by the faint light of the lamp, to contain nothing but piles upon piles of old china, and entered the room of state.

The eye at first wandered in uncertain obscurity ; and the guests cautiously proceeded over a bare oaken floor, whose dark polished surface seemed to emulate a mirror, through an apartment of formidable extent. The walls were hung with rich, but grotesque, tapestry. The ceiling, by its height and massy carving, bespoke the age of the apartment ; but the beauty of the design was lost in the gloom.

A Turkey carpet was placed in the middle of the floor; and on the middle of the carpet stood the card-table, at which two footmen, hastily summoned from the revels at Sandy Mor's, were placing chairs and cards; seemingly eager to display themselves, as if to prove that they were always at their posts.

Cards were a matter of course with Sir Sampson and his lady; but, as whist was the only game they ever played, a difficulty arose as to the means of providing amusement for the younger part of the company.

"The library is locked, but I have plenty of books here for you, my loves," said Lady Maclaughlan; and, taking one of the candles, she made a journey to the other end of the room, and entered a small turret, from which her voice was heard issuing most audibly, "All the books that should ever have been published are here. Read these, and you need read no more: all the world's in these books—humph! Here's the 'Encyclopædia Britannica,' twenty-six volumes,—'History of Scotland,' four volumes. Here's 'Floyer's Medicina Gero-comica, or the Galenic Art of preserving Old Men's Health;' 'Love's Art of Surveying and Measuring Land;' 'Transactions of the Highland Society;' 'Glass's Cookery;' 'Fencing Familiarised;' 'Observations on the Use of Bath Waters;' 'Cure for Soul Sores;' 'De Blondt's Military Memoirs;' 'Mac Ghie's Book-keeping;' 'Mead on Pestilence;' 'Astenthology, or the Art of preserving Feeble Life!'"

As she enumerated the contents of her library, she paused at the end of each title, in hopes of hearing the book called for; but she was allowed to proceed without interruption to the end of her catalogue.

"Why! what would you have, children?" cried she, in one of her sternest accents. "I don't know! Do you know yourselves? Here are two novels, the only ones I know of worth reading."

Henry gladly accepted the first volumes of " Gil Blas " and " Don Quixote ; " and, giving the latter to Lady Juliana, began the other himself. Miss Bella was settled with her hands across; and, the whist party being arranged, a solemn silence ensued.

Lady Juliana turned over a few pages of her own book, then begged Henry would exchange with her ; but both were in so different a style from the French and German school she had been accustomed to, that they were soon relinquished in disappointment and disgust.

On the table, which had been placed by the fire for her accommodation, lay an English newspaper, and to that she had recourse as a last effort at amusement. But, alas! even the dulness of Don Quixote was delight, compared to the anguish with which this fatal paper was fraught, in the shape of the following paragraph, which presented itself to the unfortunate fair one's eye :—

" Yesterday was married, by special licence, at the house of Mrs ——, his Grace the Duke of L——, to the beautiful and accomplished Miss D——. His Royal Highness the Duke of —— was gracious enough to act as father to the bride upon this occasion, and was present in person, as were their Royal Highnesses the Dukes of —— and of ——. The bride looked most bewitchingly lovely, in a simple robe of the finest Mechlin lace, with a superb veil of the same costly material, which hung down to her feet. She wore a set of pearls, estimated at thirty thousand pounds, whose chaste elegance corresponded with the rest of the dress. Immediately after the ceremony they partook of a sumptuous collation, and the happy pair set off in a chariot and four, attended by six outriders and two coaches and four.

" After spending the honeymoon at his grace's unique

villa on the Thames, their graces will receive company
at their splendid mansion in Portman Square. The
wedding paraphernalia is said to have cost ten thousand
pounds, and her grace's jewel-box is estimated at little
less than half a million."

Wretched as Lady Juliana had long felt herself to
be, her former state of mind was positive happiness
compared to what she now endured. Envy, regret,
self-reproach, and resentment, all struggled in the breast
of the self-devoted beauty, while the paper dropped
from her hand, and she cast a fearful glance around, as
if to ascertain the reality of her fate. The dreadful
certainty smote her with a sense of wretchedness too
acute to be suppressed; and, darting a look of horror
at her unconscious husband, she threw herself back in
her chair, while the scalding tears of envy, anger, and
repentance fell from her eyes.

Accustomed as Henry now was to these ebullitions
of *feeling* from his beauteous partner, he was not yet so
indifferent as to behold them unmoved, and he sought
to soothe her by the kindest expressions and most tender
epithets. These, indeed, had long since ceased to
charm away the lady's ill-humour, but they sometimes
succeeded in mollifying it. But now, their only effect
seemed to be increasing the irritation, as she turned from
all her husband's inquiries, and impatiently withdrew
her hands from his.

Astonished at a conduct so incomprehensible, Douglas
earnestly besought an explanation.

"There!" cried she at length, pushing the paper
towards him; "see there what I might have been but
for you; and then compare it with what you have
made me!"

Confounded by this reproach, Henry eagerly snatched
up the paper, and his eye instantly fell on the fatal paragraph; the poisoned dart that struck the death-blow to

all that now remained to him of happiness—the fond idea that, even amidst childish folly and capricious estrangement, still, in the main, he was beloved! With a quivering lip, and cheek blanched with mortification and indignant contempt, he laid down the paper; and, without casting a look upon, or uttering a word to, his once *adored and adoring Juliana*, quitted the apartment in all that bitterness of spirit which a generous nature must feel when it first discovers the fallacy of a cherished affection. Henry had, indeed, ceased to regard his wife with the ardour of romantic passion; nor had the solid feelings of affectionate esteem supplied its place: but he loved her still, because he believed himself the engrossing object of her tenderness; and, in that blest delusion, he had hitherto found palliatives for her folly, and consolation for all his own distresses.

To indifference he might for a time have remained insensible; because, though his feelings were strong, his perceptions were not acute. But the veil of illusion was now rudely withdrawn. He beheld himself detested where he imagined himself adored; and the anguish of disappointed affection was heightened by the stings of wounded pride and deluded self-love.

———o———

Chapter xviij.

What's done, cannot be undone; to bed, to bed, to bed!
Exit Lady Macbeth.

THE distance at which the whist party had placed themselves, and the deep interest in which their senses were involved, while the fate of the odd trick was pending, had rendered them insensible to the scene that was acting at the other extremity of the apartment. The task of administering succour to the afflicted fair one therefore devolved upon Miss Bella, whose sympathetic powers never had been called into action before. Slowly approaching the wretched Lady Juliana as she lay back in her chair, the tears coursing each other down her cheeks, she tendered her a smelling-bottle, to which her own nose and the noses of her sisters were wont to be applied whenever, as they choicely expressed it, they wanted a "fine smell." But, upon this trying occasion, she went still further; she unscrewed the stopper, unfolded a cotton handkerchief, upon which she poured a few drops of lavender-water, and offered it to her ladyship, deeming that the most elegant and efficient manner in which she could afford relief. But the well-meant offering was silently waved off; and poor Miss Bella, having done all that the light of reason suggested to her, retreated to her seat, wondering what it was her fine sister-in-law would be at.

By the time the rubber was ended, her ladyship's fears of Lady Maclaughlan had enabled her to conquer her feelings so far, that they had now sunk into a state of sullen dejection, which the good aunts eagerly interpreted into the fatigue of the journey; Miss Grizzy declaring, that although the drive was most delightful —nobody could deny that—and they all enjoyed it excessively, as indeed everybody must who had eyes in their head, — yet she must own, at the same time, that she really felt as if all her bones were broke.

A general rising therefore took place at an early hour; and Lady Juliana, attended by all the ladies of the party, was ushered into the chamber of state, which was fitted up in a style acknowledged to be truly magnificent, by all who had ever enjoyed the honour of being permitted to gaze on its white velvet bed-curtains, surmounted by the family arms, and gracefully tucked up by hands *sinister-couped* at the wrists, &c.

But, lest my fashionable readers should be of a different opinion, I shall refrain from giving an inventory of
the various articles with which this favoured ehamber
was furnished. Misses Grizzy and Jacky occupied the
green-room which had been fitted up at Sir Sampson's
birth; the curtains hung at a respectful distance from
the ground; the chimney-piece was far beyond the
reach even of the majestic Jacky's arm; and the painted
tiffany toilette was covered with a shoal of little
tortoise-shell boxes of all shapes and sizes. A grim
visage, scowling from under a Highland bonnet, graced
by a single black feather, hung on high. Miss Grizzy
placed herself before it, and, holding up the candle,
contemplated it for about the nine hundredth time, with
an awe bordering almost on adoration.

"Certainly, Sir Eneas must have been a most
wonderful man—nobody can deny that; and there can
be no question but he had the second sight to the
greatest degree—indeed, I never heard it disputed;
many of his prophecies, indeed, seem to have been
quite incomprehensible; but that is so much the more
extraordinary, you know—for instance, the one with
regard to our family," lowering her voice—"for my
part I declare I never could comprehend it; and yet
there must be something in it, too; but how any branch
from the Glenfern tree—of course, you know, that can
only mean the family tree—should help to prop Lochmarlie's walls, is what I can't conceive. If Sir
Sampson had a son, to be sure, some of the girls—for
you know it can't be any of us; at least I declare for
my own part—I'm sure even of any thing—which I
trust, in goodness, there is not the least chance of,
should ever happen to dear Lady Maclaughlan,—which,
of course, is a thing not to be thought about—and
indeed I'm quite convinced it would be very much out
of respect to dear Lady Maclaughlan, as well as friend-

ship for us, if such a thing was ever to come into his head—there can be no doubt about that."

Here the tender Grizzy got so involved in her own ideas, as to the possibility of Lady Maclaughlan's death, and the propriety of Sir Sampson's proposals, together with the fulfilling of Sir Eneas the seer's prophecy, that there is no saying how far she strayed in her self-created labyrinth. Such as choose to follow her may. For our part, we prefer accompanying the youthful Bella to her chamber, whither she was also attended by the lady of the mansion. Bella's destiny for the night lay at the top of one of those little straggling wooden stairs common in old houses, which creaked in all directions. The bed was placed in a recess dark as Erebus, and betwixt the bed and the wall was a depth profound, which Becky's eye dared not attempt to penetrate.

"You will find every thing right here, child," said Lady Maclaughlan ; " and if any thing should be wrong, you must think it right. I never suffer any thing to be thought wrong here—humph ! " Bella, emboldened by despair, cast a look towards the recess ; and, in a faint voice, ventured to inquire, " Is there no fear that Tom Jones or Gil Blas may be in that place behind the bed ? "

" And if they should," answered her hostess, in her most appalling tone, " what is that to you ? Are you a mouse, that you are afraid they will eat you ? Yes, I suppose you are. You are perhaps the princess in the fairy tale, who was a woman by day, and a mouse by night. I believe you are bewitched ! So I wish your mouseship a good night." And she descended the creaking stair, singing,—

> " Mrs Mouse, are you within ?—
> Yes, indeed, I sit and spin," &c.

till even her stentorian voice was lost in distance. Poor Bella's heart died with the retreating sounds, and only

revived to beat time with the worm in the wood.
Long and eerie was the night, as she gave herself up to
all the horrors of a superstitious mind : ghosts, grey,
black, and white, flitted around her couch—cats, half
human, held her throat—the death-watch ticked in her
ears. At length, the light of morning shed its brightening influence on the dim opaque of her understanding ;
and when all things stood disclosed in light, she shut her
eyes, and ope'd her mouth, in all the blissfulness of security.

The light of day was indeed favourable for displaying
to advantage the beauties of Lochmarlie Castle, which
owed more to nature than art. It was beautifully
situated on a smooth green bank, which rose somewhat
abruptly from the lake, and commanded a view which,
if not extensive, was yet full of variety and grandeur.

Its venerable turrets reared themselves above the
trees, which seemed coeval with them ; and the vast
magnificence of its wide-spreading lawns and extensive
forests seemed to appertain to some feudal prince's lofty
domain. But in vain were creation's charms spread
before Lady Juliana's eyes. Woods, and mountains,
and lakes, and rivers, were odious things ; and her heart
panted for dusty squares and suffocating drawing-rooms.

Something was said of departing, by the sisters, when
the party met at breakfast ; but this was immediately
negatived in the most decided manner by their hostess.

" Since you have taken your own time to come, my
dears, you must take mine to go. Thursday was the
day I invited you for, or at least wanted you for, so you
must stay Thursday, and if you will you may go away
on Friday, and my blessing go with you—humph ! "

The sisters, charmed with what they termed the
hospitality and friendship of this invitation, delightedly
agreed to remain ; and as things were at least conducted
in better style there than at Glenfern, uncomfortable as
it was, Lady Juliana found herself somewhat nearer home

there than at the family château. Lady Maclaughlan, who *could* be commonly civil in her own house, was at some pains to amuse her guests, by showing her collection of china and cabinet of gems, both of which were remarkably fine. There was also a library, a music room, a gallery containing some good pictures, and, what Lady Juliana prized still more, a billiard-table. Thursday, the destined day, at length arrived, and a large party assembled to dinner. Lady Juliana, as she half reclined on a sofa, surveyed the company with a supercilious stare, and without deigning to take any part in the general conversation that went on. It was enough that they spoke with a peculiar accent—everything they said must be barbarous ; but she was pleased once more to eat off plate, and to find herself in rooms which, though grotesque and comfortless, yet wore an air of state, and whose vastness enabled her to keep aloof from those with whom she never willingly came in contact. It was therefore with regret she saw the day of her departure arrive, and found herself once more an unwilling inmate of her only asylum, particularly as her situation now required comforts and indulgences which it was there impossible to procure.

———o———

Chapter xix.

——————————— No mother's care
Shielded my infant innocence with prayer:
*   *   *   *   *
Mother, miscall'd, farewell!

SAVAGE.

THE happy period, so long and anxiously anticipated by the ladies of Glenfern, at length arrived, and Lady Juliana presented to the house of Douglas—not, alas ! the ardently desired heir to its ancient consequence, but twin-daughters, who could only be regarded as additional burdens on its poverty.

The old gentleman's disappointment was excessive; and, as he paced up and down the parlour, with his hands in his pockets, he muttered, "Twa lasses! I ne'er heard tell the like o't! I wonder whar their tochers are to come frae?"

Miss Grizzy, in great perturbation, declared it certainly was a great pity it had so happened, but these things couldn't be helped: she was sure Lady Maclaughlan would be greatly surprised,—there could be no doubt about that.

Miss Jacky saw no cause for regret, and promised herself an endless source of delight in forming the minds and training the ideas of her infant nieces.

Miss Nicky wondered how they were to be nursed. She was afraid Lady Juliana would not be able for both, and wet-nurses had such appetites!

Henry, meanwhile, whose love had all revived in anxiety for the safety, and anguish for the sufferings, of his youthful partner, had hastened to her apartment, and, kneeling by her side, he pressed her hands to his lips with feelings of deepest emotion.

"Dearer—a thousand times dearer to me than ever," whispered he, as he fondly embraced her, "and those sweet pledges of our love!"

"Ah, don't mention them," interrupted his lady, in a languid tone. "How very provoking! I hate girls so—and two of them—oh!" and she sighed deeply. Her husband sighed too; but from a different cause. The nurse now appeared, and approached with her helpless charges; and both parents, for the first time, looked on their own offspring.

"What nice little creatures!" said the delighted father, as, taking them in his arms, he imprinted the first kiss on the innocent faces of his daughters, and then held them to their mother; who, turning from them with disgust, exclaimed, "How can you kiss them, Harry! They are so ugly, and they squall so! Oh do, for heaven's sake, take them away! And see, there is poor Psyche, quite wretched at being so long away from me—pray, put her on the bed."

"She will grow fond of her babies by and by," said poor Henry to himself, as he quitted the apartment, with feelings very different from those with which he entered it.

At the pressing solicitations of her husband, the fashionable mother was prevailed upon to attempt nursing one of her poor starving infants; but the first trial proved also the last, as she declared nothing upon earth should ever induce her to perform so odious an office; and as Henry's entreaties, and her aunt's remonstrances, served alike to irritate and agitate her, the contest was, by the advice of her medical attendant, completely given up. A wet-nurse was therefore procured; but as she refused to undertake both children, and the old gentleman would not hear of having two such incumbrances in his family, it was settled, to the unspeakable delight of the maiden sisters, that the youngest should be entrusted entirely to their management, and brought up by hand.

The consequence was such as might have been foreseen. The child, who was naturally weak and delicate at its birth, daily lost a portion of its little strength, while its continued cries declared the intensity of its sufferings, hough they produced no other effect on its unfeeling mother than her having it removed to a more distant apartment, as she could not endure to hear the cross little thing scream so for nothing. On the other hand, the more favoured twin, who was from its birth a remarkably strong lively infant, and met with all justice from its nurse, throve apace, and was pronounced by her to be the very picture of the bonnie leddie, its mamma; and then, with all the low cunning of her kind, she would launch forth into panegyrics of its beauty, and prophecies of the great dignities and honours that would one day be showered upon it; until, by her fawning and flattery, she succeeded in exciting a degree of interest which nature had not secured for it in the mother's breast.

Things were in this situation, when, at the end of three weeks, Mr and Mrs Douglas arrived to offer their congratulations on the birth of the twins. Lady Juliana received her sister-in-law in her apartment, which she had not yet quitted, and replied to her congratulations only by querulous complaints and childish murmurs.

"I am sure you are very happy in not having children," continued she, as the cries of the little sufferer reached her ear; "I hope to goodness I shall never have any more.—I wonder if any body ever had twin daughters before! and I, too, who hate girls so!"

Mrs Douglas, disgusted with her unfeeling folly, knew not what to reply, and a pause ensued; but a fresh burst of cries from the unfortunate baby again called forth its mother's indignation.

"I wish to goodness that child was gagged," cried she, holding her hands to her ears. "It has done nothing but scream since the hour it was born, and it makes me quite sick to hear it."

"Poor little dear!" said Mrs Douglas, compassionately, "it appears to suffer a great deal."

"Suffer!" repeated her sister-in-law: "what can it suffer? I am sure it meets with a great deal more attention than any person in the house. These three old women do nothing but feed it from morning to night, with every thing they can think of, and make such a fuss about it!"

"I suspect, my dear sister, you would be very sorry for yourself," said Mrs Douglas, with a smile, "were you to endure the same treatment as your poor baby; stuffed with improper food, and loathsome drugs, and bandied about from one person to another."

"You may say what you please," retorted Lady Juliana, pettishly; "but I know it's nothing but ill-temper: nurse says so, too; and it is so ugly with constantly crying, that I cannot bear to look at it:" and she turned away her head as Miss Jacky entered with the little culprit in her arms, which she was vainly endeavouring to *talk* into silence, while she dandled it in the most awkward spinster-like manner imaginable.

"Shocking! what a fright!" exclaimed the tender parent, as her child was held up to her. "Why, it is much less than when it was born, and its skin is as yellow as saffron, and it squints! Only look what a difference!" as the nurse advanced and ostentatiously displayed her charge, who had just waked out of a long sleep; its cheeks flushed with heat; its skin completely filled up; and its large eyes rolling under its already dark eyelashes.

"My missy is just her mamma's pickter," drawled out the nurse, "but the wee missy's unco like her aunties."

"Take her away," cried Lady Juliana, in a tone of despair — "I wish I could send her out of my hearing altogether, for her noise will be my death."

"Alas! what would I give to hear the blessed sound of a living child!" exclaimed Mrs Douglas, taking the infant in her arms. "And how great would be my happiness, could I call this poor rejected one mine!"

"I'm sure you are welcome to my share of the little plague," said her sister-in-law, with a laugh, "if you can prevail upon Harry to give up his."

"I would give up a great deal, could my poor child

find a mother," replied her husband, who just then entered.

"My dear brother!" cried Mrs Douglas, her eyes beaming with delight, "do you then confirm Lady Juliana's kind promise? Indeed I will be a mother to your dear baby, and love her as if she were my own; and in a month—oh! in much less time—you shall see her as stout as her sister."

Henry sighed as he thought, "why has not my poor babe such a mother of its own!" Then thanking his sister-in-law for her generous intentions, he reminded her that she must consult her husband, as few men like to be troubled with any children but their own.

"You are in the right," said Mrs Douglas, blushing at the impetuosity of feeling which had made her forget for an instant the deference due to her husband; "I shall instantly ask his permission; and he is so indulgent to all my wishes, that I have little doubt of obtaining his consent:" and, with the child in her arms, she hastened to her husband, and made known her request.

Mr Douglas received the proposal with considerable coolness; wondering what his wife could see in such an ugly squalling thing, to plague herself about it. If it had been a boy, old enough to speak and run about, there might be some amusement in it; but he could not see the use of a squalling sickly infant—and a girl, too!

His wife sighed deeply, and the tears stole down her cheeks, as she looked on the wan visage and closed eyes of the little sufferer. "Poor baby!" said she, mournfully, "you are rejected on all hands, but your misery will soon be at an end;" and she was slowly leaving the room with her helpless charge, when her husband, touched at the sight of her distress, though the feeling that caused it he did not comprehend, called to her,—"I am sure, Alicia, if you really wish to take charge of

the infant, I have no objections; only I think you will
find it a great plague, and the mother is such a fool!"

"Worse than a fool," said Mrs Douglas indignantly,
"for she hates and abjures this her poor unoffending
babe."

"Does she so?" cried Mr Douglas, every kindling
feeling roused within him at the idea of his blood being
hated and abjured; "then, hang me! if she shall have
any child of Harry's to hate, as long as I have a house
to shelter it, and a sixpence to bestow upon it,"—taking
the infant in his arms, and kindly kissing it.

Mrs Douglas smiled through her tears, as she embraced her husband, and praised his goodness and
generosity; then, full of exultation and delight, she
flew to impart the success of her mission to the parents
of her *protégé*.

Great was the surprise of the maiden-nurses at finding
they were to be bereft of their little charge.

"I declare, I think the child is doing as well as
possible," said Miss Grizzy. "To be sure, it does
yammer constantly—that can't be denied; and it is uncommonly small—nobody can dispute that. At the
same time, I am sure, I can't tell what makes it cry,
for I've given it two colic powders every day, and a
teaspoonful of Lady Maclaughlan's carminative every
three hours."

"And I've done nothing but make water-gruel and
chop rusks for it," quoth Miss Nicky, "and yet it is
never satisfied. I wonder what it would be at!"

"I know perfectly well what it would be at," said
Miss Jacky, with an air of importance. "All this crying and screaming is for nothing else but a nurse; but
it ought not to be indulged: there is no end of indulg-
ing the desires, and 'tis amazing how cunning children
are, and how soon they know how to take advantage of
people's weakness," glancing an eye of fire at Mrs

Douglas. " Were that my child, I would feed her on bread and water, before I would humour her fancies. A pretty lesson indeed, if she's to have her own way before she's a month old ! "

Mrs Douglas knew that it was in vain to attempt arguing with her aunts. She therefore allowed them to wonder, and declaim over their sucking pots, colic powders, and other instruments of torture, while she sent to the wife of one of her tenants who had lately lain in, and who wished for the situation of nurse, appointing her to be at Lochmarlie the following day. Having made her arrangements, and collected the scanty portion of clothing Mrs Nurse chose to allow, Mrs Douglas repaired to her sister-in-law's apartment, with her little charge in her arms. She found her still in bed, and surrounded with her favourites.

" So you really are going to torment yourself with that little screech-owl," said she. " Well, I must say it's very good of you ; but I am afraid you will soon tire of her. Children are such plagues ! Are they not, my darling ? " added she, kissing her pug.

" You will not say so when you have seen my little girl a month hence," said Mrs Douglas, trying to conceal her disgust for Henry's sake, who had just then entered the room. " She has promised me never to cry any more ; so give her a kiss, and let us be gone."

The high-bred mother slightly touched the cheek of her sleeping babe, extended her finger to her sister-in-law, and, carelessly bidding them good-bye, returned to her pillow and her pugs.

Henry accompanied Mrs Douglas to the carriage, and, before they parted, he promised his brother to ride over to Lochmarlie in a few days. He said nothing of his child, but his glistening eye and the warm pressure of his hand spoke volumes to the kind heart of his brother ; who assured him that Alice would be very

good to his little girl, and that he was sure she would
get quite well when she got a nurse. The carriage
drove off, and Henry, with a heavy spirit, returned to
the house to listen to his father's lectures, his aunts'
ejaculations, and his wife's murmurs.

———o———

Chapter xx.

We may boldly spend upon the hope of what
Is to come in.

Henry IV

THE birth of twin daughters awakened the young
father to a still stronger sense of the total dependence and extreme helplessness of his condition.   Yet how to remedy it he knew not : to accept
of his father's proposal was out of the question, and it
was equally impossible for him, were he ever so inclined, to remain much longer a burden on the narrow
income of the Laird of Glenfern.   One alternative only
remained, which was to address the friend and patron
of his youth, General Cameron ; and to him he therefore wrote, describing all the misery of his situation,
and imploring his forgiveness and assistance.   " The
old general's passion must have cooled by this time,"
thought he to himself, as he sealed the letter ; " and,
as he has often overlooked former scrapes, I think, after
all, he will help me out of this greatest one of all."

For once, Henry was not mistaken.   He received
an answer to his letter, in which the general—after
reviling his folly in marrying a lady of quality, up-
braiding him for the birth of his twin daughters, and
giving him some wholesome counsel as to his future
mode of life—concluded by informing him that he had
got him reinstated in his former rank in the army ; that

he should settle seven hundred per annum on him, till he saw how matters were conducted; and, in the meantime, enclosed a draught for four hundred pounds, to open the campaign.

Though this was not, according to Henry's notions, " coming down handsomely," still it was better than not coming down at all ; and, with a mixture of delight and disappointment, he flew to communicate the tidings to Lady Juliana.

" Seven hundred pounds a-year ! " exclaimed she, in raptures : " what a quantity of money ! why, we shall be quite rich, and I shall have such a beautiful house, and such pretty carriages, and give such parties, and buy so many fine things—oh dear, how happy I shall be ! "

" You know little of money, Julia, if you think seven hundred pounds will do all that," replied her husband gravely. " I hardly think we can afford a house in town ; but we may have a pretty cottage at Richmond or Twickenham ; and I can keep a curricle, and drive you about, you know ; and we may give famous good family dinners."

A dispute here ensued : her ladyship hated cottages, and curricles, and good family dinners, as much as her husband despised fancy balls, opera boxes, and chariots.

The fact was, that the one knew very nearly as much of the real value of money as the other, and Henry's *sober* scheme was just about as practicable as his wife's extravagant one.

Brought up in the luxurious profusion of a great house,—accustomed to issue her orders, and have them obeyed, Lady Juliana, at the time she married, was in the most blissful state of ignorance respecting the value of pounds, shillings, and pence. Her maid took care to have her wardrobe supplied with all things needful ; and when she wanted a new dress, or a fashionable jewel, it was only driving to Madame D.'s or Mr Y.'s, and desiring the article to be sent to herself, while the bill went to her papa.

From never seeing money in its own vulgar form, Lady Juliana had learned to consider it as a mere nominal thing; while, on the other hand, her husband, from seeing too much of it, had formed almost equally erroneous ideas of its powers. By the mistaken kindness of General Cameron, he had been indulged in all the fashionable follies of the day, and allowed to use his patron's ample fortune as if it had already been his own; nor was it until he found himself a prisoner at Glenfern from want of money, that he had ever attached the smallest importance to it. In short, both the husband and wife had been accustomed to look upon it in the same light as the air they breathed. They knew it essential to life, and concluded that it would come some way or other; either from the east or west, north or south. As for the vulgar concerns of meat and drink, servants' wages, taxes, and so forth, they never found a place in the calculations of either. Birth-day dresses, fêtes, operas, equipages, and state liveries, whirled in rapid succession through Lady Juliana's brain; while clubs, curricles, horses, and claret took possession of her husband's mind.

However much they differed in the proposed modes of showing off in London, both agreed perfectly in the necessity of going there; and Henry therefore hastened to inform his father of the change in his circumstances, and apprise him of his intention of immediately joining his regiment, the ——— Guards.

" Seven hunder pound a-year ! " exclaimed the old gentleman; " seven hunder pound ! Oo what can ye mak o' a' that siller ? Ye'll surely lay by the half o't to tocher your bairns ? Seven hunder pound a-year for doing naething ! "

Miss Jacky was afraid, unless they got some person of sense (which would not be an easy matter) to take the management of it, it would perhaps be found little enough in the long run.

Miss Grizzy declared it was a very handsome income,—nobody could dispute that; at the same time every body must allow that the money could not have been better bestowed, and she was certain—there could be no doubt about that—with the young people's good sense, and good principles, and two daughters to provide for, they would make a good use of it.

Miss Nicky observed, "there was a great deal of good eating and drinking in seven hundred a-year, if people knew how to manage it."

All was bustle and preparation throughout Glenfern Castle; and the young ladies' good-natured activity and muscular powers were again in requisition to collect the wardrobe, and pack the trunks, imperial, &c., of their noble sister.

Glenfern remarked, " that fules war fond o' flitting, for they seemed glad to leave the good quarters they were in."

Miss Grizzy declared, there was a great excuse for their being glad, poor things! young people were always so fond of a change : at the same time, it would have been quite natural for them to feel sorry too,— nobody could deny that !

Miss Jacky was astonished how any person's mind could be so callous as to think of leaving Glenfern without emotion.

Miss Nicky wondered what was to become of the christening cake she had ordered from Perth ; it might be as old as the hills before there would be another child born amongst them.

The misses were ready to weep at the disappointment of the dreaming-bread.

In the midst of all this agitation, mental and bodily, the long-looked for moment arrived. The carriage drove round ready packed and loaded ; and, absolutely screaming with delight, Lady Juliana sprang into it : as she nodded, and kissed her hand to the assembled group, she impatiently called to Henry to follow. His adieus were, however, not quite so tonish as those of his high-bred lady, for he went duly and severally through all the evolutions of kissing, embracing, shaking of hands, and promises to write ; then taking his station by the side of the nurse and child, the rest of the carriage being completely filled by the favourites, he bade a long farewell to his paternal halls and the land of his birth.

———o———

Chapter xxj.

——— For trifles, why should I displease
The man I love ?   For trifles such as these,
To serious mischiefs lead the man I love ?

HORACE.

BRIGHT prospects of future happiness, and endless plans of expense, floated through Lady Juliana's brain, and kept her temper in some degree of serenity during the journey.

Arrived in London, she expressed herself enraptured at being once more in a civilised country, and restored to the society of human creatures. An elegant house and suitable establishment were immediately provided ; and a thousand dear friends, who had completely forgotten her existence, were now eager to welcome her to her former haunts, and lead her thoughtless and willing steps in the paths of dissipation and extravagance.

Soon after their arrival, they were visited by General

Cameron. It was two o'clock, yet Lady Juliana had not appeared; and Henry, half-stretched upon a sofa, was dawdling over his breakfast, with half-a-dozen newspapers scattered round.

The first salutations over, the General demanded— " Am I not to be favoured with a sight of your lady ? Is she afraid that I am one of your country relations, and taken her flight from the breakfast-table in consequence ? "

" She has not yet made her appearance," replied Douglas; " but I will let her know you are here. I am sure she will be happy to make acquaintance with one to whom I am so much indebted."

A message was despatched to Lady Juliana, who returned for answer that she would be down immediately. Three quarters of an hour, however, elapsed ; and the general, provoked with this inattention and affectation, was preparing to depart, when the lady made her appearance.

" Juliana, my love," said her husband, " let me present you to General Cameron—the generous friend who has acted the part of a father towards me, and to whom you owe all the comforts you enjoy."

Lady Juliana slightly bowed with careless ease, and half uttered a " How d'ye do ?—very happy indeed—" as she glided on to pull the bell for breakfast. " Cupid, Cupid! " cried she to the dog, who had flown upon the general, and was barking most vehemently ; " poor darling Cupid! are you almost starved to death? Harry, do give him that muffin on your plate."

" You are very late to-day, my love," cried the mortified husband.

" I have been pestered for the last hour with Duval and the court dresses, and I could not fix on what I should like."

" I think you might have deferred the ceremony of

choosing to another opportunity.   General Cameron
has been here above an hour."

"Dear! I hope you did not wait for me—I shall
be quite shocked!" drawled out her ladyship, in a
tone denoting how very indifferent the answer would
be to her.

"I beg your ladyship would be under no uneasiness
on that account," replied the general, in an ironical
tone, which, though lost upon her, was obvious enough
to Henry.

"Have you breakfasted?" asked Lady Juliana,
exerting herself to be polite.

"Absurd, my love!" cried her husband.   "Do you
suppose I should have allowed the general to wait for
that, too, all this time, if he had not breakfasted many
hours ago?"

"How cross you are this morning, my Harry!   I
protest my Cupidon is quite ashamed of your *gros-
sièreté!* "

A servant now entered to say Mr Shagg was come
to know her ladyship's final decision about the hammer-
cloths; and the new footman was come to be engaged;
and the china merchant was below.

"Send up one of them at a time; and as to the
footman, you may say I'll have him at once," said
Lady Juliana.

"I thought you had engaged Mrs D.'s footman last
week.   She gave him the best character, did she not?"
asked her husband.

"Oh, yes, his character was good enough; but he
was a horrid cheat, for all that.   He called himself
five feet nine, and when he was measured he turned out
to be only five feet seven and a half."

"Pshaw!" exclaimed Henry, angrily.   "What
did that signify, if the man had a good character?"

"How absurdly you talk, Harry, as if a man's

character signified, who has nothing to do but stand behind my carriage! A pretty figure he would have made there beside Thomas, who is at least five feet ten!"

The entrance of Mr Shagg, bowing and scraping, and laden with cloths, lace, and fringes, interrupted the conversation.

"Well, Mr Shagg," cried Lady Juliana, "what's to be done with that odious leopard's skin? You must positively take it off my hands. I would rather never go in a carriage again than show myself in the Park with that frightful thing!"

"Certainly, my lady," replied the obsequious Mr Shagg, "anything your ladyship pleases; your ladyship can have any hammer-cloth you like; and I have accordingly brought patterns of the very newest fashions for your ladyship to make choice. Here are some uncommon elegant articles. At the same time, my lady, your ladyship must be sensible that it is impossible that we can take back the leopard's skin. It was not only cut out to fit your ladyship's coach-box—and consequently your ladyship understands it would not fit any other—but the silver feet and crests have also been affixed quite ready for use, so that the article is quite lost to us. I am confident, therefore, that your ladyship will consider of this, and allow it to be put down in your bill."

"Put it anywhere but on my coach-box, and don't bore me!" answered Lady Juliana, tossing over the patterns, and humming a tune.

"What!" said her husband, "is that the leopard's skin you were raving about last week, and are you tired of it before it has been used?"

"And no wonder. Who do you think I saw in the Park yesterday, but that old quiz Lady Denham, just come from the country, with her frightful old coach set off with a hammer-cloth precisely like the one I had ordered. Only fancy people saying, Lady Denham sets the fashion for Lady Juliana Douglas! Oh, there's confusion and despair in the thought!"

Confusion, at least, if not despair, was painted in Henry's face, as he saw the general's glance directed alternately with contempt at Lady Juliana and at himself, mingled with pity. He continued to fidget about in all directions while Lady Juliana talked nonsense to Mr Shagg, and wondered if the general never meant to go away. But he calmly kept his ground till the man was dismissed, and another introduced, loaded with china jars, monsters, and distorted tea-pots, for the capricious fair one's choice and approbation.

"Beg ten thousand pardons, my lady, for not calling yesterday, according to appointment—quite an unforeseen impediment. The Countess of Godolphin had somehow got private intelligence that I had a set of fresh commodities just cleared from the Custom-house; and, well knowing that such things are not long in hand, her la'ship came up from the country on purpose—the countess has so much taste!—she drove straight to my warehouse, and kept me a close prisoner till after your la'ship's hour; but I hope it may not be taken amiss, seeing that it is not a customary thing with us to be calling on customers, not to mention that this line of goods is not easily transported about. However, I flatter myself the articles now brought for your ladyship's inspection will not be found beneath your notice. Please to observe this choice piece—it represents a Chinese cripple, squat on the ground, with his legs crossed. Your ladyship may observe the head and chin advanced forwards, as in the act of begging. The tea pours from the open mouth; and, till your ladyship tries, you can have no idea of the elegant effect it produces."

"That is really droll," cried Lady Juliana, with a laugh of delight; "and I must have the dear sick beggar, he is so deliciously hideous."

"And here," continued Mr Brittle, "is an amazing delicate article, in the way of a jewel : a frog of Turkish agate for burning pastiles in, my lady; just such as they use in the seraglio; and, indeed, this one I may call invaluable, for it was the favourite toy of one of the widowed sultanas, till she grew devout and gave up perfumes. One of her slaves disposed of it to my foreign partner. Here it opens at the tail, where you put in the pastiles, and, closing it up, the vapour issues beautifully through the nostrils, eyes, ears, and mouth, all at once. Here, sir," turning to Douglas, "if you are curious in new workmanship, I would have you examine this. I defy any jeweller in London to come up to the fineness of these hinges, and delicacy of the carving"——

"Pshaw, hang it!" said Douglas, turning away, and addressing some remark to the general, who was provokingly attentive to everything that went on.

"Here," continued Mr Brittle, "are a set of jars, tea-pots, mandarins, sea-monsters, and pug-dogs; all of superior beauty, but such as your ladyship may have seen before."

"Oh, the dear, dear little puggies! I must have them to amuse my own darlings. I protest here is one the image of Psyche; positively I must kiss it!"

"Oh dear! I am sure," cried Mr Brittle, simpering, and making a conceited bow, "your ladyship does it and me too much honour. But here, as I was going to say, is the phœnix of all porcelain ware—the *ne plus ultra* of perfection—what I have kept in my back-room, concealed from all eyes, until your ladyship shall pronounce upon it. Somehow one of my shopmen got word of it, and told her grace of L—— (who has a

pretty taste in these things for a young lady) that I
had some particular choice article that I was keeping
for a lady that was a favourite of mine. Her grace
was in the shop the matter of a full hour and a half,
trying to wheedle me out of a sight of this rare piece ;
and I pretending not to know what her grace would be
after, but showing her thing after thing, to put it out of
her head. But she was not so easily bubbled, and at
last went away ill enough pleased. Now, my lady,
prepare all your eyes : " he then went to the door, and
returned, carrying with difficulty a large basket, which
till then had been kept by one of his own satellites.
After removing coverings of all descriptions, an uncouth group of monstrous size was displayed ; which,
on investigation, appeared to be a serpent coiled in
regular folds round the body of a tiger placed on end ;
and the whole structure, which was intended for a
vessel of some kind, was formed of the celebrated green
mottled china, invaluable to connoisseurs.

"View that well," exclaimed Mr Brittle, in a
transport of enthusiasm, "for such a specimen not one
of half the size has ever been imported to Europe.
There is a long story about this my phœnix, as I call
it ; but to be brief, it was secretly procured from one
of the temples, where, gigantic as it may seem, and
uncouth for the purpose, it was the idol's principal
tea-pot ! "

"O delicious ! " cried Lady Juliana, clasping her
hands in ecstacy ; "I will give a party for the sole purpose of drinking tea out of this machine ; and I will
have the whole room fitted up like an Indian temple.
Oh ! it will be so new ! I die to send out my cards.
The Duchess of B—— told me the other day, with
such a triumphant air, when I was looking at her two
little green jars, not a quarter the size of this, that there
was not a bit more of that china to be had for love or

money. Oh, she will be so provoked!" And she absolutely skipped for joy.

A loud rap at the door now announcing a visitor, Lady Juliana ran to the balcony, crying, "Oh, it must be Lady Gerard, for she promised to call early in the morning, that we might go together to a wonderful sale in some far-off place in the city—at Wapping, for aught I know. Mr Brittle, Mr Brittle, for the love of heaven, carry the dragon into the back drawing-room—I purchase it, remember!—make haste!—Lady Gerard is not to get a glimpse of it for the world."

The servant now entered with a message from Lady Gerard, who would not alight, begging that Lady Juliana would make haste down to her, as they had not a moment to lose. She was flying away without further ceremony than a "Pray, excuse me," to the general, when her husband called after her to know whether the child was gone out, as he wished to show her to the general.

"I don't know, indeed," replied the fashionable mother; "I haven't had time to see her to-day;" and, before Douglas could reply, she was down stairs.

A pause ensued—the general whistled a quick step, and Douglas walked up and down the room, in a pitiable state of mind, guessing pretty much what was passing in the mind of his friend, and fully sensible that it must be of a severer nature than any thing he could yet allow himself to think of his Juliana.

"Douglas," said the general, "have you made any step towards a reconciliation with your father-in-law? I believe it will become shortly necessary for your support."

"Juliana wrote twice after her marriage," replied he; "but the reception which her letters met with was not such as to encourage perseverance on our part. With regard to myself, it is not an affair in which delicacy

will permit me to be very active, as I might be accused
of mercenary motives, which I am far from having."

"Oh, of that I acquit you; but surely it ought to be
a matter of moment, even to a——Lady Juliana. The
case is now altered. Time must have accustomed him
to the idea of this imaginary affront; and, on my honour,
if he thought like a gentleman and a man of sense, I
know where he would think the misfortune lay. Nay,
don't interrupt me. The old earl must now, I say,
have cooled in his resentment; perhaps, too, his grand-
children may soften his heart; this must have occurred
to you. Has her ladyship taken any further steps since
her arrival in town?"

"I—I believe she has not; but I will put her in
mind."

"A daughter who requires to have her memory refreshed on such a subject is likely to make a valuable
wife!" said the general, drily.

Douglas felt as if it was incumbent on him to be
angry, but remained silent.

"Hark ye, Douglas," continued the general; "I
speak this for your interest. You cannot go on without
the earl's help. You know I am not on ceremony with
you; and if I refrain from saying what you see I think
about your present ruinous mode of life, it is not to spare
your feelings, but from a sense of the uselessness of any
such remonstrance. What I do give you is with good-
will; but all my fortune would not suffice to furnish
pug-dogs and deformed tea-pots for such a vitiated
taste; and if it would, hang me if it should! But
enough on this head. The earl has been in bad health,
and is lately come to town. His son too, and his lady,
are to come about the same time, and are to reside with
him during the season. I have heard Lord Lindore
spoken of as a good-natured easy man, and he would
probably enter willingly into any scheme to reinstate his

sister into his father's good graces. Think of this, and make what you can of it; and my particular advice to you personally is, try to exchange into a marching regiment: for a fellow like you, with such a wife, London is the very mischief! and so good morning to you." He snatched up his hat, and was off in a moment.

———o———

Chapter xxij.

To reckon up a thousand of her pranks,
Her pride, her wasteful spending, her unkindness,
Her scolding, pouting, . . .
Were to reap an endless catalogue.

Old Play.

WHEN Lady Juliana returned from her expedition it was so late that Douglas had not time to speak to her; and, separate engagements carrying them different ways, he had no opportunity to do so until the following morning at breakfast. He then resolved no longer to defer what he had to say, and began by reproaching her with the cavalier manner in which she had behaved to his good friend the general.

"Upon my life, Harry, you are grown perfectly savage," cried his lady. "I was most particularly civil. I wonder what you would have me to do? You know very well, I cannot have any thing to say to old men of that sort."

"I think," returned Henry, "you might have been gratified by making an acquaintance with my benefactor, and the man to whom you owe the enjoyment of your favourite pleasures. At any rate, you need not have made yourself ridiculous. May I perish, if I did not wish myself under ground while you were talking nonsense to those sneaking rascals, who wheedle you out of your money! 'Sdeath! I had a good mind to throw them and their trumpery out of the window, when I saw you make such a fool of yourself."

"A fool of myself! how foolishly you talk! And as for that vulgar awkward general, he ought to have been too much flattered. Some of the monsters were so like himself, I am sure he must have thought I took them for the love of his round bare pate."

"Upon my soul, Julia, I am ashamed of you! Do leave off this excessive folly, and try to be rational. What I particularly wished to say to you is, that your father is in town, and it will be proper that you should make another effort to be reconciled to him."

"I dare say it will," answered Lady Juliana, with a yawn.

"And you must lose no time. When will you write?"

"There's no use in writing, or indeed doing any thing in the matter. I am sure he won't forgive me."

"And why not?"

"Oh, why should he do it now? He did not forgive me when I asked him before."

"And do you think, then, for a father's forgiveness it is not worth while to have a little perseverance?"

"I am sure he won't do it; so 'tis in vain to try;" repeated she, going to the glass, and singing, "*Papa non dite di no,*" &c.

"By heavens, Julia!" cried her husband passionately, "you are past all endurance! Can nothing touch you?—nothing fix your thoughts, and make you serious for a single moment? Can I not make you understand that you are ruining yourself and me; that we have nothing to depend upon but the bounty of that man whom you disgust by your caprice, extravagance, and impertinence; and that if you don't get reconciled to your father, what is to become of you? You already

know what you have to expect from my family, and
how you like living with them."

"Heavens, Harry! what is all this tirade about?
Is it because I said papa woutdn't forgive me? I'm
sure I don't mind writing to him; I have no objection,
the first leisure moment I have; but really, in town,
one's time is so engrossed"——

At this moment her maid entered in triumph, carrying on her arms a satin dress, embroidered with gold
and flowers.

"See, my lady," cried she, "your new robe, as
madame has sent home half a day sooner than her
word; and she has disobliged several of the quality, by
not giving the pattern."

"Oh, lovely! charming! Spread it out, Gage;
hold it to the light: all my own fancy! Only look,
Harry; how exquisite! how divine!"

Harry had no time to express his contempt for embroidered robes; for just then one of his knowing
friends came, by appointment, to accompany him to
Tattersal's, where he was to bid for a famous pair of
curricle greys.

Days passed on without Lady Juliana's ever thinking
it worth while to follow her husband's advice about
applying to her father; until, a week after, Douglas
overheard the following conversation between his wife
and one of her acquaintance.

"You are going to this grand fête, of course," said
Mrs G. "I'm told it is to eclipse every thing that has
been yet seen or heard of."

"Of what fête do you speak?" demanded Lady
Juliana.

"My dear creature, how Gothic you are! Don't
you know any thing about this grand affair, that every
body has been talking of for two days? Lady Lindore
gives, at your father's house, an entertainment, which is

to be a concert, ball, and masquerade at once. All London is asked, of any distinction, *çà s'entend.* But, bless me, I beg pardon! I totally forgot that you were not on the best terms possible in that quarter—but never mind, we must have you go; there is not a person of fashion that will stay away: I must get you asked; I shall petition Lady Lindore in your favour."

"Oh, pray don't trouble yourself," cried Lady Juliana, in extreme pique. "I believe I can get this done without your obliging interference; but I don't know whether I shall be in town then."

From this moment, Lady Juliana resolved to make a vigorous effort to regain a footing in her father's house. Her first action the next morning was to write to her brother, who had hitherto kept aloof, because he could not be at the trouble of having a difference with the earl, entreating him to use his influence in promoting a reconciliation between her father and herself.

No answer was returned for four days, at the end of which time Lady Juliana received the following note from her brother:—

"Dear Julia,

"I quite agree with you in thinking that you have been kept long enough in the corner, and shall certainly tell papa that you are ready to become a good girl whenever he shall please to take you out of it. I shall endeavour to see Douglas and you soon.

"Yours affectionately,

"Lindore.

"Lady Lindore desires me to say you can have tickets for her ball, if you choose to come *en masque.*"

Lady Juliana was delighted with this billet, which she protested was every thing that was kind and generous; but the postcript was the part on which she dwelt with the greatest delight, as she repeatedly declared it was a great deal more than she expected. "You see, Harry," said she, as she tossed the note to him, "I was in the right. Papa won't forgive me; but Lindore says he will send me a ticket for the fête : it is vastly attentive of him, for I did not ask it. But I must go disguised, which is monstrous provoking, for I'm afraid nobody will know me."

A dispute here ensued. Henry swore she should not steal into her father's house as long as she was his wife. The lady insisted that she should go to her brother's fête when she was invited; and the altercation ended as altercations commonly do, leaving both parties more wedded to their own opinion than at first.

In the evening, Lady Juliana went to a large party; and, as she was passing from one room to another, she was startled by a little paper pellet thrown at her. Turning round to look for the offender, she saw her brother standing at a little distance, smiling at her surprise. This was the first time she had seen him for two years, and she went up to him with an extended hand, while he gave her a familiar nod, and a "How d'ye do, Julia?" and one finger of his hand, while he turned round to speak to one of his companions. Nothing could be more characteristic of both parties than this fraternal meeting; and from this time they were the best friends imaginable.

Chapter xxiij.

Helas! où donc chercher ou trouver le bonheur,
Nulle part tout entier, partout avec mesure!

VOLTAIRE.

SOME days before the expected fête, Lady Juliana,
at the instigation of her adviser, Lady Gerard,
resolved upon taking the field against the Duchess
of L——. Her grace had issued cards for a concert;
and, after mature deliberation, it was decided that her
rival should strike out something new, and announce a
christening for the same night.

The first intimation Douglas had of the honour intended him by this arrangement was through the medium
of the newspaper; for the husband and wife were
now much too fashionable to be at all *au fait* of each
other's schemes. His first emotion was to be extremely
surprised; the next to be exceedingly displeased; and
the last to be highly gratified at the *eclat* with which his
child was to be made a Christian. True, he had intended requesting the general to act as godfather upon
the occasion; but Lady Juliana protested she would
rather the child never should be christened at all (which
already seemed nearly to have been the case) than have
that cross vulgar-looking man to stand sponsor. Her
ladyship, however, so far conceded, that the general was
to have the honour of giving his name to the next, if a
boy, for she was now near her second confinement; and,
with this promise, Henry was satisfied to slight the only
being in the world to whom he looked for support to
himself and his children. In the utmost delight, the
fond mother drove away to consult her confidants upon
the name and decorations of the child, whom she had
not even looked at for many days.

Every thing succeeded to admiration. Amid crowds

of spectators, in all the pomp of lace and satin, surrounded by princes and peers, and handed from duchesses
to countesses, the twin daughter of Henry Douglas, and
the heroine of future story, was baptized by the names
of Adelaide Julia Geraldine.

Some months previous to this event, Lady Juliana had
received a letter from Mrs Douglas, informing her of
the rapid improvement that had taken place in her little
charge, and requesting to know by what name she should
have her christened; at the same time gently insinuating
her wish that, in compliance with the custom of the
country, and as a compliment due to the family, it should
be named after its paternal grandmother.

Lady Juliana glanced over the first line of the letter,
then looked at the signature, resolved to read the rest as
soon as she should have time to answer it; and, in the
mean time, tossed it into a drawer, amongst old visiting
cards and unpaid bills.

After vainly waiting for an answer much beyond the
accustomed time when children are baptized, Mrs
Douglas could no longer refuse to accede to the desires
of the venerable inmates of Glenfern; and, about a
month before her favoured sister received her more
elegant appellations, the neglected twin was baptized by
the name of Mary.

Mrs Douglas's letter had been enclosed in the following one from Miss Grizzy; and as it had not the good
fortune to be perused by the person to whom it was
addressed, we deem it but justice to the writer to insert
it here :—

"Glenfern Castle, July 30, 17—.

" My dearest Niece, Lady Juliana,

"I am Certain, as indeed we all are, that it will
Afford your Ladyship and our dear Nephew the greatest

Pleasure to see this letter Franked by our Worthy and
Respectable Friend Sir Sampson Maclaughlan, Bart.,
especially as it is the First he has ever franked; out of
compliment to you, as I assure you he admires you excessively, as indeed we all do.   At the same Time, you
will of course, I am sure, Sympathise with us all in the
distress Occasioned by the melancholy Death of our late
Most Obliging Member, Duncan M'Dunsmuir, Esquire,
of Dhunacrag and Auchnagoil, who you never have had
the pleasure of seeing.   What renders his death particularly distressing, is, that Lady Maclaughlan is of
opinion it was entirely owing to eating Raw oysters, and
damp feet.   This ought to be a warning to all Young
people to take care of Wet feet, and Especially eating
Raw oysters, which are certainly Highly dangerous,
particularly where there is any Tendency to Gout.   I
hope, my dear Niece, you have got a pair of Stout
walking shoes, and that both Henry and you remember
to Change your feet after Walking.   I am told Raw
Oysters are much the fashion in London at present;
but when this Fatal Event comes to be Known, it will
of course Alarm people very much, and put them upon
their guard both as to Damp Feet, and Raw oysters.
Lady Maclaughlan is in High spirits at Sir Sampson's
Success, though, at the Same Time, I assure you, she
Felt much for the Distress of poor Mr M'Dunsmuir,
and had sent him a Large Box of Pills, and a Bottle
of Gout Tincture, only two days before he died.   This
will be a great Thing for you, and especially for Henry,
my dear niece, as Sir Sampson and Lady Maclaughlan
are going to London directly to take his Seat in Parliament; and she will make a point of Paying you every
attention, and will Matronize you to the play, and any
other Public places you may wish to go; as both my
Sisters and I are of opinion you are rather Young to
matronize yourself yet, and you could not get a more

Respectable Matron than Lady Maclaughlan. I hope
Harry won't take it amiss, if Sir Sampson does not
pay him so much Attention as he might expect; but he
says that he will not be master of a moment of his own
Time in London. He will be so much taken up with
the King and the Duke of York, that he is afraid he
will Disoblige a great Number of the Nobility by it,
besides injuring his own health by such Constant application to business. He is to make a very fine Speech
in Parliament, but it is not yet Fixed what his First
Motion is to be upon. He himself wishes to move for
a New Subsidy to the Emperor of Germany; but Lady
Maclaughlan is of opinion, that it would be better to Bring
in a Bill for Building a bridge over the Water of Dlin;
which, to be sure, is very much wanted, as a Horse and
Cart were drowned at the Ford last Speat. We are
All, I am happy to Say, in excellent Health. Becky
is recovering from the Measles as well as could be
Wished, and the Rose * is quite gone out of Bella's
Face. Beenie has been prevented from Finishing a
most Beautiful Pair of bottle Sliders for your Ladyship
by a whitlow, but it is now Mending, and I hope will
be done in Time to go with Babby's Vase Carpet,
which is extremely elegant, by Sir S. and Lady Maclaughlan. This Place is in great beauty at present, and
the new Byre is completely finished. My Sisters and I
regret Excessively that Henry and you should have
seen Glenfern to such disadvantage; but when next
you favour us with a visit, I hope it will be in Summer,
and the New Byre you will think a Prodigious Improvement. Our dear Little Grand-niece is in great
health, and much improved. We reckon her Extremely like our Family, Particularly Becky; though
she has a great Look of Bella, at the Same Time, when
she Laughs. Excuse the Shortness of this Letter, my

* Erysipelas.

dear Niece, as I shall Write a much Longer one by Lady Maclaughlan.

"Meantime, I remain, my

"Dear Lady Juliana, yours and

"Henry's most affect. aunt,

"GRIZZEL DOUGLAS."

In spite of her husband's remonstrance, Lady Juliana persisted in her resolution of attending her sister-in-law's masked ball, from which she returned, worn out with amusement, and surfeited with pleasure ; protesting all the while she dawdled over her evening breakfast the following day, that there was nobody in the world so much to be envied as Lady Lindore. Such jewels! such dresses! such a house! such a husband! so easy and good-natured, and rich and generous! She was sure Lindore did not care what his wife did. She might give what parties she pleased ; go where she liked ; spend as much money as she chose ; and he would never trouble his head about the matter. She was quite certain Lady Lindore had not a single thing to wish for : *ergo*, she must be the happiest woman in the world! All this was addressed to Henry, who had, however, attained the happy art of not hearing above one word out of a hundred that happened to fall from the "angel lips of his adored Julia ; " and, having finished the newspapers, and made himself acquainted with all the blood-horses, thorough-bred *fillies*, and brood mares therein set forth, with a yawn and whistle sauntered away to G——'s, to look at the last regulation epaulettes.

Not long after, as Lady Juliana was stepping into the carriage that was to whirl her to Bond Street, she was met by her husband ; who, with a solemnity of manner that would have startled any one but his volatile lady, requested she would return with him into the house, as he wished to converse with her upon a subject of some

importance. He prevailed on her to return, upon condition that he would not detain her above five minutes:
when, shutting the drawing-room doors, he said, with
earnestness, " I think, Julia, you were talking of Lady
Lindore this morning: oblige me by repeating what
you said, as I was reading the papers, and really did
not attend much to what passed."

Her ladyship, in extreme surprise, wondered how
Harry could be so tiresome and absurd as to stop her
airing for any such purpose. She really did not know
what she said. How could she ? It was more than an
hour ago.

" Well, then, say what you think of her now," cried
Douglas, impatiently.

" Think of her ! why, what all the world must think
—that she is the happiest woman in it. She looked so
uncommonly well last night, and was in *such* spirits, in
her fancy dress, before she masked—quite the life and
soul of the assembly. After that, I lost sight of
her."

" As every one else has done—she has not been seen
since. Her favourite St Leger is missing too, and there
is hardly a doubt but they are gone off together."

Even Lady Juliana was shocked at this intelligence,
though the folly, more than the wickedness, of the thing
seemed to strike her mind ; but Henry was no nice observer, and was therefore completely satisfied with the
disapprobation she expressed for her sister-in-law's
conduct.

" I am so sorry for poor dear Lindore," said Lady
Juliana, after having exhausted herself in invectives
against his wife. " Such a generous creature as he to
be used in such a manner—it is quite shocking to think
of it ! If he had been an ill-natured stingy wretch, it
would have been nothing ; but Frederick is such a
noble-hearted creature—I dare say he would give me a

thousand pounds if I were to ask him, for he don't care about money."

"Lord Lindore takes the matter very coolly, I understand," replied her husband; "but—don't be alarmed, dear Julia—your father has suffered a little from the violence of his feelings. He has had a sort of apoplectic fit, but is not considered in immediate danger."

Lady Juliana burst into tears, desired the carriage might be put up, as she should not go out, and even declared her intention of abstaining from Mrs D.'s assembly that evening. Henry warmly commended the extreme propriety of these measures; and, not to be outdone in greatness of mind, most heroically sent an apology to a grand military dinner at the Duke of Y——'s; observing, at the same time, that, in the present state of the family, one or two friends to a quiet family dinner was as much as they should be up to.

———o———

Chapter xxib.

—— I but purpose to embark with thee
On the smooth surface of a summer sea,
While gentle zephyrs play in prosp'rous gales,
And Fortune's favour fills the swelling sails.
Henry and Emma.

HOW long these voluntary sacrifices to duty and propriety might have been made, it would not be difficult to guess; but Lady Juliana's approaching confinement rendered her seclusion more and more a matter of necessity; and, shortly after these events took place, she presented her delighted husband with a son. Henry lost no time in announcing the birth of his child to General Cameron; and, at the same time, requesting he would stand godfather, and give his name to the child. The answer was as follows :—

Hort Lodge, Berks.

"Dear Henry,

"By this time twelvemonth, I hope it will be my turn to communicate to you a similar event in my family, to that which your letter announces to me. As a preliminary step, I am just about to march into quarters for life, with a young woman, daughter to my steward. She is healthy, good-humoured, and of course vulgar; since she is no connoisseur in china, and never spoke to a pug-dog in her life.

"Your allowance will be remitted regularly from my banker until the day of my death; you will then succeed to ten thousand pounds, secured to your children, which is all you have to expect from me. If, after this, you think it worth your while, you are very welcome to give your son the name of yours faithfully, William Cameron."

Henry's consternation at the contents of this epistle was almost equalled by Juliana's indignation. The daughter of a steward!—heavens! it made her sick to think of it. It was too shocking! The man ought to be shut up. Henry ought to prevent him from disgracing his connexions in such a manner. There ought to be a law against old men marrying "——

"And young ones too," groaned Douglas, as he thought of the debts he had contracted on the faith and credit of being the general's heir; for, with all the sanguine presumption of thoughtless youth and buoyant spirits, Henry had no sooner found his fault forgiven, than he immediately fancied it forgotten, and himself completely restored to favour. His friends and the world were of the same opinion; and, as the future possessor of immense wealth, he found nothing so easy as to borrow money and contract debts, which he now saw the impossibility of ever discharging. Still he flattered himself the general might only mean to frighten him; or he might relent; or the marriage might go off; or he might not have any children; and, with these *mighty* hopes, things went on as usual for some time longer. Lady Juliana, who, to do her justice, was not of a more desponding character than her husband, had also her stock of hopes and expectations always ready to act upon. She was quite sure, that if papa ever came to his senses (for he had remained in a state of stupefaction since the apoplectic stroke), he would forgive her, and take her to live with him, now that that vile Lady Lindore was gone: or if he should never recover, she was equally sure of benefiting by his death; for, though he had said he was not to leave her a shilling, she did not believe it. She was sure papa would never do anything so cruel; and, at any rate, if he did, Lindore was so generous, he would do something very handsome for her; and so forth.

At length the bubbles burst. The same paper that stated the marriage of General William Cameron to Judith Broadcast, spinster, announced, in all the dignity of woe, the death of that most revered nobleman and eminent statesman, Augustus, Earl of Courtland.

In weak minds it has generally been remarked that no medium can be maintained. Where hope holds her dominion, she is too buoyant to be accompanied by her anchor; and between her and despair there are no gradations. Desperate, indeed, now became the condition of the misjudging pair. Lady Juliana's name was not even mentioned in her father's will, and the general's marriage rendered his settlements no longer a secret. In all the horrors of desperation, Henry now found himself daily beset by creditors of every description. At length the fatal blow came. Horses—

carriages—everything they could call their own, were seized. The term for which they held the house was expired, and they found themselves on the point of being turned into the street; when Lady Juliana, who had been for two days, as her woman expressed it, *out of one fit into another*, suddenly recovered strength to signify her desire of being conveyed to her brother's house. A hackney coach was procured, into which the hapless victim of her own follies was carried. Shuddering with disgust, and accompanied by her children and their attendants, she was set down at the noble mansion from which she had fled two years before.

Her brother, whom she fortunately found at home, lolling upon a sofa with a new novel in his hand, received her without any marks of surprise; said those things happened every day; hoped Captain Douglas would contrive to get himself extricated from this slight embarrassment; and informed his sister that she was welcome to occupy her old apartments, which had been lately fitted up for Lady Lindore. Then, ringing the bell, he desired the housekeeper might show Lady Juliana up-stairs, and put the children in the nursery; mentioned that he generally dined at eight o'clock; and, nodding to his sister as she quitted the room, returned to his book, as if nothing had occurred to disturb him from it.

In ten minutes after her entrance into Courtland House, Lady Juliana had made greater advances in *religion* and *philosophy* than she had done in the whole nineteen years of her life; for she not only perceived that "out of evil cometh good," but was perfectly ready to admit that "all is for the best," and that "whatever is, is right."

"How lucky is it for me," exclaimed she to herself, as she surveyed the splendid suite of apartments that were destined for her accommodation—"how very fortunate that things have turned out as they have done; that Lady Lindore should have run off, and that the general's marriage should have taken place just at the time of poor papa's death "—and, in short, Lady Juliana set no bounds to her self-gratulations, on the happy turn of affairs which had brought about this change in her situation.

To a heart not wholly devoid of feeling, and a mind capable of any thing like reflection, the desolate appearance of this magnificent mansion would have excited emotions of a very different nature. The apartments of the late earl, with their wide extended doors and windows, sheeted furniture, and air of dreary order, exhibited that waste and chilling aspect which marks the chambers of death; and even Lady Juliana shuddered, she knew not why, as she passed through them.

Those of Lady Lindore presented a picture not less striking, could her thoughtless successor have profited by the lesson they offered. Here was all that the most capricious fancy, the most boundless extravagance, the most refined luxury, could wish for or suggest.

" I wonder how Lady Lindore could find in her heart to leave this delicious boudoir," observed Lady Juliana to the old housekeeper.

" I rather wonder, my lady, how she could find in her heart to leave these pretty babes," returned the good woman, as a little boy came running into the room, calling " mamma, mamma ! " Lady Juliana had nothing to say to children beyond a " How d'ye do, love ? " and the child, after regarding her for a moment with a look of disappointment, ran away back to his nursery.

When Lady Juliana had fairly settled herself in her new apartments, and the tumult of delight began to subside, it occurred to her that something must be done for poor Harry, whom she had left in the hands of a brother officer, in a state little short of distraction. She accordingly went in search of her brother, to request his advice and assistance; and found him, it being nearly dark, preparing to set out on his morning's ride. Upon hearing the situation of his brother-in-law, he declared himself ready to assist Mr Douglas as far as he was able, but he had just learned from his people of business that his own affairs were somewhat involved. The late earl had expended enormous sums on political purposes—Lady Lindore had run through a prodigious deal of money, he believed; and he himself had some debts, amounting, he was told, to seventy thousand pounds. Lady Juliana was all aghast at this information, which was delivered with the most perfect *nonchalance* by the earl, while he amused himself with his Newfoundland dog. Unable to conceal her disappointment at these effects of her brother's "liberality and generosity," Lady Juliana burst into tears.

The earl's sensibility was akin to his generosity; he gave money (or rather allowed it to be taken) freely, when he had it, from indolence and easiness of temper; he hated the sight of distress in any individual, because it occasioned trouble, and was, in short, a *bore*. He therefore made haste to relieve his sister's alarm, by assuring her that these were mere trifles: that, as for Douglas's affairs, he would order his agent to arrange everything in his name—hoped to have the pleasure of seeing him at dinner—recommended to his sister to have some pheasant-pie for luncheon; and, calling Carlo, set out upon his ride.

However much Lady Juliana had felt mortified and disappointed at learning the state of her brother's finances, she began, by degrees, to extract the greatest consolation from the comparative insignificance of her own debts to those of the earl; and accordingly, in high spirits at this newly discovered and judicious source

ot comfort, she despatched the following note to her
husband :—

"DEAREST HENRY,

"I have been received in the kindest manner imaginable by Frederick, and have been put in possession
of my old apartments, which are so much altered I
should never have known them. They were furnished
by Lady Lindore, who really has a divine taste. I
long to show you all the delights of this abode. Frederick
desired me to say that he expects to see you here at
dinner, and that he will take charge of paying all our
bills whenever he gets money. Only think of his
owing a hundred thousand pounds, besides all papa's
and Lady Lindore's debts! I assure you I was
almost ashamed to tell him of ours, they sounded so
trifling ; but it is quite a relief to find other people so
much worse. Indeed, I always thought it quite
natural for us to run in debt, considering that we had
no money to pay anything, while Courtland, who is as
rich as a Jew, is so hampered. I shall expect you at
eight ; until when, adieu, *mio caro*,

"Your JULIE.

"I am quite wretched about you."

This tender and consolatory billet Henry had not
the satisfaction of receiving, having been arrested, shortly
after his wife's departure, at the suit of Mr Shagg,
for the sum of two thousand some odd hundreds,
for carriages jobbed, bought, exchanged, repaired, returned, &c.

Lady Juliana's horror and dismay at the news of her
husband's arrest was excessive. Her only ideas of confinement were taken from those pictures of the Bastille
and Inquisition that she had read so much of in French
and German novels ; and the idea of a prison was in-

dissolubly united in her mind with bread and water, chains and straw, dungeons and darkness. Callous and selfish, therefore, as she might be, she was not yet so wholly void of all natural feeling as to think with indifference of the man she had once fondly loved reduced to such a pitiable condition.

Almost frantic at the phantom of her own creation, she flew to her brother's apartment, and, in the wildest and most incoherent manner, besought him to rescue her poor Henry from chains and a dungeon.

With some difficulty Lord Courtland at length apprehended the extent of his brother-in-law's misfortune; and, with his usual *sang froid*, smiled at his sister's simplicity, assured her the King's Bench was the pleasantest place in the world; that some of his own most particular friends were there, who gave capital dinners, and led the most desirable lives imaginable.

"And will he really not be fed on bread and water, and wear chains, and sleep upon straw?" asked the tender wife, in the utmost surprise and delight. "Oh, then, he is not so much to be pitied; though I dare say he would rather get out of prison, too."

The earl promised to obtain his release the following day; and Lady Juliana. returned to her toilette, with a much higher opinion of prisons than she had ever entertained before.

Lord Courtland, for once in his life, was punctual to his promise; and even interested himself so thoroughly in Douglas's affairs, though without inquiring into any particulars, as to take upon himself the discharge of his debts, and to procure leave for him to exchange into a regiment of the line, then under orders for India.

Upon hearing of this arrangement, Lady Juliana's grief and despair, as usual, set all reason at defiance. She would not suffer her dear, dear Harry, to leave her. She knew she could not live without him—she was sure she should die ; and Harry would be sea-sick, and grow so yellow and so ugly, that, when he came back, she should never have any comfort in him again.

Henry, who had never doubted her readiness to accompany him, immediately hastened to assuage her anguish, by assuring her that it had always been his intention to take her along with him.

That was worse and worse :—she wondered how he could be so barbarous and absurd as to think of her leaving all her friends, and going to live amongst savages. She had done a great deal in living so long contentedly with him in Scotland ; but she never could, nor would, make such another sacrifice. Besides, she was sure poor Courtland could not do without her ; she knew he never would marry again ; and who would take care of his dear children, and educate them properly, if she did not? It would be too ungrateful to desert Frederick, after all he had done for them.

The pride of the man, as much as the affection of the husband, was irritated by this resistance to his will ; and a violent scene of reproach and recrimination terminated in an eternal farewell.

———0———

Chapter xxb.

In age, in infancy, from others' aid
Is all our hope; to teach us to be kind,
That nature's first, last lesson.
YOUNG.

THE neglected daughter of Lady Juliana Douglas experienced all the advantages naturally to be expected from her change of situation. Her watchful aunt superintended the years of her infancy, and all that a tender and judicious mother *could* do—

all that most mothers *think* they do—she performed. Mrs Douglas, though not a woman either of words or systems, possessed a reflecting mind, and a heart warm with benevolence towards every thing that had a being; and all the best feelings of her nature were excited by the little outcast, thus abandoned by her unnatural parent. As she pressed the unconscious babe to her bosom, she thought how blest she should have been, had a child of her own thus filled her arms; but the reflection called forth no selfish murmurs from her chastened spirit. While the tear of soft regret trembled in her eye, that eye was yet raised in gratitude to Heaven for having called forth those delightful affections which might otherwise have slumbered in her heart.

Mrs Douglas had read much, and reflected more; and many faultless theories of education had floated in her mind. But her good sense soon discovered how unavailing all theories were whose foundations rested upon the inferred wisdom of the teacher; and how intricate and unwieldy must be the machinery for the human mind where the human hand alone is to guide and uphold it. To engraft into her infant soul the purest principles of religion, was therefore the chief aim of Mary's preceptress. The fear of God was the only restraint imposed upon her dawning intellect; and from the Bible alone was she taught the duties of morality—not in the form of a dry code of laws, to be read with a solemn face on Sundays, or learned with weeping eyes as a week-day task—but, in lowly imitation of her Divine Master, adapted to her youthful capacity by judicious illustration, and familiarised to her taste by hearing its stories and precepts from the lips she best loved. Even as He,—

" Wiser by far than all the sons of men,
Yet teaching ignorance in simple speech,

> As thou would'st take an infant in thy lap
> And lesson him with his own artless tale,"—

Mrs Douglas was the friend and confidant of her pupil : to her all her hopes and fears, wishes and dreads, were confided ; and the first effort of her reason was the discovery, that, to please her aunt, she must study to please her Maker.

" *L'inutilité de la vie des femmes, est la premier source de leurs désordres.*"

Mrs Douglas was fully convinced of the truth of this observation, and that the mere selfish cares and vulgar bustle of life are not sufficient to satisfy the immortal soul, however they may serve to engross it.

A portion of Mary's time was therefore devoted to the daily practice of the great duties of life ; in administering, in some shape or other, to the wants and misfortunes of her fellow-creatures, without requiring from them that their virtue should have been immaculate, or expecting that their gratitude should be everlasting.

"It is better," thought Mrs Douglas, "that we should sometimes be deceived by others, than that we should learn to deceive ourselves ; and the charity and good-will that is suffered to lie dormant, or feed itself on speculative acts of beneficence, for want of proper objects to call it into use, will soon become the corroding rust that will destroy the best feelings of our nature."

In the family of her nurse Mary took a warm interest, but more especially in the welfare of her foster-brother, who—whether from having been robbed of his infant dues on her account, or from whatever cause—had been always a puny delicate child, altogether unlike the hardy mountain race from which he had sprung. Indeed, independent of the claim of fostership, little Angus was an interesting boy. His features and complexion were of that delicate kind which usually accompany hair of a pale golden or reddish cast, and his light-blue eyes were expressive of thought and sweetness beyond his years and station. Mary had herself taught him to read: with her first pocket-money she had bought a Bible for him, and all she learnt herself of its heavenly lore was treasured up and communicated to Angus, who, on his part, was never so happy as in listening to his dear young mistress, or in repeating to her some portion of Scripture, or psalm, or simple paraphrase, which he had committed to memory. But, as the young spirit's light increased, the bodily strength diminished, notwithstanding all that care and kindness could do. Angus gradually grew paler, and thinner, and weaker; but, so gently was life ebbing away, none deemed that death was so near.

A succession of wet stormy days had prevented Mary from visiting her *protégé* for a longer period than usual; but as soon as she could venture abroad, she hastened with her little basket of good things to the cottage of the M'Kinnons.

She was met by her nurse outside the door of the cabin, who told her, with tears, that Angus had kept his bed for two days; that he had not taken food and scarcely spoken, except to ask for his young mistress, that he might repeat to her a hymn he had learnt; and he had made his mother promise, that even if he should be asleep when she came, she was to waken him.

Mary entered, and advanced to the bed where the boy lay with his eyes closed. " I am come at last, dear Angus," said she, taking the little emaciated hand that lay on his breast; " how are you to-day?"

At the sound of her voice, a faint smile shone on his face, and he half opened his sweet, but now filmy, eyes as he softly whispered, " Dinna waken me, I'm ga'en hame;" then closed them as in sleep.*

* A real incident.

"He has fallen asleep," said Mary in a low voice to his mother, as she glided away on tiptoe; "do not disturb him, and I dare say he will be better when he awakes." But Angus awoke no more in this world; he had indeed gone to a happy, an eternal home!

How calmly sinks that child to rest!
How tranquil is his little breast!
Of such the Saviour's kingdom 's made,—
He knew it when he meekly said,
   "I'm going home!"

And where is home? oh, tell me where,
And lead *my* weary footsteps there:—
Home is with God—it is in Heaven—
Yet here to man is kindly given
   A type—a mystic home.

It is a sweet, a peaceful rest;
The Christian finds it in his breast
When Faith, and Love, and Hope unite
With holy thoughts and life upright:
   Oh, seek and find that home!

But how shall I that home attain?
Not of myself—the thought were vain;
Fast bound with earthly ties and cares,
My own vain heart and Satan's snares,
   I seek—but find no home!

Thy Saviour's love the gift bestows,
Thy thraldom well the Saviour knows;
Go—in thy bonds to him complain,
Ask—and he'll break the galling chain,
   And lead thee gently home

And may the boon to me be given,
A home on earth—a type of heaven;
Then Faith, and Hope, and Love be mine,—
Ah, no! my Saviour, all are thine:
   Lord, take thy wanderer home!

Lord! when my dying hour is near,
And weeping friends would keep me here,
Let *theirs* and *mine* this solace be,—
That none can die who live to Thee:
   Death is but going home!

———o———

Chapter xxvj.

Not but the human fabric from the birth
Imbibes a flavour of its parent earth;
As various tracts enforce a various toil,
The manners speak the idiom of their soil.

       GRAY.

ALTHOUGH Mary strenuously applied herself to the uses of life, its embellishments were by no means neglected. She was happily endowed by nature; and, under the judicious management of her aunt, made rapid though unostentatious progress in the improvement of the talents committed to her care. Without having been blessed with the advantages of a dancing-master, her step was light, and her motions free and graceful; and if her aunt had not been able to impart to her the favourite graces of the most fashionable singer of the day, neither had she thwarted the efforts of her own natural taste in forming a style full of simplicity and feeling. In the modern languages she was perfectly skilled; and if her drawings wanted the enlivening touches of the master to give them effect, as an atonement they displayed a perfect knowledge of the rules of perspective, and the study of the bust.

All this was, however, mere leather and prunella to the ladies of Glenfern; and many were the cogitations and consultations that took place on the subject of Mary's mismanagement. According to their ideas, there could be but one good system of education; and

that was the one that had been pursued with them, and
through them transmitted to their nieces.

To attend the parish church, and remember the text ;
to observe who was there, and who was *not* there ; and
to wind up the evening with a sermon stuttered and
stammered through by one of the girls (the worst reader
always piously selected, for the purpose of improving
their reading), and particularly addressed to the laird,
openly and avowedly snoring in his arm chair, though
at every pause starting up with a peevish " Weel ? "—
this was the sum total of their religious duties.   Their
moral virtues were much upon the same scale : to knit
stockings, scold servants, cement china, trim bonnets,
lecture the poor, and look up to Lady Maclaughlan,
comprised nearly their whole code.   But these were
the virtues of ripened years and enlarged understandings ;
what their pupils might hope to arrive at, but could not
presume to meddle with.   *Their* merits consisted in
being compelled to sew certain large portions of white
work ; learning to read and write in the worst manner ;
occasionally wearing a collar ; and learning the notes on
the spinnet.   These acquirements, accompanied with a
great deal of lecturing and fault-finding, sufficed for the
first fifteen years ; when the two next, passed at a provincial boarding-school, were supposed to impart every
graceful accomplishment to which women could attain.

Mrs Douglas's method of conveying instruction, it
may easily be imagined, did not square with their ideas
on that subject.   They did nothing themselves without
a bustle ; and to do a thing quietly, was to them the
same as not doing it at all—it could not be done, for
nobody had ever heard of it.   In short, like many other
worthy people, their ears were their only organs of
intelligence : they believed everything they were told ;
but, unless they were told, they believed nothing.   They
had never heard Mrs Douglas expatiate on the import-

ance of the trust reposed in her, or enlarge on the
difficulties of female education; *ergo*, Mrs Douglas
could have no idea of the nature of the duties she had
undertaken.

Their visits to Lochmarlie only served to confirm
the fact. Miss Jacky deponed, that, during the month
she was there, she never could discover when or how it
was that Mary got her lessons: luckily the child was
quick, and had contrived, poor thing! to pick up things
wonderfully, nobody knew how, for it was really
astonishing to see how little pains were bestowed upon
her; and the worst of it was, that she seemed to do
just as she liked, for nobody ever heard her reproved,
and every body knew that young people never could
have enough said to them. All this differed widely
from the *eclat* of their system, and could not fail of
causing great disquiet to the sisters.

" I declare, I'm quite confounded at all this ! " said
Miss Grizzy, at the conclusion of Miss Jacky's communication. " It really appears as if Mary, poor thing!
was getting no education at all; and yet she *can* do
things, too. I can't understand it ! And it's very odd
in Mrs Douglas to allow her to be so much neglected, for
certainly Mary's constantly with herself; which, to be
sure, shows that she is very much spoilt—nobody can
dispute that ! for although our girls are as fond of us as,
I am sure, any creatures can be, yet, at the same time,
they are always very glad—which is quite natural—to
get away from us."

" I think it's high time Mary had done something
fit to be seen," said Miss Nicky. " She is now
sixteen, past."

" Most girls of Mary's time of life, that ever *I* had
any thing to do with," replied Jacky, with a certain
wave of the head, peculiar to sensible women, " had
something to show before her age. Bella had worked

the globe long before she was sixteen; and Babby did
her filigree tea-caddy the first quarter she was at Miss
Macgowk's," glancing with triumph from the one
which hung in a gilt frame over the mantelpiece, to
the other which stood on the tea-table, shrouded in a
green bag.

"And, to be sure," rejoined Grizzy, "although
Betsy's skreen did cost a great deal of money—that
can't be denied; and her father certainly grudged it
very much at the time—there's no doubt of that; yet
certainly it does her the greatest credit, and is a great
satisfaction to us all to have these things to show. I
am sure nobody would ever think that ass was made of
crape; and how naturally it seems to be eating the
beautiful chenille thistle! I declare, I think the ass
is as like an ass as any thing can be!"

"And as to Mary's drawing," continued the narrator
of her deficiencies, "there is not one of them fit for
framing; mere scratches with a chalk pencil—what any
child might do."

"And to think," said Nicky, with indignation, "how
little Mrs Douglas seemed to think of the handsome
coloured views of Inverary and Dunkeld the girls did
at Miss Macgowk's!"

"All our girls have the greatest genius for drawing,"
observed Grizzy; "there can be no doubt of that; but
it's a thousand pities, I'm sure, that none of them seem
to like it. To be sure, they say—what I dare say is
very true—that they can't get such good paper as they
got at Miss Macgowk's; but they have showed that
they *can* do, for their drawings are quite astonishing.
Somebody lately took them to be Mr Touchup's own
doing; and I'm sure there couldn't be a greater compliment than that! I represented all that to Mrs
Douglas, and urged her very strongly to give Mary
the benefit of at least a quarter of Miss Macgowk's,

were it only for the sake of her carriage ; or, at least, to make her wear our collar."

This was the tenderest of all themes, and bursts of sorrowful exclamations ensued. The collar had long been a galling yoke upon their minds ; its iron had entered into their very souls ; for it was a collar presented to the family of Glenfern by the wisest, virtuousest, best of women and of grandmothers, the good Lady Girnachgowl; and had been worn in regular rotation by every female of the family, till now, that Mrs Douglas positively refused to subject Mary's pliant form to its thraldom. Even the laird, albeit no connoisseur in any shapes save those of his kine, was of opinion, that, since the thing was in the house, it was a pity it should be lost. Not Venus's girdle ever was supposed to confer greater charms than the Girnachgowl collar.

" It's really most distressing ! " said Miss Grizzy to her friend, Lady Maclaughlan. " Mary's back won't be worth a farthing ; and we have always been quite famous for our backs."

" Humph !—that's the reason people are always so glad to see them, child."

With regard to Mary's looks, opinions were not so decided. Mr Douglas thought her, what she was, an elegant, interesting-looking girl. The laird, as he peered at her over his spectacles, pronounced her to be but a shilpit thing, though weel aneugh, considering the ne'er-do-weels that were aught her. Miss Jacky opined, that she would have been quite a different creature had she been brought up like any other girl. Miss Grizzy did not know what to think ; she certainly was pretty —nobody could dispute that : at the same time, many people would prefer Bella's looks ; and Babby was certainly uncommonly comely. Miss Nicky thought it was no wonder she looked pale sometimes : she never supped her broth in a wise-like way at dinner; and it was a shame to hear of a girl of Mary's age being set up with tea to her breakfast, and wearing white petticoats in winter—and such roads, too !

Lady Maclaughlan pronounced (and that was next to a special revelation) that the girl would be handsome when she was forty, not a day sooner; and she would be clever, for her mother was a fool; and foolish mothers had always wise children, and *vice versâ*, "and your mother was a very clever woman, girls—humph !"

Thus passed the early years of the almost forgotten twin; blest in the warm affection and mild authority of her more than mother. Sometimes Mrs Douglas half-formed the wish that her beloved pupil should mix in society, and become known to the world; but when she reflected on the dangers of that world, and on the little solid happiness its pleasures afford, she repressed the wish, and only prayed she might be allowed to rest secure in the simple pleasures she then enjoyed. "Happiness is not a plant of this earth," said she to herself with a sigh; "but God gives peace and tranquillity to the virtuous in all situations, and under every trial. Let me, then, strive to make Mary virtuous, and leave the rest to Him who alone knoweth what is good for us !"

———o———

Chapter xxvij.

Th' immortal line in sure succession reigns,
The fortune of the family remains,
And grandsires' grandsons the long list contains.
DRYDEN'S *Virgil*

We are such stuff
As dreams are made of ; and our little life
Is rounded with a sleep.

Tempest.

BUT Mary's back, and Mary's complexion, now ceased to be the first objects of interest at Glenfern ; for, to the inexpressible delight and amazement of the sisters, Mrs Douglas, after due warning, became the mother of a son. How this event had been brought about without the prescience of Lady Maclaughlan, was past the powers of Miss Grizzy's comprehension. To the last moment, they had been sceptical ; for Lady Maclaughlan had shook her head and humphed whenever the subject was mentioned. For several months they had therefore vibrated between their own sanguine hopes and their oracle's disheartening doubt ; and, even when the truth was manifest, a sort of vague tremor took possession of their minds as to what Lady Maclaughlan would think of it.

" I declare I don't very well know how to announce this happy event to Lady Maclaughlan," said Miss Grizzy, as she sat in a ruminating posture, with her pen in her hand. " It will give her the greatest pleasure, I know that ; she has such a regard for our family, she would go any lengths for us. At the same time, every body must be sensible it is a delicate matter to tell a person of Lady Maclaughlan's skill they have been mistaken. I'm sure I don't know how she may take it ; and yet she can't suppose it will make any difference in our sentiments for her. She must be sensible we have all the greatest respect for her opinion—there can be no doubt about that."

"The wisest people are sometimes mistaken," observed Miss Jacky.

"I'm sure, Jacky, that's very true," said Grizzy, brightening up at the .brilliancy of this remark— "nobody can deny that."

"And it's better she should have been mistaken than Mrs Douglas," followed up Miss Nicky.

"I declare, Nicky, you are perfectly right; and I shall just say so at once to Lady Maclaughlan."

The epistle was forthwith commenced by the enlightened Grizelda. Miss Joan applied herself to the study of "Letters to a Young Man on his Entrance into Life," which she was determined to make herself mistress of for the benefit of her grand-nephew; and Miss Nicholas fell to reckoning all who could, would, or should be at the christening, that she might calculate upon the quantity of *dreaming-bread* that would be required. The younger ladies were busily engaged in divers and sundry disputes regarding the right of succession to a once-white lutestring negligée of their mother's, which three of them had laid their accounts with figuring in at the approaching celebration. The old gentleman was the only one in the family who partook not in the least of the general happiness. He had got into a habit of being fretted about every thing that happened, and he could not entirely divest himself of it even upon this occasion. His parsimonious turn, too, had considerably increased; and his only criterion of judging of any thing was according to what it would bring.

"Sorra tak me, if one wadna think this was the first bairn that ever was born! What's a' the fraize aboot, ye gowks? (to his daughters)—a whingin' brat! that'll

tak mair out o' fowks' pockets than e'er it'll put into
them! Mony a guid profitable beast's been brought
into the warld, and ne'er a word in its head."

All went on smoothly. Lady Maclaughlan testified
no resentment. Miss Jacky had a complete system of
manly education all ready at her finger-ends; and Miss
Nicky was more serene than could have been expected,
considering, as she did, how the servants at Lochmarlie
must be living at hack and manger. It had been decided at Glenfern that the infant heir to its consequence
could not with propriety be christened anywhere but at
the seat of his forefathers. Mr and Mrs Douglas had
good-humouredly yielded the point! and, as soon as she
was able for the change, the whole family took up their
residence for a season under the paternal roof.

Blissful visions floated around the pillows of the
happy spinsters the night preceding the christening, which
were duly detailed at the breakfast-table the following
morning.

" I declare I don't know what to think of my dream,"
began Miss Grizzy. " I dreamt that Lady Maclaughlan was upon her knees to you, brother, to get you to
take an emetic; and, just as she had mixed it up so
nicely in some of our black-currant jelly, little Norman
snatched it out of your hand, and ran away with
it."

" You're enough to turn ony body's stamick wi' your
nonsense," returned the laird gruffly.

"And I," said Miss Jacky, "thought I saw you
standing in your shirt, brother, as straight as a rash, and
good Lady Girnachgowl buckling her collar round you
with her own hands."

" I wish ye wad na deive me wi' your havers!" still
more indignantly, and turning his shoulder to the fair
dreamer, as he continued to con over the newspaper.

" And I," cried Miss Nicky, eager to get her mystic

tale disclosed, " I thought, brother, I saw you take and throw all the good dreaming-bread into the ash-hole."

" By my troth, an' ye deserve to be thrown after't! " exclaimed the exasperated laird, as he quitted the room in high wrath, muttering to himself, " Hard case—canna get peace—eat my vittals—fules—tawpies—clavers! " &c., &c.

" I declare I can't conceive why Glenfern should be so ill-pleased at our dreams," said Miss Grizzy. " Every body knows dreams are always contrary,—nobody can dispute that ; and, even were it otherwise, I'm sure I should think no shame to take an emetic, especially when Lady Maclaughlan was at the trouble of mixing it up so nicely."

" And we have all worn good Lady Girnachgowl's collar before now," said Miss Jacky.

" I think I had the worst of it, that had all my good dreaming-bread destroyed," added Miss Nicky.

" Nothing could be more natural than your dreams," said Mrs Douglas, " considering how all these subjects have engrossed you for some time past. You, aunt Grizzy, may remember how desirous you were of ad-ministering one of Lady Maclaughlan's powders to my little boy yesterday ; and you, aunt Jacky, made a point of trying Lady Girnachgowl's collar upon Mary, to convince her how pleasant it was ; while you, aunt Nicky, had experienced a great alarm in supposing your cake had been burned in the oven. And these being the most vivid impressions you had received during the day, it was perfectly natural that they should have re-tained their influence during a portion of the night."

The interpretations were received with high disdain. One and all declared they never dreamed of any thing that *had* occurred ; and therefore the visions of the night portended some extraordinary good-fortune to the family in general, and to little Norman in particular.

"The best fortune I can wish for him, and all of us, for this day, is, that he should remain quiet during the ceremony," said his mother, who was not so elated as Lady Macbeth at the predictions of the sisters.

The christening party mustered strong ; and the rites of baptism were duly performed by the Rev. Duncan M'Drone. The little Christian had been kissed by every lady in company, and pronounced by the matrons to be " a dainty little fellow ! " and by the misses to be " the sweetest lamb they had ever seen ! " The cake and wine was in its progress round the company ; when, upon its being tendered to the old gentleman, who was sitting silent in his arm-chair, he abruptly exclaimed, in a most discordant voice, " Hey ! what's a' this wastery for ? "—and, ere an answer could be returned, his jaw dropped, his eyes fixed, and the laird of Glenfern ceased to breathe !

————o————

Chapter xxbiij.

They say miracles are past ; and we have our philosophical persons to make modern and familiar things supernatural and causeless. Hence it is, that we make trifles of terrors : ensconcing ourselves into seeming knowledge, when we should submit ourselves to an unknown fear.
All's Well that Ends Well.

ALL attempts to reanimate the lifeless form proved unavailing ; and the horror and consternation that reigned in the castle of Glenfern may be imagined, but cannot be described. There is perhaps no feeling of our nature so vague, so complicated, so mysterious, as that with which we look upon the cold remains of our fellow-mortals. The dignity with which death invests even the meanest of his victims, inspires us with an awe no living thing can create. The

monarch on his throne is less awful than the beggar in
his shroud. The marble features—the powerless hand
—the stiffened limbs—oh! who can contemplate these
with feelings that can be defined? These are the
mockery of all our hopes and fears, our fondest love,
our fellest hate. Can it be, that we now shrink with
horror from the touch of that hand which but yesterday
was fondly clasped in our own? Is that tongue, whose
accents even now dwell in our ear, for ever chained in
the silence of death? These black and heavy eyelids,
are they for ever to seal up in darkness the eyes whose
glance no earthly power could restrain? And the
spirit which animated the clay, where is it now? Is it
rapt in bliss, or dissolved in woe? Does it witness our
grief, and share our sorrows? or is the mysterious tie
that linked it with mortality for ever broken? and the
remembrance of earthly scenes, are they indeed to the
enfranchised spirit as the morning dream, or the dew
upon the early flower? Reflections such as these
naturally arise in every breast. Their influence is felt,
though their import cannot always be expressed. The
principle is in all the same, however it may differ in its
operations.

In the family assembled round the lifeless form that
had so long been the centre of their domestic circle,
grief showed itself under various forms. The calm and
manly sorrow of the son; the saint-like feelings of his
wife; the youthful agitation of Mary; the weak superstitious wailings of the sisters; and the loud uncontrolled
lamentations of the daughters;—all betokened an intensity of suffering, that arose from the same source, varied
according to the different channels in which it flowed.
Even the stern Lady Maclaughlan was subdued to
something of kindred feeling; and, though no tears
dropped from her eyes, she sat by her friends, and
sought, in her own way, to soften their affliction.

The assembled guests, who had not yet been able to take their departure, remained in the drawing-room in a sort of restless solemnity, peculiar to seasons of collateral affliction, where all seek to heighten the effect upon others, and shift the lesson from themselves. Various were the surmises and speculations as to the cause of the awful transition that had just taken place.

"Glenfern was not like a man that would have gaen off in this way," said one.

"I dinna ken," said another; "I've noticed a chainge on Glenfern for a good while now."

"I agree with you, sir," said a third: "in my mind, Glenfern's been droopin' very much ever since the last tryst."

"At Glenfern's time o' life, it's no surprisin'," remarked a fourth, who felt perfectly secure of being fifteen years his junior.

"Glenfern wasna that auld, neither," retorted a fifth, whose conscience smote him with being several years his senior.

"But he had a deal of vexation from his family," said an elderly bachelor.

"Ye often see a hale stout man, like our poor friend, go like the snuff of a candle," coughed up a phthisicky gentleman.

"He was aye a tume, boss-lookin' man, ever since I mind him," wheezed out a swoln asthmatic figure.

"An' he took no care of himself," said the laird of Pettlechass. "His diet was not what it should have been at his time of life. An' he was out an' in, up an' down, in a' weathers, wet an' dry."

"Glenfern's doings had nothing to do wi' his death," said an ancient gentlewoman, with solemnity. "They must be strangers here who never heard the bod-word of the family." And she repeated, in Gaelic, words to the following effect:—

> " When Lochdow shall turn to a lin,*
> In Glenfern ye'll hear the din ;
> When frae Benmore tney snool the sna',
> O'er Glenfern the leaves will fa';
> When foreign geer grows on Benmore tap,
> Then the fir-tree will be Glenfern's hap."

" And now, ma'am, will ye be so good as point out the meanin' of this freet," said an incredulous-looking member of the company ; " for when I passed Lochdow this morning, I neither saw nor heard of a lin ; an' frae this window we can a' see Benmore wi' his white night-cap on ; an' he would hae little to do that would try to shool it aff."

" It was neither of the still water nor the stay brae that the word was spoken," said the old lady solemnly ; " *they* take no part in our doings : but knew you not that Lochdow himself had lost his sight by cataract ? and is not there dule and din enough in Glenfern to-day ? And who has not heard that Benmore has had his white locks shaven, and that he has got a fine brown wig instead ; and I'll warrant he'll have that on his old grey head the day that Glenfern's laid in his deal coffin."

The company admitted the application was too close to be resisted ; but the same sceptic (who, by the by, was only a low-country merchant, elevated by purchase to the dignity of a Highland laird) was seen to shrug his shoulders, and heard to make some sneering remarks on the days of second-sights, and such superstitious nonsense, being past. This was instantly laid hold of ; and, amongst many others of the same sort, the truth of the following story was attested by one of the party, as having actually occurred in his family within his own remembrance : —

" As Duncan M'Crae was one evening descending Benvoilloich, he perceived a funeral procession in the

* Cataract.

vale beneath. He was greatly surprised, not having heard of any death in the country; and this appeared to be the burial of some person of consequence, from the number of the attendants. He made all the haste he could to get down; and, as he drew near, he counted all the lairds of the country except my father, Sir Murdoch. He was astonished at this, till he recollected that he was away to the low country to his cousin's marriage; but he felt curious to know who it was, though some unaccountable feeling prevented him from mixing with the followers. He therefore kept on the ridge of the hill, right over their heads, and near enough to hear them speak; but, although he saw them move their lips, no sound reached his ear. He kept along with the procession in this way, till it reached the Castle Dochart burying-ground, and there it stopped. The evening was close and warm, and a thick mist had gathered in the glen, while the tops of the hills shone like gold. Not a breath of air was stirring; but the trees that grew round the burying-ground waved and soughed, and some withered leaves were swirled round and round as if by the wind. The company stood awhile to rest, and then they proceeded to open the iron gates of the burying-ground; but the lock was rusted, and would not open. Then they began to pull down part of the wall; and Duncan thought how angry his master would be at this, and he raised his voice, and shouted, and hallooed to them, but to no purpose. Nobody seemed to hear him. At last the wall was taken down, and the coffin was lifted over, and just then the sun broke out, and glinted on a new-made grave; and as they were laying the coffin in it, it gave way, and disclosed Sir Murdoch himself in his dead clothes; and then the mist grew so thick, Duncan could see no more, and how to get home he knew not; but when he entered his own door he was bathed in sweat, and white as any

corpse; and all that he could say was, that he had seen
Castle Dochart's burying.

" The following day," continued the narrator, " he
was more composed, and gave the account you have now
heard; and three days after came the intelligence of my
father's death. He had dropped down in a fit that very
evening, when entertaining a large company in honour
of his cousin's marriage; and that day week his funeral
passed through Glenvalloch exactly as described by
Duncan M'Crae, with all the particulars: the gates of
the burying-ground could not be opened; part of the
wall was taken down to admit the coffin, which received some injury, and gave way as they were placing
it in the grave."

Even the low-country infidel was silenced by the
solemnity of this story; and soon after the company
dispersed, every one panting to be the first to circulate
the intelligence of Glenfern's death.

But soon—oh, *how* soon!—" dies in human hearts
the thought of death! " Even the paltry detail which
death creates, serves to detach our minds from the cause
itself. So it was with the family of Glenfern. Their
light did not " shine inward; " and, after the first burst
of sorrow, their ideas fastened with avidity on all the
paraphernalia of affliction. Mr Douglas, indeed, found
much to do, and to direct to be done. The elder ladies
began to calculate how many yards of broad hemming
and crimped crape would be required, and to form a
muster-roll of the company; with this improvement,
that it was to be ten times as numerous as the one that
had assembled at the christening: while the young ones
busied their imaginations as to the effect of new mourning—a luxury to them hitherto unknown. Mrs Douglas
and Mary were differently affected from the other members of the family. Religion and reflection had taught
the former the enviable lesson of possessing her soul in

patience under every trial; and while she inwardly mourned the fate of the poor old man who had been thus suddenly snatched from the only world that ever had engaged his thoughts, her outward aspect was calm and serene. The impression made upon Mary's feelings was of a more powerful nature. She had witnessed suffering, and watched by sick-beds; but death, and death in so terrific a form, was new to her. She had been standing by her grandfather's chair—her head was bent to his—her hand rested upon his, when, by a momentary convulsion, she beheld the last dread change —the living man transformed into the lifeless corpse. The countenance but now fraught with life and human thoughts, in the twinkling of an eye was covered with the shades of death! It was in vain that Mary prayed, and reasoned, and strove against the feelings that had been thus powerfully excited. One object alone possessed her imagination—the image of her grandfather dying—dead; his grim features—his ghastly visage— his convulsive grasp—were ever present, by day and by night. Her nervous system had received a shock too powerful for all the strength of her understanding to contend with. Mrs Douglas sought, by every means, to soothe her feelings, and divert her attention; and flattered herself that a short time would allay the perturbation of her youthful emotions.

Five hundred persons, horse and foot, high and low, male and female, graced the obsequies of the laird of Glenfern. Benmore was there in his new wig, and the autumnal leaves dropped on the coffin as it was borne slowly along the vale!

—————o—————

Chapter xxix.

It is no diminution, but a recommendation of human nature,
that, in some instances, passion gets the better of reason, and
all that we can think is impotent against half what we feel.

Spectator.

"LIFE is a mingled yarn;" few of its afflictions
but are accompanied with some alleviation—
none of its blessings that do not bring some
alloy.   Like most other events that long have formed the
object of yearning and almost hopeless wishes, and on
which have been built the fairest structure of human
felicity, the arrival of the young heir of Glenfern produced a less extraordinary degree of happiness than had
been anticipated.   The melancholy event which had
marked the first ceremonial of his life had cast its gloom
alike on all nearly connected with him ; and when
time had dispelled the clouds of recent mourning, and
restored the mourners to their habitual train of thought
and action, somewhat of the novelty which had given
him such lively interest in the hearts of the sisters had
subsided.   The distressing conviction, too, more and
more forced itself upon them, that their advice and assistance were likely to be wholly overlooked in the nurture
of the infant mind, and management of the thriving
frame, of their little nephew.   Their active energies
therefore, driven back to the accustomed channels,
after many murmurs and severe struggles, again revolved
in the same sphere as before.   True, they sighed and
mourned for a time, but soon found occupation congenial to their nature in the little departments of life :
dressing crape ; reviving black silk ; converting narrow
hems into broad hems ; and, in short, who so busy, who
so important, as the ladies of Glenfern ?   As Madame
de Staël, or de Something, says, " they fulfilled their

destinies." Their walk lay amongst tapes and pickles ;
their sphere extended from the garret to the pantry;
and, often as they sought to diverge from it, their
instinct always led them to return to it, as the track in
which they were destined to move. There are creatures
of the same sort in the male part of the creation, but it
is foreign to my purpose to describe them at present.
Neither are the trifling and insignificant of either sex to
be treated with contempt, or looked upon as useless, by
those whom God has gifted with higher powers. In
the arrangements of an all-wise Providence, there is
nothing created in vain. Every link of that vast chain
that embraces creation helps to hold together the various
relations of life ; and all is beautiful gradation, from the
human vegetable to the glorious archangel.

If patient hope, if unexulting joy, and chastened anticipation, sanctifying a mother's love, could have secured
her happiness, Mrs Douglas would have found, in the
smiles of her infant, all the comfort her virtue deserved.
But she still had to drink of that cup of sweet and
bitter which must bathe the lips of all who breathe the
breath of life.

While the instinct of a parent's love warmed her
heart, as she pressed her infant to her bosom, the sad-
ness of affectionate and rational solicitude stifled every
sentiment of pleasure, as she gazed on the altered and
drooping form of her adopted daughter—of the child
who had already repaid the cares that had been
lavished on her, and in whom she descried the promise of a plenteous harvest from the good seed she
had sown. Though Mary had been healthy in childhood, her constitution was naturally delicate, and she
had latterly outgrown her strength. The shock she
had sustained by her grandfather's death, thus operating
on a weakened frame, had produced an effect apparently
most alarming ; and the efforts she made to exert her-

self only served to exhaust her. She felt all the watchful solicitude, the tender anxieties, of her aunt, and bitterly reproached herself with not better repaying these exertions for her happiness. A thousand times she tried to analyse and extirpate the saddening impression that weighed upon her heart.

"It is not sorrow," reasoned she with herself, "that thus oppresses me; for though I reverenced my grandfather, yet the loss of his society has scarcely been felt by me. It cannot be fear—the fear of death; for my soul is not so abject as to confine its desires to this sublunary scene. What, then, is this mysterious dread that has taken possession of me? Why do I suffer my mind to suggest to me images of horror, instead of visions of bliss? Why can I not, as formerly, picture to myself the beauty and the brightness of a soul casting off mortality? Why must the convulsed grasp, the stifled groan, the glaring eye, for ever come betwixt heaven and me?"

Alas! Mary was unskilled to answer. Hers was the season for feeling, not for reasoning. She knew not that hers was the struggle of imagination, striving to maintain its ascendency over reality. She had heard, and read, and thought, and talked of death; and even beheld its near approach; but it was of death in its fairest form—in its softest transition: and the veil had been abruptly torn from her eyes; the gloomy pass had suddenly disclosed itself before her, not strewed with flowers, but shrouded in horrors. Like all persons of sensibility, Mary had a disposition to view everything in a *beau-idéal:* whether that is a boon most fraught with good or ill, it were difficult to ascertain. While the delusion lasts, it is productive of pleasure to its possessor; but, oh! the thousand aches that heart is destined to endure, which clings to the stability, and relies on the permanency, of earthly happiness! But the youthful heart must ever remain a stranger to this saddening truth. Experience only can convince us that happiness is not a plant of this world ; and that, though many an eye had beheld its blossoms, no mortal hand hath ever gathered its fruits. This, then, was Mary's first lesson in what is called the knowledge of life, as opposed to the *beau-idéal* of a young and ardent imagination, in love with life, and luxuriating in its own happiness. And upon such a mind it could not fail of producing a powerful impression.

The anguish Mrs Douglas experienced, as she wit-nessed the changing colour, lifeless step, and forced smile of her darling *eléve*, was not mitigated by the good sense or sympathy of those around her. While Mary had prospered under her management, in the consciousness that she was fulfilling her duty to the best of her abilities she could listen with placid cheer-fulness to the broken hints of disapprobation, or forced good wishes for the success of her new-fangled schemes, that were levelled at her by the sisters. But now, when her cares seemed defeated, it was an additional thorn in her heart to have to endure the common-place wisdom and self-gratulations of the almost exulting aunts ; not that they had the slightest inten-tion of wounding the feelings of their niece, whom they really loved, but the temptation was irresistible of prov-ing that they had been in the right, and she in the wrong, especially as no such acknowledgment had yet been extorted from her.

"It is nonsense to ascribe Mary's dwining to her grandfather's death," said Miss Jacky. "We are all nearer to him in propinquity than she was, and none of our healths have suffered."

"And there's his own daughters," added Miss Grizzy, "who, of course, must have felt a great deal more than anybody else—there can be no doubt of

that. Such sensible creatures as them must feel a great
deal; but yet you see how they have got up their
spirits—I'm sure it's wonderful!"

"It shows their sense, and the effects of education,"
said Miss Jacky.

"Girls that sup their porridge will always cut a good
figure," quoth Nicky.

"With their fine feelings, I'm sure, we have all
reason to be thankful that they have been blest with
such hearty stomachs," observed Miss Grizzy: "if
they had been delicate, like poor Mary's, I'm sure, I
declare, I don't know what we would have done; for
certainly they were all most dreadfully affected at their
excellent father's death; which was quite natural, poor
things! I'm sure there was no pacifying poor Babby;
and, even yet, neither Bella nor Betsy can bear to be
left alone in a dark room. Tibby has to sleep with
them still every night; and a lighted candle too—
which is much to their credit—and yet I'm sure it's
not with reading. I'm certain—indeed, I think there's
no doubt of it—that reading does young people much
harm. It puts things into their heads that never would
have been there but for books—nobody can dispute
that! I declare, I think, reading's a very dangerous
thing. I'm certain all Mary's bad health is entirely
owing to reading. You know, we always thought she
read a great deal too much for her good."

"Much depends upon the choice of books," said
Jacky, with an air of the most profound wisdom.
"Fordyce's Sermons, and the History of Scotland, are
two of the very few books *I* would put into the hands
of a young woman. *Our* girls have read little else,"—
casting a look at Mrs Douglas, who was calmly pursuing
her work in the midst of this shower of darts, all
levelled at her.

"To be sure," returned Grizzy, "it is a thousand

pities that Mary has been allowed to go on so long; not, I'm sure, that any of us mean to reflect upon you, my dear Mrs Douglas; for of course it was all owing to your ignorance and inexperience; and that, you know, you could not help, so it was not your fault; nobody can blame you. I'm certain you would have done what was right, if you had only known better; but, of course, we must all know much better than you; because, you know, we are a great deal older, and especially Lady Maclaughlan, who has the greatest experience in the diseases of old men especially, and infants. Indeed it has been the study of her life almost; for, you know, poor Sir Sampson is never well; and, I dare say, if Mary had taken some of her nice worm lozenges, which certainly cured Duncan M'Nab's wife's daughter's little girl of the jaundice, and used that valuable growing embrocation, which we are all sensible made Babby a great deal fatter,—indeed some people thought she grew a great deal too fat, though, for my part, I think it's a good fault to be too fat,—I dare say there would have been nothing the matter with her to-day."

"Mary has been too much accustomed to spend both her time and money amongst idle vagrants," said Nicky.

"Economy of both," subjoined Jacky, with an air of humility, "I confess *I* have ever been accustomed to consider as virtues. These handsome respectable new bonnets," looking *from* Mrs Douglas, "that our girls got just before their poor father's death, were entirely the fruits of their own savings."

"And I declare," said Grizzy, who did not excel in inuendos, "I declare, for my part—although at the same time, my dear niece, I'm certain you are far from intending it—I really think it's very disrespectful to Sir Sampson and Lady Maclaughlan, in anybody, and especially such near neighbours, to give more in charity than they do : for, you may be sure, they give as much as they think proper, and they must be the best judges, and can afford to give what they please ; for Sir Sampson could buy and sell all of us a hundred times over, if he liked—there can be no doubt about that! It's long since the Lochmarlie estate was called seven thousand a-year ; and, besides that, there's the Birkendale property, and the Glenmavis estate ; and, I'm sure, I can't tell you all what ; but there's no doubt he's a man of immense fortune."

Well it was known, and frequently was it discussed, the iniquity of Mary being allowed to waste her time, and squander her money, amongst the poor, instead of being taught the practical virtues of making her own gowns, and of hoarding up her pocket-money for some selfish gratification.

In colloquies such as these, day after day passed on, without any visible improvement taking place in her health. Only one remedy suggested itself to Mrs Douglas, and that was to remove her to the south of England for the winter. Milder air, and change of scene, she had no doubt would prove efficacious ; and her opinion was confirmed by that of the celebrated Dr ———, who having been summoned to the laird of Pettlechass, had paid a visit at Glenfern *en passant*. How so desirable an event was to be accomplished, was the difficulty. By the death of his father, a variety of business, and an extent of farming, had devolved upon Mr Douglas, which obliged him to fix his residence at Glenfern, and rendered it impossible for him to be long absent from it. Mrs Douglas had engaged in the duties of a nurse to her little boy, and to take him or leave him was equally out of the question.

In this dilemma, the only resource that offered was that of sending Mary for a few months to her mother.

True, it was a painful necessity; for Mrs Douglas seldom heard from her sister-in-law, and when she did, her letters were short and cold. She sometimes desired a "kiss to her (Mrs Douglas's) little girl;" and once, in an extraordinary fit of good humour, had actually sent a locket with her hair in a letter by post, for which Mrs Douglas had to pay something more than the value of the present. This was all that Mary knew of her mother, and the rest of her family were still greater strangers to her. Her father remained in a distant station in India, and was seldom heard of. Her brother was gone to sea; and though she had written repeatedly to her sister, her letters remained unnoticed. Under these circumstances, there was something revolting in the idea of obtruding Mary upon the notice of her relations, and trusting to their kindness even for a few months; yet her health, perhaps her life, was at stake, and Mrs Douglas felt she had scarcely a right to hesitate.

"Mary has, perhaps, been too long an alien from her own family," said she to herself: "this will be a means of her becoming acquainted with them, and of introducing her to that sphere in which she is probably destined to walk. Under her uncle's roof she will surely be safe, and in the society of her mother and sister she cannot be unhappy. New scenes will give a stimulus to her mind; the necessity of exertion will brace the languid faculties of her soul; and a few short months, I trust, will restore her to me such, and even superior to what she was. Why, then, should I hesitate to do what my conscience tells me ought to be done? Alas! it is because I selfishly shrink from the pain of separation, and am unwilling to relinquish, even for a season, one of the many blessings heaven has bestowed upon me." And Mrs Douglas, noble and disinterested as ever, rose superior to the weakness that

she felt was besetting her.   Mary listened to her communication with a throbbing heart, and eyes suffused
with tears : to part from her aunt was agony; but to
behold her mother—she to whom she owed her existence,—to embrace a sister too—and one for whom
she felt all those mysterious yearnings which twins are
said to entertain towards each other,—Oh ! there was
rapture in the thought ; and Mary's buoyant heart
fluctuated between the extremes of anguish and delight.

The venerable sisters received the intelligence with
much surprise.   They did not know very well what to
say about it : there was much to be said both for and
against it.   Lady Maclaughlan had a high opinion of
English air ; but then they had heard the morals of the
people were not so good, and there were a great many
dissipated young men in England ; though, to be sure,
there was no denying but the mineral waters were excellent : and, in short, it ended in Miss Grizzy's sitting
down to concoct an epistle to Lady Maclaughlan ; in
Miss Jacky's beginning to draw up a code of instructions for a young woman upon her entrance into life ;
and Miss Nicky hoping, that, if Mary did go, she
would take care not to bring back any extravagant
English notions with her.   The younger set debated
amongst themselves how many of them would be invited to accompany Mary to England ; and from thence
fell to disputing the possession of a brown hair-trunk,
with a flourished D, in brass letters, on the top.

Mrs Douglas, with repressed feelings, set about offering the sacrifice she had planned ; and in a letter to
Lady Juliana, descriptive of her daughter's situation,
she sought to excite her tenderness without creating an
alarm.   How far she succeeded, will be seen hereafter.
In the meantime, we must take a retrospective glance at
the last seventeen years of her ladyship's life.

Chapter XXX.

Her " only labour was to kill the time ;
And labour dire it is, and weary woe."
Castle of Indolence.

YEARS had rolled on, amidst heartless pleasures and joyless amusements, but Lady Juliana was made neither the wiser nor the better by added years and increased experience. Time had in vain turned his glass before eyes still dazzled with the gaudy allurements of the world, for she took "no note of time," but as the thing that was to take her to the Opera and the Park, and that sometimes hurried her excessively, and sometimes bored her to death. At length she was compelled to abandon her chase after happiness, in the only sphere where she believed it was to be found. Lord Courtland's declining health unfitted him for the dissipation of a London life ; and, by the advice of his physician, he resolved upon retiring to a country seat which he possessed in the vicinity of Bath. Lady Juliana was in despair at the thoughts of this sudden wrench from what she termed life : but she had no resource ; for though her good-natured husband gave her the whole of General Cameron's allowance, that merely served as pin-money ; and though her brother was perfectly willing that she and her children should occupy apartments in his house, yet he would have been equally acquiescent had she proposed to remove from it. Lady Juliana had a sort of instinctive knowledge of this, which prevented her from breaking out into open remonstrance. She therefore contented herself with being more than usually peevish and irascible to her servants and children ; and talking to her friends of the prodigious sacrifice she was about to make for her brother and his family, as if it had been

the cutting off of a hand, or the plucking out of an eye.
To have heard her, any one unaccustomed to the
hyperbole of fashionable language would have deemed
Botany Bay the nearest possible point of destination.
Parting from her fashionable acquaintances was tearing
herself from all she loved—quitting London was bidding adieu to the world.   Of course there could be no
society where she was going, but still she would do her
duty—she would not desert dear Frederick and his
poor children !   In short, no martyr was ever led to
the stake with half the notions of heroism and self-
devotion as those with which Lady Juliana stepped into
the barouche that was to conduct her to Beech Park.
In the society of piping bullfinches, pink canaries, grey
parrots, gold-fish, green squirrels, Italian greyhounds,
and French poodles, she sought a refuge from despair.
But even these varied charms, after a while, failed to
please : the bullfinches grew hoarse—the canaries turned
yellow—the parrots became stupid—the gold-fish grew
dim—the squirrels were cross—the dogs fought ; even
a shell-grotto, that was constructing, fell down ; and by
the time the aviary and conservatory were filled, they
had lost their interest.   The children were the next
subjects for her ladyship's *ennui* to discharge itself upon.
Lord Courtland had a son, some years older, and a
daughter nearly of the same age as her own.   It suddenly occurred to her that they must be educated,
and that she would educate the girls herself.   As the
first step, she engaged two governesses, French and
Italian ;—modern treatises on the subject of education
were ordered from London—looked at, admired, and
arranged on gilded shelves and sofa-tables : and, could
their contents have exhaled with the odours of their
Russian leather bindings, Lady Juliana's dressing-room
would have been, what Sir Joshua Reynolds says every
seminary of learning *is;* "an atmosphere of floating

knowledge." But amidst this splendid display of human lore, THE BOOK found no place. She *had* heard of the Bible, however, and even knew it was a book appointed to be read in churches, and given to poor people, along with Rumford soup and flannel shirts; but as the rule of life—as the book that alone could make wise unto salvation, this Christian parent was ignorant as the Hottentot or Hindoo.

Three days beheld the rise, progress, and decline of Lady Juliana's whole system of education; and it would have been well for the children had the trust been delegated to those better qualified to discharge it. But neither of the preceptresses were better skilled in the only true knowledge. Signora Cicianai was a bigoted Catholic, whose faith hung upon her beads; and Madame Grignon was an *esprit fort*, who had no faith in any thing but *le plaisir*. But the signora's singing was heavenly, and madame's dancing was divine; and what lacked there more?

So passed the first years of being trained for immortality. The children insensibly ceased to be children, and Lady Juliana would have beheld the increasing height and beauty of her daughter with extreme disapprobation, had not that beauty, by awakening her ambition, also excited her affection, if the term affection could be applied to that heterogeneous mass of feelings and propensities that "shape had none distinguishable." Lady Juliana had fallen into an error, very common with wiser heads than hers—that of mistaking the *effect* for the *cause*. She looked no farther than to her union with Henry Douglas for the foundation of all her unhappiness—it never once occurred to her, that her marriage was only the *consequence* of something previously wrong; she saw not the headstrong passions that had impelled her to please herself—no matter at what price. She thought not of the want of principle

—she blushed not at the want of delicacy, that had led
her to deceive a parent, and elope with her lover. She
therefore considered herself as having fallen a victim to
love; and could she only save her daughter from a
similar error, she might yet by her means retrieve her
fallen fortune. To implant principles of religion and
virtue in her mind, was not within the compass of her
own; but she could scoff at every pure and generous
affection—she could ridicule every disinterested attachment—and she could expatiate on the never-fading joys
that attend on wealth and titles, jewels and equipages—
and all this she did in the belief that she was acting the
part of a most wise and tender parent! The seed, thus
carefully sown, promised to bring forth an abundant
harvest. At eighteen, Adelaide Douglas was as heartless and ambitious as she was beautiful and accomplished
—but the surface was covered with flowers, and who
would have thought of analysing the soil?

It sometimes happens, that the very means used, with
success, in the formation of one character, produce a
totally opposite effect upon another. The mind of Lady
Emily Lindore had undergone exactly the same process
in its formation as that of her cousin; yet in all things
they differed. Whether it were the independence of
high birth, or the pride of a mind conscious of its own
powers, she had hitherto resisted the sophistry of her
governesses, and the solecisms of her aunt. But her
notions of right and wrong were too crude to influence
the general tenor of her life, or operate as restraints upon
a naturally high spirit, and impetuous temper. Not all
the united efforts of her preceptresses had been able to
form a manner for their pupil; nor could their authority
restrain her from saying what she thought, and doing
what she pleased; and, in spite of both precept and
example, Lady Emily remained as insupportably natural
and sincere as she was beautiful and *piquante*. At six

years old, she had declared her intention of marrying her cousin, Edward Douglas ; and at eighteen, her words were little less equivocal. Lord Courtland, who never disturbed himself about any thing, was rather diverted with this juvenile attachment ; and Lady Juliana, who cared little for her son, and still less for her niece, only wondered how people could be such fools as to think of marrying for love, after she had told them how miserable it would make them.

———o———

Chapter xxxj.

Unthought-of frailties cheat us in the wise ;
The fool lies hid in inconsistencies.

POPE.

And for unfelt imaginations
They often feel a world of restless cares.

SHAKSPEARE.

SUCH were the female members of the family to whom Mary was about to be introduced. In her mother's heart she had no place, for of her absent husband and neglected daughter she seldom thought ; and their letters were scarcely read, and rarely answered. Even good Miss Grizzy's elaborate epistle, in which were curiously entwined the death of her brother, and the birth and christening of her grand-nephew, in a truly Gordian manner, remained disentangled. Had her ladyship only read to the middle of the seventh page, she would have learned the indisposition of her daughter, with the various opinions thereupon ; but poor Miss Grizzy's labours were vain, for her letter remains a dead letter to this day. Mrs Douglas was therefore the first to convey the unwelcome intelligence, and to suggest to the mind of the mother that her alienated daughter still retained some claims upon her care and affection; and, although this was done with all the tenderness and delicacy of a gentle and enlightened mind, it called forth the most bitter indignation from Lady Juliana.

She almost raved at what she termed the base ingratitude and hypocrisy of her sister-in-law. After the sacrifice she had made in giving up her child to her when she had none of her own, it was a pretty return to send her back only to die. But she saw through it. She did not believe a word of the girl's illness: that was all a trick to get rid of her. Now they had a child of their own, they had no use for hers . but she was not to be made a fool of in such a way, and by such people, &c., &c.

" If Mrs Douglas is so vile a woman," said the provoking Lady Emily, " the sooner my cousin is taken from her the better."

" You don't understand these things, Emily," returned her aunt impatiently.

" What things ? "

" The trouble and annoyance it will occasion me to take charge of the girl at this time."

" Why at this time more than at any other ? "

" Absurd, my dear ! how can you ask so foolish a question ? Don't you know that you and Adelaide are both to bring out this winter, and how can I possibly do you justice with a dying girl upon my hands ? "

" I thought you suspected it was all a trick," continued the persecuting Lady Emily.

" So I do ; I haven't the least doubt of it. The whole story is the most improbable stuff I ever heard."

" Then you will have less trouble than you expect."

" But I hate to be made a dupe of, and imposed upon by low cunning. If Mrs Douglas had told me candidly she wished me to take the girl, I should have thought nothing of it; but I can't bear to be treated like a fool."

" I don't see any thing at all unbecoming in Mrs Douglas's treatment."

" Then, what can I do with a girl who has been educated in Scotland? She must be vulgar—all Scotch women are so. They have red hands and rough voices; they yawn, and blow their noses, and talk and laugh loud, and do a thousand shocking things. Then, to hear the Scotch brogue—oh, heavens! I should expire every time she opened her mouth!"

" Perhaps my sister may not speak so *very* broad," kindly suggested Adelaide in her sweetest accents.

" You are very good, my love, to think so; but no-body can live in that odious country without being infected with its *patois*. I really thought I should have caught it myself; and Mr Douglas (no longer Henry) became quite gross in his language, after living amongst his relations."

" This is really too bad," cried Lady Emily, indig-nantly. " If a person speaks sense and truth, what does it signify in what accent they are spoken? And whether your ladyship chooses to receive your daughter here or not, I shall, at any rate, invite my cousin to my father's house." And, snatching up a pen, she instantly began a letter to Mary.

Lady Juliana was highly incensed at this freedom of her niece; but she was a little afraid of her, and there-fore, after some sharp altercation, and with infinite violence done to her feelings, she was prevailed upon to write a decently civil sort of a letter to Mrs Douglas, consenting to receive her daughter for a *few months;* firmly resolving in her own mind to conceal her from all eyes and ears while she remained, and to return her to her Scotch relations early in the summer.

This worthy resolution formed, she became more serene, and awaited the arrival of her daughter with as much firmness as could reasonably have been expected.

Little weened the good ladies of Glenfern the ungracious reception their *protégé* was likely to experience from her mother; for, in spite of the defects of her education, Mary was a general favourite in the family; and, however they might solace themselves by depreciating her to Mrs Douglas, to the world in general, and their young female acquaintances in particular, she was upheld as an epitome of every perfection above and below the sun. Had it been possible for them to conceive that Mary could have been received with anything short of rapture, Lady Juliana's letter might, in some measure, have opened the eyes of their understanding; but to the guileless sisters it seemed everything that was proper. Sorry for the necessity Mrs Douglas felt of parting with her adopted daughter—was "prettily expressed;" had no doubt it was merely a slight nervous affection—"was kind and soothing;" and the assurance, more than once repeated, that her friends might rely upon her being returned to them in the course of a very few months, "showed a great deal of feeling and consideration." But as their minds never maintained a just equilibrium long upon any subject, but, like falsely-adjusted scales, were ever hovering and vibrating at either extreme—so they could not rest satisfied in the belief that Mary was to be happy—there must be something to counteract that stilling sentiment; and that was the apprehension that Mary would be spoilt. This, for the present, was the pendulum of their imaginations.

"I declare, Mary, my sisters and I could get no sleep last night for thinking of you," said Miss Grizzy; "we are all certain that Lady Juliana especially, but indeed all your English relations, will think so much of you—from not knowing you, you know—which will be quite natural, that my sisters and I have taken it into our heads—but I hope it won't be the case, as you have a great deal of good sense of your own—that they will quite turn your head."

"Mary's head is on her shoulders to little purpose," followed up Miss Jacky, "if she can't stand being made of when she goes amongst strangers; and she ought to know by this time, that a mother's partiality is no proof of a child's merit."

"You hear that, Mary," rejoined Miss Grizzy: "so I'm sure I hope you won't mind a word what your mother says to you,—I mean about yourself; for, of course, you know, she can't be such a good judge of you as us, who have known you all your life. As to other things, I dare say she is very well informed about the country, and politics, and these sort of things—I'm certain Lady Juliana knows a great deal."

"And I hope, Mary, you will take care and not get into the daadlin' handless ways of the English women," said Miss Nicky; "I wouldn't give a pin for an English woman."

"And I hope you will never look at an Englishman, Mary," said Miss Grizzy, with equal earnestness; "take my word for it, they are a very dissipated unprincipled set of young men—so you may think what it would be for all of us if you was to marry any of them." And tears streamed from the good spinster's eyes, at the bare supposition of such a calamity.

"Don't be afraid, my dear aunt," said Mary, with a kind caress; "I shall come back to you your own 'Highland Mary.' No Englishman, with his round face and trim meadows, shall ever captivate me. Heath-covered hills, and high cheek-bones, are the charms that must win my heart."

"I'm delighted to hear you say so, my dear Mary," said the literal-minded Grizzy. "Certainly nothing can

be prettier than the heather when it's in flower; and
there is something very manly—nobody can dispute that
—in high cheek-bones: and besides, to tell you a secret,
Lady Maclaughlan has a husband in her eye for you;—
we, none of us, can conceive who it is, but, of course,
he must be suitable in every respect; for you know
Lady Maclaughlan has had two husbands herself, so,
of course, she must be an excellent judge of a good
husband."

"Or a bad one," said Mary, "which is the same
thing. Warning is as good as example."

Mrs Douglas's ideas and those of her aunts did not
coincide upon this occasion more than upon most others.
In her sister-in-law's letter she flattered herself she saw
only fashionable indifference; and she fondly hoped that
would soon give way to a tenderer sentiment, as her
daughter became known to her. At any rate, it was
proper that Mary should make the trial, and, whichever
way it ended, it must be for her advantage.

"Mary has already lived too long in these mountain
solitudes," thought she; "her ideas will become
romantic, and her taste fastidious. If it is dangerous to
be too early initiated into the ways of the world, it is perhaps equally so to live too long secluded from it. Should
she win herself a place in the heart of her mother and
sister, it will be so much happiness gained; and should
it prove otherwise, it will be a lesson learnt—a hard one,
indeed! but hard are the lessons we must all learn in the
school of life!" Yet Mrs Douglas's fortitude almost
failed her as the period of separation approached.

It had been arranged by Lady Emily that a carriage
and servants should meet Mary at Edinburgh, whither
Mr Douglas was to convey her. The cruel moment
came; and mother, sister, relations, friends, all the
bright visions which Mary's sanguine spirit had conjured
up to soften the parting pang, all were absorbed in one

agonising feeling—one overwhelming thought. Oh!
who that, for the first time, has parted from the parent
whose tenderness and love were entwined with our
earliest recollections, whose sympathy had soothed our
infant sufferings, whose fondness had brightened our
infant felicity;—who, that has a heart, but must have
felt it sink beneath the anguish of a first farewell! Yet
bitterer still must be the feelings of the parent upon
committing the cherished object of her cares and affections to the stormy ocean of life. When experience
points to the gathering cloud and rising surge which may
soon assail her defenceless child, what can support the
mother's heart but trust in Him whose eye slumbereth
not, and whose power extendeth over all! It was this
pious hope, this holy confidence, that enabled this more
than mother to part from her adopted child with a
resignation which no earthly motive could have imparted
to her mind.

It seems almost profanation to mingle with her elevated feelings the coarse, yet simple, sorrows of the
aunts, old and young, as they clung around the nearly
lifeless Mary, each tendering the parting gift they had
kept as a solace for the last.

Poor Miss Grizzy was more than usually incoherent,
as she displayed "a nice new umbrella, that could be
turned into a nice walking-stick, or any thing;" and
"a dressing-box, with a little of every thing in it;"
and, with a fresh burst of tears, Mary was directed
where she would *not* find eye-ointment, and where she
was *not* to look for court-plaster.

Miss Jacky was more composed, as she presented a
flaming copy of "Fordyce's Sermons to Young Women,"
with a few suitable observations; but Miss Nicky could
scarcely find voice to tell, that the housewife she now
tendered had once been Lady Girnachgowl's, and that
it contained Whitechapel needles of every size and

number.   The younger ladies had clubbed for the purchase of a large locket, in which was enshrined a lock
from each subscriber, tastefully arranged by the ———
jeweller, in the form of a wheatsheaf, upon a blue ground.
Even old Donald had his offering, and, as he stood
tottering at the chaise-door, he contrived to get a "bit
snishin mull" laid on Mary's lap, with a "Bless her
bonny face, an' may she ne'er want a good sneesh!"

   The carriage drove off, and for a while Mary's eyes
were closed in anguish.

———o———

Chapter xxxii.

> Farewell to the mountains, high cover'd with snow;
> Farewell to the straths, and green valleys below;
> Farewell to the forests, and wild hanging woods;
> Farewell to the torrents, and loud roaring floods!
>
> *Scotch Song.*

HAPPILY in the moral world, as in the material
one, the warring elements have their prescribed
bounds, and "the flood of grief decreaseth when
it can swell no higher;" but it is only by retrospection
we can bring ourselves to believe in this obvious truth.
The young and untried heart hugs itself in the bitterness of its emotions, and takes a pride in believing that
its anguish can end but with its existence; and it is
not till time hath almost steeped our senses in forgetful-
ness, that we discover the mutability of all human
passions.

   But Mary left it not to the slow hand of time to
subdue in some measure the grief that swelled her heart.
Had she given way to selfishness, she would have sought
the free indulgence of her sorrow as the only mitigation
of it; but she felt also for her uncle.   He was depressed

at parting with his wife and child, and he was taking a long and dreary journey entirely upon her account. Could she therefore be so selfish as to add to his uneasiness by a display of her sufferings? No—she would strive to conceal it from his observation, though to overcome it was impossible. Her feelings must ever remain the same, but she would confine them to her own breast; and she began to converse with, and even strove to amuse, her kind-hearted companion. Ever and anon, indeed, a rush of tender recollections came across her mind, and the soft voice and the bland countenance of her maternal friend seemed for a moment present to her senses; and then the dreariness and desolation that succeeded as the delusion vanished, and all was stillness and vacuity! Even self-reproach shot its piercing sting into her ingenuous heart: levities, on which, in her usual gaiety of spirit, she had never bestowed a thought, now appeared to her as crimes of the deepest dye. She thought how often she had slighted the counsels and neglected the wishes of her gentle monitress; how she had wearied of her good old aunts, their cracked voices, the drowsy hum of their spinning wheels, the rasping sound of their shaping-scissors, and the everlasting *tic-a-tic* of their knitting-needles; how coarse and vulgar she had sometimes deemed the younger ones; how she had mimicked Lady Maclaughlan, and caricatured Sir Sampson; and "even poor dear old Donald," said she, as she summed up the catalogue of her crimes, "could not escape my insolence and ill-nature. How clever I thought it to sing 'Haud awa frae me, Donald,' and how affectedly I shuddered at everything he touched!"—and the "sneeshin mull" was bedewed with tears of affectionate contrition. But every painful sentiment was for a while suspended in admiration of the magnificent scenery that was spread around them. Though summer had fled, and few even of autumn's graces remained, yet over the august features of mountain scenery the seasons have little control.   Their charms depend not upon richness of verdure, or luxuriance of foliage, or any of the mere prettinesses of nature ; but, whether wrapped in snow, or veiled in mist, or glowing in sunshine, their lonely grandeur remains the same ; and the same feelings fill and elevate the soul in contemplating these mighty works of an Almighty hand.

> O Nature! all thy seasons please the eye
> Of him who sees a Deity in all.

The eye is never weary of watching the thousand varieties of light and shade, as they flit over the mountain, or gleam upon the water ; while the ear is satisfied with the majestic silence of solitude, or charmed with the " wild roarings of nature," as heard in the hollow murmur of the wind, or the hoarse gurgling of innumerable mountain-streams.

Others besides Mary seemed to have taken a fanciful pleasure in combining the ideas of the mental and elemental world ; for, in the dreary dwelling where they were destined to pass the night, she found inscribed the following lines :—

> " The busy winds war 'mid the waving boughs,
>   And darkly rolls the heaving surge to land ;
>   Among the flying clouds the moon-beam glows
>   With colours foreign to its softness bland.

> " Here, one dark shadow melts, in gloom profound,
>   The towering Alps—the guardians of the Lake ;
>   There, one bright gleam sheds silver light around,
>   And shows the threat'ning strife that tempests wake.

> " Thus o'er my mind a busy memory plays,
>   That shakes the feelings to their inmost core ;
>   Thus beams the light of Hope's fallacious rays,
>   When simple confidence can trust no more.

> " So one dark shadow shrouds each by-gone hour,
> So one bright gleam the coming tempest shows ;
> *That* tells of sorrows, which, though past, still lower,
> And *this* reveals th' approach of future woes.   C."

While Mary was trying to decipher these somewhat mystic lines, her uncle was carrying on a colloquy in Gaelic with their hostess. The consequences of the consultation were not of the choicest description, consisting of braxy * mutton, raw potatoes, wet bannocks, hard cheese, and whisky. Very differently would the travellers have fared, had the good Nicky's intentions been fulfilled. She had prepared with her own hands a moorfowl-pie and potted nowt's-head, besides a profusion of what she termed " trifles, just for Mary, poor thing ! to divert herself with upon the road." But, alas ! in the anguish of separation the covered basket had been forgot, and the labour of Miss Nicky's hands fell to be consumed by the family, though Miss Grizzy protested, with tears in her eyes, " that it went to her heart like a knife, to eat poor Mary's puffs and snaps."

Change of air and variety of scene failed not to produce the happiest effects upon Mary's languid frame and drooping spirits. Her cheek already glowed with health, and was sometimes dimpled with smiles. She still wept, indeed, as she thought of those she had left ; but often while the tear trembled in her eye its course was arrested by wonder, or admiration, or delight,—for every object had its charms for her. Her cultivated taste and thoughtful mind could descry beauty in the form of a hill, and grandeur in the foam of the wave, and elegance in the weeping birch as it dipped its now almost leafless boughs in the mountain stream. These simple pleasures, unknown alike to the sordid mind and vitiated taste, are ever exquisitely enjoyed by

> —— one whose heart the holy forms
> Of young Imagination have kept pure.

* Sheep that have died a natural death, and been salted

Chapter xxxiij.

Her native sense improved by reading,
Her native sweetness by good breeding.

DURING their progress through the Highlands, the travellers were hospitably entertained at the mansions of the country gentlemen, where old-fashioned courtesy and modern comfort combined to cheer the stranger-guest. But upon *coming out*, as it is significantly expressed by the natives of these mountain regions, viz., entering the low country, they found they had only made a change of difficulties. In the Highlands they were always sure, that wherever there was a house, that house would be to them a home; but on a fair day in the little town of G—— they found themselves in the midst of houses, and surrounded by people, yet unable to procure rest or shelter.

At the only inn the place afforded, they were informed the horses were all out, and the house quite full; while the driver asserted, what indeed was apparent, "that his beasts warna fit to gang the length o' their foot farther—no for the king himsel'."

At this moment, a stout, florid, good-humoured-looking man passed, whistling " Roy's Wife " with all his heart; and, just as Mr Douglas was stepping out of the carriage to try what could be done, the same person, evidently attracted by curiosity, repassed, changing his tune to " There's cauld kail in Aberdeen."

He started at sight of Mr Douglas; then eagerly grasping his hand, " Ah! Archie Douglas, is this you? " exclaimed he, with a loud laugh, and hearty shake. " What! you haven't forgot your old school-fellow, Bob Gawffaw? "

A mutual recognition now took place, and much pleasure was manifested on both sides at this unexpected rencontre. No time was allowed to explain their embarrassments, for Mr Gawffaw had already tipped the post-boy the wink (which he seemed easily to comprehend); and, forcing Mr Douglas to resume his seat in the carriage, he jumped in himself.

"Now for Howffend, and Mrs Gawffaw! ha, ha, ha! This will be a surprise upon her. She thinks I'm in my barn all this time—ha, ha, ha!"

Mr Douglas here began to express his astonishment at his friend's precipitation, and his apprehensions as to the trouble they might occasion Mrs Gawffaw; but bursts of laughter and broken expressions of delight were the only replies he could procure from his friend.

After jolting over half a mile of very bad road, the carriage stopped at a mean vulgar-looking mansion, with dirty windows, ruinous thatched offices, and broken fences.

Such was the picture of still life. That of animated nature was not less picturesque. Cows bellowed, and cart-horses neighed, and pigs grunted, and geese gabbled, and ducks quacked, and cocks and hens flapped and fluttered promiscuously, as they mingled, in a sort of yard, divided from the house by a low dike, possessing the accommodation of a crazy gate, which was bestrode by a parcel of bare-legged boys.

"What are you about, you lazy rascals!" called Mr Gawffaw to them.

"Naething," answered one.

"We're just takin' a heize on the yett," answered another.

"I'll heize ye, ye scoundrels!" exclaimed the incensed Mr Gawffaw, as he burst from the carriage; and, snatching the driver's whip from his hand, flew after the more nimble-footed culprits.

Finding his efforts to overtake them in vain, he returned to the door of his mansion, where stood his guests, waiting to be ushered in. He opened the door himself, and led the way to a parlour, which was quite of a piece with the exterior of the dwelling. A dim dusty table stood in the middle of the floor, heaped with a variety of heterogeneous articles of dress, and an exceeding dirty volume of a novel lay open amongst them. The floor was littered with shapings of flannel, and shreds of gauzes, ribands, &c. The fire was almost out, and the hearth was covered with ashes.

After insisting upon his guests being seated, Mr Gawffaw walked to the door of the apartment, and hallooed out, "Mrs Gawffaw—ho! May, my dear! —I say, Mrs Gawffaw!"

A low, croaking, querulous voice was now heard in reply,—"For any sake, Mr Gawffaw, make less noise! have mercy on the walls of your house, if you've none on my poor head!" And thereupon entered Mrs Gawffaw, a cap in one hand, which she appeared to have been trying on—a smelling-bottle in the other.

She possessed a considerable share of insipid, and somewhat faded, beauty, but disguised by a tawdry trumpery style of dress, and rendered almost disgusting by the air of affectation, folly, and peevishness, that overspread her whole person and deportment. She testified the utmost surprise and coldness at sight of her guests; and, as she entered, Mr Gawffaw rushed out, having descried something passing in the yard that called for his interposition. Mr Douglas was therefore under the necessity of introducing himself and Mary to their ungracious hostess; briefly stating the circumstances that had led them to be her guests, and dwelling, with much warmth, on the kindness and hospitality of her husband in having relieved them from their embarrassment. A gracious smile, or what was intended as such, beamed over Mrs Gawffaw's face at first mention of their names.

"Excuse me, Mr Douglas," said she, making a profound reverence to him, and another to Mary, while she waved her hand for them to be seated. "Excuse me, Miss Douglas; but, situated as I am, I find it necessary to be very distant to Mr Gawffaw's friends sometimes. He is a thoughtless man, Mr Douglas; a very thoughtless man. He makes a perfect inn of his house. He never lies out of the town, trying who he can pick up and bring home with him. It is seldom I am so fortunate as to see such guests as Mr and Miss Douglas of Glenfern Castle in my house,"—with an elegant bow to each, which, of course, was duly returned. "But Mr Gawffaw would have shown more consideration, both for you and me, had he apprised me of the honour of your visit, instead of bringing you here in this ill-bred, unceremonious manner. As for me, I am too well accustomed to him to be hurt at these things now. He has kept me in hot water, I may say, since the day I married him!"

In spite of the conciliatory manner in which this agreeable address was made, Mr Douglas felt considerably disconcerted, and again renewed his apologies, adding something about hopes of being able to proceed.

"Make no apologies, my dear sir," said the lady, with what she deemed a most bewitching manner; "it affords me the greatest pleasure to see any of your family under my roof. I meant no reflection on you; it is entirely Mr Gawffaw that is to blame, in not having apprised me of the honour of this visit, that I might not have been caught in this *déshabille;* but I was really so engaged by my studies," pointing to the dirty novel, "that I was quite unconscious of the lapse of time." The guests felt more and more at a loss what to say. But the lady was at none. Seeing Mr Douglas still standing with his hat in his hand, and his eye directed towards the door, she resumed her discourse:

"Pray be seated, Mr Douglas—I beg you will sit off the door. Miss Douglas, I entreat you will walk in to the fire—I hope you will consider yourself as quite at home"—another elegant bend to each. "I only regret that Mr Gawffaw's folly and ill-breeding should have brought you into this disagreeable situation, Mr Douglas. He is a well-meaning man, Mr Douglas, and a good-hearted man; but he is very deficient in other respects, Mr Douglas."

Mr Douglas, happy to find any thing to which he could assent, warmly joined in the eulogium on the excellence of his friend's heart. It did not appear, however, to give the satisfaction he expected. The lady resumed with a sigh,—"Nobody can know Mr Gawffaw's heart better than I do, Mr Douglas. It *is* a good one, but it is far from being an elegant one; it is one in which I find no congeniality of sentiment with my own. Indeed, Mr Gawffaw is no companion for me, nor I for him, Mr Douglas—he is never happy in my society; and I really believe he would rather sit down with the tinklers on the road-side, than spend a day in my company."

A deep sigh followed; but its pathos was drowned in the obstreperous "ha, ha, ha!" of her joyous help-mate, as he bounced into the room, wiping his forehead:

"Why, May, my dear, what have you been about to-day? Things have been all going to the deuce. Why didn't you hinder these boys from sweein' the gate off its hinges, and "——

"Me hinder boys from sweein' gates, Mr Gawffaw! Do I look like as if I was capable of hindering boys from sweein' gates, Miss Douglas?"

"Well, my dear, you ought to look after your pigs a

little better. That jade, black Jess, has trod a parcel of them to death, ha, ha, ha! and "——

"Me look after pigs, Mr Gawffaw! I'm really astonished at you!" again interrupted the lady, turning pale with vexation. Then, with an affected giggle, appealing to Mary,—"I leave you to judge, Miss Douglas, if I look like a person made for running after pigs!"

"Indeed," thought Mary, "you don't look like as if you could do anything half so useful."

"Well, never mind the pigs, my dear; only don't give us any of them for dinner—ha, ha, ha!—and, May, when will you let us have it?"

"Me let you have it, Mr Gawffaw! I'm sure I don't hinder you from having it when you please, only you know I prefer late hours myself. I was always accustomed to them in my poor father's life-time—he never dined before four o'clock; and I seldom knew what it was to be in my bed before twelve o'clock at night, Miss Douglas, till I married Mr Gawffaw."

Mary tried to look sorrowful, to hide the smile that was dimpling her cheek.

"Come, let us have something to eat in the meantime, my dear."

"I'm sure you may eat the house, if you please, for me, Mr Gawffaw! What would you take, Miss Douglas? Pull the bell,—softly, Mr Gawffaw! you do every thing so violently."

A dirty maid-servant, with bare feet, answered the summons.

"Where's Tom?" demanded the lady, well knowing that Tom was afar off at some of the farm operations.

"I ken na whar he's. He'll be aether at the patatees, or the horses, I'se warran. Div ye want him?"

" Bring some glasses," said her mistress, with an air
of great dignity. " Mr Gawffaw, you must see about the
wine yourself, since you have sent Tom out of the way."

Mr Gawffaw and his handmaid were soon heard in
an adjoining closet ; the one wondering where the screw
was, the other vociferating for a knife to cut the bread ;
while the mistress of this well-regulated mansion sought
to divert her guests' attention from what was passing,
by entertaining them with complaints of Mr Gawffaw's
noise, and her maid's insolence, till the parties appeared
to speak for themselves.

After being refreshed with some very sour wine and
stale bread, the gentlemen set off on a survey of the
farm, and the ladies repaired to their toilettes. Mary's
simple dress was quickly adjusted ; and, upon descending, she found her uncle alone in what Mrs Gawffaw
had shown to her as the drawing-room. He guessed
her curiosity to know something of her hosts ; and
therefore briefly informed her that Mrs Gawffaw was
the daughter of a trader in some manufacturing town,
who had lived in opulence, and died insolvent. During
his life, his daughter had eloped with Bob Gawffaw,
then a gay lieutenant in a marching regiment, who had
been esteemed a very lucky fellow in getting the pretty
Miss Croaker, with the prospect of ten thousand pounds.
None thought more highly of her husband's good
fortune than the lady herself ; and though *her* fortune
never was realised, she gave herself all the airs ot
having been the making of his. At this time, Mr
Gawffaw was a reduced lieutenant, living upon a small
paternal property, which he pretended to farm ; but the
habits of a military life, joined to a naturally social disposition, were rather inimical to the pursuits of agricul-
ture, and most of his time was spent in loitering about
the village of G——, where he generally contrived,
either to pick up a guest or procure a dinner.

Mrs Gawffaw despised her husband—had weak nerves and headaches—was above managing her house —read novels—dyed ribands—and altered her gowns according to every pattern she could see or hear of.

Such were Mr and Mrs Gawffaw ; one of the many ill-assorted couples in this world—joined, not matched. A sensible man would have curbed her folly and peevishness : a good-tempered woman would have made his home comfortable, and rendered him more domestic.

The dinner was such as might have been expected from the previous specimens—bad of its kind, cold, ill-dressed, and slovenly set down ; but Mrs Gawffaw seemed satisfied with herself and it.

" This is very fine mutton, Mr Douglas, and not under-done to most people's tastes—and this fowl, I have no doubt, will eat well, Miss Douglas, though it is not so white as some I have seen."

" The fowl, my dear, looks as if it had been the great-grandmother of this sheep—ha, ha, ha ! "

" For any sake, Mr Gawffaw, make less noise, or my head will split in a thousand pieces ! " putting her hands to it, as if to hold the frail tenement together. This was always her refuge when at a loss for a reply.

A very ill-concocted pudding next called forth her approbation.

" This pudding should be good ; for it is the same I used to be so partial to in my poor father's life-time ! when I was used to every delicacy, Miss Douglas, that money could purchase."

" But you thought me the greatest delicacy of all, my dear, ha, ha, ha ! for you left all your other deli-cacies for me, ha, ha, ha !—what do you say to that, May ?—ha, ha, ha ! "

May's reply consisted in putting her hands to her head, with an air of inexpressible vexation ; and, find-ing all her endeavours to be elegant frustrated by the

overpowering vulgarity of her husband, she remained
silent during the remainder of the repast ; solacing herself with complacent glances at her yellow silk gown,
and adjusting the gold chains and necklaces that adorned
her bosom.

Poor Mary was doomed to a *tête-à-tête* with her
during the whole evening ; for Mr Gawffaw was too
happy *with* his friend, and *without* his wife, to quit the
dining-room till a late hour ; and then he was so much
exhilarated, that she could almost have joined Mrs
Gawffaw in her exclamation of " For any sake, Mr
Gawffaw, have mercy on my head ! "

The night, however, like all other nights, had a
close ; and Mrs Gawffaw, having once more enjoyed the
felicity of finding herself in company at twelve o'clock
at night, at length withdrew ; and having apologised,
and hoped, and feared, for another hour in Mary's
apartment, she finally left her to the blessings of solitude
and repose.

As Mr Douglas was desirous of reaching Edinburgh
the following day, he had, in spite of the urgent remonstrances of his friendly host, and the elegant importunities of his lady, ordered the carriage at an early
hour ; and Mary was too eager to quit Howffend to
keep it waiting. Mr Gawffaw was in readiness to
hand her in, but fortunately Mrs Gawffaw's head did
not permit of her rising. With much the same hearty
laugh that had welcomed their meeting, honest Gawffaw
now saluted the departure of his friend ; and, as he
leant whistling over his gate, he ruminated sweet and
bitter thoughts as to the destinies of the day—whether
he should solace himself with a good dinner, and the
company of Bailie Merrythought, at the Cross-Keys
in G———, or put up with cold mutton, and May, at
home.

Chapter xxxib.

Edina! Scotia's darling seat!
All hail thy palaces and tow'rs,
Where once, beneath a monarch's feet,
Sat Legislation's sov'reign pow'rs!
                                    BURNS.

THE travellers had viewed with interest the memorable localities of Stirling Castle, and looked with delight from its rocky ramparts on the magnificent panorama which lay stretched around. They now stood amidst the mouldering walls of Linlithgow palace, as the setting sun gilded them with its last rays, and shed its mellow radiance over the green bank on which they stand. *That* is now crumbling into mere masses of mossy herbage; yet there may still be traced those terraced gardens where once flourished England's proud rose and France's fair *fleur-de-lis,* but where Scotland's wild blue-bell now hangs its lonely head. The farewell gleam of light quivered on the stems of the aged sycamores which surmount the grassy knolls, and whose shrivelled arms and scanty foliage seem, to the fanciful eye, as though now, in their old age, stretched forth to guard the kingly walls which had once sheltered their green heads from the storm. The tranquil waters of the fair Loch lay in deep-blue shadow beneath. It was a scene to be remembered, and Mary felt the impressiveness of the contrast, as she turned from the enduring loveliness of nature to retrace her steps through the gloom and vacuity of the roofless towers and desolate halls of this, once the fairest " beyond compare " of Scotland's pleasant palaces.

But the young enthusiast's feelings were still more vividly excited on entering the Scottish metropolis. An inhabitant of London or Paris would smile to hear

Edinburgh styled a great city; but, to one born and
bred amid nature's solitudes, its size seemed vast, its
buildings noble, its beauty (as in truth it is) surpassing.
But beyond all these were the historic and romantic
associations which crowded upon her mind, and to
which youth and imagination love to give "a local
habitation and a name;" and visions of olden time
seemed to start into life, with all their picturesque
pageantry.

"And this was once a gay court!" thought she, as
they traversed the dull arcades of its deserted palace,
and listened to the dreary sounds of the sentinel's footsteps. "How changed since that bright epoch when
here shone the

> Star of the Stuart line—accomplish'd James!

And here, where all is now so sad and still, were once

> The banquet and the song;
> By day the tourney, and by night
> The merry dance trac'd fast and light,
> The masquers quaint, the pageant bright,
> The revel loud and long!

And on this very spot on which I now stand once stood
the hapless Mary Stuart, in all her bright and queenly
beauty! *Her* eye beheld the same objects on which
mine now rests; *her* hand has touched the draperies
which I now hold in mine:—these frail memorials
remain; but what, alas! remains of Scotland's queen,
but blood-stained records and a blighted fame!"

Even the fatal chamber, the scene of Rizzio's
murder, possessed a nameless charm for Mary's vivid
imagination. She had not entirely escaped the super-
stitions of the country in which she had lived; and she
readily yielded her assent to the asseverations of her
guide, as to its being the *bonâ fide* blood of David

Rizzio, which, for nearly three hundred years, had resisted all human efforts to efface it.

"My credulity is so harmless," said she, in answer to her uncle's attempt to laugh her out of her belief, "that I surely may be permitted to indulge it—especially since, I confess, I feel a sort of indescribable pleasure in it."

"*You* take a pleasure in the sight of blood!" exclaimed Mr Douglas, in astonishment,—"you, who turn pale at sight of a cut finger, and shudder at a leg of mutton with the juice in it!"

"Oh, mere modern vulgar blood is very shocking," answered Mary, with a smile; "but observe how this is mellowed by time into a tint that could not offend the most fastidious fine lady: besides," added she, in a graver tone, "I own I love to believe in things supernatural; it seems to connect us more with another world, than when everything is seen to proceed in the mere ordinary course of nature, as it is called. I cannot bear to imagine a dreary chasm betwixt the inhabitants of this world and beings of a higher sphere; I love to fancy myself surrounded by"——

"I wish you would remember you are surrounded by rational beings, and not fall into such rhapsodies," said her uncle, glancing at a party, who stood near them, jesting upon all the objects which Mary had been regarding with so much veneration. "But, come, you have been long enough here. Let us try whether a breeze on the Calton Hill will not dispel these cobwebs from your brain."

The day, though cold, was clear and sunny; and the lovely spectacle before them shone forth in all its gay magnificence. The blue waters lay calm and motionless. The opposite shores glowed in a thousand varied tints of wood and plain, rock and mountain, cultered field, and purple moor. Beneath, the old town reared its dark brow, and the new one stretched its golden lines; while, all around, the varied charms of nature lay scattered in that profusion which nature's hand alone can bestow.

"Oh! this is exquisite!" exclaimed Mary, after a long pause, in which she had been riveted in admiration of the scene before her. "And you are in the right, my dear uncle. The ideas which are inspired by the contemplation of such a spectacle as this, are far—oh, how far!—superior to those excited by the mere works of art. There, I can, at best, think but of the inferior agents of Providence: here, the soul rises from nature up to nature's God."

"You will certainly be taken for a Methodist, Mary, if you talk in this manner," said Mr Douglas, with some marks of disquiet, as he turned round at the salutation of a fat elderly gentleman, whom he presently recognised as Bailie Broadfoot.

The first salutations over, Mr Douglas's fears of Mary having been overheard recurred, and he felt anxious to remove any unfavourable impression with regard to his own principles, at least, from the mind of the enlightened magistrate.

"Your fine views here have set my niece absolutely raving," said he with a smile; "but I tell her it is only in romantic minds that fine scenery inspires romantic ideas. I dare say many of the worthy inhabitants of· Edinburgh walk here with no other idea than that of sharpening their appetites for dinner."

"Nae doot," said the bailie, "it's a most capital place for that. Were it no' for that, I ken nae muckle use it would be of."

"You speak from experience of its virtues in that respect, I suppose?" said Mr Douglas, gravely.

"'Deed as to that, I canna compleen. At times, to be sure, I am troubled with a little kind of squeamishness after our public interteenments: but three rounds o' the hill sets a' to rights." Then observing Mary's eyes exploring, as he supposed, the town of Leith, "You see that prospeck to nae advantage the day, miss," said he. "If the glass-houses had been workin', it would have looked as weel again. Ye hae nae glass-houses in the Highlands; na, na."

The bailie had a share in the concern; and the volcanic clouds of smoke that issued from thence were far more interesting subjects of speculation to him than all the eruptions of Vesuvius or Etna. But there was nothing to charm the lingering view to-day; and he therefore proposed their taking a look at Bridewell, which, next to the smoke from the glass-houses, he reckoned the object most worthy of notice. It was, indeed, deserving of the praises bestowed upon it; and Mary was giving her whole attention to the details of it, when she was suddenly startled by hearing her own name wailed in piteous accents from one of the lower cells, and, upon turning round, she discovered in the prisoner the son of one of the tenants of Glenfern. Duncan M'Free had been always looked upon as a very honest lad in the Highlands, but he had left home to push his fortune as a pedlar; and the temptations of the low country having proved too much for his virtue, poor Duncan was now expiating his offence in durance vile.

"I shall have a pretty account of you to carry to Glenfern," said Mr Douglas, regarding the culprit with his sternest look.

"O, 'deed, sir, it's no' my fau't!" answered Duncan, blubbering bitterly; "but there's nae freedom at a' in this country. Och, an' I were oot o't! Ane canna ca' their head their ain in't; for ye canna lift the bouk o' a prin, but they're a' upon ye." And a fresh burst of sorrow ensued.

Finding the *peccadillo* was of a venial nature, Mr

Douglas besought the bailie to use his interest to procure the enfranchisement of this his vassal, which Mr Broad-foot, happy to oblige a customer, promised should be obtained on the following day ; and Duncan's emotions being rather clamorous, the party found it necessary to withdraw.

" And noo," said the bailie, as they emerged from this place of dole and durance, " will ye step up to the Monument, and tak a rest and some refreshment ? "

" Rest and refreshment in a monument ! " exclaimed Mr Douglas. " Excuse me, my good friend, but we are not inclined to bait there yet a while."

The bailie did not comprehend the joke, and he proceeded in his own drawling humdrum accent to assure them that the Monument was a most convenient place.

" It was erected in honour of Lord Nelson's memory," said he, " and is let to a pastry-cook and confectioner, where you can always find some trifles to treat the ladies, such as pies and custards, and berries, and these sort of things ; but we passed an order in the cooncil that there should be nothing of a spiritous nature introduced, for, if once spirits got admittance, there's no' saying what might happen."

This was a fact which none of the party were disposed to dispute ; and the bailie, triumphing in his dominion over the spirits, shuffled on before, to do the honours of the place, appropriated at one and the same time to the manes of a hero and the making of minced pies. The regale was admirable ; and Mary could not help thinking times were improved, and that it was a better thing to eat tarts in Lord Nelson's monument, than to have been poisoned in Julius Cæsar's.

———o———

Chapter xxxb.

Having a tongue rough as a cat, and biting like an adder, and all their reproofs are direct scoldings, their common intercourse is open contumely.

JEREMY TAYLOR.

" THOUGH last, not least of Nature's works, I must now introduce you to a friend of mine," said Mr Douglas, as, the bailie having made his bow, they bent their steps towards the Castle Hill. " Mrs Violet Macshake is an aunt of my mother's, whom you must often have heard of, and the last remaining branch of the noble race of Girnachgowl."

" I am afraid she is rather a formidable person, then?" said Mary.

Her uncle hesitated—" No, not formidable—only rather particular, as all old people are; but she is very good-hearted."

" I understand, in other words, she is very disagreeable. All ill-tempered people, I observe, have the character of being good-hearted; or else all good-hearted people are ill-tempered,—I cannot tell which."

" It is more than reputation with her," said Mr Douglas, " for she is, in reality, a very good-hearted woman, as I experienced when a boy at college. Many a crown-piece and half-guinea I used to get from her: —many a scold, to be sure, went along with them; but that, I dare say, I deserved. Besides, she is very rich, and I am her reputed heir; therefore, gratitude and self-interest combine to render her extremely amiable in my estimation."

They had now reached the airy dwelling where Mrs Macsnake resided, and having rung, the door was at length most deliberately opened by an ancient, sour-visaged, long-waisted female, who ushered them into an

apartment, the *coup d'œil* of which struck a chill to
Mary's heart.   It was a good-sized room, with a bare
sufficiency of small-legged dining-tables, and lank hair-
cloth chairs, ranged in high order round the walls.
Although the season was advanced, and the air piercing
cold, the grate stood smiling in all the charms of polished
steel ; and the mistress of the mansion was seated by the
side of it in an arm-chair, still in its summer position.
She appeared to have no other occupation than what her
own meditations afforded ; for a single glance sufficed
to show, that not a vestige of book or work was harboured
there.   She was a tall large-boned woman, whom even
Time's iron hand had scarcely bent, as she merely stooped
at the shoulders.   She had a drooping snuffy nose—a
long turned-up chin—small quick grey eyes ; and her face
projected far beyond her figure, with an expression of
shrewd restless curiosity.   She wore a mode (not *à-la-
mode*) bonnet, and cardinal of the same ; a pair of clogs
over her shoes, and black silk mittens on her arms.

As soon as she recognised Mr Douglas, she welcomed
him with much cordiality, shook him long and heartily
by the hand—patted him on the back—looked into his
face with much seeming satisfaction ; and, in short, gave
all the demonstrations of gladness usual with gentlewomen of a certain age.   Her pleasure, however, appeared to be rather an *impromptu* than an habitual feeling ; for, as the surprise wore off, her visage resumed its
harsh and sarcastic expression, and she seemed eager to
efface any agreeable impression her reception might have
excited.

" An' wha thought o' seein' you ? " said she, in a
quick gabbling voice ; " what's brought you to the
toon ?   Are ye come to spend your honest faither's
siller, ere he's weel cauld in his grave, poor man ? "

Mr Douglas explained, that it was upon account of
his niece's health.

" Health ! " repeated she, with a sardonic smile, " it
wad mak an ool laugh to hear the wark that's made
aboot young fowk's health noo-a-days. I wonder what
ye're aw made o'," grasping Mary's arm in her great
bony hand—" a wheen puir, feckless windlestraes—ye
maun awa to Ingland for your healths.—Set ye up ! I
wunder what cam o' the lasses i' my time, that but to
bide at hame ? And whilk o' ye will e'er live to see
ninety-sax, like me ?—Health ! he, he ! "

Mary, glad of a pretence to indulge the mirth the old
lady's manner and appearance had excited, joined most
heartily in the laugh.

" Tak aff your bannet, bairn, an' let me see your face ;
wha can tell what like ye are, wi' that snule o' a thing
on your head ? " Then, after taking an accurate survey
of her face, she pushed aside her pelisse—" Weel, it's a
mercy, I see you hae neither the red head nor the muckle
feet o' the Douglases. I kenna whether your father has
them or no. I ne'er set een on him : neither him nor
his braw leddy thought it worth their while to ask after
me ; but I was at nae loss, by aw accounts."

" You have not asked after any of your Glentern
friends," said Mr Douglas, hoping to touch a more
sympathetic chord.

" Time enough—will ye let me draw my breath,
man ?—fowk canna say awthing at ance. An' ye but
to hae an Inglish wife too, a Scotch lass wadna serve
ye. An' your wean, I'se warran', it's ane o' the
world's wonders—it's been unca lang o' cummin'—
he, he ! "

" He has begun life under very melancholy auspices,
poor fellow ! " said Mr Douglas, in allusion to his
father's death.

" An' wha's faut was that ?—I ne'er heard tell the
like o't, to hae the bairn kirsened an' its grandfaither
deein' ! — But fowk are neither born, nor kirsened,

nor do they wad or dee as they used to do—awthing's changed."

" You must, indeed, have witnessed many changes," observed Mr Douglas, rather at a loss how to utter any thing of a conciliatory nature.

" Changes !—weel a wat, I sometimes wunder if it's the same waurld, an' if it's my ain head that's upon my shoothers."

" But with these changes you must also have seen many improvements?" said Mary, in a tone of diffidence.

" Impruvements ! " turning sharply round upon her, " what ken ye about impruvements, bairn? A bonny impruvement, or else no, to see tyleyors and sclaters leavin', whar I mind dukes an' yearls ! An' that great glowrin' new toon there," pointing out of her windows, " whar I used to sit an' look out at bonny green parks, and see the cows milket, and the bits o' bairnies rowin' an' tummlin', an' the lasses trampin' in their tubs—what see I noo, but stane an' lime, an' stoor an' dirt, an' idle cheils, an' dinket-oot madams prancin'.—Impruvements, indeed ! "

Mary found she was not likely to advance her uncle's fortune by the judiciousness of her remarks, therefore prudently resolved to hazard no more. Mr Douglas, who was more *au fait* to the prejudices of old age, and who was always amused with her bitter remarks when they did not touch himself, encouraged her to continue the conversation by some observation on the prevailing manners.

" Manners ! " repeated she, with a contemptuous laugh, " what caw ye manners noo, for I dinna ken? ilk ane gangs bang in to their neebor's house, an' bang out o't, as it war a chynge-house ; an' as for the master o't, he's no o' sae muckle value as the flunky behind his chyre. In my grandfaither's time, as I hae heard him tell, ilka master o' a faamily had his ain seat in his ain house, ay! an' sat wi' his hat on his head before the best o' the land, an' had his ain dish, an' was ay helpit first, an' keepit up his authority as a man should do. Paurents war paurents then—bairns dardna set up their gabs before them than as they do now. They ne'er presumed to say their heads war their ain i' thae days; —wife an' servants—retainers an' childer, aw trummelt i' the presence o' their head."

Here a long pinch of snuff caused a pause in the old lady's harangue; but, after having duly wiped her nose with her coloured handkerchief, and shook off all the particles that might be presumed to have lodged upon her cardinal, she resumed:—

"An' nae word o' ony o' your sisters gawn to get husbands yet? They tell me they're but coorse lasses: an' wha'll tak ill-farred, tocherless queans, where there's wealth o' bonny faces an' lang purses i' the market?— he, he!" Then resuming her scrutiny of Mary— "An' I'se warran' ye'll be looking for an Inglish sweetheart too; that'll be what's takin' ye awa to Ingland."

"On the contrary," said Mr Douglas, seeing Mary was too much frightened to answer for herself—"On the contrary, Mary declares she will never marry any but a true Highlander; one who wears the dirk and plaid, and has the second-sight. And the nuptials are to be celebrated with all the pomp of feudal times; with bagpipes, and bonfires, and gatherings of clans, and roasted sheep, and barrels of whisky, and "——

"Weel a wat an she's i' the right there," interrupted Mrs Macshake, with more complacency than she had yet shown. "They may caw them what they like, but there's nae weddins now. Wha's the better o' them but innkepers and chaise - drivers? I wudnae count mysel married i' the hiddlins way they gang aboot it noo."

"I dare say you remember these things done in a very different style?" said Mr Douglas.

"I dinna mind them when they war at the best; but I hae heard my mother tell what a bonny ploy was at her weddin'. I canna tell you how mony was at it; mair than the room wad haud, ye may be sure, for every relation an' friend o' baith sides war there, as weel they should; an' aw in full dress: the leddies in their hoops on, an' some o' them had sat up aw night te hae their heads drest; for they hadnae thae pooket-like taps ye hae noo," looking with contempt at Mary's Grecian contour. "An' the bride's gown was aw sewed ow'r wi' favors, frae the tap down to the tail, an' aw round the neck, an' about the sleeves; and, as soon as the ceremony was ow'r, ilk ane ran, an' rugget an' rave at her for the favors, till they hardly left the gown upon her back. Then they didnae run awa as they do now, but six an' thirty o' them sat down to a grand dinner, and there was a ball at night, an' ilka night till Sabbath cam round; an' than the bride an' the bridegroom, drest in their weddin' suits, and aw their friends in theirs wi' their favors on their breasts, walked in procession to the kirk. An' was nae that something like a weddin'? It was worth while to be married i' thae days—he, he!" *

"The wedding seems to have been admirably conducted," said Mr Douglas, with much solemnity. "The christening, I presume, would be the next distinguished event in the family."

"Troth, Archie—an' ye should keep your thumb upon christenins as lang's ye live; yours was a bonny christening or else no! I hae heard o' mony things, but a bairn christened whan its grandfather was in the dead-thraw, I ne'er heard tell o' before." Then

* These particulars were taken from the MS. reminiscences of an old lady—one of the aristocracy of her day.

observing the indignation that spread over Mr Douglas's face, she quickly resumed, "An' so you think the kirsnin' was the next ploy?—Na; the cryin was a ploy, for the leddies didnae keep themselves up than as they do now; but the day after the bairn was born, the leddy sat up in her bed, wi' her fan in her hand; an' aw her friends cam an' stood round her an' drank her health an' the bairn's. Than, at the leddy's recovery, there was a graund supper gien that they caw'd the *cummerfeals*, an' there was a great pyramid o' hens at the tap o' the table, an' anither pyramid o' ducks at the foot, an' a muckle stoup fu' o' posset i' the middle, an' aw kinds o' sweeties doon the sides; an' as soon as ilk ane had eatin' their fill, they aw flew to the sweeties, an' fought, an' strave, an' wrastled for them, leddies an' gentlemen an' aw; for the brag was, wha could pocket maist; an' whiles they wad hae the cloth aff the table, an' awthing in the middle of the floor, and the chairs upside down. Oo! muckle gude diversion, I'se warran', was at the *cummerfeals*.—Than whan they had drank the stoup dry, that ended the ploy. As for the kirsnin', that was aye whar it should be—in the house o' God, an' aw the kith an' kin by in full dress, an' a band o' maiden kimmers aw in white; an' a bonny sight it was, as I've heard my mother tell."

Mr Douglas, who was now rather tired of the old lady's reminiscences, availed himself of the opportunity of a fresh pinch to rise and take leave.

"Oo, what's takin' ye awa, Archie, in sic a hurry? Sit doon there," laying her hand upon his arm, "an' rest ye, an' tak a glass o' wine, an' a bit bread; or may be," turning to Mary, "ye wad rather hae a drap broth to warm ye. What gars ye look sae blae, bairn? I'm sure it's no cauld; but ye're just like the rest: ye gang aw skiltin' about the streets half naked, an' than ye maun sit an' birsle yoursels before the fire at hame."

She had now shuffled along to the further end of the room, and, opening a press, took out wine, and a plateful of various-shaped articles of bread, which she handed to Mary.

" Hae, bairn—tak a cookie—tak it up-—what are ye fear'd for !—it'll no bite ye.—Here's t'ye, Glenfern, an' your wife, an' your wean ; puir thing, it's no had a very chancy ootset, weel a wat."

The wine being drunk, and the cookies discussed, Mr Douglas made another attempt to withdraw, but in vain.

" Canna ye sit still a wee, an' let me ask after my auld friends at Glenfern ? How's Grizzy, an' Jacky, an' Nicky ?—aye workin' awa at the drugs ! I ne'er gied a bawbee for drugs aw my days, an' see if ony of them will rin a race wi' me whan they're near five score."

Mr Douglas here paid some compliments upon her appearance, which were pretty graciously received ; and added that he was the bearer of a letter from his aunt Grizzy, which he would send along with a roebuck and brace of moor-game.

" If your roebuck's nae better than your last, atweel it's no worth the sendin' : poor dry fissinless stuff, no worth the chewin' ; weel a wat, I begrudged my teeth on't. Your muirfowl war nae that ill, but they're no worth the carryin' ; they're dog-cheap i' the market now, so it's nae great compliment. If ye had brought me a leg o' gude mutton, or a cauler salmon, there would hae been some sense in't ; but ye're ane o' the fowk that'll ne'er harry yoursel' wi' your presents ; it's but the pickle powther they cost ye, an' I'se warran' ye're thinkin' mair o' your ain diversion than o' my stamick, whan ye're at the shootin' o' them, poor beasts."

Mr Douglas had borne the various indignities levelled against himself and his family with a philosophy that had no parallel in his life before, but to this attack upon his game he was not proof. His colour rose, his eyes flashed fire, and something resembling an oath burst from his lips as he strode indignantly towards the door.

His friend, however, was too nimble for him. She stepped before him, and, breaking into a discordant laugh, as she patted him on the back, " So I see ye're just the auld man, Archie,—aye ready to tak' the strums, an' ye dinna get aw thing your ain way. Mony a time I had to fleech you out o' the dorts whan ye was a callant. Do ye mind how ye was affronted because I set you doon to a cauld pigeon-pie an' a tanker o' tippenny, ae night to your foweroors, before some leddies?—he, he, he! Weel a wat, ye're wife maun hae her ain adoos to manage ye, for ye're a cumstairy chield, Archie."

Mr Douglas still looked as if he was irresolute whether to laugh or be angry.

" Come, come, sit ye doon there, till I speak to this bairn," said she, as she pulled Mary into an adjoining bed-chamber, which wore the same aspect of chilly neatness as the one they had quitted. Then, pulling a huge bunch of keys from her pocket, she opened a drawer, out of which she took a pair of diamond ear-rings. " Hae, bairn," said she, as she stuffed them into Mary's hand; " they belanged to your father's grand-mother. She was a gude woman, an' had four-an'-twenty sons and dochters, an' I wish you nae war for-tune than just to hae as mony. But mind ye," with a shake of her bony finger, " they maun a' be Scots. If I thought ye wad marry ony pock-puddin', fient haed wad ye hae gotten frae me.—Now, haud your tongue, and dinna deive me wi' thanks," almost pushing her into the parlour again; " and since ye're gaun awa' the morn, I'll see nae mair o' you—so fare ye weel. But, Archie, ye maun come an' tak your breakfast wi' me.—I have

muckle to say to you; but ye manna be sae hard upon
my baps as ye used to be," with a facetious grin to her
mollified favourite, as they shook hands and parted.

"Well, how do you like Mrs Macshake, Mary?"
asked her uncle, as they walked home.

"That is a cruel question, uncle," answered she,
with a smile. "My gratitude and my taste are at such
variance," displaying her splendid gift, "that I know
not how to reconcile them."

"That is always the case with those whom Mrs
Macshake has obliged," returned Mr Douglas. "She
does many liberal things, but in so ungracious a manner,
that people are never sure whether they are obliged or
insulted by her. But the way in which she receives
kindness is still worse. Could any thing equal her impertinence about my roebuck?—I have a good mind
never to enter her door again!"

Mary could scarcely preserve her gravity at her
uncle's indignation, which seemed so disproportioned to
the cause. But, to turn the current of his ideas, she
remarked, that he had certainly been at pains to select
two admirable specimens of her countrywomen tor her.

"I don't think I shall soon forget either Mrs
Gawffaw or Mrs Macshake," said she laughing.

"I hope you won't carry away the impression, that
these two *lusus naturæ* are specimens of Scotch women?"
said her uncle. "The former, indeed, is rather a sort
of weed that infests every soil—the latter, to be sure, is
an indigenous plant. I question if she would have
arrived at such perfection in a more cultivated field, or
genial clime. She was born at a time when Scotland
was very different from what it is now. Female education was little attended to, even in families of the highest
rank; consequently, the ladies of those days possess a
raciness (or it may be a coarseness) in their manners and
ideas that we should vainly seek for in this age of culti-

vation and refinement. Had your time permitted, you could have seen much good society here, equal, perhaps, to what is to be found any where else, as far as mental cultivation is concerned. But you will have leisure for that when you return."

Mary acquiesced with a sigh. *Return* was to her still a melancholy-sounding word. It reminded her of all she had left—of the anguish of separation—the dreariness of absence; and all these painful feelings were renewed, in their utmost bitterness, when the time approached for her to bid adieu to her uncle. Lord Courtland's carriage, and two respectable-looking servants, awaited her; and the following morning she commenced her journey, in all the anguish of a heart that fondly clings to its native home.

———o———

Chapter xxxbj.

—— Nor only by the warmth
And soothing sunshine of delightful things,
Do minds grow up and flourish.

AKENSIDE.

So found is worse than lost.

ADDISON.

AFTER parting with the last of her beloved relatives, Mary tried to think only of the happiness that awaited her in a reunion with her mother and sister, and she gave herself up to the blissful reveries of a young and ardent imagination. Mrs Douglas had sought to repress, rather than excite, her sanguine expectations; but vainly is the experience of others employed in moderating the enthusiasm of a glowing heart. Experience *cannot* be imparted: we may render the youthful mind prematurely cautious, or meanly suspicious, but the experience of a pure and enlightened mind is the result of observation, matured by time.

The journey, like most modern journeys, was performed in comfort and safety; and, late one evening, Mary found herself at the goal of her wishes—at the threshold of the house that contained her mother! One idea filled her mind; but that idea called up a thousand emotions.

"I am now to meet my mother!" thought she; and, unconscious of every thing else, she was assisted from the carriage, and conducted into the house. A door was thrown open, but, shrinking from the glare of light and sound of voices that assailed her, she stood dazzled and dismayed, till she beheld a figure approaching that she guessed to be her mother. Her heart beat violently—a film was upon her eyes—she made an effort to reach her mother's arms, and sank lifeless on her bosom!

Lady Juliana, for such it was, doubted not but that her daughter was really dead; for, though she talked of fainting every hour of the day herself, still, what is emphatically called a *dead faint*, was a spectacle no less strange than shocking to her. She was, therefore, sufficiently alarmed and overcome to behave in a very interesting manner; and some yearnings of pity even possessed her heart, as she beheld her daughter's lifeless form extended before her—her beautiful, though inanimate, features half hid by the profusion of golden ringlets that fell around her. But these kindly feelings were of short duration; for no sooner was the nature of her daughter's insensibility ascertained, than all her former hostility returned, as she found every one's attention directed to Mary, and she herself entirely overlooked in the general interest she had excited; and her displeasure was still further increased, as Mary, at length slowly unclosing her eyes, stretched out her hands, and faintly articulated—"My mother!"

"Mother! What a hideous vulgar appellation!" thought the fashionable parent to herself! and, instead of answering her daughter's appeal, she hastily proposed that she should be conveyed to her own apartment: then, summoning her maid, she consigned her to her care, slightly touching her cheek as she wished her good night, and returned to the card-table. Adelaide, too, resumed her station at the harp, as if nothing had happened; but Lady Emily attended her cousin to her room —embraced her again and again, as she assured her she loved her already, she was so like her dear Edward; then, after satisfying herself that everything was comfortable, affectionately kissed her, and withdrew.

Bodily fatigue got the better of mental agitation; and Mary slept soundly, and awoke refreshed. "Can it be," thought she, as she tried to collect her bewildered thoughts, "can it be that I have really beheld my mother—that I have been pressed to her heart—that she has shed tears over me while I lay unconscious in her arms?—Mother! what a delightful sound; and how beautiful she seemed! yet I have no distinct idea of her, my head was so confused; but I have a vague recollection of something very fair, and beautiful, and seraph-like, covered with silver drapery and flowers, and with the sweetest voice in the world. Yet that must be too young for my mother—perhaps it was my sister, and my mother was too much overcome to meet her stranger-child. Oh! how happy must I be with such a mother and sister!"

In these delightful cogitations Mary remained till Lady Emily entered.

"How well you look this morning, my dear cousin!" said she, flying to her; "you are much more like my Edward than you were last night. Ah! and you have got his smile too! You must let me see that very often."

"I am sure I shall have cause," said Mary, returning her cousin's affectionate embrace, "but at present I
feel anxious about my mother and sister. The agitation of our meeting, and my weakness, I fear, has been
too much for them:" and she looked earnestly in
Lady Emily's face for a confirmation of her fears.

"Indeed, you need be under no uneasiness on
their account," returned her cousin, with her usual
bluntness; "their feelings are not so easily disturbed:
you will see them both at breakfast, so come along."

The room was empty; and again Mary's sensitive
heart trembled for the welfare of those already so dear
to her; but Lady Emily did not appear to understand
the nature of her feelings.

"Have a little patience, my dear!" said she, with
something of an impatient tone, as she rang for breakfast; "they will be here at their usual time. Nobody
in this house is a slave to hours, or *gêné* with each
other's society. Liberty is the motto here : everybody
breakfasts when and where they please. Lady Juliana,
I believe, frequently takes hers in her dressing-room;
papa never is visible till two or three o'clock; and
Adelaide is always late."

"What a selfish cold-hearted thing is grandeur!"
thought Mary, as Lady Emily and she sat like two
specks in the splendid saloon, surrounded by all that
wealth could purchase or luxury invent; and her
thoughts reverted to the pious thanksgiving, and affectionate meeting, that graced their social meal in the
sweet sunny breakfast-room at Lochmarlie.

Some of those airy nothings, without a local habitation, who are always to be found flitting about the
mansions of the great, now lounged into the room; and
soon after Adelaide made her *entrée*. Mary, trembling
violently, was ready to fall upon her sister's neck; but
Adelaide seemed prepared to repel every thing like a

scène; for, with a cold but sweet "I hope you are better this morning?" she seated herself at the opposite side of the table.   Mary's blood rushed back to her heart—her eyes filled with tears, she knew not why, for she could not analyse the feelings that swelled in her bosom.   She would have shuddered to *think* her sister unkind, but she *felt* she was so.

"It can only be the difference of our manners," sighed she to herself: "I am sure my sister loves me, though she does not show it in the same way I should have done;" and she gazed with the purest admiration and tenderness on the matchless beauty of her face and form.   Never had she beheld any thing so exquisitely beautiful; and she longed to throw herself into her sister's arms, and tell her how she loved her.   But Adelaide seemed to think the present company wholly unworthy of her regard; for, after having received the adulation of the gentlemen, as they severally paid her a profusion of compliments upon her appearance, "Desire Tomkins," said she, to a footman, "to ask Lady Juliana for 'The Morning Post,' and the second volume of 'Le ——,' of the French novel I am reading, and say she shall have it again when I have finished it."

"In what different terms people may express the same meaning!" thought Mary: "had I been sending a message to my mother, I should have expressed myself quite differently; but, no doubt, my sister's meaning is the same, though she may not use the same words."

The servant returned with the newspaper, and the novel would be sent when it could be found.

"Lady Juliana never reads like any body else," said her daughter; "she is for ever mislaying books.   She has lost the first volumes of the two last novels that came from town, before I had even seen them."

This was uttered in the softest sweetest tone imagin-

able, and as if she had been pronouncing a panegyric.
Mary was more and more puzzled.

"What can be my sister's meaning here?" thought
she; "the words seem almost to imply censure, but that
voice and smile speak the sweetest praise. How truly
Mrs Douglas warned me never to judge of people by
their words!"

At that moment the door opened, and three or
four dogs rushed in, followed by Lady Juliana, with a
volume of a novel in her hand. Again Mary found
herself assailed by a variety of powerful emotions—she
attempted to rise; but, pale and agitated, she sank back
in her chair.

Her agitation was unmarked by her mother, who did
not even appear to be sensible of her presence; for with
a graceful bend of her head to the company in general,
she approached Adelaide, and, putting her lips to her
forehead, "How do you do, love? I am afraid you
are very angry with me about that teazing Le ——. I
can't conceive where it can be; but here is the third
volume, which is much prettier than the second."

"I certainly shall not read the third volume before
the second," said Adelaide, with her usual serenity.

"Then I shall order another copy from town, my
love; or, I dare say, I could tell you the story of the
second volume: it is not at all interesting, I assure you.
Hermisilde, you know——but I forget where the first
volume left off." Then directing her eyes to Mary,
who had summoned strength to rise, and was slowly
venturing to approach her, she extended a finger towards her. Mary eagerly seized her mother's hand, and
pressed it with fervour to her lips; then hid her face
on her shoulder to conceal the tears that burst from her
eyes.

"Absurd, my dear!" said her ladyship in a peevish
tone, as she disengaged herself from her daughter;

"you must really get the better ot this foolish weakness; these *scènes* are too much for me. I was most
excessively shocked last night, I assure you; and you
ought not to have quitted your room to-day."

Poor Mary's tears congealed in her eyes at this tender
salutation, and she raised her head as if to ascertain
whether it really proceeded from her mother; but, instead of the angelic vision she had pictured to herself,
she beheld a face which, though once handsome, now
conveyed no pleasurable feeling to the heart.

Late hours, bad temper, and rouge, had done much
to impair Lady Juliana's beauty. There still remained
enough to dazzle a superficial observer, but not to satisfy
the eye used to the expression of all the best affections
of the soul. Mary almost shrank from the peevish
inanity pourtrayed on her mother's visage, as a glance
of the mind contrasted it with the mild benevolence of
Mrs Douglas's countenance; and, abashed and disappointed, she remained mournfully silent.

"Where is Dr Redgill?" demanded Lady Juliana
of the company in general.

"He has got scent of a turtle at Admiral Yellowchops'," answered Mr P.

"How provoking," rejoined her ladyship, "that he
should be out of the way the only time I have wished
to see him since he came to the house!"

"Who is this favoured individual, whose absence
you are so pathetically lamenting, Julia?" asked Lord
Courtland, as he indolently sauntered into the
room.

"That disagreeable Dr Redgill. He has gone
somewhere to eat turtle, at the very time I wished to
consult him about"——

"The propriety of introducing a new niece to your
lordship," said Lady Emily, as with affected solemnity
she introduced Mary to her uncle. Lady Juliana

frowned—the earl smiled—saluted his niece—hoped she had recovered from the fatigue of the journey— remarked it was very cold, and then turned to a parrot, humming, " Pretty Polly, say," &c.

Such was Mary's first introduction to her family ; and those only who have felt what it was to have the genial current of their souls chilled by neglect, or changed by unkindness, can sympathise in the feelings of wounded affection—when the overflowings of a generous heart are confined within the narrow limits ot its own bosom, and the offerings of love are rudely rejected by the hand most dear to them.

Mary was too much intimidated by her mother's manner towards her, to give way, in her presence, to the emotions that agitated her ; but she followed her sister's steps as she quitted the room, and, throwing her arms around her, sobbed, in a voice almost choked with the excess of her feelings, " My sister, love me !—oh ! love me ! " But Adelaide's heart, seared by selfishness and vanity, was incapable of loving anything in which self had no share ; and, for the first time in her life, she felt awkward and embarrassed. Her sister's stream- ing eyes and supplicating voice spoke a language to which she was a stranger ; for art is ever averse to recognise the accents of nature. Still less is it capable of replying to them ; and Adelaide could only wonder at her sister's agitation, and think how unpleasant it was ; and say something about " overcome," and " *eau- de-Cologne*," and " composure ; " which was all lost upon Mary as she hung upon her neck, every feeling wrought to its highest tone by the complicated nature of those emotions which swelled her heart. At length, making an effort to regain her composure, " Forgive me, my sister ! " said she. " This is very foolish—to weep when I ought to rejoice—and I do rejoice—and I know I shall be so happy yet ! " But, in spite of the faint smile that accompanied her words, tears again burst from her eyes.

"I am sure I shall have infinite pleasure in your society," replied Adelaide, with her usual sweetness and placidity, as she replaced a ringlet in its proper position; "but I have unluckily an engagement at this time. You will, however, be at no loss for amusement: you will find musical instruments there," pointing to an adjacent apartment; "and here are new publications, and *portefeuilles* of drawings you will perhaps like to look over:" and so saying, she disappeared.

"Musical instruments and new publications!" repeated Mary, mechanically, to herself: "what have I to do with them?—O, for one kind word from my mother's lips!—one kind glance from my sister's eye!"

And she remained overwhelmed with the weight of those emotions which, instead of pouring into the hearts of others, she was compelled to concentrate in her own. Her mournful reveries were interrupted by her kind friend Lady Emily; but Mary deemed her sorrow too sacred to be betrayed even to her, and therefore, rallying her spirits, she strove to enter into those schemes of amusement suggested by her cousin for passing the day. But she found herself unable for such continued exertion; and, hearing a large party was expected to dinner, she retired, in spite of Lady Emily's remonstrances, to her own apartment, where she sought a refuge from her thoughts, in writing to her friends at Glenfern.

Lady Juliana looked in upon her as she passed to dinner. She was in a better humour, for she had received a new dress which was particularly becoming, as both her maid and her glass had attested.

Again Mary's heart bounded towards the being to whom she owed her birth; yet, afraid to give utterance to her feelings, she could only regard her with silent admiration, till a moment's consideration converted that into a less pleasing feeling, as she observed, for the first time, that her mother wore no mourning.

Lady Juliana saw her astonishment, and, little guessing the cause, was flattered by it. "Your style of dress is very obsolete, my dear," said she, as she contrasted the effect of her own figure and her daughter's in a large mirror; "and there's no occasion for you to wear black here. I shall desire my woman to order some things for you; though perhaps there won't be much occasion, as your stay here is to be short; and, of course, you won't think of going out at all. *Apropos,* you will find it dull here by yourself, won't you? I shall leave you my darling Blanche for a companion," kissing a little French lap-dog, as she laid it in Mary's lap; "only you must be very careful of her, and coax her, and be very, very good to her; for I would not have my sweetest Blanche vexed, not for the world!" And, with another long and tender salute to her dog, and a "Good by, my dear!" to her daughter, she quitted her to display her charms to a brilliant drawing-room, leaving Mary to solace herself in her solitary chamber with the whines of a discontented lap-dog.

———o———

Chapter xxxvij.

C'est un personage illustre dans son genre, et qui a porté le talent de bien nourrir jusques où il pouvoit aller;——il ne semble né que pour la digestion.—LA BRUYERE.

IN every season of life, grief brings its own peculiar antidote along with it. The buoyancy of youth soon repels its deadening weight—the firmness of manhood resists its weakening influence—the torpor of old age is insensible to its most acute pangs.

In spite of the disappointment she had experienced the preceding day, Mary arose the following morning with fresh hopes of happiness springing in her heart.

"How foolish I was," thought she, "to view so seriously what, after all, must be merely difference of manner; and how illiberal to expect every one's manners should accord exactly with my ideas! but, now that I have got over the first impression, I dare say I shall find every body quite amiable and delightful."

And Mary quickly reasoned herself into the belief, that she only could have been to blame. With renovated spirits, she therefore joined her cousin, and accompanied her to the breakfasting saloon. The visitors had all departed, but Dr Redgill had returned, and seemed to be at the winding-up of a solitary but voluminous meal. He was a very tall corpulent man, with a projecting front, large purple nose, and a profusion of chin.

"Good morning, ladies!" mumbled he, with a full mouth, as he made a feint of half-rising from his chair. "Lady Emily, your servant—Miss Douglas, I presume —hem! allow me to pull the bell for your ladyship," as he sat without stirring hand or foot; then after it was done—" 'pon my honour, Lady Emily, this is not using me well. Why did you not desire me?—and you are so nimble—I defy any man to get the start of you."

"I know you have been upon hard service, doctor, and therefore I humanely wished to spare you any additional fatigue," replied Lady Emily.

"Fatigue! pooh! I'm sure I mind fatigue as little as any man. Besides, it's really nothing to speak of; I have merely rode from my friend Admiral Yellowchops' this morning."

"I hope you passed a pleasant day there yesterday?"

"So so—very so so," returned the doctor, drily.

"Only so so, and a turtle in the case!" exclaimed Lady Emily.

"Pooh!—as to that, the turtle was neither here nor there. I value turtle as little as any man. You may be sure it wasn't for that I went to see my old friend Yellowchops. It happened, indeed, that there *was* a turtle, and a very well-dressed one, too; but where five-and-thirty people (one half of them ladies, who, of course, are always helped first) sit down to dinner, there's an end of all rational happiness, in my opinion."

"But at a turtle feast you have surely something much better. You know you may have rational happiness any day over a beef-steak."

"I beg your pardon—that's not such an easy matter. I can assure you it is a work of no small skill to dress a beef-steak handsomely; and, moreover, to eat it in perfection, a man must eat it by himself. If once you come to exchange words over it, it is useless. I once saw the finest steak I ever clapt my eyes upon completely ruined by one silly scoundrel asking another if he liked fat. If he liked fat!—what a question for one rational being to ask another! The fact is, a beef-steak is like a woman's reputation; if once it is breathed upon, it's good for nothing!"

"One of the stories with which my nurse used to amuse my childhood," said Mary, "was that of having seen an itinerant conjurer dress a beef-steak on his tongue."

The doctor suspended the morsel he was carrying to his mouth, and for the first time regarded Mary with looks of unfeigned admiration.

"'Pon my honour, and that was as clever a trick as ever I heard of! You are a wonderful people, you Scotch—a very wonderful people—but pray, was she at any pains to examine the fellow's tongue?"

"I imagine not," said Mary: "I suppose the love

of science was not strong enough to make her run the
risk of burning her fingers."

"It's a thousand pities," said the doctor, as he
dropped his chin with an air of disappointment. "I
am surprised none of your Scotch *savans* got hold of
the fellow, and squeezed the secret out of him. It
might have proved an important discovery—a very important discovery;—and your Scotch are not apt to let
anything escape them—a very searching shrewd people
as ever I knew—and that's the only way to arrive at
knowledge. A man must be of a stirring mind if he
expects to do good."

"A poor woman below wishes to see you, sir," said
a servant.

"These poor women are perfect pests to society,"
said the doctor, as his nose assumed a still darker hue;
"there is no resting upon one's seat for them—always
something the matter! They burn, and bruise, and
hack themselves and their brats, one would really think,
on purpose to give trouble."

"I have not the least doubt of it," said Lady Emily;
"they must find your sympathy so soothing."

"As to that, Lady Emily, if you knew as much
about poor women as I do, you wouldn't think so much
of them as you do. Take my word for it—they are,
one and all of them, a very greedy ungrateful set, and
require to be kept at a distance."

"And also to be kept waiting. As poor people's
time is their only wealth, I observe you generally make
them pay a pretty large fee in that way."

"That is not really what I should have expected
from you, Lady Emily. I must take the liberty to
say, your ladyship does me the greatest injustice. You
must be sensible how ready I am to fly," rising as if he
had been glued to his chair, "when there is any real
danger. I'm sure it was only last week I got up as

soon as I had swallowed my dinner, to see a man who had fallen down in a fit; and now I am going to this woman, who, I dare say, has nothing the matter with her, before my breakfast is well down my throat."

"Who is that gentleman?" asked Mary, as the doctor at length, with much reluctance, shuffled out of the room.

"He is a sort of medical aid-de-camp of papa's," answered Lady Emily; "who, for the sake of good-living, has got himself completely domesticated here. He is vulgar, selfish, and *gourmand*, as you must already have discovered; but these are accounted his greatest perfections, as papa, like all indolent people, must be diverted, and *that* he never is by genteel sensible people. He requires something more *piquant*, and nothing fatigues him so much as the conversation of a common-place sensible man—one who has the skill to keep his foibles out of sight. Now, what delights him in Dr Redgill, there is no *retenu*—any child who runs may read his character at a glance."

"It certainly does not require much penetration," said Mary, "to discover the doctor's master passion: love of ease, and self-indulgence, seem to be the predominant features of his mind; and he looks as if, when he sat in an arm-chair, with his toes on the fender, and his hands crossed, he would not have an idea beyond 'I wonder what we shall have for dinner to-day.'"

"I'm glad to hear you say so, Miss Douglas," said the doctor, catching the last words as he entered the room, and taking them to be the spontaneous effusions of the speaker's own heart; "I rejoice to hear you say so. Suppose we send for the bill of fare,"—pulling the bell; and then to the servant who answered the summons, "Desire Grillade to send up his bill—Miss Douglas wishes to see it."

"Young ladies are much more housewifely in Scotland than they are in this country," continued the doctor, seating himself as close as possible to Mary,—"at least they were when I knew Scotland: but that's not yesterday; and it's much changed since then, I dare say. I studied physic in Edinburgh, and went upon a *tower* through the Highlands. I was very much pleased with what I saw, I assure you. Fine country in some respects—Nature has been very liberal."

Mary's heart leapt within her at hearing her dear native land praised even by Dr Redgill, and her conscience smote her for the harsh and hasty censures she had passed upon him. "One who can admire the scenery of the Highlands," thought she, "must have a mind. It has always been observed, that only persons of taste were capable of appreciating the peculiar charms of mountain scenery. A London citizen, or a Lincolnshire grazier, sees nothing but deformity in the sublime works of nature;" *ergo*, reasoned Mary, "Dr Redgill must be of a more elevated way of thinking than I had supposed." The entrance of Lady Juliana prevented her expressing the feelings that were upon her lips; but she thought what pleasure she should have in resuming the delightful theme with the good doctor at another opportunity.

———o———

Chapter xxxviij.

Alas! fond child,
How are thy thoughts beguil'd
To hope for honey from a nest of wasps?

QUARLES.

AFTER slightly noticing her daughter, and carefully adjusting her favourites, Lady Juliana began :—

"I am anxious to consult you, Dr Redgill, upon the

state of this young person's health.—You have been excessively ill, my dear, have you not ? (My sweetest Blanche, do be quiet!) You had a cough, I think, and every thing that was bad.—And as her friends in Scotland have sent her to me for a short time, entirely on account of her health—(my charming Frisk, your spirits are really too much!)—I think it quite proper that she should be confined to her own apartment during the winter, that she may get quite well and strong against spring. As to visiting, or going into company, that, of course, must be quite out of the question.— You can tell Dr Redgill, my dear, all about your complaints yourself."

Mary tried to articulate, but her feelings rose almost to suffocation, and the words died upon her lips.

"Your ladyship confounds me," said the doctor, pulling out his spectacles, which, after duly wiping, he adjusted on his nose, and turned their beams full on Mary's face—"I really never should have guessed there was any thing the matter with the young lady. She does look a *leetle* delicate, to be sure—changing colour, too ;—but hand cool—eye clear—pulse steady, a *leetle* impetuous, but that's nothing ; and the appetite good. I own I was surprised to see you cut so good a figure at the toast ; after the delicious meals you have been accustomed to in the north, you must find it miserable picking here. An English breakfast," glancing with contempt at the eggs, muffins, toast, preserves, &c. &c. he had collected round him, "is really a most insipid meal : if I did not make a rule of rising early and taking regular exercise, I doubt very much if I should be able to swallow a mouthful—there's nothing to whet the appetite here ; and it's the same every where ; as Yellowchops says, our breakfasts are a disgrace to England. One would think the whole nation was upon a regimen of tea and toast—from the

Land's End to Berwick-on-Tweed, nothing but tea
and toast ! Your ladyship must really acknowledge the
prodigious advantage the Scotch possess over us in that
respect."

" I thought the breakfasts, like everything else in
Scotland, extremely disgusting," replied her ladyship,
with indignation.

" Ha ! well, that really amazes me. The people I
give up—they are dirty and greedy; the country, too,
is a perfect mass of rubbish ; and the dinners not fit
for dogs—the cookery, I mean ; as to the materials,
they are admirable. But the breakfasts ! that's what
redeems the land—and every country has its own
peculiar excellence. In Argyleshire you have the
Lochfine herring—fat, luscious, and delicious, just out
of the water, falling to pieces with its own richness—
melting away like butter in your mouth. In Aberdeen-
shire you have the Finnan haddo', with a flavour all its
own, vastly relishing—just salt enough to be *piquant,*
without parching you up with thirst. In Perthshire
there is the Tay salmon, kippered, crisp, and juicy—a
very magnificent morsel—a *leetle* heavy, but that's easily
counteracted by a tea-spoonful of the Athole whisky.
In other places you have the exquisite mutton of the
country, made into hams of a most delicate flavour ;
flour scones, soft and white ; oat-cake, thin and crisp ;
marmalade and jams of every description ; and ——
But I beg pardon !—your ladyship was upon the subject
of this young lady's health. 'Pon my honour ! I can
see little the matter—we were just going to look over
the bill together when your ladyship entered. I see it
begins with that eternal *soupe santé,* and that paltry
potage-au-riz—this is the second day within a week
Monsieur Grillade has thought fit to treat us with
them ; and it's a fortnight yesterday since I have seen
either oyster or turtle soup upon the table. 'Pon my

honour ! such inattention is infamous. I know Lord
Courtland detests *soupe santé*, or, what's the same thing,
he's quite indifferent to it—for I take indifference and
dislike to be much the same : a man's indifference to
his dinner is a serious thing, and so I shall let Monsieur
Grillade know." And the doctor's chin rose and fell
like the waves of the sea.

" What is the name of the physician at Bristol, who
is so celebrated for consumptive complaints ? " asked
Lady Juliana of Adelaide. " I shall send for him ; he
is the only person I have any reliance upon. I know
he always recommends confinement for consumption."

Tears dropped from Mary's eyes. Lady Juliana
regarded her with surprise and severity.

" How very tiresome ! I really can't stand these
perpetual *scènes*. Adelaide, my love, pull the bell for
my *eau de Cologne*. Dr Redgill, place the screen there.
This room is insufferably hot. My dogs will literally
be roasted alive ! " and her ladyship fretted about in all
the perturbation of ill-humour.

"'Pon my honour ! I don't think the room hot,"
said the doctor, who, from a certain want of tact, and
opacity of intellect, never comprehended the feelings of
others : " I declare I have felt it much hotter when
your ladyship has complained of the cold : but there's
no accounting for people's feelings. If you would
move your seat a *leetle* this way, I think you would be
cooler ; and as to your daughter "——

" I have repeatedly desired, Dr Redgill, that you
will not use these familiar appellations when you address
me or any of my family ! " interrupted Lady Juliana,
with haughty indignation.

" I beg pardon," said the doctor, nowise discomposed
at this rebuff.—" Well, with regard to Miss—Miss—
this young lady, I assure your ladyship you need be
under no apprehensions on her account. She's a *leetle*

nervous, that's all; take her about, by all means—all young ladies love to go about and see sights. Show her the pump-room, and the ball-room, and the shops, and the rope-dancers, and the wild beasts, and there's no fear of her. I never recommend confinement to man, woman, or child. It destroys the appetite—and our appetite is the best part of us. What would we be without appetites? Miserable beings! worse than the beasts of the field!"—And away shuffled the doctor to admonish Monsieur Grillade on the iniquity of neglecting this the noblest attribute of man.

"It appears to me excessively extraordinary," said Lady Juliana, addressing Mary, "that Mrs Douglas should have alarmed me so much about your health, when it seems there's nothing the matter with you. She certainly showed very little regard for my feelings. I can't understand it; and I must say, if you are not ill, I have been most excessively ill-used by your Scotch friends." And, with an air of great indignation, her ladyship swept out of the room, regardless of the state into which she had thrown her daughter.

Poor Mary's feelings were now at their climax, and she gave way to all the repressed agony that swelled her heart. Lady Emily, who had been amusing herself at the other end of the saloon, and had heard nothing of what had passed, flew towards her at sight of her suffering, and eagerly demanded of Adelaide the cause.

"I really don't know," answered Adelaide, lifting her beautiful eyes from her book with the greatest composure; "Lady Juliana is always cross of a morning."

"Oh, no!" exclaimed Mary, trying to regain her composure, "the fault is mine. I—I have offended my mother, I know not how. Tell me!—O tell me, how I can obtain her forgiveness?"

"Obtain her forgiveness!" repeated Lady Emily, indignantly, "for what?"

" Alas ! I know not, but in some way I have displeased my mother ; her looks—her words—her manner
—all tell me how dissatisfied she is with me ; while to
my sister, and even to her very dogs "—— Here
Mary's agitation choked her utterance.

" If you expect to be treated like a dog, you will
certainly be disappointed," said Lady Emily. " I
wonder Mrs Douglas did not warn you of what you
had to expect. She must have known something of
Lady Juliana's ways, and it would have been as well
had you been better prepared to encounter them."

Mary looked hurt, and, making an effort to conquer
her emotion, she said, " Mrs Douglas never spoke of
my mother with disrespect, but she did warn me against
expecting too much from her affection. She said I had
been too long estranged from her, to have retained my
place in her heart ; but still "——

" You could not foresee the reception you have met
with ? Nor I, neither. Did you, Adelaide ? "

" Lady Juliana is sometimes so odd," answered her
daughter, in her sweetest tone, " that I really am seldom
surprised at anything she does ; but all this *fracas*
appears to me perfectly absurd, as nobody minds anything she says."

" Impossible ! " exclaimed Mary, " my duty must
ever be to reverence my mother—my study should be to
please to her, if I only knew how ; and oh ! would she
but suffer me to love her ! "——

" My dear cousin," said Lady Emily, " you speak a
very sweet, but an unknown language here : we none
of us make the least pretence to love and reverence
each other — quite the reverse, as Adelaide knows :
being reasonable people, all we aim at is, to keep from
hating and despising one another ;—so give me all the
love you have brought with you from your warm-hearted
highland, and I will keep it till I find some one more

worthy than myself to bestow it upon. As for reverence, truly I cannot, at this moment, recommend any individual in this family to whom I think it is due. But, my dear cousin, do not weep at my nonsense ; you will understand us all by-and-by, and find, perhaps, that we are not so very bad as we appear ; only we don't yet quite understand each other,—is it not so, Adelaide ? "

But Adelaide regarded her sister for a moment with a look of surprise, then rose and left the room, humming an Italian air.

Lady Emily remained with her cousin, but she was a bad comforter ; her indignation against the oppressor was always much stronger than her sympathy with the oppressed, and she would have been more in her element scolding the mother than soothing the daughter.

But Mary had not been taught to trust to mortals weak as herself for support in the hour of trial : she knew her aid must come from a higher source, and in solitude she sought for consolation.

" This must be all for my good," sighed she, " else it would not be. I had drawn too bright a picture of happiness—already it is blotted out with my tears. I must set about replacing it with one of soberer colours."

Alas ! Mary knew not how many a fair picture of human felicity had shared the same fate as hers !

END OF VOL. I.

MARRIAGE.

——— ✳ ———

Chapter xxxix.

They were in sooth a most enchanting train;
——————————— skilful to unite
With evil good, and strew with pleasure pain.
Castle of Indolence.

IN writing to her maternal friend, Mary did not
follow the mode usually adopted by young ladies
of the heroic cast, viz. that of giving a minute
and circumstantial detail of their own complete wretchedness, and abusing, in terms highly sentimental, every
member of the family with whom they are associated.
Mary knew, that to breathe a hint of her own unhappiness would be to embitter the peace of those she loved;
and she therefore strove to conceal from their observation the disappointment she had experienced. Many
a sigh was heaved, however, and many a tear was
wiped away ere a letter could be composed that would
carry pleasure to the dear group at Glenfern; for she
felt, though she dared not even to herself express it.——

To me more dear, congenial to my heart,
One native charm than all the gloss of art.

She could say nothing of her mother's tenderness, or

her sister's affection ; but she dwelt upon the elegance of the one, and the beauty of the other. She could not boast of the warmth of her uncle's reception, but she praised his good-humour, and enlarged upon Lady Emily's kindness and attention. Even Dr Redgill's admiration of Scotch breakfasts was given as a *bonne bouche* for her good old aunts.

" I declare," said Miss Grizzy, as she ended her fifth perusal of the letter, " Mary must be a happy creature ! Everybody must allow—indeed I never heard it disputed, that Lady Juliana is a most elegant being ; and I dare say she is greatly improved since we saw her, for you know that it is a long time ago."

" The mind may improve after a certain age," replied Jacky, with one of her wisest looks, " but I doubt very much if the person does."

" If the inside had been like the out, there would have been no need for improvement," observed Nicky.

" I'm sure you are both perfectly right," resumed the sapient Grizzy ; " and I have not the least doubt but that our dear niece is a great deal wiser than when we knew her : nobody can deny but she is a great deal older ; and you know people always grow wiser as they grow older, of course."

" They *ought* to do it," said Jacky, with emphasis.

" But there's no fool like an old fool," quoth Nicky.

" What a delightful creature our charming niece Adelaide must be, from Mary's account," said Grizzy ; " only I can't conceive how her eyes come to be black. I'm sure there's not a black eye amongst us. The Kilnacroish family are black, to be sure ; and Kilnacroish's great grandmother was first cousin, once removed, to our grandfather's aunt by the mother's side : it's wonderful the length that resemblances run in some old families ; and I really can't account for our niece Adelaide's black eyes naturally, any other way than just through the Kilnacroish family; for I'm quite convinced it's from us she takes them; children always take their eyes from their father's side: every body knows that Becky's, and Bella's, and Babby's are all as like their poor father's as they can stare."

"There's no accounting for the varieties of the human species," said Jacky.

"And like's an ill mark," observed Nicky.

"And only think of her being so much taller than Mary, and twins!—I declare it's wonderful. I should have thought—indeed I never doubted—that they would have been exactly the same size. And such a beautiful colour, too, when we used to think Mary rather pale—it's very unaccountable!"

"You forget," said Jacky, who had not forgot the insult offered to her nursing system eighteen years before; "you forget that I always predicted what would happen."

"I never knew any good come of changes," said Nicky.

"I'm sure that's very true," rejoined Grizzy; "and we have great reason to thank our stars that Mary is not a perfect dwarf, which I really thought she would have been for long, till she took a shooting, summer was a year."

"But she'll shoot no more," said Jacky, with a shake of the head that might have vied with Jove's imperial nod; "England's not the place for shooting."

"The English women are all poor droichs," said Nicky, who had seen three in the course of her life.

"It's a great matter to us all, however, and to herself too, poor thing! that Mary should be so happy," resumed Grizzy. "I'm sure I don't know what she would have done, if Lord Courtland had been an ill-tempered harsh man, which, you know, he might just as easily have been; and it would really have been very hard upon poor Mary—and Lady Emily such a sweet creature, too! I'm sure we must all allow we have the greatest reason to be thankful; there can be no doubt about that!"

"I don't know," said Jacky; "Mary was petted enough before; I wish she may have a head to stand any more."

"She'll be ten times nicer than ever," quoth Nicky.

"There is some reason, to be sure, that can't be denied, to be afraid of that; at the same time, Mary has a great deal of sense of her own when she chooses; and it's a great matter for her, and indeed for all of us, that she is under the eye of such a sensible worthy man as that Dr Redgill. Of course, we may be sure, Lord Courtland will keep a most elegant table, and have a great variety of sweet things, which are certainly very tempting for young people; but I have no doubt but Dr Redgill will look after Mary, and see that she doesn't eat too many of them."

"Dr Redgill must be a very superior man," pronounced Jacky, in her most magisterial manner.

"If I could hear of a private opportunity," exclaimed Nicky, in a transport of generosity, "I would send them one of our hams, and a nice little pig * of butter —the English are all great people for butter."

The proposal was hailed with rapture by both sisters in a breath; and it was finally settled, that, to those tender pledges of Nicky's, Grizzy should add a bottle of Lady Maclaughlan's latest invented lotion, while Miss Jacky was to compose the epistle that was to accompany them.

The younger set of aunts were astonished that Mary had said nothing about lovers and offers of marriage, as they had always considered going to England as synonymous with going to be married.

* Jar.

To Mrs Douglas's more discerning eye, Mary's happiness did not appear in so dazzling a light as to the weaker optics of her aunts.

" It is not like my Mary," thought she, " to rest so much on mere external advantages ; surely, her warm affectionate heart cannot be satisfied with the *grace* of a mother, and the *beauty* of a sister : these she might admire in a stranger ; but where we seek for happiness, we better prize more homely attributes.   Yet Mary is so open and confiding, I think she could not have concealed from me, had she experienced a disappointment."

Mrs Douglas was not aware of the effect of her own practical lessons ; and that, while she was almost unconsciously practising the quiet virtues of patience, and fortitude, and self-denial, and unostentatiously sacrificing her own wishes to promote the comfort of others— her example, like a kindly dew, was shedding its silent influence on the embryo blossoms of her pupil's heart.

——o——

Chapter xi.

—— So the devil prevails often ; *opponit nubem*, he claps a cloud between ; some little objection ; a stranger is come ; or my head aches ; or the church is too cold ; or I have letters to write ; or I am not disposed ; or it is not yet time ; or the time is past : these, and such as these, are the clouds the devil claps between heaven and us ; but these are such impotent objections, that they were as soon confuted, as pretended, by all men that are not fools, or professed enemies of religion.

JEREMY TAYLOR.

LADY JULIANA had in vain endeavoured to obtain a sick certificate for her daughter, that would have authorised her consigning her to the oblivion of her own apartment.   The physicians, whom she consulted, all agreed, for once, in recommending a

totally different system to be pursued; and her displeasure, in consequence, was violently excited against
the medical tribe in general, and Dr Redgill in particular.   For that worthy she had, indeed, always entertained a most thorough contempt and aversion; for he
was poor, ugly, and vulgar, and these were the three
most deadly sins in her calendar.   The object of her
detestation was, however, completely insensible to its
effects.   The doctor, like Achilles, was vulnerable but
in one part, and over that she could exercise no control.   She had nothing to do with the *menage*—possessed no influence over Lord Courtland, nor authority
over Monsieur Grillade.   She differed from himself as
to the dressing of certain dishes; and, in short, he
summed up her character in one emphatic sentence,
that, in his idea, conveyed severer censure than all that
Pope or Young ever wrote—" I don't think she has the
taste of her mouth ! "

Thus thwarted in her scheme, Lady Juliana's dislike
to her daughter rather increased than diminished: and
it was well for Mary, that lessons of forbearance had
been early infused into her mind; for her spirit was
naturally high, and would have revolted from the
tyranny and injustice with which she was treated, had
she not been taught the practical duties of Christianity,
and that "patience, with all its appendages, is the sum-
total of all our duty that is proper to the day of
sorrow."

Not that Mary sought, by a blind compliance with all
her mother's follies and caprices, to ingratiate herself
into her favour—even the motive she would have
deemed insufficient to have sanctified the deed.   And
the only arts she employed to win a place in her parent's
heart, were ready obedience, unvarying sweetness, and
uncomplaining submission.

Although Mary possessed none of the sour bigotry

of a narrow mind, she was yet punctual in the discharge
of her religious duties; and the Sunday following her
arrival, as they sat at breakfast she inquired of her cousin
at what time the church-service began?

"I really am not certain—I believe it is late," replied her cousin, carelessly. "But why do you ask?"

"Because I wish to be there in proper time."

"But we scarcely ever go in winter—never, indeed,
to the parish church, it is so cold—and we are rather
distant from any other; so you must say your prayers at
home."

"I should certainly prefer going to church," said
Mary.

"Going to church!" exclaimed Dr Redgill. "I
wonder what makes people so keen of going to church!
For my part, I declare I would just as soon think of
going into my grave in this weather. Take my word
for it, churches and churchyards are rather too nearly
related."

"In such a day as this," said Mary, "so dry and
sunny, I am sure there can be no danger."

"Take your own way, Miss Mary," said the doctor;
"but I think it my duty to let you know my opinion of
churches. I look upon them as extremely prejudicial
to the health. They are, invariably, either too hot or
too cold; you are either stewed or starved in them;
and, till some improvement takes place, I assure you my
foot shall never enter one of them. In fact, they are
perfect receptacles of human infirmities. I can tell one
of your church-going ladies at a glance: they have all
rheumatisms in their shoulders, and colds in their heads,
and swelled faces. Besides, it's a poor country church
—there's nothing to be seen after you do go."

"I assure you, Lady Juliana will be excessively
annoyed if you go," said Lady Emily, as Mary rose
to leave the room.

" Surely my mother cannot be displeased at my attending church ! " said Mary, in astonishment.

" Yes, she can, and most certainly will. She never goes herself now to the parish church, since she had a quarrel with Dr Barlow, the clergyman ; and she can't bear any of the family to attend him."

" And you have my sanction for staying away, Miss Mary," added the doctor.

" Is he a man of bad character ? " asked Mary, as she stood irresolute whether to proceed.

" Quite the reverse. He is a very good man ; but he was scandalised at Lady Juliana's bringing her dog to church one day, and wrote her what she conceived a most insolent letter about it.—But here comes your lady-mamma, and the culprit in question."

" Your ladyship is just come in time to settle a dispute here," said the doctor, anxious to turn her attention from a hot muffin, which had just been brought in, and which he meditated appropriating to himself : " I have said all I can say—(Was you looking at the toast, Lady Emily ?)—I must now leave it to your ladyship to convince this young lady of the risk she runs in going to church this cold day."

The doctor gained his point. The muffin was upon his own plate, while Lady Juliana directed her angry look towards her daughter.

" Who talks of going to church ? " inquired she, peevishly.

Mary gently expressed her wish to be permitted to attend divine service.

" No—I can't permit it—the weather is much too cold for going to church. I don't intend to go myself, and I don't approve of your going."

" It is the only place I shall ask to go to," said Mary, timidly ; " but I have always been accustomed to attend church, and—— "

"Your Scotch customs can be no rule here," interrupted her mother, angrily. "I, too, have been accustomed to attend church when circumstances permit, which they don't do at present. When I go, you shall accompany me."

"I am sure I shall not suffer from going—the day is so fine, and I feel quite well"——

"You have made a wonderfully rapid recovery," said her ladyship, in a tone which brought tears to poor Mary's eyes; "but Dr Redgill is of a different opinion, and disapproves of your attending church: and, besides, I disapprove of any of my family going there; I consider the clergyman is quite a Methodist."

"I assure you the Methodists are gaining ground very fast," said the doctor, with his mouth full; "'pon my word, I think we had all need to look about us—'tis very alarming!"

"Pray, doctor, what is so alarming in the apprehension?" inquired Lady Emily.

"What is so alarming! 'Pon my honour, Lady Emily, I'm astonished to hear you ask such a question!"—muttering to himself, "zealots—fanatics—enthusiasts—bedlamites! I'm sure everybody knows what Methodists are—and we'll be all Methodists before long, I can tell you, if we don't take care!"

"Indeed!" exclaimed Lady Emily; "then who knows, doctor, but we may yet see you the founder of a sect—the Redgill Methodists?—it sounds well—a Redgillian! most euphonious, is it not?" addressing Lady Juliana with an air of affected softness.

But her ladyship was too much enraged to notice her; so, turning to Mary with repressed feelings and assumed dignity, she said,—

"There has been a great deal too much said on this subject. I take it for granted you have a prayer-book, and can read the church service, and"——

"And there are plenty of good sermons in the house," interposed the doctor, who, like many other people, thought he was always doing a meritorious action when he could dissuade anybody from going to church. "I saw a volume somewhere not long ago; and, at any rate, there's the 'Spectator,' if you want Sunday's reading—some of the papers there are as good as any sermon you'll get from Dr Barlow."

Mary, with fear and hesitation, made another attempt to overcome her mother's prejudice, but in vain.

"I desire I may hear no more about it!" cried she, raising her voice. "The clergyman is a most improper person. I won't suffer any of my family to attend his church; and it does not suit me at all times to go to a greater distance,—certainly not to-day; and therefore, once for all, I won't hear another syllable on the subject."

This was said in a tone and manner not to be disputed, and Mary felt her resolution give way before the displeasure of her mother. A contest of duties was new to her, and she could not all at once resolve upon fulfilling one duty at the expense of another. "Besides," thought she, "my mother thinks she is in the right. Perhaps, by degrees, I may bring her to think otherwise; and it is surely safer to try to conciliate, than to determine to oppose."

As for Lady Juliana, she exulted in the wise and judicious manner in which she had exercised her authority, and felt her consequence greatly increased by a public display of it: power being an attribute she was very seldom invested with now. Indeed, to do her ladyship justice, she was most feelingly alive to the duty to parents, though that such a commandment existed seemed quite unknown to her till she became a mother. But she made ample amends for former deficiencies now : as to hear her expatiate on the subject, one would have deemed it the only duty necessary to be practised, either by Christian or heathen, and that, like charity, it comprehended every virtue, and was a covering for every sin. But there are many more sensible people than her ladyship, who entertain the same sentiments, and, by way of variety, reverse the time and place of their duties. When they are children, they make many judicious reflections on the duties of parents; when they become parents, they then acquire a wonderful insight into the duties of children. In the same manner, husbands and wives are completely alive to the duties incumbent upon each other; and the most ignorant servant is fully instructed in the duty of a master. But we shall leave Lady Juliana to pass over the duties of parents, and ponder upon those of children; while we give the conclusion of an argument which had been carrying on between Lady Emily and Doctor Redgill. How it had commenced did not appear; but the doctor's voice was raised as if to bring it to a triumphant termination.

"The French, madam, in spite of your prejudices, are a very superior people to us. I don't speak of their religion—that we have nothing to do with; but their skill and knowledge in arts and sciences are infinitely higher than ours. Every man in France is a first-rate cook; in fact, they are a nation of cooks; and one of our late travellers informs us, that for one thing they have discovered no fewer than three hundred methods of dressing eggs—three hundred different methods of dressing eggs!"

"That is just two hundred and ninety-nine ways more than enough," said Lady Emily; "give me the good old English character, and a plain boiled fresh egg, and you are welcome to the whole tribe of French encyclopedists and gastronomists, with all their ennobling discoveries. Indeed, I desire no other variety of the produce of a hen, till it takes the form of a chicken."

Doctor Redgill lowered his eyebrows, and drew up his chin, but disdained to waste more argument upon so tasteless a being. "To talk sensibly to a woman," muttered he, " is like feeding chickens upon turtle soup —they can't stand it ! "

————o————

Chapter xlj.

Hail, Sabbath ! thee I hail, the poor man's friend !
GRAHAME.

—— Thy creatures have been my books; but thy Scriptures much more. I have sought thee in thy courts, fields, and gardens, but I have found thee in thy temples.
LORD BACON

ANOTHER Sabbath came, and Mary found she had made no progress in obtaining the desired permission. She therefore began seriously to commune with her own heart as to the course she ought to pursue; praying at the same time for that direction from above, without which all communings are vain.

The commandment of "Honour thy father and thy mother" had been deeply imprinted on her mind, and few possessed higher notions of filial reverence; but there was another divine precept which came also to her heart, "Whosoever loveth father and mother more than me cannot be my disciple."

"But I may honour and obey my mother, without loving her more than my Saviour," argued she with herself, in hopes of lulling her conscience by this reflection. "But again," thought she, "the Scripture says, 'He that keepeth my commandments, he it is that loveth me.'" Then she felt the necessity of owning

that if she obeyed the commands of her mother when
in direct opposition to the will of God, she gave
one of the Scripture proofs of either loving or fearing
her parent upon earth more than her Father which is in
heaven. But eager to reconcile impossibilities,—viz.
the will of an ungodly parent with the commands of her
Maker, Mary thought of another argument to calm her
conscience. " The Bible," said she, " says nothing positive about the necessity of attending public worship, and,
as Lady Emily says, I may say my prayers just as well at
home." Again, however, passages of Holy Writ rose
to her recollection. " Lift up your hands in the
sanctuary, and bless the Lord." " I will come into
thy house in the multitude of thy mercy ; and in thy
fear will I worship toward thy holy temple." " For-
sake not the assembling of yourselves together."
" Where two or three are gathered together in my
name, there will I be in the midst of them ; " &c.
&c. But, alas ! two or three never were gathered
together at Beech Park, except upon parties of pleasure,
games of hazard, or purposes of conviviality.

The result of Mary's deliberations was, a firm
determination to do what she deemed her duty,
however painful. She therefore went in search of
Lady Emily, hoping to prevail upon her to use her
influence with Lady Juliana to grant the desired permission ; or should she fail in obtaining it, she trusted
her resolution would continue strong enough to enable
her to brave her mother's displeasure in this act of con-
scientious disobedience. She met her cousin, with her
bonnet on, prepared to go out.

" Dear Lady Emily," said she, " let me entreat of
you to use your influence with my mother, to persuade
her to allow me to go to church."

" In the first place," answered her cousin, " you
may know that I have no influence ;—in the second,

that Lady Juliana is never to be persuaded into anything ;—in the third, I really can't suppose you are
serious in thinking it a matter of such vast moment
whether or not you go to church."

"Indeed I do," answered Mary, earnestly. "I have
been taught to consider it as such ; and "——

"Pshaw ! nonsense ! these are some of your stiff-
necked Presbyterian notions. I shall really begin to
suspect you are a Methodist ; and yet you are not at
all like one."

"Pray, tell me," said Mary, with a smile, "what
are your ideas of a Methodist ?"

"Oh ! thank Heaven, I know little about them !—
almost as little as Dr Redgill, who, I verily believe,
could scarcely tell the difference between a Catholic
and a Methodist, except that the one dances, and
t'other prays.   But I am rather inclined to believe
a Methodist is a sort of a scowling, black - browed,
hard-favoured creature, with lank hair combed straight
upon its flat forehead, and that twirls its thumbs, and
turns up its eyes, and speaks through its nose ; and, in
short, is every thing that you are not, except in this
matter—of going to church.   So, to avert all these evil
signs from falling upon you, I shall make a point of
your keeping company with me for the rest of the
day."

Again Mary became serious, as she renewed her
entreaties to her cousin to intercede with Lady Juliana
that she might be allowed to attend *any* church.

"Not for kingdoms ! " exclaimed she. " Her
ladyship is in one of her most detestable humours
to-day ; not that I should mind that, if it was anything of real consequence that I had to compass for
you. A ball, for instance—I should certainly stand
by you there ; but I am really not so fond of mischief
as to enrage her for nothing ! "

" Then I fear I must go to church without leave,"
said Mary, in a melancholy tone.

" If you are to go at all, it must certainly be without
it; but (not to torment you any longer) here is the
carriage which I ordered for the purpose of carrying us
to church. You shall go under my auspices. I am
quite ready to bear all the blame, and to suffer the full
penalty of her ladyship's wrath; so, you see, I have
something of the spirit of a martyr in me. Now get
your cloak, and let us be gone."

Mary warmly thanked her cousin, and hastening to
obey her injunctions, they were speedily on their way
to church. The road lay by the side of a river; and
though Mary's taste had been formed upon the wild
romantic scenery of the Highlands, she yet looked with
pleasure on the tamer beauties of an English landscape.
And though accustomed to admire even

> "Rocks where the snow flake reposes,"

she had also taste, though of a less enthusiastic kind,
for the

> "Gay landscapes and gardens of roses,"

which, in this more genial clime, bloomed even under
winter's sway. The carriage drove smoothly along,
and the sound of the church-bells fell at intervals on
the ear,

> " In cadence sweet, now dying all away; "

and at the holy sound, Mary's heart flew back to the
peaceful vale and primitive kirk of Lochmarlie, where
all her happy sabbaths had been passed.

> " If ought there be upon this rude bad earth,
>   Which angels from their happy spheres above
>   Could lean and listen to,
>   It were those peaceful sounds."

The view now opened upon the village church,

beautifully situated on the slope of a green hill. Parties of straggling villagers, in their holiday suits, were descried in all directions : some already assembled in the church-yard, others swarming the sheltered lanes and neat foot-paths which led through the meadows. Old age was there in clean, though antiquated garments, with its silver locks, faded cheek, and feeble step, moving slowly along. And there were the hale and hearty, in man's vigour and woman's matronly prime, and ruddy youths and fair maidens, and blooming boys and girls, walking sedately hand in hand ; and the prim charity-school troops, casting wistful side-glances at the free step and wider range of those happy little ones, who feared no harsh chidings from their parent's lips for their occasional harmless deviations from the beaten track. But to Mary's eyes the well-clothed English rustic, trudging carefully along the smooth path, was a far less picturesque object than the bare-footed Highland girl, bounding lightly over trackless heath-covered hills ; and the well-preserved glossy blue coat seemed a poor substitute for the varied drapery of the graceful plaid. So much do early associations tincture all our future ideas.

They had now reached the church—a grave antique-looking building, whose grey ivy-mantled tower proclaimed, not worldly pomp, but heavenly hope, while its meek low-browed porch seemed to echo the hallowed invitation of Him, whose temple is all space, " Come unto me, all ye that are weary and heavy laden, and I will give you rest."

Mary loved the simple ritual of her native land, but she felt and acknowledged the excellence and impressive solemnity of England's church service. Perhaps in every form of Christian worship, the devout heart will find something suited to its wants ; in none will it find all things in perfect accordance with its feelings.

The service was performed in a simple and reverent manner. The prayers were not, perhaps, what is called "beautifully *read!*" but they were felt as the breathings of a lowly, penitent, and devout spirit, in deep prostration in the awful presence of its God. But how discordant—how *unholy* sounded to Mary's unaccustomed ear, the irreverent responses of the clerk, as he gabbled over those sacred echoes which, if heard at all, ought to come from the hearts and lips of a praying people.

The sermon was delivered with the same scriptural simplicity and fervent unction, as coming from the heart of one deeply impressed with the importance of the divine truths he proclaimed, and earnest in enforcing their moral influence in the personal holiness of all who profess to believe them. The organ was good, and Mary felt how well its sublime melody was adapted to solemnize the mind in its approach to God. But the singing was (as is commonly the case) meagre and defective; and surely all must admit that no *merely* instrumental music, however fine that may be, can be so acceptable to the Hearer of prayer and of praise as the voices of his intelligent creatures, combining symphony of voice with sympathy of heart, such as *ought* to be in every Christian congregation. The one, however exquisite, is but the mere vibration of matter on the outward senses, but to render

"The deep worship of the living soul,"

" in the noble psalms of David, as sung by the mingled voices of a large congregation, swelling often to a sublime volume of sound, elevating the mind and quickening the feelings beyond all studied excitements of art,"* is as the melody of heaven begun upon earth.

Far different sounds than those of peace and praise

* Joanna Baillie.

awaited her return.   Lady Juliana, apprised of this open
act of rebellion, was in all the paroxysms incident to a
little mind, on discovering the impotence of its power.
She rejected all attempts at reconciliation ; raved about
ingratitude and disobedience ; declared her determination of sending Mary back to her vulgar Scotch relations
one moment—the next protested she should never see
those odious Methodists again—then she was to take her
to France, and shut her up in a convent, &c., till, after
uttering all the incoherencies usual with ladies in a
passion, she at last succeeded in raving herself into a fit
of hysterics.

Poor Mary was deeply affected at this (to her) tre-
mendous display of passion.   She who had always been
used to the mild placidity of Mrs Douglas, and who
had seen her face sometimes clouded with sorrow, but
never deformed by anger—what a spectacle, to behold
a parent subject to the degrading influence of an un-
governable temper !   Her very soul sickened at the
sight ; and while she wept over her mother's weakness,
she prayed that the Power which stayed the ocean's
wave would mercifully vouchsafe to still the wilder
tempests of human passion.

————o————

Chapter xlij.

Why, all delights are vain ; but that most vain,
Which, with pain purchased, doth inherit pain.
                                                SHAKSPEARE.

IN addition to her mother's implacable wrath, and
unceasing animadversion, Mary found she was
looked upon as a sort of alarming character by the
whole family.   Lord Courtland seemed afraid of being
drawn into a religious controversy every time he ad-

dressed her. Dr Redgill retreated at her approach, and eyed her askance, as much as to say, " 'Pon my honour, a young lady that can fly in her mother's face about such a trifle as going to church, is not very safe company." And Adelaide shunned her more than ever, as if afraid of coming in contact with a professed Methodist. Lady Emily, however, remained stanch to her; and though she had her own private misgivings as to her cousin's creed, she yet stoutly defended her from the charge of Methodism, and maintained that, in many respects, Mary was no better than her neighbours.

" Well, Mary," cried she, as she entered her room one day with an air of exultation, " here is an opportunity for you to redeem your character. There," throwing down a card, " is an invitation for you to a fancy ball."

Mary's heart bounded at the mention of a ball. She had never been at one, and it was pictured in her imagination in all the glowing colours with which youth and inexperience deck untried pleasures.

" O how charming! " exclaimed she, with sparkling eyes; " how my aunts Becky and Bella will love to hear an account of a ball.—And a fancy ball!—what is that?"

Lady Emily explained to her the nature of the entertainment, and Mary was in still greater raptures.

" It will be a perfect scene of enchantment, I have no doubt," continued her cousin, " for Lady M. understands giving balls, which is what every one does not; for there are dull balls as well as dull everythings else in the world. But come, I have left Lady Juliana and Adelaide in grand debate as to their dresses. We must also hold a cabinet council upon ours. Shall I summon the inimitable Slash to preside?"

The mention of her mother recalled Mary's thoughts

from the festive scene to which they had already
flown.

"But are you *quite* sure," said she, "that I shall
have my mother's consent to go?"

"Quite the contrary," answered her cousin, coolly;
"she won't hear of your going. But what signifies that?
you could go to church in spite of her, and surely you
can't think her consent of much consequence to a ball?"

Poor Mary's countenance fell, as the bright vision of
her imagination melted into air.

"Without my mother's permission," said she, "I
shall certainly not think of, or even wish"—with a
sigh—"to go to the ball; and if she has already refused it, that is enough."

Lady Emily regarded her with astonishment. "Pray,
is it only on Sundays you make a point of disobeying
your mother?"

"It is only when I conceive a higher duty is required
of me," answered Mary.

"Why, I confess I used to think that to honour
one's father and mother *was* a duty, till you showed
me the contrary. I have to thank you for ridding me
of that vulgar prejudice. And now, after setting me
such a noble example of independence, you seem to
have got a new light on the subject yourself."

"My obedience and disobedience both proceed from
the same source," answered Mary. "My first duty, I
have been taught, is to worship my Maker—my next
to obey my mother. My own gratification never can
come in competition with either."

"Well, I really can't enter into a religious controversy with you; but it seems to me, the sin, if it is
one, is precisely the same, whether you play the naughty
girl in going to one place or another. I can see no
difference."

"To me it appears very different," said Mary;

" and therefore I should be inexcusable were I to choose the evil, believing it to be such."

" Say what you will," cried her cousin, pettishly, " you will never convince me there can be any harm in disobeying such a mother as yours ; so unreasonable, so ———"

" The Bible makes no exceptions," interrupted Mary, gently ; " it is not because of the reasonableness of our parents' commands that we are required to obey them, but because it is the will of God."

" You certainly are a Methodist—there's no denying it. I have fought some hard battles for you, but I see I must give you up : the thing won't conceal." This was said with such an air of vexation, that Mary burst into a fit of laughter.

" And yet you are the oddest compound," continued her cousin ; " so gay and comical, and so little given to be shocked and scandalised at the wicked ways of others, or to find fault and lecture—or, in short, to do any of the insufferable things that your good people are so addicted to. I really don't know what to think of you."

" Think of me as a creature with too many faults of her own, to presume to meddle with those of others," replied Mary, smiling at her cousin's perplexity.

" Well, if all good people were like you, I do believe I should become a saint myself. If you are right, I must be wrong ; but fifty years hence we shall settle that matter with spectacles on nose, over our bohea. In the meantime, the business of the ball-room is much more pressing : we really must decide upon something. Will you choose your own style, or shall I leave it to Madame Trieur to do us up exactly alike ?"

" You have only to choose for yourself, my dear cousin," answered Mary. " You know I have no interest in it—at least not till I have received my mother's permission."

"I have told you already there is no chance of obtaining it. I had a *brouillerie* with her on the subject before I came to you."

"Then I entreat you will not say another word. It is a thing of so little consequence, that I am quite vexed to think that my mother should have been disturbed about it. Dear Lady Emily, if you love me, promise that you will not say another syllable on the subject."

"And this is all the thanks I get for my trouble and vexation!" exclaimed Lady Emily, angrily; "but the truth is, I believe you think it would be a sin to go to a ball; and as for dancing—Oh shocking!—that would be absolute——. I really can't say the bad word you good people are so fond of using."

"I understand your meaning," answered Mary, laughing; "but, indeed, I have no such apprehensions. On the contrary, I am very fond of dancing; so fond, that I have often taken Aunt Nicky for my partner in a strathspey, rather than sit still; and, to confess my weakness, I should like very much to go to a ball."

"Then you must and shall go to this one. It is really a pity that you should have enraged Lady Juliana so much by that unfortunate church-going; but for that, I think she might have been managed; and even now I should not despair, if you would, like a good girl, beg pardon for what is past, and promise never to do so any more."

"Impossible!" replied Mary. "You surely cannot be serious in supposing I would barter a positive duty for a trifling amusement?"

"Oh, hang duties! they are odious things. And as for your amiable, dutiful, virtuous Goody Two-Shoes characters, I detest them. They never would go down with me, even in the nursery; with all the attractions of a gold watch, and coach-and-six, they were ever my abhorrence, as every species of canting and hypocrisy still is."

Then, struck with a sense of her own violence and impetuosity, contrasted with her cousin's meek unreproving manner, Lady Emily threw her arms around her, begging pardon, and assuring her she did not mean her.

"If you had," said Mary, returning her embrace, "you would only have told me what I am in some respects. Dull and childish I know I am; for I am not the same creature I was at Lochmarlie,"—and a tear trembled in her eye as she spoke—"and troublesome, I am sure, you have found me."

"No, no!" eagerly interrupted Lady Emily; "you are the reverse of all that. You are the picture of my Edward, and everything that is excellent and engaging; and I see, by that smile, you will go to the ball—there's a darling!"

Mary shook her head.

"I'll tell you what we can do," cried her persevering patroness; "we can go as masks, and Lady Juliana shall know nothing about it. That will save the scandal of an open revolt, or a tiresome dispute. Half the company will be masked; so, if you keep your own secret, nobody will find it out. Come, what characters shall we choose?"

"That of Janus, I think, would be the most suitable for me," said Mary. Then, in a serious tone, she added, "I can neither disobey nor deceive my mother. Therefore, once for all, my dear cousin, let me entreat of you to be silent on a subject on which my mind is made up. I am perfectly sensible of your kindness, but any further discussion will be very painful to me."

Lady Emily was now too indignant to stoop to remonstrance. She quitted her cousin in great anger, and poor Mary felt as if she had lost her only friend.

"Alas!" sighed she, "how difficult it is to do
right, when even the virtues of others throw obstacles
in our way! and how easy our duties would be, could
we kindly aid one another in the performance of
them!"

But such is human nature. The real evils of life,
of which we so loudly complain, are few in number,
compared to the daily, hourly pangs we inflict on one
another.

Lady Emily's resentment, though violent, was short-
lived; and, in the certainty that either the mother
would relent, or the daughter rebel, she ordered a dress
for Mary; but the night of the ball arrived, and both
remained unshaken in their resolution. With a few
words, Adelaide might have obtained the desired permission for her sister, but she chose to remain neuter,
coldly declaring she never interfered in quarrels.

Mary beheld the splendid dresses and gay countenances of the party for the ball with feelings free from
envy, though perhaps not wholly unmixed with regret.
She gazed with the sincerest admiration on the extreme
beauty of her sister, heightened as it was by the fantastic
elegance of her dress, and contrasted with her own pale
visage and mourning habiliments.

"Indeed," thought she, as she turned from the
mirror, with rather a mournful smile, "my aunt Nicky
was in the right: I certainly am a poor *shilpit* thing."

As she looked again at her sister, she observed that
her ear-rings were not so handsome as those she had
received from Mrs Mackshake, and she instantly
brought them, and requested Adelaide would wear
them for that night.

"I have looked with more respect upon ear-rings,"
said she, with a smile, "since I somewhere read of a
pretty fancy of the ancients, who, it seems, sent a
present of them to their friends on their birth-days, in

token that they should consecrate their ears to amity,
and (as the old *tome* expressed it) 'preoccupate them
against slander.' "

Adelaide took them with her usual coolness—remarked how very magnificent they were—wished some
old woman would take it into her head to make her
such a present; and, as she clasped them in her ears,
regarded herself with increased complacency. The
hour of departure arrived; Lord Courtland and Lady
Juliana were at length ready, and Mary found herself
left to a *tête-à-tête* with Dr Redgill; and, strange as it
may seem, neither in a sullen nor melancholy mood.
But after a single sigh, as the carriage drove off, she
sat down with a cheerful countenance to play at back-
gammon with the doctor.

The following day, she heard of nothing but the
ball and its delights; for both her mother and cousin
sought (though from different motives) to heighten her
regret at not having been there. But Mary listened to
the details of all she had missed with perfect fortitude,
and only rejoiced to hear they had all been so happy.

——o——

Chapter xliij.

Day follows night. The clouds return again
After the falling of the latter rain;
But to the aged blind shall ne'er return
Grateful vicissitude: She still must mourn
The sun, and moon, and every starry light,
Eclipsed to her, and lost in everlasting night.
PRIOR.

AMONGST the numerous letters and parcels with
which Mary had been entrusted by the whole
county of ——, there was one she had received
from the hands of Lady Maclaughlan, with a strict

injunction to be the bearer of it herself; and as even Lady Maclaughlan's wishes now wore an almost sacred character in Mary's estimation, she was very desirous of fulfilling this her parting charge. But, in the thraldom in which she was kept, she knew not how that was to be accomplished. She could not venture to wait upon the lady to whom it was addressed, without her mother's permission; and she was aware, that to ask was upon every occasion only to be refused. In this dilemma, she had recourse to Lady Emily; and, showing her the letter, craved her advice and assistance.

"Mrs Lennox, Rose Hall," said her cousin, reading the superscription. "Oh, I don't think Lady Juliana will care a straw about your going there. She is merely an unfortunate blind old lady, whom everybody thinks it a bore to visit — myself, I'm afraid, amongst the number. We ought to have called upon her ages ago —so I shall go with you now."

Permission for Mary to accompany her was easily obtained; for Lady Juliana considered a visit to Mrs Lennox as an act of penance rather than of pleasure; and Adelaide protested that the very mention of her name gave her the vapours. There certainly was nothing that promised much gratification in what Mary had heard; and yet she already felt interested in this unfortunate blind lady, whom everybody thought it a bore to visit, and she sought to gain some more information respecting her. But Lady Emily, though possessed of warm feelings, and kindly affections, was little given to frequent the house of mourning, or sympathise with the wounded spirit; and she yawned, as she declared she was sorry for poor Mrs Lennox, and would have made a point of seeing her oftener, could she have done her any good.

"But what can I possibly say to her," continued she, "after losing her husband, and having I don't know how many sons killed in battle, and her only daughter dying of a consumption, and herself going blind in consequence of her grief for all these misfortunes—What can I possibly do for her, or say to her? Were I in her situation, I am sure I should hate the sight and sound of any human being, and should give myself up entirely to despair."

" That would be but a pagan sacrifice," said Mary.

" What would you do in such desperate circumstances?" demanded Lady Emily.

" I would hope," answered Mary, meekly.

" But, in poor Mrs Lennox's case, that would be to hope though hope were lost; for what can she hope for now? She has still something to fear, however, as I believe she has one son remaining, who is in the brunt of every battle; of course, she has nothing to expect but accounts of his death."

" But she may hope that Heaven will preserve him, and ——"

" That you will marry him. That would do excellently well, for he is as brave as a real Highlander, though he has the misfortune to be only half a one. His father, General Lennox, was a true Scot to the very tip of his tongue, and as proud and fiery as any chieftain need be. *His* death, certainly, was an improvement in the family. But there is Rose Hall, with its pretty shrubberies, and nice parterres;—what do you say to becoming its mistress?"

" If I am to lay snares," answered Mary, laughing, " it must be for nobler objects than hedge-row elms and hillocks green."

" Oh! it must be for black crags and naked hills! Your country really does vastly well to rave about! Lofty mountains and deep glens, and blue lakes and roaring rivers, are mighty fine sounding things; but I suspect corn fields and barn yards are quite as comfortable neighbours : so take my advice, and marry Charles Lennox."

Mary only answered by singing, " My heart's in the Highlands, my heart is not here," &c. as the carriage drew up.

" This is the property of Mrs Lennox," said Lady Emily, in answer to some remark of her companion's : " she is the last of some ancient stock ; and you see the family taste has been treated with all due respect."

Rose Hall was indeed perfectly English : it was a description of place of which there are few in Scotland ; for it wore the appearance of antiquity, without the too usual accompaniments of devastation or decay : neither did any incongruities betray vicissitude of fortune, or change of owner ; but the taste of the primitive possessor seemed to have been respected through ages, by his descendants ; and the ponds remained as round, and the hedges as square, and the grass walks as straight, as the day they had been planned. The same old-fashioned respectability was also apparent in the interior of the mansion : the broad heavy oaken stair-case shone in all the lustre of bees' wax ; and the spacious sitting-room, into which they were ushered, had its due allowance of Vandyke portraits, massive chairs, and china jars, standing much in the same positions they had been placed in a hundred years before.

To the delicate mind the unfortunate are always objects of respect : as the ancients held sacred those places which had been blasted by lightning, so the feeling heart considers the afflicted as having been touched by the hand of God himself. Such were the sensations with which Mary found herself in the presence of the venerable Mrs Lennox—venerable rather through affliction than age ; for sorrow, more than time, had dimmed the beauty of former days, though enough still remained to excite interest and engage affection in the mournful, yet gentle expression of her countenance, and the speaking silence of her darkened eyes. On hearing the names of her visitors, she arose, and, guided by a little girl, who had been sitting at her feet, advanced to meet them, and welcomed them with a kindness and simplicity of manner, that reminded Mary of the home she had left, and the maternal tenderness of her beloved aunt. She delivered her credentials, which Mrs Lennox received with visible surprise; but laid the letter aside without any comments.

Lady Emily began some self-accusing apologies for the length of time that had intervened since her last visit; but Mrs Lennox gently interrupted her.

"Do not blame yourself, my dear Lady Emily," said she, "for what is so natural at your age; and do not suppose I am so unreasonable as to expect that the young and the gay should seek for pleasure in the company of an old blind woman: at your time of life, I would not have courted distress any more than you."

"At every time of life," said Lady Emily, "I am sure you must have been a very different being from what I am, or ever shall be."

"Ah! you little know what changes adversity makes on the character," said Mrs Lennox, mournfully; "and may you never know—unless it is for your good."

"I doubt much if I shall ever be good on any terms," answered Lady Emily, in a half melancholy tone; "I don't think I have the elements of goodness in my composition: but here is my cousin, who is fit to stand proxy for all the virtues," placing her cousin's hand in that of the old lady as she spoke.

Mrs Lennox involuntarily turned her mild but sightless eyes towards Mary, then heaved a sigh, and shook her head, as she was reminded of her deprivation. Mary was too much affected to speak; but she pressed her hand with fervour to her lips, while her eyes overflowed with tears. The language of sympathy is soon understood. Mrs Lennox seemed to feel the tribute of pity and respect that flowed from Mary's warm heart, and from that moment they felt towards each other that indefinite attraction, which, however it may be ridiculed, certainly does sometimes influence our affections.

"That is a picture of your son, Colonel Lennox, is it not?" asked Lady Emily; "I mean the one that hangs below the lady in the satin gown with the bird in her hand."

Mrs Lennox answered in the affirmative; then added, with a sigh, "and when I could look on that face, I forgot all I had lost; but I was too fond, too proud a mother. Look at it, my dear," taking Mary's hand, and leading her to the well-known spot, while her features brightened with an expression which showed maternal vanity was not yet extinct in the mourner's heart. "He was only eighteen," continued she, "when that was done; and many a hot sun has burned on that fair brow, and many a fearful sight has met those sweet eyes, since then; and sadly that face may be changed; but I shall never see it more!"

"Indeed," said Lady Emily, affecting to be gay, while a tear stood in her eye, "it is a very dangerous face to look on; and I should be afraid to trust myself with it, were not my heart already pledged; as for my cousin Mary, there is no fear of her falling a sacrifice to hazel eyes and chesnut hair—her imagination is all on the side of sandy locks and frosty grey eyes; and I should doubt if Cupid himself would have any chance with her, unless he appeared in tartan plaid and Highland bonnet."

"Then my Charles would have some," said Mrs Lennox, with a faint smile, "for he has lately been promoted to the command of a Highland regiment."

"Indeed!" said Lady Emily, "that is very gratifying, and you have reason to be proud of Colonel Lennox; he has distinguished himself upon every occasion."

"Ah! the days of my pride are now past," replied Mrs Lennox, with a sigh; "'tis only the more honour, the greater danger, and I am weary of such bloody honours. See there!" pointing to another part of the room, where hung a group of five lovely children, "three of these dear heads were laid low in battle; the fourth, my Louisa, died of a broken heart for the loss of her brothers. Ah! what can human power or earthly honours do, to cheer the mother who has wept over her children's graves? But there *is* a power," raising her darkened eyes to heaven, "that can sustain even a mother's heart; and here," laying her hand upon an open Bible, "is the balm he has graciously vouchsafed to pour into the wounded spirit. My comfort is not that my boys died nobly, but that they died Christians."

Lady Emily and Mary were both silent from different causes. The former was at a loss what to say—the latter felt too much affected to trust her voice with the words of sympathy that hovered on her lips.

"I ought to beg your pardon, my dears," said Mrs Lennox, after a pause, "for talking in this serious manner to you, who cannot be supposed to enter into sorrows to which you are strangers. But you must excuse me, though my heart does sometimes run over."

"Oh, do not suppose," said Mary, making an effort to conquer her feelings, "that we are so heartless as to refuse to take a part in the afflictions of others—surely none can be so selfish—and might I be allowed to come often—very often—" She stopped and blushed; for she felt that her feelings were carrying her further than she was warranted to go.

Mrs Lennox kindly pressed her hand.—" Ah, God

hath, indeed, sent some into the world, whose province it is to refresh the afflicted, and lighten the eyes of the disconsolate—such, I am sure, you would be to me—for I feel my heart revive at the sound of your voice; it reminds me of my heart's darling, my Louisa! and the remembrance of her, though sad, is still sweet. Come to me, then, when you will, and God's blessing, and the blessing of the blind and desolate will reward you."

Lady Emily turned away, and it was not till they had been some time in the carriage, that Mary was able to express the interest this visit had excited, and her anxious desire to be permitted to renew it.

"It is really an extraordinary kind of delight, Mary, that you take in being made miserable," said her cousin, wiping her eyes; "for my part, it makes me quite wretched to witness suffering that I can't relieve; and how can you or I possibly do poor Mrs Lennox any good? We can't bring back her sons?"

"No; but we can bestow our sympathy, and that, I have been taught, is always a consolation to the afflicted."

"I don't quite understand the nature of that mysterious feeling called sympathy. When I go to visit Mrs Lennox, she always sets me a-crying, and I try to set her a-laughing—is that what you call sympathy?"

Mary smiled, and shook her head.

"Then, I suppose, it is sympathy to sigh and blow one's nose—is that it? or what is it?"

Mary declared that she could not define it; and Lady Emily insisted she could not comprehend it.

"You will, some day or other," said Mary; "for none, I believe, have ever passed through life without feeling, or at least requiring its support; and it is well, perhaps, that we should know betimes how to receive, as well as how to bestow it."

" I don't see the necessity at all. I know I should hate mortally to be what you call sympathised with; indeed, it appears to me the height of selfishness in anybody to like it. If I am wretched, it would be no comfort to me to make everybody else wretched."

" But they would not be wretched if they thought they were alleviating your sorrow by sharing it with you," said Mary.

" It would be no alleviation to my sorrow to be for ever carrying it about, like a baby with her doll, calling upon every one to admire it."

" Even that were better than to sit sullenly in a corner, and mope over it."

" Hem,—well, suppose I were wretched,—that I were to lose some one very dear to me,—can you figure my taking refuge in the sympathy of Dr Redgill?"

" If you were to lose your dinner, you might depend upon it," said Mary; " which proves that all have some sympathetic chord in their nature, which, if rightly struck, will ' yield fine issue.' "

" Very well said, Miss Mary," replied Lady Emily, mimicking the doctor's tone and manner, " 'pon my honour that's very well said, ' only a *leetle* too severe.' "

" Well, here is a sentiment to make amends," said Mary, with a smile, " I don't know whose it is, or whether I repeat it verbatim, but it is to this effect: ' Sorrow, like a stream, loses itself in many channels; and joy, like a sunbeam, reflects with greater force from the breast of a friend.' "

" Well, I can only repeat, were I in Mrs Lennox's place, I would have more spirit than to speak about my misfortunes."

" But Mrs Lennox does not appear to be what you call a spirited character. She seems all sweetness, and——"

" O sweet enough, certainly! But hers is a sort of an Eolian harp sweetness, that lulls me to sleep. I tire to death of people who have only two or three notes in their character. By the by, Mary, you have a tolerable compass yourself, when you choose, though I don't think you have science enough for a *bravura ;* there I certainly have the advantage of you, as I flatter myself my mind is a full band in itself. My kettle-drums and trumpets I keep for Lady Juliana, and I am quite in the humour for giving her a flourish to-day. I really require something of an exhilarating nature, after Mrs Lennox's dead march."

An unusual bustle seemed to pervade Beech Park as the carriage stopped, and augured well for its mistress's intention of being more than usually vivacious. It was found to be occasioned by the arrival of her brother Lord Lindore's servants and horses, with the interesting intelligence that his lordship would immediately follow ; and Lady Emily, wild with delight, forgot every thing, in the prospect of embracing her brother.

"How does it happen," said Mary, when her cousin's transports had a little subsided, "that you, who are in such ecstacies at the idea of seeing your brother, have scarcely mentioned his name to me?"

"Why, to tell you the truth, I fear I was beginning to forget there was such a person in the world. I have not seen him since I was ten years old. At that time he went to college, and from thence to the Continent : so all I remember of him is, that he was very handsome, and very good-humoured ; and all that I have heard of him is, that wherever he goes he is the ' glass of fashion, and the mould of form '—not that he is much of a Hamlet, I've a notion, in other respects—so pray put off that Ophelia phiz, and don't look as if you were of ladies most deject and wretched, when everybody else is gay and happy. Come, give your last sigh to the Lennox, and your first smile to Lindore."

"That is sympathy," said Mary.

Chapter xlib.

Quelle fureur, dit-il, quel aveugle caprice
Quand le dîner est prêt——.

BOILEAU.

"I HOPE your lordship has no thoughts of waiting dinner for Lord Lindore?" asked Dr Redgill, with a face of alarm, as seven o'clock struck, and neither dinner nor Lord Lindore appeared.

"I have no thoughts upon the subject," answered Lord Courtland, as he turned over some new caricatures, with as much *nonchalance* as if it had been mid-day.

"That's enough, my lord; but I suspect Mr Marshall, in his officiousness, takes the liberty of thinking for you, and that we shall have no dinner without orders," rising to pull the bell.

"We ought undoubtedly to wait for Frederick," said Lady Juliana; "it is of no consequence when we sit down to table."

A violent yell from the sleeping Beauty on the rug, sounded like a summary judgment on her mistress.

"What is the meaning of this?" cried her ladyship, flying to the offended fair one, in all the transports of pity and indignation; "how can you, Dr Redgill, presume to treat my dog in such a manner?"

"Me treat your ladyship's dog!" exclaimed the doctor, in well-feigned astonishment—"'Pon my honour!—I'm quite at a loss!—I'm absolutely confounded!"

"Yes, I saw you plainly give her a kick, and ——"

"Me kick Beauty!—after that!—'Pon my honour I should just as soon have thought of kicking my own grandmother. I did give her a *leetle*—a very *leetle* shove, just with the point of my toe, as I was going to pull the bell, but it couldn't have hurt a fly. I assure you

it would be one of the last actions of my life to treat
Beauty ill—Beauty!—poor Beauty!"—affecting to
pat and soothe, by way of covering his transgression.
But neither Beauty nor her mistress were to be taken
in by the doctor's cajoleries. The one felt, and the
other saw, the indignity he had committed, and his
caresses and protestations were all in vain. The fact
was, the doctor's indignation was so raised by Lady
Juliana's remark, made in all the plenitude of a late
luncheon, that, had it been herself instead of her favourite, he could scarcely have refrained from this testimony
of his detestation and contempt. But, much as he
despised her, he felt the necessity of propitiating her at
this moment, when dinner itself depended upon her
decision; for Lord Courtland was perfectly neutral,
Lady Emily was not present, and a servant waited to
receive orders.

"I really believe it's hunger that's vexing her, poor
brute!" continued he, with an air of unfeigned sympathy; "she knows the dinner hour as well as any of
us. Indeed, the instinct of dogs in that respect is
wonderful—Providence has really—a—hem!—indeed
it's no joke to tamper with dogs, when they've got the
notion of dinner in their heads. A friend of mine had a
very fine animal—just such another as poor Beauty there
—she had always been accustomed, like Beauty, to
attend the family to dinner at a particular hour; but
one day, by some accident, instead of sitting down at
five, she was kept waiting till half-past six; the consequence was, the disappointment operating upon an
empty stomach, brought on an attack of the hydrophobia,
and the poor thing was obliged to be shot the following
morning. I think your lordship said—dinner," in a
loud voice to the servant; and Lady Juliana, though
still sullen, did not dissent.

For an hour the doctor's soul was in a paradise still

more substantial than a Turk's; for it was lapt in the richest of soups and *ragoûts*, and secure of their existence, it smiled at ladies of quality, and defied their lap-dogs.

Dinner passed away, and supper succeeded; and breakfast, dinner, and supper, revolved, and still no Lord Lindore appeared. But this excited no alarm in the family; it was Lord Courtland's way, and it was Lady Juliana's way, and it was all their ways, not to keep to their appointed time, and they therefore experienced none of the vulgar consternation incident to common minds, when the expected guest fails to appear. Lady Emily indeed, wondered, and was provoked, and impatient, but she was not alarmed; and Mary amused herself with contrasting, in her own mind, the difference of her aunts' feelings in similar circumstances.

"Dear aunt Grizzy would certainly have been in tears these two days, fancying the thousand deaths Lord Lindore must have died; and aunt Jacky would have been inveighing from morning till night against the irregularities of young men; and aunt Nicky would have been lamenting that the black cock had been roasted yesterday, or that there would be no fish for to-morrow." And the result of Mary's comparison was, that her aunts' feelings, however troublesome, were better than no feelings at all. "They are, to be sure, something like brambles," thought she; "they fasten upon one in every possible way, but still they are better than the faded exotics of fashionable life."

At last, on the third day, when dinner was nearly over, and Dr Redgill was about to remark for the third time, "I think it's as well we did not wait for Lord Lindore," the door opened, and, without warning or bustle, Lord Lindore walked calmly into the room.

Lady Emily, uttering an exclamation of joy, threw

herself into his arms.   Lord Courtland was roused to
something like animation, as he cordially shook hands
with his son; Lady Juliana flew into raptures at the
beauty of his Italian greyhound; Adelaide, at the first
glance, decided, that her cousin was worthy of falling
in love with her; Mary thought on the happiness of
the family re-union; and Dr Redgill offered up a silent
thanksgiving, that this fracas had not happened ten
minutes sooner, otherwise the woodcocks would have
been as cold as death.   Chairs were placed by the
officious attendants in every possible direction; and the
discarded first course was threatening to displace the
third : but Lord Lindore seemed quite insensible to all
these attentions; he stood surveying the company with
a *nonchalance*, that had nothing of rudeness in it, but
seemed merely the result of high-bred ease.   His eye,
for a moment, rested upon Adelaide.   He then slightly
bowed and smiled, as in recognition of their juvenile
acquaintance.

" I really can't recommend either the turtle-soup or
the venison to your lordship to-day," said Dr Redgill,
who experienced certain uneasy sensations at the idea
of beholding them resume their stations, something
resembling those which Macbeth testified at sight of
Banquo's ghost, or Hamlet on contemplating Yorick's
skull—"after travelling, there is nothing like a light
dinner; allow me to recommend this *pretty leetle cuisse
de poulet en papillote*—and here are some fascinating
beignets d'abricots—quite foreign."

" If there is any roast beef or boiled mutton to be
had, pray let me have it," said Lord Lindore, waving
off the zealous *maître d'hotel*, as he kept placing dish
after dish before him.

" Roast beef, or boiled mutton ! " ejaculated the
doctor, with a sort of internal convulsion; " he is
certainly mad."

"How did you contrive to arrive without being heard by me, Frederick?" asked Lady Emily; "my ears have been wide open these two days and three nights, watching your approach."

"I walked from Newberry-house," answered he, carelessly: "I met Lord Newberry two days ago, as I was coming here, and he persuaded me to alter my course, and accompany him home."

"Vastly flattering to your friends here," said Lady Emily, in a tone of pique.

"What! you walked all the way from Newberry," exclaimed the Earl, "and the ground covered with snow? How could you do such a foolish thing?"

"Simply because, as the children say, I liked it," replied Lord Lindore, with a smile.

"That's just of a piece with his liking to eat boiled mutton," muttered the doctor to Mary; "and yet to look at him, one would really not expect such gross stupidity."

There certainly was nothing in Lord Lindore's appearance that denoted either coarseness of taste or imbecility of mind. On the contrary, he was an elegant - looking young man, rather slightly formed, and of the middle size, possessing that ease and grace in all his movements, which a perfect proportion alone can bestow. There was nothing foreign or *recherché*, either in his dress or deportment; both were plain, even to simplicity; yet an almost imperceptible air of *hauteur* was mingled with the good-humoured indifference of his manner. He spoke little, and seemed rather to endure than to be gratified by attentions; his own were chiefly directed to his dog, as he was more intent on feeding it, than on answering the questions that were put to him. There never was anything to be called conversation at the dinner-table at Beech Park; and the general practice was in no danger of being departed from on the present occasion. The earl hated to converse—it was a bore; and he now merely exchanged a few desultory sentences with his son, as he ate his olives and drank his claret. Lady Juliana, indeed, spoke even more than her usual quantity of nonsense, but nobody listened to it. Lady Emily was somewhat perplexed in her notions about her brother. He was handsome and elegant, and appeared good-humoured and gentle; yet something was wanting to fill up the measure of her expectations, and a latent feeling of disappointment lurked in her heart. Adelaide was indignant that he had not instantly paid her the most marked attention, and revenged herself by her silence. In short, Lord Lindore's arrival seemed to have added little or nothing to the general stock of pleasure; and the effervescence of joy—the rapture of *sensation*, like some subtle essence, had escaped almost as soon as it was perceived.

" How stupid everybody always is at a dinner table!" exclaimed Lady Emily, rising abruptly with an air of chagrin. " I believe it is the fumes of the meat that dulls one's senses, and renders them so detestable. I long to see you in the drawing-room, Frederick. I've a notion you are more of a carpet-knight, than a knight of the round table; so pray," in a whisper as she passed, " leave papa to be snored asleep by Dr Redgill, and do you follow us—here's metal more attractive," pointing to the sisters, as they quitted the room; and she followed without waiting for her brother's reply.

Chapter xlb.

Io dubito, Signor M. Pietro, che il mio Cortegiano non sarà stato altro che fatica mia, e fastidio degli amici.—BALDASSARRE CASTIGLIONE.

LORD LINDORE was in no haste to avail himself of his sister's invitation; and when he did, it was evident his was a "mind not to be changed by place;" for he entered more with the air of one who was tired of the company he had left, than expecting pleasure from the society he sought.

"Do come and entertain us, Lindore," cried Lady Emily, as he entered; "for we are all heartily sick of one another. A snow storm, and a lack of company, are things hard to be borne; it is only the expectancy of your arrival that has kept us alive these two days, and now pray don't let us die away of the reality."

"You have certainly taken a most effectual method of sealing my lips," said her brother, with a smile.

"How so?"

"By telling me that I am expected to be extremely entertaining, since every word I utter can only serve to dispel the illusion, and prove that I am gifted with no such miraculous power."

"I don't think it requires any miraculous power either to entertain or to be entertained. For my part, I flatter myself I can entertain any man, woman, or child, in the kingdom, when I choose; and as for being entertained, that is still an easier matter. I seldom meet with anybody who is not entertaining, either from their folly, or their affectation, or their stupidity, or their vanity; or, in short, something of the ridiculous, that renders them not merely supportable, but positively amusing."

"How extremely happy you must be!" said Lord Lindore.

"Happy! no—I don't know that my feelings precisely amount to happiness neither; for at the very time
I'm most diverted, I'm sometimes disgusted too, and
often provoked. My spirits get chafed, and ——"

"You long to box the ears of all your acquaintances,"
said her brother, laughing. "Well, no matter — there
is nothing so enviable as a facility of being amused, and
even the excitement of anger is perhaps preferable to the
stagnation of indifference."

"Oh, thank Heaven! I know nothing about indifference—I leave that to Adelaide."

Lord Lindore turned his eyes with more animation
than he had yet evinced towards his cousin, who sat
reading, apparently paying no attention to what was
going on. He regarded her for a considerable time
with an expression of admiration, but Adelaide, though
she was conscious of his gaze, calmly pursued her
studies.

"Come, you positively must do something to signalize
yourself. I assure you, it is expected of you that you
should be the soul of the company. Here is Adelaide
waltzes like an angel, when she can get a partner to her
liking."

"But I waltz like a mere mortal," said Lord Lindore, seating himself at a table, and turning over the
leaves of a book.

"And I am engaged to play at billiards with my
uncle," said Adelaide, rising with a blush of indignation.

"Shall we have some music, then? Can you bear
to listen to our croakings, after the warbling of your
Italian nightingales?" asked Lady Emily.

"I should like very much to hear you sing," answered
her brother, with an air of the most perfect indifference.

"Come then, Mary, do you be the one to 'untwist
the chains that tie the hidden soul of harmony.' Give
us your Scotch Exile, pray? It is tolerably appropriate

to the occasion, though an English one would have been
still more so ; but, as you say, there is nothing in this
country to make a song about."

Mary would rather have declined, but she saw a refusal would displease her cousin, and she was not accustomed to consult her own inclination in such frivolous
matters ; she therefore seated herself at the harp, and
sang one or two of the following verses :—

THE EXILE.

The weary wanderer may roam
   To seek for bliss in change of scene;
Yet still the loved idea of his home,
   And of the days he there has seen,
Pursue him with a fond regret,
Like rays from suns that long have set.

'Tis not the sculptor's magic art,
   'Tis not th' heroic deeds of yore,
That fill and gratify the heart.
   No! 'tis affection's tender lore—
The thought of friends, and love's first sigh,
When youth, and hope, and health were nigh.

What though on classic ground we tread,
   What though we breathe a genial air—
Can these restore the bliss that's fled?
   Is not remembrance ever there?
Can any soil protect from grief,
Or any air breathe soft relief?

No! the sick soul, that wounded flies
   From all its early thoughts held dear,
Will more some gleam of memory prize,
   That draws the long-lost treasure near;
And warmly presses to its breast
The very thought that mars its rest.

Some mossy stone, some torrent rude,
   Some moor unknown to worldly ken;
Some weeping birches, fragrant wood,
   Or some wild roebuck's fern-clad glen;—
Yes! these his aching heart delight,
These bring his country to his sight.

Ere the song was begun, Lord Lindore had sauntered away to the billiard-room, singing, "Oh! Giove Omnipotente!" and seemingly quite unconscious that any attentions were due from him in return. But there, even Adelaide's charms failed to attract. In spite of the variety of graceful movements practised before him— the beauty of the extended arm, the majestic step, and the exclamations of the enchanting voice, Lord Lindore kept his station by the fire, in a musing attitude, from which he was only roused occasionally by the caresses of his dog. At supper it was still worse : he placed himself by Mary, and when he spoke, it was only of Scotland.

"Well! what do you think of Lindore?" demanded Lady Emily of her aunt and cousins, as they were about to separate for the night. "Is he not charming?"

"Perfectly so!" replied Lady Juliana, with all the self-importance of a fool. "I assure you I think very highly of him. He is a very charming, clever young man—perfectly beautiful, and excessively amiable ; and his attention to his dog is quite delightful—it is so uncommon to see men at all kind to their dogs. I assure you I have known many who were absolutely cruel to them—beat them and starve them, and did a thousand shocking things ; and——"

"Pray, Adelaide, what is your opinion of my brother?"

"Oh, I—I—have no doubt he is extremely amiable," replied Adelaide, with a gentle yawn. "As mamma says, his attentions to his dog prove it."

"And you, Mary, are your remarks to be equally judicious and polite?"

Mary, in all the sincerity of her heart, said she thought him by much the handsomest and most elegant-looking man she had ever seen. And there she stopped.

" Yes ; I know all that.   But—however, no matter
—I only wish he may have sense enough to fall in love
with you, Mary.   How happy I should be to see you
Lady Lindore !—*En attendant*—you must take care of
your heart, for I hear he is *un peu volage*—and, moreover, that he admires none but *les dames Mariées*.   As
for Adelaide, there is no fear of her ; she will never
cast such a pearl away upon one who is merely, no
doubt, *extremely amiable*," retorting Adelaide's ironical
tone.

" Then you may feel equally secure upon my
account," said Mary, " as I assure you I am in still
less danger of losing mine, after the warning you have
given."

This off-hand sketch of her brother's character,
which Lady Emily had thoughtlessly given, produced
the most opposite effects on the minds of the sisters.
With Adelaide, it increased his consequence and en-
hanced his value.   It would be no vulgar conquest to
fix and reform one who was notorious for his inconstancy and libertine principles ; and, from that moment,
she resolved to use all the influence of her charms to
captivate and secure the heart of her cousin.   In Mary's
well-regulated mind, other feelings arose.   Although
she was not one of the outrageously virtuous, who
storm and rail at the very mention of vice, and deem it
contamination to hold any intercourse with the erring
and faulty, she yet possessed proper ideas of the distinction to be drawn ; and the hope of finding a friend
and brother in her cousin, now gave way to the feeling,
that in future she could only consider him as a mere
common acquaintance.

————o————

Chapter xlvj.

On sera ridicule et je n'oserai rire!

BOILEAU.

IN honour of her brother's return, Lady Emily resolved to celebrate it with a ball; and, always prompt in following up her plans, she fell to work immediately with her visiting list.

"Certainly," said she, as she scanned it over, "there never was any family so afflicted in their acquaintances as we are. At least one half of the names here belong to the most insufferable people on the face of the earth. The Claremonts, and the Edgerfields, and the Bouveries, and the Sedleys, and a few more, are very well; but can anything, in human form, be more insupportable than the rest; for instance, that wretch Lady Placid?"

"Does her merit lie only in her name, then?" asked Mary.

"You shall judge for yourself, when I have given you a slight sketch of her character. Lady Placid, in the opinion of all sensible persons in general, and myself in particular, is a vain, weak, conceited, vulgar egotist. In her own eyes she is a clever, well-informed, elegant, amiable woman; and though I have spared no pains to let her know how detestable I think her, it is all in vain: she remains as firmly entrenched in her own good opinion, as folly and conceit can make her, and I have the despair of seeing all my buffetings fall blunted to the ground. She reminds me of some odious fairy or genii I have read of, who possessed such a power in their person, that every hostile weapon levelled against them was immediately turned into some agreeable present—stones became balls of silk—arrows, flowers —swords, feathers, &c. Even so it is with Lady

Placid: The grossest insult that could be offered, she would construe into an elegant compliment—the very crimes of others, she seems to consider as so much incense offered up at the shrine of her own immaculate virtue. I'm certain she thinks she deserves to be canonized for having kept out of Doctors' Commons. Never is any affair of that sort alluded to, that she does not cast such a triumphant look towards her husband, as much as to say, 'O thou most fortunate of men, here am I, the paragon of faithful wives and virtuous matrons!' Were I in his place, I should certainly throw a plate at her head. And here, you may take this passing remark—How much more odious people are who have radical faults, than those who commit, I do not say positive crimes, but occasional weaknesses. Even a noble nature may fall into a great error; but what is that to the ever-enduring pride, envy, malice, and conceit of a little mind. Yes—I would, at any time, rather be the fallen, than the one to exult over the fall of another. Then, as a mother, she is, if possible, still more meritorious. 'A woman (this is the way she talks), a woman has nobly performed her part to her country, and for posterity, when she has brought a family of fine healthy children into the world.' I can't agree with you, I reply; I think many mothers have brought children into the world, who would have been much better out of it. A mother's merit must depend solely upon how she brings up her children (hers are the most spoiled brats in Christendom). 'There I perfectly agree with you, Lady Emily. As you observe, it is not every mother who does her duty by her children. Indeed, I may say to you, it is not every one that will make the sacrifices for their family I have done; but I am richly repaid. My children are everything I could wish them to be!'—Everything of hers, as a matter of course, must be superior to every other person's, and even what she is obliged to share in common with others, acquires some miraculous charm in operating upon her.   Thus, it is impossible for any-one to imagine the delight she takes in bathing; and as for the sun, no mortal can conceive the effect it has upon her.   If she was to have the plague, she would assure you it was owing to some peculiar virtue in her blood; and if she was to be put in the pillory, she would ascribe it entirely to her great merit.   If her coachman was to make her a declaration of love, she would impute it to the boundless influence of her charms; that every man who sees her does not declare his passion is entirely owing to the well-known severity of her morals, and the dignity of her deportment.   If she is amongst the first invited to my ball, that will be my eagerness to secure her; if the very last, it will be a mark of my friendship, and the easy footing we are upon.   If not invited at all, then it will be my jealousy. In short, the united strength of worlds would not shake that woman's good opinion of herself; and the intoler-able part of it is, there are so many fools in this one, that she actually passes with the multitude for being a charming sweet-tempered woman—always the same—always pleased and contented.   Contented! just as like contentment as the light emitted by putridity resembles the divine halo!   But too much of her—Let her have a card, however.

"Then comes Mrs Wiseacre, that renowned law-giver, who lavishes her advice on all who will receive it, without hope of fee or reward, except that of being thought wiser than anybody else.   But, like many more deserving characters, she meets with nothing but in-gratitude in return; and the wise sentences that are for ever hovering around her pursed-up mouth, have only served to render her insupportable.   This is her mode of proceeding—'If I might presume to advise Lady

Emily;' or, 'if my opinion could be supposed to have
any weight;' or, 'if my experience goes for anything;'
or, 'I'm an old woman now, but I think I know something of the world;' or, 'if a friendly hint of mine
would be of any service:'—then when very desperate,
it is, 'however averse I am to obtrude my advice, yet,
as I consider it my duty, I must for once;' or, 'it
certainly is no affair of mine, at the same time I must
just observe,' &c. &c.   I don't say that she insists,
however, upon your swallowing all the advice she crams
you with; for provided she has the luxury of giving it,
it can make little difference how it is taken; because
whatever befalls you, be it good or bad, it is equally a
matter of exultation to her.   Thus, she has the satisfaction of saying, 'if poor Mrs Dabble had but followed
my advice, and not have taken that draught of Dr
Doolittle's, she would have been alive to-day, depend
upon it;' or, if Sir Thomas Speckle had but taken
advantage of a friendly hint I threw out some time ago,
about the purchase of the Drawrent estate, he might
have been a man worth ten thousand a year at this
moment;' or, 'if Lady Dull hadn't been so infatu-
ated as to neglect the caution I gave her about Bob
Squander, her daughter might have been married to
Nabob Gull.'

"But there is a strange contradiction about Mrs
Wiseacre, for though it appears that all her friends'
misfortunes proceed from neglecting her advice, it is no
less apparent, by her account, that her own are all
occasioned by following the advice of others.   She is
for ever doing foolish things, and laying the blame upon
her neighbours.   Thus, 'had it not been for my friend
Mrs Jobbs there, I never would have parted with my
house for an old song as I did;' or, 'it was entirely
owing to Miss Glue's obstinacy, that I was robbed of
my diamond necklace;' or, 'I have to thank my

friend, Colonel Crack, for getting my carriage smashed
to pieces.'   In short, she has the most comfortable
repository of stupid friends to have recourse to, of anybody I ever knew.   Now, what I have to warn you
against, Mary, is the sin of ever listening to any of her
advices.   She will preach to you about the pinning of
your gown, and the curling of your hair, till you would
think it impossible not to do exactly what she wants
you to do.   She will inquire with the greatest solicitude
what shoemaker you employ, and will shake her head
most significantly when she hears it is any other than
her own.   But if ever I detect you paying the smallest
attention to any of her recommendations, positively I
shall have done with you."

Mary laughingly promised to turn a deaf ear to all
Mrs Wiseacre's wisdom; and her cousin proceeded:—

"Then here follows a swarm 'as thick as idle motes
in sunny ray,' and much of the same importance,
methinks, in the scale of being.   Married ladies only
celebrated for their good dinners, or their pretty equipages, or their fine jewels.   How I should scorn to be
talked of as the creature of my coachmaker, or the
appendage to my soups or pearls!   Then there are the
daughters of these ladies—misses, who are mere misses,
and nothing more.   Oh! the insipidity of a mere miss!
a soft simpering thing, with pink cheeks, and pretty
hair, and fashionable clothes;—*sans* eyes for anything
but lovers—*sans* ears for anything but flattery—*sans*
taste for anything but balls—*sans* brains for anything at
all!   Then there are ladies who are neither married
nor young, and who strive with all their might to talk
most delightfully, that the charms of their conversation
may efface the marks of the crow's feet; but 'all these
I passen by, and nameless numbers moe.'   And now
comes the Hon. Mrs Downe Wright, a person of considerable shrewdness and penetration—vulgar, but un-

affected. There is no politeness, no gentleness in her heart; but she possesses some warmth, much honesty, and great hospitality. She has acquired the character of being,—Oh, odious thing!—a clever woman! There are two descriptions of clever women, observe; the one is endowed with corporeal cleverness—the other with mental, and I don't know which of the two is the greater nuisance to society; the one torments you with her management—the other with her smart sayings; the one is for ever rattling her bunch of keys in your ears—the other electrifies you with the shock of her wit; and both talk *so* much and *so* loud, and are such egotists, that I rather think a clever woman is even a greater term of reproach than a good creature. But to return to that clever woman, Mrs Downe Wright: she is a widow, left with the management of an only son—a common-place, weak young man. No one, I believe, is more sensible of his mental deficiencies than his mother; but she knows that a man of fortune is, in the eyes of the many, a man of consequence; and she therefore wisely talks of it as his chief characteristic. To keep him in good company, and get him well married, is all her aim; and this, she thinks, will not be difficult, as he is very handsome—possesses an estate of ten thousand a-year—and succeeds to some Scotch Lord Something's title.—There's for you, Mary! She once had views of Adelaide, but Adelaide met the advances with so much scorn, that Mrs Downe Wright declared she was thankful she had shown the cloven foot in time; for that she never would have done for a wife to her William. Now you are the very thing to suit, for you have no cloven feet to show."

" Or, at least, you are not so quick-sighted as Mrs Downe Wright. You have not spied them yet, it seems," said Mary, with a smile.

" Oh, as to that, if you had them, I should defy you,

or any one, to hide them from me. When I reflect upon the characters of most of my acquaintances, I sometimes think nature has formed my optics only to see disagreeables."

" That must be a still more painful faculty of vision than even the second-sight," said Mary ; " but I should think it depended very much upon yourself to counteract it."

" Impossible ! my perceptions are so peculiarly alive to all that is obnoxious to them, that I could as soon preach my eyes into blindness, or my ears into deafness, as put down my feelings with chopping logic.   If people *will* be affected and ridiculous, why must I live in a state of warfare with myself, on account of the feelings they rouse within me ? "

" If people *will* be irritable," said Mary, laughing, " why must others sacrifice their feelings to gratify them ? "

" Because mine are natural feelings and theirs are artificial.   A very saint must sicken at sight of affectation, you'll allow.   Vulgarity, even innate vulgarity, is bearable—stupidity itself is pardonable—but affectation is never to be endured or forgiven."

" It admits of palliation, at least," answered Mary. " I dare say there are many people who would have been pleasing and natural in their manners, had not their parents and teachers interfered.   There are many, I believe, who have not courage to show themselves such as they are—some who are naturally affected—and many, very many, who have been taught affectation as a necessary branch of education."

" Yes—as my governess would have taught me ; but, thank Heaven ! I got the better of them.   *Fascinating* was what they wanted to make me ; but whenever the word was mentioned, I used to knit my brows, and frown upon them in such a sort ! The frown, I know, sticks by me; but no matter, a frowning brow is better than a false heart, and I defy any one to say that I am fascinating."

"There certainly must be some fascination about you, otherwise I should never have sat so long listening to you," said Mary, as she rose from the table at which she had been assisting to dash off the At-Homes.

"But you *must* listen to me a little longer," cried her cousin, seizing her hand to detain her: "I have not got half through my detestables yet; but, to humour you, I shall let them go for the present. And now, that you mayn't suppose I am utterly insensible to excellence, you must suffer me to show you, that I can and do appreciate worth, when I can find it. I confess, my talent lies fully as much in discovering the ridiculous as the amiable; and I am equally ready to acknowledge it is a fault, and no mark of superior wit or understanding; since it is much easier to hit off the glaring caricature lines of deformity, than the finer and more exquisite touches of beauty, especially for one who reads as he runs—the sign-posts are sure to catch the eye. But now for my favourite—no matter for her name—it would frighten you were you to hear it. In the first place, she is, as some of your old divines say, *hugely religious;* but then she keeps her piety in its proper place, and where it ought to be—in her very soul. It is never a stumbling-block in other people's way, or interfering with other people's affairs. Her object is to *be,* not to *seem,* religious; and there is neither hypocrisy nor austerity necessary for that. She is forbearing, without meanness—gentle, without insipidity—sincere, without rudeness. She practises all the virtues herself, and seems quite unconscious that others don't do the same. She is, if I may trust the expression of her eye, almost as much alive to the ridiculous as I am; but she is only diverted where I am pro-

voked.   She never bestows false praise, even upon her
friends; but a simple approval from her is of more
value than the finest panegyric from another.   She
never finds occasion to censure or condemn the conduct
of any one, however flagrant it may be in the eyes of
others ; because she seems to think virtue is better expressed by her own actions than by her neighbour's
vices.   She cares not for admiration, but is anxious to
do good and give pleasure.   To sum up the whole, she
could listen with patience to Lady Placid; she could
bear to be advised by Mrs Wiseacre; she could stand
the scrutiny of Mrs Downe Wright; and, hardest task
of all," (throwing her arms around Mary's neck,)
" she can bear with all my ill-humour and impertinence."

———o———

Chapter xlvij.

" Have I then not tears for thee, my *mother* ?
  Can I forget thy cares from helpless years—
  Thy tenderness for me ? an eye still beamed
  With love ? "

                                  THOMSON.

THE arrival of Lord Lindore brought an influx of
         visitors to Beech Park ; and, in the unceasing
         round of amusement that went on, Mary found
herself completely overlooked.   She therefore gladly
took advantage of her insignificance to pay frequent
visits to Mrs Lennox, and easily prevailed with Lady
Juliana to allow her to spend a week there occasionally.
In this way, the acquaintance soon ripened into the
warmest affection on both sides.   The day seemed
doubly dark to Mrs Lennox that was not brightened
by Mary's presence ; and Mary felt all the drooping
energies of her heart revive in the delight of administering to the happiness of another.

Mrs Lennox was one of those gentle, amiable beings, who engage our affections far more powerfully than many possessed of higher attributes. Her understanding was not strong—neither had it been highly cultivated according to the ideas of the present time; but she had a benevolence of heart, and a guileless simplicity of thought, that shamed the pride of wit, and pomp of learning. Bereft of all external enjoyments, and destitute of great mental resources, it was retrospection and futurity that gilded the dark evening of her days, and shed their light on the dreary realities of life. She loved to recall the remembrance of her children—to tell of their infant beauties, their growing virtues—and to retrace scenes of past felicity which memory loves to treasure in the heart.

"Oh! none but a mother can tell," she would exclaim, "the bitterness of those tears which fall from a mother's eyes!—all other sorrows seem natural, but—God forgive me!—surely it is not natural that the old should weep for the young. Ah! when I saw myself surrounded by my children, little did I think that death was so soon to seal their eyes—sorrow mine! and yet I would rather have suffered all than have stood in the world a lonely being.—Yes—my children revered His power and believed in His name, and, thanks to His mercy, I feel assured they are now angels in heaven! Here," taking some papers from a writing-box, "my Louisa speaks to me even from the tomb!—These are the words she wrote but a few hours before her death. Read them to me; for it is not every voice I can bear to hear uttering her last thoughts."—Mary read as follows:—

FOR EVER GONE.

For ever gone! oh, chilling sound!
　That tolls the knell of hope and joy!
Potent with torturing pang to wound
　But not in mercy to destroy.

For ever gone! what words of grief--
  Replete with wild mysterious woe!
The Christian kneels to seek relief—
  A Saviour died—— It is not so.

For a brief space we sojourn here,
  And life's rough path we journey o'er;
Thus was it with the friend so dear,
  That is not lost, but sped before.

For ever gone! oh, madness wild
  Dwells in that drear and Atheist doom!
But death of horror is despoil'd,
  When heaven shines forth beyond the tomb.

For ever gone! oh, dreadful fate!
  Go visit nature—gather thence
The symbols of man's happier state,
  Which speaks to every mortal sense.

The leafless spray, the wither'd flower,
  Alike with man, own death's embrace;
But bursting forth, in summer hour,
  Prepare anew to run life's race.

And shall it be, that man alone
  Dies, never more to rise again!
Of all creation, highest one,
  Created but to live in vain?

For ever gone! oh, dire despair!—
  Look to the heavens, the earth, the sea—
Go, read a Saviour's promise there—
  Go, heir of Immortality!

From such communings as these the selfish would
have turned with indifference; but Mary's generous
heart was ever open to the overflowings of the wounded
spirit. She had never been accustomed to lavish the
best feelings of her nature on frivolous pursuits, or
fictitious distresses; but had early been taught to consecrate them to the best, the most ennobling purposes
of humanity—even to the comforting of the weary soul

—the binding of the bruised heart. Yet Mary was no rigid moralist. She loved amusement as the *amusement* of an imperfect existence, though her good sense, and still better principles, taught her to reject it as the *business* of an immortal being.

Several weeks passed away, during which Mary had been an almost constant inmate at Rose Hall; but the day of Lady Emily's *fête* arrived, and with something of hope and expectation fluttering at her heart, she anticipated her *début* in the ball-room. She repaired to the breakfast-table of her venerable friend, with even more than usual hilarity; but, upon entering the apartment, her gaiety fled; for she was struck with the emotion visible on the countenance of Mrs Lennox; her meek but tearful eyes were raised to heaven, and her hands were crossed on her bosom, as if to subdue the agitation of her heart. Her faithful attendant stood by her with an open letter in her hand.

Mary flew towards her; and as her light step and soft accents met her ear, she extended her arms towards her.

"Mary, my child, where are you?" exclaimed she, as she pressed her with convulsive eagerness to her heart—"My son!—my Charles!—to-morrow I shall see him—See him! Oh, God help me! I shall never see him more!" And she wept in all the agony of contending emotions, suddenly and powerfully excited.

"But you will hear him—you will hold him to your heart—you will be conscious that he is beside you," said Mary, soothingly.

"Yes, thank God! I shall once more hear the voice of a living child! Oh, how often do those voices ring in my heart, that are all hushed in the grave! I am used to it now—but to think of his returning to this wilderness! When last he left it, he had father, brothers, sister—and now, all—all gone!"

"Indeed it will be a sad return," said the old house-keeper, as she wiped her eyes; "for the colonel doated on his sister, and she on him, and his brothers too! Dearly they all loved one another. How in this very room have I seen them chase each other up and down in their pretty plays, with their papa's cap and sword, and say they would be soldiers!"

Mary motioned the good woman to be silent; then turning to Mrs Lennox, she sought to soothe her into composure, and turned, as she always did, the bright side of the picture to view, by dwelling on the joy her son would experience in seeing her. Mrs Lennox shook her head mournfully.

"Alas! he cannot have joy in seeing me, such as I am. I have too long concealed from him my dreary doom: he knows not that these poor eyes are sealed in darkness! Ah! he will seek to read a mother's fondness there, and he will find all cold and silent."

"But he will also find you resigned—even contented," said Mary, while her tears dropped on the hand she held to her lips.

"Yes; God knows, I do not repine at his will. It is not for myself these tears fall; but my son!—How will he bear to behold the mother he so loved and honoured, now blind, bereft, and helpless!" And the wounds of her heart seemed to bleed afresh at the excitement of even its happiest emotions—the return of a long absent, much-loved son.

Mary exerted all the powers of her understanding, all the tenderness of her heart, to dispel the mournful images that pressed on the mind of her friend; but she found it was not so much her *arguments* as her *presence* that produced that effect; and to leave her in her present situation seemed impossible. In the agitation of her spirits, she had wholly forgotten the occasion that called for Mary's absence, and she implored her to remain with her till the arrival of her son, with an earnestness that was irresistible.

The thoughts of her cousin's displeasure, should she absent herself upon such an occasion, caused Mary to hesitate; yet her feelings would not allow her to name the cause.

"How unfeeling it would sound to talk of balls at such a time!" thought she; "what a painful contrast must it present!—surely Lady Emily will not blame me, and no one will miss me——" And, in the ardour of her feelings, she promised to remain. Yet she sighed as she sent off her excuse, and thought of the pleasures she had renounced; but the sacrifice made, the regrets were soon passed; and she devoted herself entirely to soothing the agitated spirits of her venerable friend.

It is perhaps the simplest and most obvious truth, skilfully administered, that, in the season of affliction, produces the most salutary effects upon our mind. Mary was certainly no logician, and all that she could say, might have been said by another; but there is something in the voice and manner that carries an irresistible influence along with it—something that tells us our sorrows are felt and understood, not coldly seen and heard. Mary's well-directed exertions were repaid with success; she read, talked, played, and sang, not in her gayest manner, but in that subdued strain which harmonized with the feelings, while it won upon the attention, and she had at length the satisfaction of seeing the object of her solicitude restored to her usual state of calm confiding acquiescence.

"God bless you, my dear Mary!" said she, as they were about to separate for the night—"He only can repay you for the good you have done me this day!"

"Ah!" thought Mary, as she tenderly embraced her, "such a blessing is worth a dozen balls!"

At that moment the sound of a carriage was heard, and an unusual bustle took place below; but scarcely had they time to notice it, ere the door flew open, and Mrs Lennox found herself locked in the arms of her son.

For some minutes the tide of feeling was too strong for utterance, and "My mother!" "My son!" were the only words that either could articulate. At length, raising his head, Colonel Lennox fixed his eyes on his mother's face, with a gaze of deep and fearful inquiry—but no returning glance spoke there. With that mournful vacuity, peculiar to the blind, which is a thousand times more touching than all the varied expression of the living orb, she continued to regard the vacant space which imagination had filled, with the image she sought in vain to behold.

At this confirmation of his worst fears, a shade of the deepest anguish overspread the countenance of her son. He raised his eyes, as in agony to heaven—then threw himself on his mother's bosom; and as Mary hurried from the apartment, she heard the sob which burst from his manly heart, as he exclaimed, "My dear mother! do I indeed find you thus?"

———o———

Chapter xlviij.

"There is more complacency in the negligence of some men, than in what is called the good-breeding of others; and the little absences of the heart are often more interesting and engaging than the punctilious attention of a thousand professed sacrificers to the graces."—HENRY MACKENZIE.

POWERFUL emotions are the certain levellers of ordinary feelings. When Mary met Colonel Lennox in the breakfast-room the following morning, he accosted her, not with the ceremony of a stranger, but with the frankness of a heart careless of common forms; and spoke of his mother with indications of sensibility, which he vainly strove to repress. Mary knew that she had sought to conceal her real situation from him: but it seemed a vague suspicion of the truth had crossed his mind, and having, with difficulty, obtained a short leave of absence, he had hastened to have either his hopes or fears realized.

"And, now that I know the worst," said he, "I know it only to deplore it. Far from alleviating, my presence seems rather to aggravate my poor mother's misfortune. Oh! it is heart-rending to see the striving of these longing eyes to look upon the face of those she loves!"

"Ah!" thought Mary, "were they to behold that face now, how changed would it appear!" as she contrasted it with the portrait that hung immediately over the head of the original. The one in all the brightness of youth—the radiant eyes—the rounded cheek—the fair, open brow—spoke only of hope, and health, and joy. Those eyes were now dimmed by sorrow; the cheek was wasted with toil; the brow was clouded by cares. Yet, "as it is the best part of beauty which a picture cannot express,"* so there is something superior to the mere charms of form and colour; and an air of high-toned feeling, of mingled vivacity and sensibility, gave a dignity to the form, and an expression to the countenance, which more than atoned for the want of youth's more brilliant attributes.

At least so thought Mary; but her comparisons were interrupted by the entrance of Mrs Lennox. Her son flew towards her, and taking her arm from that of her attendant, led her to her seat, and sought to render her those little offices which her helplessness required.

* Lord Bacon.

"My dear Charles," said she, with a smile, as he tried to adjust her cushions, "your hands have not been used to this work. Your arm is my best support, but a gentler hand must smooth my pillow. Mary, my love, where are you? Give me your hand.' Then placing it in that of her son—"Many a tear has this hand wiped from your mother's eyes! "

Mary, blushing deeply, hastily withdrew it. She felt it as a sort of appeal to Colonel Lennox's feelings, and a sense of wounded delicacy made her shrink from being thus recommended to his gratitude. But Colonel Lennox seemed too much absorbed in his own painful reflections, to attach such a meaning to his mother's words; and though they excited him to regard Mary for a moment with peculiar interest, yet, in a little while, he relapsed into the mournful reverie from which he had been roused.

Colonel Lennox was evidently not a show-off character. He seemed superior to the mere vulgar aim of making himself agreeable—an aim which has much oftener its source in vanity than in benevolence. Yet he exerted himself to meet his mother's cheerfulness; though as often as he looked at her, or raised his eyes to the youthful group that hung before them, his changing hue and quivering lip betrayed the anguish he strove to hide.

Breakfast ended, Mary rose to prepare for her departure, in spite of the solicitations of her friend, that she should remain till the following day.

"Surely, my dear Mary," said she, in an imploring accent, "you will not refuse to bestow one day of happiness upon me?—and it is *such* a happiness to see my Charles and you together. I little thought that ever I should have been so blessed. Ah! I begin to think God has yet some good in store for my last days! Do not then leave me just when I am beginning to taste of

joy! "—And she clung to her with that pathetic look
which Mary had ever found irresistible.

But, upon this occasion, she steeled her heart against
all supplication. It was the first time she had ever
turned from the entreaty of old age or infirmity, and
those only who have lived in the habitual practice of
administering to the happiness of others, can conceive
how much it costs the generous heart to resist even the
weaknesses of those it loves. But Mary felt she had
already sacrificed too much to affection, and she feared
the reproaches and ridicule that awaited her return to
Beech Park. She therefore gently, though steadily,
adhered to her resolution, only softening it by a promise
of returning soon.

"What an angel goes there!" exclaimed Mrs
Lennox to her son, as Mary left the room to prepare
for her departure. "Ah! Charles, could I but hope
to see her yours!"

Colonel Lennox smiled—"That must be when I am
an angel myself, then. A poor weather-beaten soldier
like me must be satisfied with something less."

"But is she not a lovely creature?" asked his
mother, with some solicitude.

"Angels, you know, are always fair," replied Colonel
Lennox, laughingly, trying to parry this attack upon his
heart.

"Ah! Charles, that is not being serious! But
young people now are different from what they were in
my day,—there is no such thing as falling in love now
—you are all so cautious!"

And the good old lady's thoughts reverted to the
time when the gay and gallant Captain Lennox had
fallen desperately in love with her, as she danced a
minuet in a blue satin *sacque* and Bologna hat, at a
county ball.

"You forget, my dear mother, what a knack I had

at falling in love ten years ago.   Since then, I confess,
I have got rather out of the way of it ; but a little, a
very little practice, I am sure, will make me as expert as
ever ; and then I promise you shall have no cause to
complain of my caution."

Mrs Lennox sighed, and shook her head.   She had
long cherished the hope, that if ever her son came
home, it would be to fall in love with and marry her
beloved Mary ; and she had dwelt upon this favourite
scheme till it had taken entire possession of her mind.
In the simplicity of her heart, she also imagined that it
would greatly help to accelerate the event, were she to
suggest the idea, to her son, as she had no doubt but
that the object of her affections must necessarily become
the idol of his.   So little did she know of human
nature, that the very means she used to accomplish her
purpose were the most effectual she could have contrived to defeat it.   Such is man, that his pride revolts
from all attempts to influence his affections.   The weak
and the undiscerning, indeed, are often led to "choose
love by another's eyes ; " but the lofty and independent
spirit loves to create for itself those feelings which lose
half their charms when their source is not in the depths
of their own heart.

It was with no slight mortification that Mrs Lennox
saw Mary depart without having made the desired impression on the heart of her son ; or, what was still
more to be feared, of his having secured himself a place
in her favour.   But, again and again, she made Mary
repeat her promise of returning soon, and spending some
days with her.   "And then," thought she, "things
will all come right.   When they live together, and see
each other constantly, they cannot possibly avoid loving
each other, and all will be as it should be.   God grant
I may live to see it ! "   And hope softened the pang
of disappointment.

Chapter xlix.

'Qui vous a pu plonger dans cette humeur chagrine,
A-t-on par quelque edit réformé la cuisine?'

BOILEAU.

MARY'S inexperienced mind expected to find on her return to Beech Park, some vestige of the pleasures of the preceding night—some shadows at least of gaiety, to show what happiness she had sacrificed—what delight her friends had enjoyed; but, for the first time, she beheld the hideous aspect of departed pleasure. Drooping evergreens, dying lamps, dim transparencies, and faded flowers, met her view as she crossed the hall, while the public rooms were covered with dust from the chalked floors, and wax from the droppings of the candles. Everything, in short, looked tawdry and forlorn. Nothing was in its place—nothing looked as it used to do—and she stood amazed at the disagreeable metamorphose all things had undergone.

Hearing some one approach, she turned, and beheld Dr Redgill enter.

"So—it's only you, Miss Mary!" exclaimed he, in a tone of chagrin. "I was in hopes it was some of the women-servants. 'Pon my soul, it's disgraceful to think that, in this house, there is not a woman stirring yet! I have sent five messages by my man, to let Mrs Brown know that I have been waiting for my breakfast these two hours; but this nonsensical ball has turned everything upside down!—You are come to a pretty scene," continued he, looking round with a mixture of fury and contempt,—"a very pretty scene! Just look at these rags!" kicking a festoon of artificial roses that had fallen to the ground. "Can anything be more despicable?—and to think that rational creatures in possession of their senses should take pleasure in the sight of such trumpery!—I—I—declare it confounds me! I really used to think Lady Emily (for this is all her doing) had some sense—but such a display of folly as this—!"

"Pshaw!" said Mary, "it is not fair in us to stand here analysing the dregs of gaiety after the essence is gone. I dare say this was a very brilliant scene last night."

"Brilliant scene, indeed!" repeated the doctor, in a most wrathful accent: "I really am amazed—I—yes—brilliant enough—if you mean that there was a glare of light enough to blind the devil. I thought my eyes would have been put out, the short time I staid; indeed, I don't think this one has recovered it yet," advancing a fierce blood-shot eye almost close to Mary's. "Don't you think it looks a *leetle* inflamed, Miss Mary?"

Mary gave it as her opinion that it did. "Well, that's all I've got by this business, but I never was consulted about it. I thought it my duty, however, to give a *leetle* hint to the Earl, when the thing was proposed. 'My lord,' says I, 'your house is your own; you have a right to do what you please with it; burn it—pull it down—make a purgatory of it, if you think proper;—but, don't give a ball in it!' The ball was given, and you see the consequences. A ball! and what's a ball, that a whole family should be thrown into disorder for it?"

"I dare say, to those who are engaged in it, it is a very delightful amusement at the time."

"Delightful fiddlestick! 'Pon my soul, I'm surprised at you, Miss Mary! I thought your staying away was a pretty strong proof of your good sense; but I—hem!—Delightful amusement, indeed! to see human creatures twirling one another about all night like so many monkeys, making perfect mountebanks of themselves. Really, I look upon dancing as a most degrading and a most immoral practice. 'Pon my honour, I—*I* couldn't have the face to waltz, I know; and it's all on account of this delightful amusement," with a convulsive shake of his chin, "that things are in this state—myself kept waiting for my breakfast two hours and a half beyond my natural time; not that I mind myself at all—that's neither here nor there—and if I was the only sufferer, I'm sure I should be the very last to complain; but I own it vexes—it distresses me —'pon my honour, I can't stand seeing a whole family going to destruction!"

The doctor's agitation was so great that Mary really pitied him.

"It is rather hard that you cannot get any breakfast, since you had no enjoyment in the ball," said she. "I dare say, were I to apply to Mrs Brown, she would trust me with her keys; and I shall be happy to officiate for her in making your tea."

"Thank you, Miss Mary," replied the doctor, coldly. "I'm very much obliged to you: it is really a very polite offer on your part; but—hem!—you might have observed that I never take tea to breakfast, —I keep that for the evening: most people, I know, do the reverse, but they're in the wrong. Coffee is too nutritive for the evening. The French themselves are in an error there. That woman, that Mrs Brown, knows what I like; in fact, she's the only woman I ever met with who could make coffee—coffee that I thought drinkable. She knows that—and she knows that I like it to a moment—and yet——"

Here the doctor blew his nose, and Mary thought she perceived a tear twinkle in his eye. Finding she was incapable of administering consolation, she was about to quit the room, when the doctor, recovering himself, called after her.

"If you happen to be going the way of Mrs Brown's room, Miss Mary, I would take it very kind, if you could just contrive to let her know what time of day it is; and that I have not tasted a mouthful of anything since last night at twelve o'clock, when I took a *leetle* morsel of supper in my own room."

Mary took advantage of the deep sigh that followed to make her escape; and as she crossed the vestibule, she descried the doctor's man, hurrying along with a coffee-pot, which she had no doubt would pour consolation into his master's soul.

As Mary was aware of her mother's dislike to introduce her into company, she flattered herself she had for once done something to merit her approbation, by having absented herself on this occasion. But Mary was a novice in the ways of temper, and had yet to learn, that to study to please, and to succeed, are very different things. Lady Juliana had been decidedly averse to her appearing at the ball, but she was equally disposed to take offence at her having staid away; besides, she had not been pleased herself, and her glass told her she looked jaded and ill. She was, therefore, as her maid expressed it, in a most particular bad temper; and Mary had to endure reproaches, of which she could only make out, that although she ought not to have been present, she was much to blame in having been absent. Lady Emily's indignation was in a different style. There was a heat and energy in her anger, that never failed to overwhelm her victim at once. But it was more tolerable than the tedious, fretful, ill-humour of the other; and after she had fairly exhausted herself in invective, and ridicule, and insolence, and drawn tears from her cousin's eyes by the bitterness of her language, she heartily embraced her—vowed she liked her better than any body in the world—and that she was a fool for minding anything she said to her.

"I assure you," said she, "I was only tormenting you a little, and you must own you deserve that; but you can't suppose I meant half what I said; that is a *bétise* I can't conceive you guilty of. You see I am much more charitable in my conclusions than you. You have no scruple in thinking me a wretch, though I am too good-natured to set you down for a fool. Come, brighten up, and I'll tell you all about the ball.—How I hate it, were it only for having made your nose red! But really, the thing in itself was detestable; Job himself must have gone mad at the provocations I met with. In the first place, I had set my heart upon introducing you with *eclât*; and instead of which you preferred psalm-singing with Mrs Lennox, or sentiment with her son—I don't know which. In the next place, there was a dinner in Bath, that kept away some of the best men; then, after waiting an hour and a half for Frederick to begin the ball with Lady Charlotte M., I went myself to his room, and found him lounging by the fire with a volume of Rousseau in his hand, not dressed, and quite surprised that I should think his presence at all necessary; and when he did make his *entré*, conceive my feelings at seeing him single out Lady Placid as his partner! I certainly would rather have seen him waltzing with a hyena! I don't believe he knew or cared whom he danced with—unless, perhaps, it had been Adelaide, but she was engaged—and, by the by, there certainly is some sort of a *liaison* there —how it will end, I don't know—it depends upon themselves; for I'm sure the course of their love may run smooth if they choose—I know of nothing to interrupt it. Perhaps, indeed, it may become stagnate from that very circumstance; for you know, or perhaps you don't know, 'there is no spirit under heaven that works with such delusion.'"

Mary would have felt rather uneasy at this intelli-

gence, had she believed it possible for her sister to be in
love; but she had ever appeared to her so insensible to
every tender emotion and generous affection, that she
could not suppose even love itself was capable of making
any impression on her heart. When, however, she saw
them together, she began to waver in her opinion.
Adelaide, silent and disdainful to others, was now gay
and enchanting to Lord Lindore, and looked as if she
triumphed in the victory she had already won. It was
not so easy to ascertain the nature of Lord Lindore's
feelings towards his cousin, and time only developed
them.

———o———

Chapter I.

"Les douleurs muettes et stupides sont hors d'usage; on
pleure, on récite, on répète, on est si touchée de la mort de son
mari, qu'on n'en oublie pas la moindre circonstance."—LA
BRUYERE.

"PRAY put on your Lennox face this morning,
Mary," said Lady Emily one day to her
cousin, "for I want you to go and pay a
funereal visit with me to a distant relation, but un-
happily a near neighbour of ours, who has lately lost
her husband. Lady Juliana and Adelaide ought to
go, but they won't, so you and I must celebrate, as we
best can, the obsequies of the Honourable Mr Sufton."

Mary readily assented; and when they were seated
in the carriage, her cousin began—

"Since I am going to put you in the way of a trap,
I think it but fair to warn you of it. All traps are
odious things, and I make it my business to expose them
wherever I find them. I own it chafes my spirit to
see even sensible people taken in by the clumsy machinery
of such a woman as Lady Matilda Sufton: so here she
is in her true colours. Lady Matilda is descended

from the ancient and illustrious family of Altamont. To have a fair character is, in her eyes, much more important than to deserve it. She has prepared speeches for every occasion ; and she expects they are all to be believed,—she has studied attitudes, and imagines they are to pass for *impromptu* feelings,—in short, she is a *show* woman—the world is her theatre, and from it she looks for the plaudits due to her virtue—for with her, the reality and the semblance are synonymous. She has a grave and imposing air, which keeps the timid at a distance ; and she delivers the most common truths as if they were the most profound aphorisms. To degrade herself is her greatest fear ; or, to use her own expression, there is nothing so degrading as associating with our inferiors—that is, our inferiors in rank and wealth—for with her all other gradations are incomprehensible. With the lower orders of society she is totally unacquainted — she knows they are meanly clothed and coarsely fed—consequently they are mean. She is proud, both by nature and principle ; for she thinks it is the duty of every woman of family to be proud, and that humility is only a virtue in the *canaille*. Proper pride she calls it, though I rather think it ought to be *pride-proper*, as I imagine it is a distinction that was unknown before the introduction of heraldry. The only true knowledge, according to her creed, is the knowledge of the world, by which she means a knowledge of the most courtly etiquette—the manners and habits of the great, and the newest fashions in dress. Ignoramuses might suppose she entered deeply into things, and was thoroughly acquainted with human nature : no such thing—the only wisdom she possesses, like the owl, is the look of wisdom, and that is the very part of it which I detest. Passions or feelings she has none ; and to love she is an utter stranger. When somewhat ' in the sear and yellow leaf,' she married Mr

Sufton, a silly old man, who had been dead to the
world for many years. But after having had him
buried alive in his own chamber till his existence was
forgot, she had him disinterred for the purpose of giving
him a splendid burial in good earnest. That done, her
duty is now to mourn, or appear to mourn, for the
approbation of the world : and now you shall judge for
yourself, for here is Sufton House. Now for the trap-
pings and the weeds of woe."

Aware of her cousin's satirical turn, Mary was not
disposed to yield conviction to her representation, but
entered Lady Matilda's drawing-room with a mind
sufficiently unbiassed to allow her to form her own
judgment ; but a very slight survey satisfied her that the
picture was not overcharged. Lady Matilda sat in an
attitude of woe—a crape-fan and open prayer-book lay
before her—her cambric handkerchief was in her hand
—her mourning-ring was upon her finger—and the tear,
not unbidden, stood in her eye. On the same sofa,
and side by side, sat a tall, awkward, vapid-looking
personage, whom she introduced as her brother, the
Duke of Altamont. His grace was flanked by an
obsequious looking gentleman, who was slightly named,
as General Carver ; and at a respectful distance was
scated a sort of half-caste gentlewoman, something between the confidential friend and humble companion, who
was incidentally mentioned as " my good Mrs Finch."

Her ladyship pressed Lady Emily's hand—

" I did not expect, my dearest young friend, after
the blow I have experienced—I did not expect I
should so soon have been enabled to see my friends ;
but I have made a great exertion. Had I consulted
my own feelings, indeed !—but there is a duty we owe
to the world—there is an example we are all bound to
show—but such a blow ! " Here she had recourse to
her handkerchief.

" Such a blow ! " echoed the duke.

" Such a blow ! " re-echoed the general.

" Such a blow ! " reverberated Mrs Finch.

" The most doating husband ! I may say he lived but in my sight. Such a man ! "

" Such a man ! " said the duke.

" Such a man ! " exclaimed the general.

" Oh ! such a man ! " sobbed Mrs Finch, as she complacently dropped a few tears. At that moment, sacred to tender remembrance, the door opened, and Mrs Downe Wright was announced. She entered the room as if she had come to profane the ashes of the dead, and insult the feelings of the living. A smile was upon her face ; and, instead of the silent pressure, she shook her ladyship heartily by the hand, as she expressed her pleasure at seeing her look so well.

" Well ! " repeated the lady ; " that is wonderful, after what I have suffered—but grief, it seems, will not kill ! "

" I never thought it would," said Mrs Downe Wright ; " but I thought your having been confined to the house so long might have affected your looks. However, I am happy to see that is not the case, as I don't recollect ever to have seen you so fat."

Lady Matilda tried to look her into decency, but in vain. She sighed, and even groaned ; but Mrs Downe Wright would not be dolorous, and was not to be taken in, either by sigh or groan, crape-fan, or prayer-book. There was nobody her ladyship stood so much in awe of as Mrs Downe Wright. She had an instinctive knowledge that she knew her, and she felt her genius repressed by her, as Julius Cæsar's was by Cassius. They had been very old acquaintances, but never were cordial friends, though many worthy people are very apt to confound the two. Upon this occasion, Mrs Downe Wright certainly did ; for, availing herself of this privilege, she took off her cloak, and said, "'Tis so long since I have seen you, my dear; and since I see you so well, and able to enjoy the society of your friends, I shall delay the rest of my visits, and spend the morning with you."

"That is truly kind of you, my dear Mrs Downe Wright," returned the mourner, with a countenance in which real woe was now plainly depicted; "but I cannot be so selfish as to claim such a sacrifice from you."

"There is no sacrifice in the case, I assure you, my dear," returned Mrs Downe Wright: "this is a most comfortable room; and I could go nowhere, that I would meet a pleasanter little circle," looking round.

Lady Matilda thought herself undone. "Looking well—fat—comfortable room—pleasant circle"—rung in her ears, and caused almost as great a whirl in her brain as noses, lips, handkerchiefs, did in Othello's. Mrs Downe Wright, always disagreeable, was now perfectly insupportable. She had disconcerted all her plans—she was a bar to all her studied speeches—even an obstacle to all her sentimental looks—yet to get rid of her was impossible. In fact, Mrs Downe Wright was far from being an amiable woman. She took a malicious pleasure in tormenting those she did not like; and her skill in this art was so great, that she even deprived the tormented of the privilege of complaint. She had a great insight into character, and she might be said to read the very thoughts of her victims. Making a desperate effort to be herself again, Lady Matilda turned to her two young visitors, with whom she had still some hopes of success.

"I cannot express how much I feel indebted to the sympathy of my friends upon this trying occasion—an occasion, indeed, that called for sympathy."

"A most melancholy occasion!" said the duke.

"A most distressing occasion!" exclaimed the general.

"Never was greater occasion!" moaned Mrs Finch.

Her ladyship wiped her eyes, and resumed—

"I feel that I act but a melancholy part, in spite of every exertion. But my kind friend Mrs Downe Wright's spirits will, I trust, support me. She knows what it is to lose ——"

Again her voice was buried in her handkerchief, and again she recovered and proceeded—

"I ought to apologize for being thus overcome; but my friends, I hope, will make due allowance for my situation. It cannot be expected that I should at all times find myself able for company."

"Not at all!" said the duke; and the two satellites uttered their responses.

"You are able for a great deal, my dear!" said the provoking Mrs Downe Wright; "and I have no doubt but, with a very little exertion, you could behave as if nothing had happened."

"Your partiality makes you suppose me capable of a great deal more than I am equal to," answered her ladyship, with a real hysteric sob. "It is not every one who is blessed with the spirits of Mrs Downe Wright."

"What woman can do, you dare; who dares do more, is none!" said the general, bowing with a delighted air at this brilliant application.

Mrs Downe Wright charitably allowed it to pass, as she thought it might be construed either as a compliment or a banter. Visitors flocked in, and the insufferable Mrs Downe Wright declared to all, that her ladyship was astonishingly well; but without the appropriate whine, which gives proper pathos, and generally accompanies this hackneyed speech. Mrs Finch, indeed, laboured hard to counteract the effect of this injudicious cheerfulness, by the most orthodox sighs, shakes of the head, and confidential whispers, in which "wonderful woman!"—"prodigious exertion!"—"perfectly over-come!"—"suffer for this afterwards!"—were audibly heard by all present; but even then Mrs Downe Wright's drawn-up lip and curled nose spoke daggers. At length the tormentor recollected an engagement she had made elsewhere, and took leave, promising to return, if possible, the following day. Her friend, in her own mind, took her measures accordingly. She resolved to order her own carriage to be in waiting, and if Mrs Downe Wright put her threat in execution, she would take an airing. True, she had not intended to have been able for such an exertion for at least a week longer; but, with the blinds down, she thought it might have an interesting effect.

The enemy fairly gone, Lady Matilda seemed to feel like a person suddenly relieved from the night-mare; and she was beginning to give a fair specimen of her scenic powers, when Lady Emily, seeing the game was up with Mrs Downe Wright, abruptly rose to depart.

"This has been a trying scene for you, my sweet young friends!" said her ladyship, taking a hand of each.

"It has indeed!" replied Lady Emily, in a tone so significant as made Mary start.

"I know it would—youth is always so full of sympathy. I own I have a preference for the society of my young friends on that account. My good Mrs Finch, indeed, is an exception; but worthy Mrs Downe Wright has been almost too much for me."

"She *is* too much!" said the duke.

"She is a great deal too much!" said the general.

"She is a vast deal too much!" said Mrs Finch.

"I own I have been rather overcome by her!" with a deep-drawn sigh, which her visitors hastily availed them-

selves of to make their retreat. The duke and the
general handed Lady Emily and Mary to their carriage.

" You find my poor sister wonderfully composed,"
said the former.

" Charming woman, Lady Matilda ! " ejaculated
the latter ; " her feelings do honour to her head and
heart ! "

Mary sprung into the carriage as quick as possible, to
be saved the embarrassment of a reply ; and it was not
till they were fairly out of sight, that she ventured to
raise her eyes to her cousin's face. There the expression of ill humour and disgust were so strongly depicted, that she could no longer repress her risible
emotions, but gave way to a violent fit of laughter.

" How ! " exclaimed her companion, " is this the
only effect ' Matilda's moan ' has produced upon you ?
I expected your taste for grief would have been highly
gratified by this affecting representation."

" My appetite, you ought rather to say," replied
Mary ; " taste implies some discrimination, which you
seem to deny me."

" Why, to tell you the truth, I do look upon you as
a sort of intellectual ghoul—you really do remind me of
the lady in the Arabian Nights, whose taste or appetite,
which you will, led her to scorn everything that did not
savour of the church-yard."

" The delicacy of your comparison is highly flattering," said Mary ; " but I must be duller than the fat
weed, were I to give my sympathy to such as Lady
Matilda Sufton."

" Well, I'm glad to hear you say so ; for I assure
you, I was in pain lest you should have been taken in,
notwithstanding my warning, to say something *larmoyante*—or join the soft echo—or heave a sigh—or
drop a tear—or do something, in short, that would have
disgraced you with me for ever. At one time, I must

do you the justice to own, I thought I saw you with difficulty repress a smile, and then you blushed so, for fear you had betrayed yourself! The smile I suppose has gained you one conquest—the blush another. How happy you, who can hit the various tastes so easily! Mrs Downe Wright whispered me as she left the room, ‘What a charming intelligent countenance your cousin has!’ While my Lord Duke of Altamont observed, as he handed me along, ‘What a very sweet modest-looking girl Miss Douglas was!’ So take your choice—Mrs William Downe Wright, or Duchess of Altamont!’’

‘‘Duchess of Altamont, to be sure,’’ said Mary: ‘‘and then such a man! Oh! such a man!’’

———o———

Chapter Ij.

"For marriage is a matter of more worth
Than to be dealt with in attorneyship."
                          SHAKSPEARE.

‘‘ ALLOW me to introduce to you, ladies, that most high and puissant Princess, her Grace the Duchess of Altamont, Marchioness of Norwood, Countess of Penrose, Baroness of, &c. &c.,’’ cried Lady Emily, as she threw open the drawing-room door, and ushered Mary into the presence of her mother and sister, with all the demonstrations of ceremony and respect. The one frowned—the other coloured.

‘‘ How very absurd!’’ cried Lady Juliana, angrily.

‘‘ How very amusing!’’ cried Adelaide, contemptuously.

‘‘ How very annoying!’’ cried Lady Emily; ‘‘ to think that this little Highlander should bear aloft the ducal crown, while you and I, Adelaide, must sneak about in shabby straw bonnets," throwing down her own in pretended indignation. "Then to think, which is almost certain, of her viceroying it some day; and you and I, and all of us, being presented to her majesty—having the honour of her hand to kiss—retreating from the royal presence upon our heels—oh! ye Sylphs and Gnomes!" and she pretended to sink down overwhelmed with mortification.

Lady Emily delighted in tormenting her aunt and cousin, and she saw that she had completely succeeded. Mary was disliked by her mother, and despised by her sister; and any attempt to bring her forward, or raise her to a level with themselves, never failed to excite the indignation of both. The consequences were always felt by her, in the increased ill-humour and disdainful indifference with which she was treated; and on the present occasion, her injudicious friend was only brewing phials of wrath for her. But Lady Emily never looked to future consequences—present effect was all she cared for; and she went on to relate seriously as she called it, but in the most exaggerated terms, the admiration which the duke had expressed for Mary, and her own firm belief that she might be duchess when she chose; "that is, after the expiry of his mourning for the late duchess. Every one knows that he is desirous of having a family, and is determined to marry the moment propriety permits—he is now decidedly on the look-out, for the year must be very near a close; and then,—hail Duchess of Altamont!"

"I must desire, Lady Emily, you will find some other subject for your wit, and not fill the girl's head with folly and nonsense—there is a great deal too much of both there already."

"Take care what you say of the future representative of majesty; this may be high treason yet; only I trust your grace will be as generous as Henry the

Fifth was, and that the Duchess of Altamont will
not remember the offences committed against Mary
Douglas."

Lady Juliana, to whom a jest was an outrage, and
raillery incomprehensible, now started up, and, as she
passionately swept out of the room, threw down a stand
of hyacinths, which, for the present, put a stop to Lady
Emily's diversion.

The following day Mrs Downe Wright arrived with
her son, evidently primed for falling in love at first
sight. He was a handsome young man, gentle, and
rather pleasing in his manners; and Mary, to whom
his intentions were not so palpable, thought him by no
means deserving of the contempt her cousin had expressed for him.

" Well ! " cried Lady Emily, after they were gone,
" the plot begins to thicken—lovers begin to pour in,
but all for Mary—how mortifying to you and me,
Adelaide ! At this rate, we shall have nothing to
boast of in the way of disinterested attachment—
nobody refused !—nothing renounced !—By and by
Edward will be reckoned a very good match for *me*,
and *you* will be thought greatly married, if you succeed
in securing Lindore : *poor* Lord Lindore, as it seems
that wretch Placid calls him."

Adelaide heard all her cousin's taunts in silence, and
with apparent coolness; but they rankled deep in a
heart already festering with pride, envy, and ambition.
The thoughts of her sister—and that sister so inferior
to herself—attaining a more splendid alliance, was not
to be endured. True, she loved Lord Lindore, and
imagined herself beloved in return; but even that was
not sufficient to satisfy the craving passions of a perverted mind. She did not, indeed, attach implicit
belief to all that her cousin said on the subject; but
she was provoked and irritated at the mere supposition

of such a thing being possible; for it is not merely the jealous whose happiness is the sport of trifles light as air —every evil thought, every unamiable feeling, bears about with it the bane of that enjoyment after which it vainly aspires.

Mary felt the increasing ill-humour which this subject drew upon her, without being able to penetrate the cause of it; but she saw that it was displeasing to her mother and sister, and that was sufficient to make her wish to put a stop to it. She therefore earnestly entreated Lady Emily to end the joke.

" Excuse me," replied her ladyship, " I shall do no such thing. In the first place, there happens to be no joke in the matter: I'm certain, seriously certain, or certainly serious, which you like, that you may be Duchess of Altamont, if you please. It could be no common admiration that prompted his Grace to an original and spontaneous effusion of it. I have met with him before, and never suspected that he had an innate idea in his head. I certainly never heard him utter anything half so brilliant before—it seemed quite like the effect of inspiration."

" But I cannot conceive, even were it as you say, why my mother should be so displeased about it. She surely cannot suppose me so silly, as to be elated by the unmeaning admiration of any one, or so meanly aspiring as to marry a man I could not love, merely because he is a Duke. She was incapable of such a thing herself: she cannot then suspect me."

" It seems as impossible to make you enter into the characters of your mother and sister, as it would be to teach them to comprehend yours; and far be it from me to act as interpreter betwixt your understandings. If you cannot even imagine such things as prejudice, narrow-mindedness, envy, hatred, and malice, your ignorance is bliss, and you had better remain in it. But

you may take my word for one thing, and that is, that
'tis a much wiser thing to resist tyranny than to submit
to it. Your patient Grizzels make nothing of it, except
in little books : in real life they become perfect pack-
horses, saddled with the whole offences of the family.
Such will you become, unless you pluck up spirit, and
dash out.   Marry the Duke, and drive over the necks
of all your relations ; that's my advice to you."

" And you may rest assured that when I follow your
advice, it shall be in whole, not in part."

" Well, situated so detestably as you are, I rather
think the best thing you could do, would be to make
yourself Duchess of Altamont.   How disdainful you
look !   Come, tell me honestly now, would you really
refuse to be your Grace, with ninety thousand per
annum, and remain simple Mary Douglas, ' passing
rich with forty pounds a-year ' perhaps ? "

" Unquestionably," said Mary.

" What ! you really pretend to say you would not
marry the Duke of Altamont ? " cried Lady Emily.
" Not that I would take him myself ; but as you and I,
though the best of friends, differ widely in our sentiments on most subjects, I should really like to know
how it happens that we agree in this one.   Very
different reasons, I dare say, lead to the same conclusion ; but I shall generously give you the advantage
of hearing mine first.   I shall say nothing of being
engaged — I shall even banish that idea from my
thoughts ; but were I free as air—unloving and un-
loved—I would refuse the Duke of Altamont ; first,
because he is old—no, that is not it—but my objections
are so many, I must give you them in pairs, else I
should never come to the end.   First, then, he is dull
and stupid ; second, he is obstinate and unconvincible ;
third, he is proud and pompous ; fourth, he is old and
ugly ; fifth (and that may stand for a thousand), he

carries his *bétise* so far as to think all that the Lady
Matilda says and does must be 'the wisest, virtuousest,
discreetest, best;'—to conclude, he wants that inimitable *Je ne sçais quoi*, which I consider as a necessary
ingredient in the matrimonial cup. I shall not, in
addition to these defects, dwell upon his unmeaning
stare—his formal bow—his little senseless simper, &c.
&c. &c. All these enormities, and many more of the
same stamp, I shall pass by, as I have no doubt they
had their due effect upon you as well as me; but then
I am not, like you, under the torments of Lady
Juliana's authority. Were that the case, I should
certainly think it a blessing to become Duchess of
anybody to-morrow."

"And can you really imagine," said Mary, "that
for the sake of shaking off my mother's authority, I
would impose upon myself chains still heavier, and even
more binding? Can you suppose I would so far forfeit
my honour and truth, as that I would swear to love,
honour, and obey, where I could feel neither love nor
respect; and where cold, heartless obedience would be
all of my duty I could hope to fulfil?"

"Love!" exclaimed Lady Emily; "can I credit
my ears? Love! did you say? I thought that had
only been for naughty ones, such as me; and that saints
like you would have married for anything and everything but love. Prudence, I thought, had been the
word with you proper ladies—a prudent marriage!
Come, confess, is not that the climax of virtue in the
creed of your school?"

"I never learnt the creed of any school," said Mary,
"nor ever heard any one's sentiments on the subject,
except my dear Mrs Douglas's."

"Well, I should like to hear your oracle's opinion,
if you can give it in short-hand."

"She warned me there was a passion, which was

very fashionable, and which I should hear a great deal of, both in conversation and books, that was the result of indulged fancy, warm imaginations, and ill-regulated minds; that many had fallen into its snares, deceived by its glowing colours and alluring name; that —— "

"A very good sermon, indeed!" interrupted Lady Emily; "but, no offence to Mrs Douglas, I think I could preach a better myself. Love is a passion that has been much talked of, often described, and little understood. Cupid has many counterfeits going about the world, who pass very well with those whose minds are capable of passion, but not of love. These Birmingham Cupids have many votaries amongst boarding-school misses, militia officers, and milliners' apprentices; who marry upon the mutual faith of blue eyes and scarlet coats; have dirty houses and squalling children, and hate each other most delectably. Then there is another species for more refined souls, which owes its birth to the works of Rousseau, Göethe, Cottin, &c. : its success depends very much upon rocks, woods, and waterfalls; and it generally ends in daggers, pistols, poison, or Doctors' Commons. But there, I think, Lindore would be more eloquent than me, so I shall leave it for him to discuss that chapter with you. But, to return to your own immediate concerns.—Pray, are you then positively prohibited from falling in love? Did Mrs Douglas only dress up a scarecrow to frighten you, or had she the candour to show you Love himself in all his majesty?"

"She told me," said Mary, "that there was a love which even the wisest and most virtuous need not blush to entertain—the love of a virtuous object, founded upon esteem, and heightened by similarity of tastes, and sympathy of feelings, into a pure and devoted attachment :—unless I feel all this, I shall never fancy myself in love."

"Humph! I can't say much as to the similarity of tastes and sympathy of souls between the duke and you; but surely you might contrive to feel some love and esteem for a coronet and ninety thousand a year."

"Suppose I did," said Mary, with a smile, "the next point is to honour; and surely he is as unlikely to excite that sentiment as the other. Honour ———"

"I can't have a second sermon upon honour. 'Can honour take away the grief of a wound?' as Falstaff says. Love is the only subject I care to preach about; though, unlike many young ladies, we can talk about other things too; but as to this duke, *I* certainly 'had rather live on cheese and garlic, in a windmill far, than feed on cates, and have him talk to me in any summer-house in Christendom;' and now I have had Mrs Douglas's second-hand sentiments upon the subject—I should like to hear your own."

"I have never thought much upon the subject," said Mary; "my sentiments are therefore all at second-hand, but I shall repeat to you what I think is *not* love, and what *is*." And she repeated these pretty and well-known lines:—

CARELESS AND FAITHFUL LOVE.

To sigh—yet feel no pain—
To weep—yet scarce know why,
To sport an hour with beauty's chain,
Then throw it idly by:
To kneel at many a shrine,
Yet lay the heart on none;
To think all other charms divine,
But those we just have won:—
This is love—careless love—
Such as kindleth hearts that rove.

To keep one sacred flame
Through life unchill'd, unmoved;
To love in wint'ry age the same
That first in youth we loved:

To feel that we adore
With such refined excess,
That though the heart would break with more,
We could not live with less:—
This is love—faithful love—
Such as saints might feel above.

"And such as I do feel, and will always feel, for my Edward," said Lady Emily.—"But there is the dressing bell!" And she flew off, singing,

"To keep one sacred flame," &c.

————o————

Chapter lij.

"Some, when they write to their friends, are all affection; some are wise and sententious; some strain their powers for efforts of gaiety; some write news, and some write secrets— but to make a letter without affection, without wisdom, without gaiety, without news, and without a secret, is doubtless the great epistolic art."—Dr Johnson.

AN unusual length of time had elapsed since Mary had heard from Glenfern, and she was beginning to feel some anxiety on account of her friends there, when her apprehensions were dispelled by the arrival of a large packet, containing letters from Mrs Douglas and aunt Jacky. The former, although the one that conveyed the greatest degree of pleasure, was perhaps not the one that would be most acceptable to the reader. Indeed, it is generally admitted, that the letters of single ladies are infinitely more lively and entertaining than those of married ones—a fact which can neither be denied nor accounted for. The following is a faithful transcript from the original letter in question.

"Glenfern Castle, ——shire, N.B.
Feb. 19th, 18—.

"My dear Mary,

"Yours was *received* with *much* pleasure, as it is *always* a satisfaction to your friends *here* to know that you are *well* and doing *well*. We all *take* the most *sincere* interest in your *health*, and also in your *improvements* in other *respects*. But I am *sorry* to say they do not quite *keep* pace with *our* expectations. I must therefore *take* this opportunity of *mentioning* to you a *fault* of yours, *which*, though a very great *one* in itself, is one *that* a very slight *degree* of attention on your *part*, will, I have *no* doubt, enable you to *get* entirely the *better of*. It is fortunate for *you*, my dear Mary, that you have *friends* who are always ready to point *out* your errors to you. For *want* of that *most* invaluable *blessing*, viz. a sincere *friend*, many a *one* has gone out of the *world*, no wiser, in many *respects*, than when they *came* into it. But that, I flatter *myself*, will not be your *case*, as you cannot *but* be sensible of the great *pains* my sisters and I have *taken* to point out your *faults* to you from the hour of your birth. The *one* to which I particularly *allude* at present is, the constant omission of *proper* dates to your *letters*, by which means we are all of us very often *brought* into *most* unpleasant *situations*. As an *instance* of it, our *worthy* minister, Mr M'Drone, happened to be *calling* here the very *day* we received your last *letter*. After *hearing* it read, he most *naturally* inquired the date of it; and I *cannot* tell you how *awkward* we all *felt* when we were *obliged* to confess it had *none!* And since I am *upon* that subject, I think it much *better* to tell you candidly that I *do* not think your *hand* of write by any *means* improved. It does not *look* as if you *bestowed* that pains upon it which you *undoubtedly* ought to do; for without *pains*, I can assure

you, Mary, you *will* never do any *thing* well.   As our
admirable *grandmother*, good Lady Girnachgowl, *used*
to say, pains *makes* gains, and so it was *seen* upon her;
for it was entirely *owing* to her *pains* that the Girnachgowl estate was relieved, and *came* to be what it is now,
viz. a most valuable and *highly* productive property.

  " I know there are *many* young *people* who are very
apt to think it *beneath* them to take *pains ;* but I sincerely trust, my dear Mary, you have *more* sense than
to be so very *foolish*.   Next to a good distinct *hand* of
write, and *proper* stops (which I observe you never *put*),
the thing *most* to be attended to is your style, *which* we
all think might *be* greatly *improved* by a *little* reflection
on your *part*, joined to a *few* judicious *hints* from your
friends.   We are *all* of opinion that your *periods* are too
short, and also *that* your expressions are *deficient* in
dignity.   *Neither* are you sufficiently circumstantial in
your *intelligence*, even upon subjects of the highest *importance*.   Indeed, upon some *subjects*, you *communicate*
no information whatever, which is *certainly* very extraordinary in a *young* person, who ought to be naturally
extremely communicative.   Miss M'Pry, who is here
upon a *visit* to us at *present*, is perfectly *astonished* at
the total *want* of news in your *letters*.   She has a *niece*
residing in the neighbourhood of *Bath*, who sends her
regular lists of the company there, and also an *account*
of the most *remarkable* events that take *place* there.
Indeed, had it not been for Patty M'Pry, we never
would have *heard* a *syllable* of the celebrated *Lady*
Travers's elopement with *Sir* John Conquest ; and, indeed, I cannot *conceal* from you, that we have heard
more as to what goes on in Lord Courtland's *family*,
through Miss Patty M'Pry, than *ever* we have heard
from you, *Mary*.

  " In short, I *must* plainly tell you, *however* painful
you may *feel* it, that not one of us is ever a *whit* the

wiser after reading your *letters* than we *were* before.
But I am *sorry* to say this is not the *most* serious part
of the *complaint* we have to *make* against you. We are
all *willing* to find excuses for you, even *upon* these points,
but I must *confess*, your neglecting to *return* any answers
to certain inquiries of your aunt's, *appears* to me perfectly inexcusable. Of *course*, you must *understand*,
that I allude to that *letter* of your aunt Grizzy's, dated
the 17th of December, wherein she *expressed* a strong
desire that you should endeavour to make yourself *mistress* of Dr Redgill's opinion with *respect* to lumbago,
as she is extremely anxious to *know* whether he *considers* the seat of the disorder to be in the bones or the
sinews ; and undoubtedly it is of the greatest *consequence*
to procure the *opinion* of a sensible well-informed English *physician*, upon a subject of such vital *importance.*
Your aunt Nicky, also, in a letter, *dated* the 22nd of
December, requested to be *informed* whether Lord
Courtland (like our *great* landholders) kills his own
mutton, and if so, *what* becomes of *all* the *sheep heads*,
as Miss P. M'P. insinuates in a *letter* to her aunt, that
the *servants* there are suspected of being *guilty* of great
abuses on that *score ;* but there you also *preserve* a most
unbecoming, and I own I think *somewhat* mysterious
silence.

"And now, my dear Mary, *having* said all that *I*
trust is necessary to *recall* you to a sense of *your* duty,
I *shall* now communicate to you a *piece* of intelligence,
which, I am certain, will *occasion* you the *most* unfeigned
pleasure, viz. the prospect there is of your soon *beholding* some of your friends from this *quarter* in Bath.
Our valuable friend and *neighbour*, Sir Sampson, has
been rather (we think) worse than *better* since you left
us. He is now *deprived* of the entire use of one leg.
He *himself* calls his *complaint* a morbid rheumatism ;
but Lady Maclaughlan *assures* us it is a rheumatic

palsy, and she has now *formed* the resolution of *taking* him *up* to Bath early in the ensuing *spring*. And not only that, but she has most considerately *invited* your aunt Grizzy to accompany them, *which*, of course, she is to do with the greatest *pleasure*. We are therefore all extremely *occupied* in getting your aunt's things *put* in order for such an *occasion ;* and you must *accept* of that as an apology for none of the girls *being* at leisure to write *you* at present, and *likewise* for the shortness of *this* letter. But be assured we will all *write* you fully by Grizzy. Meantime, all *unite* in kind remembrance to *you*. And I *am*, my dear Mary, your most affectionate aunt, JOAN DOUGLAS."

"P.S.—Upon *looking* over your letter, I am much *struck* with your X's. You surely *cannot* be so ignorant as *not* to know that a well *made x* is neither more nor *less* than two *c*'s joined together back to back, *instead* of these senseless crosses you *seem* so fond of; and as to *your z*'s, I defy any *one* to distinguish them *from* your *y*'s. I trust you will *attend* to this, and show that it *proceeds* rather from want of proper *attention* than *from* wilful airs. J. D."

"P.S.—Miss P. M'Pry *writes* her aunt that *there* is a strong *report* of Lord Lindore's marriage to our *niece* Adelaide ; but *we* think that is *impossible*, as you certainly *never* could have omitted to *inform* us of a circumstance *which* so deeply concerns *us*. If so, I must *own* I shall think you quite *unpardonable*. At the *same* time, it *appears* extremely improbable *that* Miss M'P. *would* have mentioned *such* a thing to her *aunt*, without having good *grounds* to go upon. J.D."

Mary could not entirely repress her mirth while she read this catalogue of her crimes, but she was, at the same time, eager to expiate her offences, real or imaginary, in the sight of her good old aunt; and she immediately sat down to the construction of a letter after the model prescribed, though with little expectation of being able to cope with the intelligent Miss P. M‘P., in the extent of her communications. Her heart warmed at the thoughts of seeing again the dear familiar face of aunt Grizzy, and of hearing the tones of that voice, which, though sharp and cracked, still sounded sweet in memory's ear. Such is the power that early associations ever retain over the kind and unsophisticated heart. But she was aware how differently her mother would feel on the subject, as she never alluded to her husband's family but with indignation or contempt; and she therefore resolved to be silent with regard to aunt Grizzy's prospects for the present.

———o———

Chapter liii.

——As in apothecaries' shops all sorts of drugs are permitted to be, so may all sorts of books be in the library ; and as they out of vipers, and scorpions, and poisonous vegetables, extract often wholesome medicaments for the life of mankind, so out of whatsoever book, good instruction and examples may be acquired.—DRUMMOND *of Hawthornden.*

MARY'S thoughts had often reverted to Rose Hall since the day she had last quitted it, and she longed to fulfil her promise to her venerable friend, but a feeling of delicacy, unknown to herself, withheld her. "She will not miss me while she has her son with her," said she to herself; but, in reality, she dreaded her cousin's raillery, should she continue to visit there as frequently as before. At length a favourable opportunity occurred: Lady Emily, with great exultation, told her the Duke of Altamont was to dine at Beech Park the following day, but that

she was to conceal it from Lady Juliana and Adelaide;
"for assuredly," said she, "if they were apprised of it,
they would send you up to the nursery as a naughty
girl, or, perhaps, down to the scullery, and make a
Cinderella of you. Depend upon it, you would not get
leave to show your face in the drawing-room."

"Do you really think so?" asked Mary.

"I know it. I know Lady Juliana would torment
you till she had set you a-crying, and then she would
tell you, you had made yourself such a fright, that you
were not fit to be seen, and so order you to your own
room. You know very well it would not be the first
time that such a thing has happened."

Mary could not deny the fact; but, sick of idle
altercation, she resolved to say nothing, but walk over
to Rose Hall the following morning. And this she
did, leaving a note for her cousin, apologizing for her
flight.

She was received with rapture by Mrs Lennox.

"Ah! my dear Mary," said she, as she tenderly
embraced her, "you know not, you cannot conceive,
what a blank your absence makes in my life! When
you open your eyes in the morning, it is to see the
light of day, and the faces you love, and all is brightness around you. But, when I awake, it is still to
darkness. My night knows no end. 'Tis only when
I listen to your dear voice that I forget I am blind."

"I should not have staid so long from you," said
Mary, "but I knew you had Colonel Lennox with
you, and I could not flatter myself you would have
even a thought to bestow upon me."

"My Charles is, indeed, every thing that is kind and
devoted to me. He walks with me, reads to me,
talks to me, sits with me for hours, and bears with all
my little weaknesses as a mother would with her sick
child; but still there are a thousand little feminine

attentions he cannot understand—I would not that he did. And then to have him always with me seems so selfish; for, gentle and tender-hearted as he is, I know he bears the spirit of an eagle within him; and the tame monotony of my life can ill accord with his active habits. Yet he says he is happy with me, and I try to make myself believe him."

"Indeed," said Mary, "I cannot doubt it. It is always a happiness to be with those we love, and who we know love us, under any circumstances; and it is for that reason I love so much to come to my dear Mrs Lennox," caressing her as she spoke.

"Dearest Mary, who would not love you? Oh! could I but see—could I but hope—"

"You must hope every thing you desire," said Mary, gaily, and little guessing the nature of her good friend's hopes; "I do nothing but hope." And she tried to check a sigh, as she thought how some of her best hopes had been already blighted by the unkindness of those whose love she had vainly strove to win.

Mrs Lennox's hopes were already upon her lips, when the entrance of her son fortunately prevented their being for ever destroyed by a premature disclosure. He welcomed Mary with an appearance of the greatest pleasure, and looked so much happier and more animated than when she last saw him, that she was struck with the change, and began to think he might almost stand a comparison with his picture.

"You find me still here, Miss Douglas," said he, "although my mother gives me many hints to be gone, by insinuating what, indeed, cannot be doubted, how very ill I supply your place; but," turning to his mother, "you are not likely to be rid of me for some time, as I have just received an additional leave of absence; but for that, I must have left you to-morrow."

"Dear Charles! you never told me so. How could you conceal it from me! how wretched I should have been had I dreamed of such a thing!"

"That is the very reason for which I concealed it, and yet you reproach me. Had I told you there was a chance of my going, you would assuredly have set it down for a certainty, and so have been vexed for no purpose."

"But your remaining was a chance too," said Mrs Lennox, who could not all at once reconcile herself even to an *escape* from danger; "and think, had you been called away from me without any preparation!— Indeed, Charles, it was very imprudent."

"My dearest mother, I meant it in kindness: I could not bear to give you a moment's certain uneasiness for an uncertain evil. I really cannot discover either the use or the virtue of tormenting one's self by anticipation. I should think it quite as rational to case myself in a suit of mail, by way of security to my person, as to keep my mind perpetually on the rack of anticipating evil. I perfectly agree with that philosopher who says, if we confine ourselves to general reflections on the evils of life, *that* can have no effect in preparing us for them; and if we bring them home to us, *that* is the certain means of rendering ourselves miserable."

"But they will come, Charles," said his mother, mournfully, "whether we bring them or not."

"True, my dear mother; but when misfortune does come, it comes commissioned from a higher power, and it will ever find a well-regulated mind ready to receive it with reverence, and submit to it with resignation. There is something, too, in real sorrow, that tends to enlarge and exalt the soul; but the imaginary evils of our own creating can only serve to contract and depress it."

Mrs Lennox shook her head—" Ah! Charles, you

may depend upon it your reasoning is wrong, and you will be convinced of it some day."

"I am convinced of it already. I begin to fear this discussion will frighten Miss Douglas away from us. *There* is an evil anticipated! Now, do you, my dear mother, help me to avert it; where that can be done, it cannot be too soon apprehended."

As Colonel Lennox's character unfolded itself, Mary saw much to admire in it; and it is more than probable the admiration would soon have been reciprocal, had it been allowed to take its course. But good Mrs Lennox would force it into a thousand little channels prepared by herself, and love itself must have been quickly exhausted by the perpetual demands that were made upon it. Mary would have been deeply mortified had she suspected the cause of her friend's solicitude to show her off; but she was a stranger to match-making in all its bearings—had scarcely ever read a novel in her life, and, consequently, was not at all aware of the necessity there was for her falling in love with all convenient speed. She was, therefore, sometimes amused, though oftener ashamed, at Mrs Lennox's panegyrics, and could not but smile as she thought how aunt Jacky's wrath would have been kindled, had she heard the extravagant praises that were bestowed on her most trifling accomplishments.

"You must sing my favourite song to Charles, my love—he has never heard you sing. Pray do: you did not use to require any entreaty from me, Mary! Many a time you have gladdened my heart with your songs, when, but for you, it would have been filled with mournful thoughts!"

Mary finding, whatever she did or did *not*, she was destined to hear only her own praises, was glad to take refuge at the harp, to which she sang the following ancient ditty :—

" Sweet day ! so cool, so calm, so bright,
The bridal of the earth and sky,
Sweet dews shall weep thy fall to-night,
                    For thou must die.

Sweet rose ! whose hue, angry and brave,
Bids the rash gazer wipe his eye,
Thy root is ever in its grave ;
                    And thou must die.

Sweet spring ! full of sweet days and roses,
A box where sweets compacted lie,
My music shows you have your closes,
                    And all must die.

Only a sweet and virtuous soul,
Like season'd timber, never gives ;
But when the whole world turns to coal,
                    Then chiefly lives.

"That," said Colonel Lennox, "is one of the many
exquisite little pieces of poetry which are to be found,
like ' jewels in an Ethiop's ear,' in my favourite Izaak
Walton. The title of the book offers no encourage-
ment to female readers, but I know few works from
which I rise with such renovated feelings of benevolence and good-will. Indeed, I know no author who
has given, with so much *naïveté*, so enchanting a picture
of a pious and contented mind. Here," taking the
book from a shelf, and turning over the leaves, "is one
of the passages which has so often charmed me :—
'That very hour which you were absent from me, I
sat down under a willow by the waterside, and considered what you had told me of the owner of that
pleasant meadow in which you left me—that he has a
plentiful estate, and not a heart to think so ; that he
has at this time many law-suits depending—and that
they both damped his mirth, and took up so much of
his time and thoughts, that he himself had not leisure
to take that sweet comfort, I, who pretended no title

to them, took in his fields; for I could there sit quietly, and, looking in the water, see some fishes sport themselves in the silver streams, others leaping at flies of several shapes and colours. Looking on the hills, I could behold them spotted with woods and groves; looking down upon the meadows, I could see, here a boy gathering lilies and lady-smocks, and there a girl cropping culverkeys and cowslips, all to make garlands suitable to this present month of May. These, and many other field-flowers, so perfumed the air, that I thought that very meadow like that field in Sicily, of which Diodorus speaks, where the perfumes arising from the place make all dogs that hunt in it to fall off and lose their scent. I say as I thus sat joying in my own happy condition, and pitying this poor rich man, that owned this and many other pleasant groves and meadows about me, I did then thankfully remember what my Saviour said, that the *meek possess the earth*— or, rather, they enjoy what the others possess and enjoy not; for anglers and meek-spirited men are free from those high, those restless thoughts, which corrode the sweets of life; and they, and they only, can say, as the poet has happily expressed it—

> ' Hail, blest estate of lowliness!
> Happy enjoyments of such minds
> As, rich in self-contentedness,
> Can, like the reeds in roughest winds,
> By yielding, make that blow but small,
> By which proud oaks and cedars fall.' "

"There is both poetry and painting in such prose as this," said Mary; "but I should certainly as soon have thought of looking for a pearl necklace in a fish pond, as of finding pretty poetry in a treatise upon the art of angling."

"That book was a favourite of your father's, Charles," said Mrs Lennox; "and I remember, in

our happiest days, he used to read parts of it to me.
One passage, in particular, made a strong impression
upon me, though I little thought then it would ever
apply to me. It is upon the blessings of sight. Indulge
me by reading it to me once again."

Colonel Lennox made an effort to conquer his
feelings, while he read as follows:

"What would a blind man give to see the pleasant
rivers, and meadows, and flowers, and fountains, that
we have met with! I have been told, that if a man
that was born blind could attain to have his sight for
but only one hour during his whole life, and should, at
the first opening of his eyes, fix his sight upon the sun
when it was in its full glory, either at the rising or the
setting, he would be so transported and amazed, and so
admire the glory of it, that he would not willingly turn
his eyes from that first ravishing object, to behold all
the other various beauties this world could present to
them. And this, and many other like objects, we
enjoy daily, and for most of them, because they be so
common, most men forget to pay their praises; but
let not us, because it is a sacrifice so pleasing to Him
that made the sun, and us, and gives us showers and
flowers——"

A deep sigh from Mrs Lennox made her son look
up: Her eyes were bathed in tears.

He threw his arms around her. "My dearest
mother!" cried he, in a voice choked with agitation, "how cruel—how unthinking—thus to remind
you——"

"Do not reproach yourself for my weakness, dear
Charles; but I was thinking, how much rather, could
I have my sight but for one hour, I would look upon
the face of my own child, than on all the glories of the
creation!"

Colonel Lennox was too deeply affected to speak.

He pressed his mother's hand to his lips—then rose abruptly, and quitted the room. Mary succeeded in soothing her weak and agitated spirits into composure; but the chord of feeling had been jarred, and all her efforts to restore it to its former tone, proved abortive for the rest of the day.

———o———

Chapter lib.

Friendship is constant in all other things
Save in the office and affairs of love;
Therefore all hearts in love use their own tongues;
Let every eye negotiate for itself,
And trust no agent.

Much Ado About Nothing.

THERE was something so refreshing in the domestic peacefulness of Rose Hall, when contrasted with the heartless bustle of Beech Park, that Mary felt too happy in the change to be in any hurry to quit it. But an unfortunate discovery soon turned all her enjoyment into bitterness of heart; and Rose Hall, from being to her a place of rest, was suddenly transformed into an abode too hateful to be endured.

It happened, one day as she entered the drawing-room, Mrs Lennox was, as usual, assailing the heart of her son in her behalf. A large Indian screen divided the room, and Mary's entrance was neither seen nor heard till she was close by them.

"O, certainly, Miss Douglas is all that you say— very pretty—very amiable—and very accomplished," said Colonel Lennox, with a sort of half-suppressed yawn, in answer to an eulogium of his mother's.

"Then why not love her? Ah! Charles, promise me that you will at least try!" said the good old lady, laying her hand upon his with the greatest earnestness.

This was said when Mary was actually standing before her. To hear the words, and to feel their application, was as a flash of lightning; and, for a moment, she felt as if her brain was on fire. She was alive but to one idea, and that the most painful that could be suggested to a delicate mind. She had heard herself recommended to the love of a man who was indifferent to her. Could there be such a humiliation —such a degradation? Colonel Lennox's embarrass- ment was scarcely less; but his mother saw not the mischief she had done, and she continued to speak without his having the power to interrupt her. But her words fell unheeded on Mary's ear—she could hear nothing but what she had already heard. Colonel Lennox rose and respectfully placed a chair for her, but the action was unnoticed—she saw only herself a suppliant for his love; and, insensible to every thing but her own feelings, she turned and hastily quitted the room without uttering a syllable. To fly from Rose Hall, never again to enter it, was her first resolution; yet how was she to do so without coming to an ex- planation, worse even than the cause itself; for she had that very morning yielded to the solicitations of Mrs Lennox, and consented to remain till the follow- ing day.

"Oh!" thought she, as the scalding tears of shame, for the first time, dropped from her eyes, "what a situation am I placed in! To continue to live under the same roof with the man whom I have heard solicited to love me; and how mean—how despicable must I appear in his eyes—thus offered—rejected! How shall I ever be able to convince him that I care not for his love—that I wished it not—that I would refuse, scorn it to-morrow, were it offered to me. Oh!

could I but tell him so; but he must ever remain a stranger to my real sentiments—*he* might reject—but *I* cannot disavow! And yet, to have him think that I have all this while been laying snares for him—that all this parade of my acquirements was for the purpose of gaining his affections!—Oh! how blind and stupid I was, not to see through the injudicious praises of Mrs Lennox! I should not then have suffered this degradation in the eyes of her son!"

Hours passed away unheeded by Mary, while she was giving way to the wounded sensibility of a naturally high spirit and acute feelings, thus violently excited in all their first ardour. At length, she was recalled to herself, by hearing the sound of a carriage, as it passed under her window; and, immediately after, she received a message to repair to the drawing-room to her cousin Lady Emily.

"How fortunate!" thought she; "I shall now get away—no matter how or where, I shall go, never again to return." And, unconscious of the agitation visible in her countenance, she hastily descended, impatient to bid an eternal adieu to her once-loved Rose Hall. She found Lady Emily and Colonel Lennox together. Eyes less penetrating than her cousin's would easily have discovered the state of poor Mary's mind, as she entered the room; her beating heart—her flushed cheek and averted eye, all declared the perturbation of her spirits, and Lady Emily regarded her for a moment with an expression of surprise that served to heighten her confusion.

"I have no doubt I am a very unwelcome visitor here to all parties," said she; "for I come—how shall I declare it!—to carry you home, Mary, by command of Lady Juliana."

"No, no!" cried Mary, eagerly; "you are quite welcome. I am quite ready—I was wishing—I was waiting—" Then, recollecting herself, she blushed still deeper at her own precipitation.

" There is no occasion to be so vehemently obedient," said her cousin ; " *I* am not quite ready, neither am I wishing or waiting to be off in such a hurry. Colonel Lennox and I had just set about reviving an old acquaintance, begun I can't tell when, and broken off when I was a thing in the nursery, with a blue sash and red fingers. I have promised him that when he comes to Beech Park, you shall sing him my favourite Scotch song, ' Should auld acquaintance be forgot.' I would sing it myself, if I could ; but I think every English woman, who pretends to sing Scotch songs, ought to have the bow-string ; " then turning to the harpsichord, she began to play it with exquisite taste and feeling.

" There," said she, rising with equal levity ; " is not that worth all the formal bows—and ' recollects to have had the pleasure '—and ' long time since I had the honour '—and such sort of hateful reminiscences, that make one feel nothing but that they are a great deal older, and uglier, stupider, and more formal than they were so many years before."

" Where the early ties of the heart remain unbroken," said Colonel Lennox, with some emotion, " such remembrances do indeed give it back all its first freshness ; but it cannot be to every one a pleasure to have its feelings awakened, even by tones such as these."

There was nothing of austerity in this ; on the contrary, there was so much sweetness mingled with the melancholy which shaded his countenance, that even Lady Emily was touched, and for a moment silent. The entrance of Mrs Lennox relieved her from her embarrassment. She flew towards her, and taking her hand, " My dear Mrs Lennox, I feel very much as if I were come here in the capacity of an executioner ;—

no, not exactly that, but rather a sort of constable or
bailiff;—for I am come on the part of Lady Juliana
Douglas, to summon you to surrender the person of her
well-beloved daughter, to be disposed of as she in her
wisdom may think fit."

"Not to-day, surely?" cried Mrs Lennox in
alarm; "to-morrow——"

"My orders are peremptory—the suit is pressing,"
with a significant smile to Mary; "this day—oh, ye
hours!" looking at a timepiece, "this very minute,
come, Mary—are you ready—*cap-a-pie?*"

At another time, Mary would have thought only of
the regrets of her venerable friend at parting with her;
but now she felt only her own impatience to be gone,
and she hastily quitted the room to prepare for her
departure.

On returning to it, Colonel Lennox advanced to
meet her, evidently desirous of saying something, yet
labouring under great embarrassment.

"Were it not too selfish and presumptuous," said
he, while his heightened colour spoke his confusion,
"I would venture to express a hope that your absence
will not be very long from my poor mother."

Mary pretended to be very busy collecting her work,
drawings, &c., which lay scattered about, and merely
bent her head in acknowledgment. Colonel Lennox
proceeded—

"I am aware of the sacrifice it must be to such as
Miss Douglas, to devote her time and talents to the
comforting of the blind and desolate; and I cannot
express — she cannot conceive — the gratitude — the
respect—the admiration, with which my heart is filled
at such proofs of noble disinterested benevolence on her
part."

Had Mary raised her eyes to those that vainly sought
to meet hers, she would there have read all, and more

than had been expressed; but she could only think,
" he has been entreated to love me!" and at that
humiliating idea, she bent her head still lower, to hide
the colour that dyed her cheek to an almost painful
degree, while a sense of suffocation at her throat prevented her disclaiming, as she wished to do, the merit
of any sacrifice. Some sketches of Lochmarlie lay
upon a table, at which she had been drawing the day
before; they had ever been precious in her sight till
now, but they only excited feelings of mortification, as
she recollected having taken them from her *portefeuille*
at Mrs Lennox's request, to show to her son.

This was part of the parade by which I was to
win him," thought she, with bitterness; and scarcely
conscious of what she did, she crushed them together,
and threw them into the fire. Then hastily advancing
to Mrs Lennox, she tried to bid her farewell; but, as
she thought it was for the last time, tears of tenderness
as well as pride stood in her eyes.

" God bless you, my dear child!" said the unsuspecting Mrs Lennox, as she held her in her arms.
" And God *will* bless you in his way—though his
ways are not as our ways. I cannot urge you to
return to this dreary abode. But oh, Mary! think
sometimes in your gaiety, that when you do come,
you bring gladness to a mournful heart, and lighten
eyes that never see the sun!"

Mary, too much affected to reply, could only wring
the hand of her venerable friend, as she tore herself
from her embrace, and followed Lady Emily to the
carriage. For some time they proceeded in silence.
Mary dreaded to encounter her cousin's eyes, which
she was aware were fixed upon her with more than
their usual scrutiny. She therefore kept hers steadily
employed in surveying the well-known objects the road
presented. At length her ladyship began in a grave tone.

" You appear to have had very stormy weather at Rose Hall ? "

" Very much so," replied Mary, without knowing very well what she said.

" And we have had nothing but calms and sunshine at Beech Park. Is not that strange ? "

" Very."

" I left the barometer very high—not quite at *settled calm*—that would be too much ; but I find it very low indeed—absolutely below nothing."

Mary now did look up in some surprise ; but she hastily withdrew from the intolerable expression of her cousin's eyes.

" Dear Lady Emily ! " cried she, in a deprecating tone.

" Well, what more ? You can't suppose I'm to put up with hearing my own name ; I've heard that fifty times to-day already from Lady Juliana's parrot — come, your face speaks volumes. I read a declaration of love in the colour of your cheeks—a refusal in the height of your nose—remorse in the twinkling of your eye—a sort of general agitation in the quiver of your lip—and the *déréglement* of your hair. Now for your pulse—a *leetle* hasty, as Dr Redgill would say ; but let your tongue declare the rest."

Mary would fain have concealed the cause of her distress from every human being, as she felt as if degraded still lower by repeating it to another ; and she remained silent, struggling with her emotions.

" 'Pon my honour, Mary, you really do use great liberties with my patience and good nature. I appeal to yourself whether I might not just as well have been reading one of Tully's orations to a mule all this while. Come, you must really make haste to tell your tale, for I am dying to disclose mine. Or shall I begin ? No —that would be inverting the order of nature, or

custom, which is the same thing—beginning with the
farce and ending with the tragedy—so *commencez au
commencement, m' amie.*"

Thus urged, Mary at length, and with much hesitation, related to her cousin the humiliation she had
experienced. "And after all," said she, as she ended,
"I am afraid I behaved very like a fool; and yet what
could I do? In my situation what would you have
done?"

"Done! why I should have taken the old woman
by the shoulders, and cried Boh! in her ear. And so
this is the mighty matter! You happen to overhear
Mrs Lennox, good old soul! recommending you as a
wife to her son—what could be more natural? except
his refusing to fall head and ears in love before he had
time to pull his boots off. And then to have a wife
recommended to him! and all your perfections set
forth, as if you had been a laundry maid: an early
riser, neat worker, regular attender upon church!—
Ugh!—I must say, I think his conduct quite meritorious. I could almost find in my heart to fall in love
with him myself, were it for no other reason than because he is not such a Tommy Goodchild as to be in
love at his mamma's bidding—that is, loving his mother
as he does—for I see he could cut off a hand, or pluck
out an eye, to please her, though he can't or won't give
her his heart and soul to dispose of as she thinks proper."

"You quite misunderstand me," said Mary, with
increasing vexation; "I did not mean to say anything
against Colonel Lennox. I did not wish—I never
once thought or cared whether he liked me or not."

"That says very little for you: you must have a
very bad taste if you care more for the mother's liking
than the son's. Then what vexes you so much? Is
it at having made the discovery that your good old
friend is a—a—I beg your pardon—a bit of a goose?

Well, never mind, since you don't care for the man, there's no mischief done. You have only to change the *dramatis personæ*: fancy that you overheard me recommending you to Dr Redgill for your skill in cookery—you'd only have laughed at that—so why should you weep at t'other? However, one thing I must tell you, whether it adds to your grief or not, I did remark that Charles Lennox looked very lover-like towards you; and, indeed, this sentimental passion he has put you in becomes you excessively. I really never saw you look so handsome before; it has given an energy and *esprit* to your countenance, which is the only thing it wants. You are very much obliged to him, were it only for having kindled such a fire in your eyes, and raised such a carnation in your cheek. It would have been long before good *larmoyante* Mrs Lennox would have done as much for you. I shouldn't wonder were he to fall in love with you after all."

Lady Emily little thought how near she was to the truth when she talked in this random way. Colonel Lennox saw the wound he had innocently inflicted on Mary's feelings, and a warmer sentiment than any he had hitherto experienced had sprung up in his heart. Formerly, he had merely looked upon her as an amiable sweet-tempered girl; but when he saw her roused to a sense of her own dignity, and marked the struggle betwixt tender affection and offended delicacy, he formed a higher estimate of her character, and a spark was kindled that wanted but opportunity to blaze into a flame, pure and bright as the shrine on which it burned. Such is the waywardness and caprice of even the best affections of the human breast.

———o———

Chapter XV.

—— C'est a moi de *choisir* mon gendre;
Toi, tel qu'il est, c'est à toi de le prendre;
De vous aimer, si vous pouvez tous deux,
Et d'obéir à tout ce que je veux.

L'Enfant Prodigue.

"AND now," said Lady Emily, "that I have listened to your story, which, after all, is really a very poor affair, do you listen to mine. The heroine in both is the same, but the hero differs by some degrees. Know, then, as the ladies in novels say, that the day which saw you depart from Beech Park was the day destined to decide your fate, and dash your hopes, if ever you had any, of becoming Duchess of Altamont. The duke arrived, I know, for the express purpose of being enamoured of you; but, alas! you were not—and there was Adelaide, *so* sweet!—*so* gracious!—*so* beautiful!—the poor gull was caught, and is now, I really believe, as much in love as it is in the nature of a stupid man to be. I must own she has played her part admirably, and has made more use of her time than I, with all my rapidity, could have thought possible. In fact, the duke is now all but her declared lover, and that merely stands upon a point of punctilio."

"But Lord Lindore!" exclaimed Mary, in astonishment.

"Why, that part of the story is what I don't quite comprehend. Sometimes I think it is a struggle with Adelaide. Lindore, poor, handsome, captivating on one hand; his grace, rich, stupid, magnificent, on the other. As for Lindore, he seems to stand quite aloof. Formerly, you know, he never used to stir from her side, or notice any one else: now he scarcely notices her, at least in the presence of the duke. Sometimes he affects to look unhappy, but I believe it is mere affectation. I doubt if he ever thought seriously of Adelaide, or indeed anybody else, that he could have in a straightforward, Ally Croker sort of a way— but something too much of this. While all this has been going on in one corner, there comes regularly every day Mr William Downe Wright, looking very much as if he had lost his shoe-string or pocket-handker-chief, and had come there to look for it. I had some suspicion of the nature of the loss, but was hopeful he would have the sense to keep it to himself. No such thing; he yesterday stumbled upon Lady Juliana all alone, and, in the weakest of his weak moments, in-formed her that the loss he had sustained was no less than the loss of that precious jewel, his heart; and that the object of his search was no other than that of Miss Mary Douglas to replace it! He even carried his *bêtise* so far as to request her permission, or her influence, or, in short, something that her ladyship never was asked for by any mortal in their senses before, to aid him in his pursuit. You know how it delights her to be dressed in a little brief authority; so you may conceive her transports at seeing the sceptre of power thus placed in her hands. In the heat of her pride she makes the matter known to the whole house-hold; Redgills, cooks, stable boys, scullions, all are quite *au fait* to your marriage with Mr Downe Wright; so I hope you'll allow that it was about time you should be made acquainted with it yourself. But why so pale and frightened-looking?"

Poor Mary was indeed shocked at her cousin's in-telligence. With the highest feelings of filial rever-ence, she found herself perpetually called upon either to sacrifice her own principles or to act in direct opposition to her mother's will; and, upon this

occasion, she saw nothing but endless altercation await-
ing her : for her heart revolted from the indelicacy of
such measures, and she could not for a moment brook
the idea of being *bestowed* in marriage. But she had
little time for reflection. They were now at Beech
Park ; and, as she alighted, a servant informed her,
Lady Juliana wished to see her in her dressing-room
immediately. Thither she repaired with a beating
heart and agitated step. She was received with
greater kindness than she had ever yet experienced
from her mother.

"Come in, my dear," cried she, as she extended
two fingers to her, and slightly touched her cheek.
"You look very well this morning—much better than
usual. Your complexion is much improved. At the
same time, you must be sensible how few girls are
married merely for their looks—that is, married well
—unless, to be sure, their beauty is something *à mer-
veilleuse*—such as your sister's, for instance. I assure
you, it is an extraordinary piece of good fortune in a
merely pretty girl to make what is vulgarly called a
good match. I know, at least, twenty really very nice
young women at this moment who cannot get themselves established."

Mary was silent; and her mother, delighted at her
own good sense and judicious observations, went on—

"That being the case, you may judge how very
comfortable I must feel at having managed to procure
for you a most excessive good establishment—just the
very thing I have long wished, as I have felt quite at
a loss about you of late, my dear. When your sister
marries, I shall, of course, reside with her ; and, as I
consider your *liaison* with those Scotch people as completely at an end, I have really been quite wretched as
to what was to become of you. I can't tell you,
therefore, how excessively relieved I was when Mr

Downe Wright yesterday asked my permission to address you. Of course, I could not hesitate an instant; so you will meet him at dinner as your accepted. By the by, your hair is rather blown. I shall send Fanchon to dress it for you. You have really got very pretty hair; I wonder I never remarked it before. Oh! and Mrs Downe Wright is to wait upon me to-morrow, I think; and then, I believe, we must return the visit. There is a sort of etiquette, you know, in all these matters: that is the most unpleasant part of it; but when that is over, you will have nothing to think of but ordering your things."

For a few minutes, Mary was too much confounded by her mother's rapidity to reply. She had expected to be urged to accept of Mr Downe Wright; but to be told that was actually done for her, was more than she was prepared for. At length she found voice to say, that Mr Downe Wright was almost a stranger to her, and she must therefore be excused from receiving his addresses at present.

"How excessively childish!" exclaimed Lady Juliana, angrily. "I won't hear of anything so perfectly foolish. You know (or, at any rate, I do) all that is necessary to know. I know that he is a man of family and fortune, heir to a title, uncommonly handsome, and remarkably sensible and well-informed. I can't conceive what more you would wish to know!"

"I should wish to know something of his character —his principles—his habits—temper, talents—in short, all those things on which my happiness would depend."

"Character and principles!—one would suppose you were talking of your footman! Mr Downe Wright's character is perfectly good. I never heard anything against it. As to what you call his principles, I must confess my ignorance. I really can't tell whether he is a Methodist; but I know he is a gentleman—has a

large fortune—is very good-looking—and is not at all
dissipated, I believe.   In short, you are most excessively fortunate in meeting with such a man."

"But I have not the slightest partiality for him,"
said Mary, colouring.   "It cannot be expected that I
should, when I have not been half a dozen times in his
company.   I must be allowed some time before I can
consent even to consider——"

"I don't mean that you are to marry to-morrow.
It may probably be six weeks, or two months, before
everything can be arranged."

Mary saw she must speak boldly.

"But I must be allowed much longer time before I
can consider myself as sufficiently acquainted with Mr
Downe Wright, to think of him at all in that light.
And even then—he may be very amiable, and yet"—
hesitating—"I may not be able to love him as I
ought."

"Love!" exclaimed Lady Juliana, her eyes sparkling with anger; "I desire I may never hear that word
again from any daughter of mine.   I am determined I
shall have no disgraceful love-marriages in the family.
No well-educated young woman ever thinks of such
a thing now, and I won't hear a syllable on the
subject."

"I shall never marry anybody, I am sure, that you
disapprove of," said Mary, timidly.

"No; I shall take care of that.   I consider it the
duty of parents to establish their children properly in the
world, without any regard to their ideas on the subject.
I think I must be rather a better judge of the matter
than you can possibly be, and I shall therefore make a
point of your forming what I consider a proper alliance.
Your sister, I know, won't hesitate to sacrifice her own
affections to please me.   She was most excessively attached to Lord Lindore—everybody knew that; but

she is convinced of the propriety of preferring the Duke of Altamont, and won't hesitate in sacrificing her own feelings to mine. But, indeed, she has ever been all that I could wish—so perfectly beautiful, and, at the same time, so excessively affectionate and obedient. She approves entirely of your marriage with Mr Downe Wright, as indeed all your friends do. I don't include *your* friend Lady Emily in that number. I look upon her as a most improper companion for you, and the sooner you are separated from her the better. So now, good bye for the present. You have only to behave as other young ladies do upon those occasions, which, by the by, is generally to give as much trouble to their friends as they possibly can."

There are some people who, furious themselves at opposition, cannot understand the possibility of others being equally firm and decided in a gentle manner. Lady Juliana was one of those who always expect to carry their point by a raised voice and sparkling eyes; and it was with difficulty Mary, with her timid air and gentle accents, could convince her that she was determined to judge for herself in a matter in which her happiness was so deeply involved. When at last brought to comprehend it, her ladyship's indignation knew no bounds, and Mary was accused, in the same breath, with having formed some low connection in Scotland, and of seeking to supplant her sister, by aspiring to the Duke of Altamont; and, at length, the conference ended pretty much where it began. Lady Juliana resolved that her daughter should marry to please her, and her daughter equally resolved not to be be driven into an engagement from which her heart recoiled.

———o———

Chapter lvj.

Qu'on vante en lui la foi, l'honneur, la probité;
Qu'on prise sa candeur et sa civilité;
Qu'il soit doux, complaisant, officieux, sincere:
On le veut, j'y souscris, et suis pret à me taire.

                                        BOILEAU.

WHEN Mary entered the drawing-room, she
found herself, without knowing how, by the
side of Mr Downe Wright. At dinner it
was the same; and, in short, it seemed an understood
thing, that they were to be constantly together.

There was something so gentle and unassuming in
his manner, that, almost provoked as she was by the
folly of his proceedings, she found it impossible to
resent it by her behaviour towards him; and, indeed,
without being guilty of actual rudeness, of which she
was incapable, it would not have been easy to have
made him comprehend the nature of her sentiments.
He appeared perfectly satisfied with the toleration he
met with; and, compared to Adelaide's disdainful
glances, and Lady Emily's biting sarcasms, Mary's
gentleness and civility might well be mistaken for en-
couragement. But even under the exhilarating influence
of hope and high spirits, his conversation was so insipid
and common-place, that Mary found it almost a relief
to turn to Dr Redgill. It was evident the doctor was
aware of what was going on, for he regarded her with
that increased respect due to the future mistress of a
splendid establishment. Between the courses he made
some complimentary allusions to Highland mutton and
red deer, and he even carried his attentions so far as to
whisper, at the very first mouthful, that *les côtelettes de
saumon* were superb, when he had never been known to
commend anything to another, until he had fully dis-

cussed it himself. On the opposite side of the table sat
Adelaide and the Duke of Altamont, the latter looking
still more heavy and inanimate than ever. The operation of eating over, he seemed unable to keep himself
awake, and every now and then yielded to a gentle
slumber, from which, however, he was instantly recalled at the sound of Adelaide's voice, when he exclaimed, "Ah! charming—very charming, ah!"—
Lady Emily looked *from* them as she hummed some
part of Dryden's ode—

> " Aloft in awful state
>   The godlike hero sat, &c.
> The lovely Thais by his side,
> Look'd like a blooming eastern bride."

Then, as his Grace closed his eyes, and his head sunk
on his shoulder—

> " With ravish'd ears
>   The monarch hears,
>   Assumes the god,
>   Affects to nod."

Lady Juliana, who would have been highly incensed,
had she suspected the application of the words, was so
unconscious of it, as to join occasionally in singing
them, to Mary's great confusion, and Adelaide's manifest displeasure.

When they returned to the drawing-room, "Heavens!
Adelaide," exclaimed her cousin, in an affected manner,
"what are you made of? Semelé herself was but a
mere cinder-wench to you! How can you stand such
a Jupiter—and not scorched! not even singed, I protest!" pretending to examine her all over. "I vow,
I trembled at your temerity—your familiarity with the
imperial nod was fearful. I every instant expected to
see you turned into a live coal."

"I did burn," said Adelaide, indignantly, "but it

was with shame to see the mistress of a house forget
what was due to her father's guests."

"There's a slap on the cheek for me! Mercy! how
it burns!—No, I did not forget what was due to my
father's guests; on the contrary, I consider it due to
them to save them if I can, from the snares that I see
set for them. I have told you that I abhor all traps,
whether for the poor simple mouse that comes to steal
its bit of cheese, or for the dull elderly gentleman who
falls asleep with a star on his breast."

"This is one of the many kind and polite allusions
for which I am indebted to your ladyship," said Adelaide, haughtily; "but I trust the day will come when
I shall be able to discharge what I owe you."

And she quitted the room, followed by Lady Juliana,
who could only make out that Lady Emily had been
insolent, and that Adelaide was offended. A pause
followed.

"I see you think I am in the wrong, Mary, I can
read that in the little reproachful glance you gave me
just now. Well, perhaps I am; but I own it chafes
my spirit to sit and look on such a scene of iniquity—
Yes, iniquity I call it, for a woman to be in love with
one man, and at the same time laying snares for another.
You may think, perhaps, that Adelaide has no heart to
love anything; but she has a heart, such as it is,
though it is much too fine for everyday use, and therefore it is kept locked up in a marble casket, quite out
of reach of you or me. But I'm mistaken if Frederick
has not made himself master of it! Not that I should
blame her for that, if she would be honestly and sted-
fastly in love with him. But how despicable to see
her, with her affections placed upon one man, at the
same time lavishing all her attentions on another—and
that other, if he had been plain John Altamont, Esq.,
she would not have been commonly civil to! And

apropos of civility—I must tell you, if you mean to refuse your hero, you were too civil by half to him. I observed you at dinner; you sat perfectly straight, and answered everything he said to you."

" What could I do ? " asked Mary, in some surprise.

" I'll tell you what I would have done, and have thought the most honourable mode of proceeding; I should have turned my back upon him, and have merely thrown him a monosyllable now and then over my shoulder."

" I could not be less than civil to him, and I am sure I was not more ? "

" Civility is too much for a man one means to refuse. You'll never get rid of a weak man by civility. Whenever I had any reason to apprehend a lover, I thought it my duty to turn short upon him and give him a snarl at the outset, which rid me of him at once. But I really begin to think I manage these matters better than anybody else.—' Where I love, I profess it, where I hate, in every circumstance I dare proclaim it.' "

Mary tried to defend her sister, in the first place; but though her charity would not allow her to censure, her conscience whispered there was much to condemn, and she was relieved from what she felt a difficult task, when the gentlemen began to drop in.

In spite of all her manœuvres, Mr Downe Wright contrived to be next her, and whenever she changed her seat, she was sure of his following her. She had also the mortification of overhearing Lady Juliana tell the duke, that Mr Downe Wright was the accepted lover of her youngest daughter — that he was a man of large fortune — and heir to his uncle, Lord Glenallan !

" Ah ! a nephew of my Lord Glenallan's ! Indeed —a pretty young man—like the family !—Poor Lord

Glenallan !—I knew him very well : He has had the palsy since then, poor man—ah ! "

The following day Mary was compelled to receive Mrs Downe Wright's visit ; but she was scarcely conscious of what passed, for Colonel Lennox arrived at the same time, and it was equally evident that his visit was also intended for her.   She felt that she ought to appear unconcerned in his presence, and she tried to be so, but still the painful idea would recur, that he had been solicited to love her, and, unskilled in the arts of even innocent deception, she could only try to hide her agitation under the coldness of her manner.

" Come, Mary," cried Lady Emily, as if in answer to something Colonel Lennox had addressed to her in a low voice, " do you remember the promise I made Colonel Lennox, and which it rests with you to perform ? "

" I never consider myself bound to perform the promises of others," replied Mary, gravely.

" In some cases that may be a prudent resolution, but, in the present, it is surely an unfriendly one," said Colonel Lennox.

" A most inhuman one ! " cried Lady Emily, " since you and I, it seems, cannot commence our friendship without something sentimental to set us going.   It rests with you, Mary, to be the founder of our friendship ; and if you manage the matter well, that is, sing in your best manner, we shall perhaps make it a triple alliance, and admit you as third."

" As every man is said to be the artificer of his own fortune, so every one, I think, had best be the artificer of their own friendship," said Mary, trying to smile, as she pulled her embroidery frame towards her, and began to work.

" Neither can be the worse of a good friend to help them on," observed Mrs Downe Wright.

"But both may be materially injured by an injudicious one," said Colonel Lennox; "and although, on this occasion, I am the greatest sufferer by it, I must acknowledge the truth of Miss Douglas's observation: Friendship and love, I believe, will always be found to thrive best when left to themselves."

"And so ends my novel, elegant, and original plan, for striking up a sudden friendship," cried Lady Emily. "Pray, Mr Downe Wright, can you suggest anything better for the purpose than an old song?"

Mr Downe Wright, who was not at all given to suggesting, looked a little embarrassed.

"Pull the bell, William, for the carriage," said his mother; "we must now be moving." And with a general obeisance to the company, and a significant pressure of the hand to Mary, she withdrew her son from his dilemma. Although a shrewd, penetrating woman, she did not possess that tact and delicacy necessary to comprehend the finer feelings of a mind superior to her own; and in Mary's averted looks and constrained manner, she saw nothing but what she thought quite proper and natural in her situation. "As for Lady Emily," she observed, "there would be news of her and that fine dashing-looking Colonel yet, and Miss Adelaide would, perhaps, come down a pin before long."

Soon after Colonel Lennox took his leave, in spite of Lady Emily's pressing invitation for him to spend the day there, and meet her brother, who had been absent for some days, but was now expected home. He promised to return again soon, and departed.

"How very handsome Colonel Lennox looked to-day!" said she, addressing Mary; "and how perfectly unconscious, at least indifferent, he seems about it! It is quite refreshing to see a handsome man who is neither a fool nor a coxcomb."

"Handsome ! no, I don't think he is very hand-some," said Lady Juliana : " Rather dark, don't you think, my love ? " turning to Adelaide, who sat apart at a table writing, and had scarcely deigned to lift her head all the time.

"Whom do you mean ?　The man who has just gone out ?　Is his name Lennox ?　Yes, he is rather handsome."

" I believe you are right; he certainly is good-looking, but in a peculiar style.　I don't quite like the expression of his eye, and he wants that air *distingué*, which, indeed, belongs exclusively to persons of birth."

" He has perfectly the air of a man of fashion," said Adelaide, in a decided tone, as if ashamed to agree with her mother.　" Perhaps *un peu militaire*, but nothing at all professional."

" Lennox !—it is a Scotch name," observed Lady Juliana, contemptuously.

" And to cut the matter short," said Lady Emily, as she was quitting the room, " the man who has just gone out is Colonel Lennox, and not the Duke of Altamont."

After a few more awkward, indefinite sorts of visits, in which Mary found it impossible to come to an explanation, she was relieved, for the present, from the assiduities of her lover.　Lady Juliana received a note from Mrs Downe Wright, apologizing for what she termed her son's unfortunate absence at such a critical time ; but he had received accounts of the alarming illness of his uncle Lord Glenallan, and had, in con-sequence, set off instantly for Scotland, where she was preparing to follow ; concluding with particular regards to Miss Mary—hopes of being soon able to resume their pleasant footing in the family, &c. &c.

" How excessively well arranged it will be, that old man's dying at this time," said her ladyship, as she tossed the note to her daughter; "Lord Glenallan will sound so much better that Mr Downe Wright. The name I have always considered as the only objectionable part: You are really most prodigiously fortunate."

Mary was now aware of the folly of talking reason to her mother, and remained silent; thankful for the present peace this event would ensure her, and almost tempted to wish that Lord Glenallan's doom might not speedily be decided.

———o———

Chapter lvij.

It seems it is as proper to our age
To cast beyond ourselves in our opinions,
As it is common for the younger sort
To lack discretion.

Hamlet.

LORD LINDORE and Colonel Lennox had been boyish acquaintances, and a sort of superficial intimacy was soon established between them, which served as the ostensible cause of his frequent visits at Beech Park. But to Mary, who was more alive to the difference of their · characters and sentiments than any other member of the family, this appeared very improbable, and she could not help suspecting, that love for the sister, rather than friendship for the brother, was the real motive by which he was actuated. In a half jesting manner she mentioned her suspicions to Lady Emily, who treated the idea with her usual ridicule.

"I really could not have supposed you so extremely missy-ish, Mary," said she, "as to imagine, that because two people like each other's society, and talk, and laugh together a little more than usual, that they must needs be in love! I allow I am partial to Colonel Lennox, *very* partial; but so I am to you, and to all I like. I am not even ashamed to acknowledge a preference for him, and yet I am not in love with him, nor he with me. I believe he loves me much the same as he did eleven years ago, when I was a little wretch, that used to pull his hair and spoil his watch. And as for me, you know that I consider myself quite as an old woman—at least as a married one; and he is perfectly *au fait* to my engagement with Edward. I have even shown him his picture, and some of his letters."

Mary looked incredulous.

"You may think as you please, but I tell you it is so. In my situation, I should scorn to have Colonel Lennox, or anybody else in love with me. As to his liking to talk to me, pray, who else can he talk to? Adelaide would sometimes *condescend* indeed; but he won't be condescended to, that's clear, even by a duchess. With what mock humility he meets her airs! how I adore him for it! Then you are such a pillar of ice!—so shy and unsociable when he is present!—and, by the by, if I did not despise recrimination as the *pis aller* of all conscious misses, I would say you are much more the object of his *attention*, at least, than I am. Several times I have caught him looking very earnestly at you, when, by the laws of good-breeding, his eyes ought to have been fixed exclusively upon me; and—"

"Pshaw!" interrupted Mary, colouring, "that is mere absence—nothing to the purpose—or, perhaps," forcing a smile, "he may be *trying* to love me!"

Mary thought of her poor old friend, as she said this, with bitterness of heart. It was long since she had seen her; and when she had last inquired for her, her son had said he did not think her well, with a look Mary could not misunderstand. She had heard him make an appointment with Lord Lindore for the following day, and she took the opportunity of his certain absence to visit his mother. Mrs Lennox, indeed, looked ill, and seemed more than usually depressed. She welcomed Mary with her usual tenderness, but even her presence seemed to fail of inspiring her with gladness.

Mary found she was totally unsuspicious of the cause of her estrangement, and imputed it to a very different one.

"You have been a great stranger, my dear!" said she, as she affectionately embraced her; "but at such a time I could not expect you to think of me."

"Indeed," answered Mary, equally unconscious of her meaning, "I have thought much and often, very often, of you, and wished I could have come to you; but—" she stopped, for she could not tell the truth, and would not utter a falsehood.

"I understand it all," said Mrs Lennox, with a sigh. "Well—well—God's will be done!" Then, trying to be more cheerful, "Had you come a little sooner, you would have met Charles. He is just gone out with Lord Lindore. He was unwilling to leave me, as he always is, and when he does, I believe it is as much to please me as himself. Ah! Mary, I once hoped that I might have lived to see you the happy wife of the best of sons. I may speak out now, since that is all over. It has been willed otherwise, and may you be rewarded in the choice you have made!"

Mary was struck with consternation to find that her supposed engagement with Mr Downe Wright had spread even to Rose Hall; and in the greatest confusion she attempted to deny it. But after the acknowledgment she had just heard, she acquitted herself awkwardly; for she felt as if an open explanation would only serve to revive hopes that never could be realised, and subject Colonel Lennox and herself to future perplexities. Nothing but the whole truth would have sufficed to undeceive Mrs Lennox, for she had had the intelligence of Mary's engagement from Mrs Downe Wright herself, who, for better security of what she already considered her son's property, had taken care to spread the report of his being the accepted lover before she left the country. Mary felt all the unpleasantness of her situation. Although detesting deceit and artifice of every kind, her confused and stammering denials seemed rather to corroborate the fact; but she felt that she could not declare her resolution of never bestowing her hand upon Mr Downe Wright, without seeming, at the same time, to court the addresses of Colonel Lennox. Then how painful—how unjust to herself, as well as cruel to him, to have it for an instant believed that she was the betrothed of one whose wife she was resolved she never would be!

In short, poor Mary's mind was a complete chaos; and, for the first time in her life, she found it impossible to determine which was the right course for her to pursue. Even in the midst of her distress, however, she could not help smiling at the *naiveté* of the good old lady's remarks.

"He is a handsome young man, I hear," said she, still in allusion to Mr Downe Wright,—"has a fine fortune, and an easy temper. All these things help people's happiness, though they cannot make it; and his choice of you, my dear Mary, shows that he has some sense."

"What an eulogium!" said Mary, laughing and blushing. "Were he really to me what you suppose, I must be highly flattered; but I must again assure you, it is not using Mr Downe Wright well to talk of him as anything to me. My mother, indeed——"

"Ah! Mary, my dear, let me advise you to beware of being led, even by a mother, in such a matter as this. God forbid that I should ever recommend disobedience towards a parent's will; but I fear you have yielded too much to yours. I said, indeed, when I heard it, that I feared undue influence had been used; for that I could not think William Downe Wright would ever have been the choice of your heart. Surely parents have much to answer for, who mislead their children in such an awful step as marriage!"

This was the severest censure Mary had ever heard drop from Mrs Lennox's lips; and she could not but marvel at the self-delusion that led her thus to condemn in another the very error she had committed herself; but under such different circumstances, that she would not easily have admitted it to be the same. *She* sought for the happiness of her son, while Lady Juliana, she was convinced, wished only her own aggrandizement.

"Yes, indeed," said Mary, in answer to her friend's observation, "parents ought, if possible, to avoid even forming wishes for their children—hearts are wayward things, even the best of them." Then more seriously she added, "and, dear Mrs Lennox, do not either blame my mother or pity me; for be assured, with my heart only will I give my hand; or rather, I should say, with my hand only will I give my heart: And now good-bye," cried she, starting up and hurrying away, as she heard Colonel Lennox's voice in the hall.

She met him on the stair, and would have passed on with a slight remark, but he turned with her, and finding she had dismissed the carriage, intending to walk home, he requested permission to attend her. Mary declined; but snatching up his hat, and whistling his dogs, he set out with her in spite of her remonstrances to the contrary.

"If you persist in refusing my attendance," said he, "you will inflict an incurable wound upon my vanity. I shall suspect you are ashamed of being seen in such company. To be sure, myself, with my shabby jacket, and my spattered dogs, do form rather a ruffian-like escort; and I should not have dared to have offered my services to a fine lady—but you are not a fine lady, I know;" and he gently drew her arm within his as they began to ascend a hill.

This was the first time Mary had found herself alone with Colonel Lennox, since that fatal day which seemed to have divided them for ever. At first she felt uneasy and embarrassed, but there was so much good sense and good feeling in the tone of his conversation; it was so far removed either from pedantry or frivolity, that all disagreeable ideas soon gave way to the pleasure she had in conversing with one whose turn of mind seemed so similar to her own; and it was not till she had parted from him at the gate of Beech Park, she had time to wonder, how she could possibly have walked two miles *tête-à-tête* with a man whom she had heard solicited to love her.

From that day Colonel Lennox's visits insensibly increased in length and number; but Lady Emily seemed to appropriate them entirely to herself; and certainly all the flow of his conversation, the brilliancy of his wit, were directed to her; but Mary could not but be conscious that his looks were much oftener rivetted on herself, and if his attentions were not such as to attract general observation, they were such as she could not fail of perceiving, and being unconsciously gratified by.

"How I admire Charles Lennox's manner to you, Mary!" said her cousin; "after the awkward dilemma you were both in, it was no easy matter to know how to proceed: a vulgar-minded man would either have oppressed you with his attentions, or insulted you by his neglect, while he steers so gracefully free from either extreme; and I observe you are the only woman upon whom he deigns to bestow *les petits soins.* How I despise a man who is ever on the watch to pick up every silly Miss's fan or glove, that she thinks it pretty to drop! No—the woman he loves, whether his mother or his wife, will always be distinguished by him were she amongst queens and empresses; not by his silly vanity or vulgar fondness, but by his marked and gentlemanlike attentions towards her. In short, the best thing you can do, is to make up your quarrel with him —take him for all in all—you won't meet with such another—certainly not amongst your Highland lairds, by all that I can learn; and, by the by, I do suspect he is, now, as you say, trying to love you; and let him —you will be very well repaid if he succeeds."

Mary's heart swelled at the thoughts of submitting to such an indignity, especially as she was beginning to feel conscious that Colonel Lennox was not quite the object of indifference to her that he ought to be; but her cousin's remarks only served to render her more distant and reserved to him than ever.

———o———

Chapter lviij.

What dangers ought'st thou not to dread,
When Love, that's blind, is by blind Fortune led?
COWLEY.

AT length the long-looked for day arrived. The Duke of Altamont's proposals were made in due form, and in due form accepted. Lady Juliana seemed now touching the pinnacle of earthly

joy ; for, next to being greatly married herself, her
happiness centred in seeing her daughter at the head
of a splendid establishment. Again visions of bliss
hovered around her, and " Peers and Dukes, and all
their sweeping train," swam before her eyes, as she
anticipated the brilliant results to herself from so noble
an alliance ; for self was still, as it had ever been, her
ruling star, and her affection for her daughter was the
mere result of vanity and ambition.

The ensuing weeks were passed in all the bustle of
preparations necessarily attendant on the nuptials of the
great. Every morning brought from town, dresses,
jewels, patterns, and packages of all descriptions.
Lady Juliana was in ecstacies, even though it was
but happiness in the second person. Mary watched
her sister's looks with the most painful solicitude, for
from her lips she knew she never would learn the
sentiments of her heart. But Adelaide was aware
she had a part to act, and she went through it with
an ease and self-possession that seemed to defy all
scrutiny. Once or twice, indeed, her deepening colour
and darkening brow betrayed the feelings of her heart,
as the Duke of Altamont and Lord Lindore were
brought into comparison ; and Mary shuddered to
think that her sister was even now ashamed of the
man whom she was soon to vow to love, honour, and
obey. She had vainly tried to lead Adelaide to the
subject. Adelaide would listen to nothing which she
had reason to suppose was addressed to herself; but
either with cool contempt took up a book, or left the
room, or, with insolent affectation, would put her hands
to her head, exclaiming, " *Mes oreilles n'etoient pas
faites pour les entretiens serieux.*"

All Mary's worst fears were confirmed a few days
before that fixed for the marriage. As she entered the
music room, she was startled to find Lord Lindore and

Adelaide alone. Unwilling to suppose that her presence would be considered as an interruption, she seated herself at a little distance from them, and was soon engrossed by her task, that of copying music. Adelaide, too, had the air of being deeply intent upon some trifling employment; and Lord Lindore, as he sat opposite to her, with his head resting upon his hands, had the appearance of being engaged in reading. All were silent for some time; but as Mary happened to look up, she saw Lord Lindore's eyes fixed earnestly upon her sister, and with a voice of repressed feeling, he repeated, "*Ah! je le sens, ma Julie! si'l falloit renoncer à vous, il n'y auroit plus pour moi d'autre sejour ni d'autre saison;*" and throwing down the book, he quitted the room. Adelaide, pale and agitated, rose as if to follow him; then, recollecting herself, she rushed from the apartment by an opposite door. Mary followed, vainly hoping, that in this moment of excited feeling, she might be induced to open her heart to the voice of affection; but Adelaide was a stranger to sympathy, and saw only the degradation of confessing the struggle she endured in choosing betwixt love and ambition. That her heart was Lord Lindore's, she could not conceal from herself, though she would not confess it to another; and that other the tenderest of sisters, whose only wish was to serve her. Mary's tears and entreaties were therefore in vain, and, at Adelaide's repeated desire, she at length quitted her, and returned to the room she had left.

She found Lady Emily there with a paper in her hand. "Lend me your ears, Mary," cried she, "while I read these lines to you. Don't be afraid, there are no secrets in them, or at least none that you or I will be a whit the wiser for, as they are truly in a most mystic strain. I found them lying upon this table, and they are in Frederick's hand-writing, for I see he affects the *soupirant* at present, and it seems there has been a sort of a sentimental farce acted between Adelaide and him. He pretends, that although distractedly in love with her, he is not so selfish as even to wish her to marry him in preference to the Duke of Altamont; and Adelaide, not to be outdone in heroics, has also made it out that it is the height of virtue in her to espouse the Duke of Altamont, and sacrifice all the tenderest affections of her heart to duty!—Duty! yes, the duty of being a duchess, and of living in state and splendour with the man she secretly despises, to the pleasure of renouncing both for the man she loves, and so they have parted; and here, I suppose, is Lindore's lucubrations upon it, intended as a *souvenir* for Adelaide, I presume. Now, night visions befriend me!—

> The time returns when o'er my wilder'd mind
> A thraldom came which did each sense enshroud;
> Not that I bowed in willing chain confined,
> But that a soften'd atmosphere of cloud
> Veil'd every sense—conceal'd th' impending doom.
> 'Twas mystic night, and I seem'd borne along
> By pleasing dread—and in a doubtful gloom,
> Where fragrant incense and the sound of song,
> And all fair things we dream of, floated by,
> Lulling my fancy like a cradled child,
> Till that the dear and guileless treachery
> Made me the wretch I am—so lost, so wild—
> A mingled feeling, neither joy nor grief,
> Dwelt in my heart—I knew not whence it came,
> And—but that, woe is me! 't was passing brief,
> Even at this hour I fain would feel the same!
> I track'd a path of ffowers—but flowers among
> Were hissing serpents and drear birds of night,
> That shot across and scared with boding cries;
> And yet deep interest lurk'd in that affright,
> Something endearing in those mysteries,
> Which bade me still the desperate joy pursue,
> Heedless of what might come—when from mine eyes
> The clouds should pass, or what might then accrue.

The cloud *has* pass'd—the blissful power is flown,
The flowers are wither'd—wither'd all the scene.
But ah! the dear delusions I have known,
Are present still, with loved though alter'd mien.
I tread the self-same path in heart unchanged,
But changed now is all that path to me,
For where 'mong flowers and fountains once I ranged,
Are barren rocks and savage scenery!

Mary felt it was in vain to attempt to win her sister's
confidence, and she was too delicate to seek to wrest her
secrets from her; she therefore took no notice of this
effusion of love and disappointment, which she concluded
it to be.

Adelaide appeared at dinner as usual. All traces of
agitation had vanished, and her manner was as cool and
collected as if all had been peace and tranquillity at
heart. Lord Lindore's departure was slightly noticed.
It was generally understood, that he had been rejected
by his cousin, and his absence at such a time was
thought perfectly natural; the duke merely remarking,
with a vacant simper, "So, Lord Lindore is gone—
Ah! poor Lord Lindore!"

Lady Juliana had, in a very early stage of the business, fixed in her own mind that she, as a matter of
course, would be invited to accompany her daughter
upon her marriage; indeed, she always looked upon it
as a sort of triple alliance, that was to unite her as in-
dissolubly to the fortunes of the Duke of Altamont, as
though she had been his wedded wife. But the time
drew near, and in spite of all her hints and manœuvres,
no invitation had yet been extorted from Adelaide.
The Duke had proposed to her to invite her sister, and
even expressed something like a wish to that effect;
for though he felt no positive pleasure in Mary's
society, he was yet conscious of a void in her absence.
She was always in good humour—always gentle and
polite—and, without being able to tell why, his Grace

always felt more at ease with her than with anybody
else. But his selfish bride seemed to think that the
joys of her elevation would be diminished, if shared
even by her own sister, and she coldly rejected the
proposal. Lady Juliana was next suggested—for the
duke had a sort of vague understanding that his safety
lay in a multitude. With him, as with all stupid people,
company was society, words were conversation—and
all the gradations of intellect, from Sir Isaac Newton
down to Dr Redgill, were to him unknown. But
although, as with most weak people, obstinacy was his
forte, he was here again compelled to yield to the will
of his bride, as she also declined the company of her
mother for the present. The disappointment was somewhat softened to Lady Juliana, by the sort of indefinite
hopes that were expressed by her daughter of seeing
her in town when they were fairly established; but
until she had seen Altamont House, and knew its
accommodations, she could fix nothing; and Lady
Juliana was fain to solace herself with this dim perspective, instead of the brilliant reality her imagination
had placed within her grasp. She felt, too, without
comprehending, the imperfectness of all earthly felicity.
As she witnessed the magnificent preparations for her
daughter's marriage, it recalled the bitter remembrance
of her own—and many a sigh burst from her heart as
she thought, "Such as Adelaide is, I might have been,
had I been blest with such a mother, and brought up
to know what was for my good!"

The die was cast.—Amidst pomp and magnificence,
elate with pride, and sparkling with jewels, Adelaide
Douglas reversed the fate of her mother; and while
her affections were bestowed on another, she vowed, in
the face of Heaven, to belong only to the Duke of
Altamont!

"Good bye, my dearest love!" said her mother, as

she embraced her with transport, "and I shall be with you very soon; and, above all things, try to secure a good opera-box for the season. I assure you it is of the greatest consequence."

The duchess impatiently hurried from the congratulations of her family, and throwing herself into the splendid equipage that awaited her, was soon lost to their view.

―――o―――

Chapter lix.

Every white will have it its black,
And every sweet its sour:

AS Lady Juliana experienced. Her daughter was Duchess of Altamont, but Grizzy Douglas had arrived in Bath!—The intelligence was communicated to Mary in a letter. It had no date, but was as follows:—

"MY DEAR MARY,

"You will See from the Date of this, that we are at last Arrived here, after a very long journey, which you of Course Know it is from this to our Part of the country; at the same Time, it was uncommonly Pleasant, and we all enjoyed it very Much, only poor Sir Sampson was so ill that we Expected him to Expire every minute, which would have made it Extremely unpleasant for dear Lady Maclauchlan. He is now, I am happy to say, greatly Better, though still so Poorly, that I am much Afraid you will see a very Considerable change upon him. I sincerely hope, my dear Mary, that you will make a proper Apology to Lady Juliana for my not going to Beech Park (where I know I would be made most Welcome) directly—but I am certain she will Agree with me that it would be

Highly Improper in me to leave Lady M'Lauchlan when she is not at all Sure how long Sir Sampson may Live; and it would Appear very Odd if I was to be out of the way at such a time as That. But you may Assure her, with my Kind love, and indeed all our Loves (as I am sure None of us can ever forget the Pleasant time she spent with us at Glenfern in my Poor brother's lifetime, before you was Born) that I will Take the very first Opportunity of Spending some Time at Beech Park before leaving Bath, as we Expect the Waters will set Sir Sampson quite on his Feet again. It will be a happy Meeting, I am certain, with Lady Juliana and all of us, as it is Eighteen years this spring since we have Met. You may be sure I have a great Deal to tell you and Lady Juliana too, about all Friends at Glenfern, whom I left all quite Well. Of course, the Report of Bella's and Betsy's marriages Must have reached Bath by this time, as it will be three Weeks to-day since we left our part of the country; but in case it has not reached you, Lady M'Laughlan is of opinion that the Sooner you are made Acquainted with it the Better, especially as there is no doubt of it. Bella's marriage, which is in a manner fixed by this time, I dare say, though of Course it will not take place for some time, is to Captain M'Nab of some Regiment, but I'm sure I Forget which, for there are so many Regiments, you know, it is Impossible to remember them All; but he is quite a Hero, I know that, as he is been in Several battles, and had Two of his front Teeth Knocked out at one of them, and was much complimented about it, besides being Six feet and I Can't tell how many inches high; and he Says, he is quite Certain of getting Great promotion—at any Rate a pension for it, so there is no Fear of him.

"Betsy has, if Possible, been still More fortunate

than her Sister, although you know Bella was always reckoned the Beauty of the Family, though some People certainly preferred Betsy's Looks too. She has made a Complete conquest of Major M'Tavish, of the Militia, who, Independent of his rank, which is certainly very High, has also distinguished himself very much, and shewed the Greatest bravery once when there was a Very serious Riot about the raising the Potatoes a penny a peck, when there was no Occasion for it, in the town of Dunoon; and it was very much talked of at the Time, as well as Being in all the Newspapers. This gives us all the Greatest Pleasure, as I am certain it will also Do Lady Juliana, and you, my dear Mary. At the same time, we Feel very much for poor Baby, and Beenie, and Becky, as they Naturally, and indeed all of us, Expected they would, of Course, be married first; and it is certainly a great Trial for them to See their younger sisters married before them. At the same Time, they are Wonderfully supported, and Behave with Astonishing firmness; and I Trust, my dear Mary, you will do the Same, as I have no Doubt you will All be married yet, as I am sure you Richly deserve it when it Comes. I hope I will see you Very soon, as Lady M'Laughlan, I am certain, will make you most Welcome to call. We are living in Most elegant Lodgings—all the Furniture is quite New, and perfectly Good. I do not know the Name of the street yet, as Lady M'Lauchlan, which is no wonder, is not fond of being Asked many questions when she is Upon a Journey; and, indeed, makes a Point of never Answering any, which, I dare say, is the Best way. But, of Course, anybody will Tell you where Sir Sampson Maclauchlan, Baronet, of Lochmarlie Castle, ———shire, N.B., lives; and, if You are at any Loss, it has a Green door, and a most Elegant Balcony. I must now bid you adieu, my dear Mary, as I Am so soon to See yourself. Sir Sampson and Lady M'Lauchlan unite with Me in Best compliments to the Family at Beech Park. And, in kind love to Lady Juliana and you, I remain, My dear Mary, your most affectionate Aunt,   " GRIZZEL DOUGLAS."

" P.S. I have a long letter for you from Mrs Douglas, which is in my Trunk, that is coming by the ——— Carrier, and unless he is stopped by the Snow, I Expect he will be here in ten days."

With the idea of Grizzy was associated in Mary's mind all the dear familiar objects of her happiest days, and her eyes sparkled with delight at the thoughts of again beholding her.

"Oh! when may I go to Bath to dear aunt Grizzy?" exclaimed she, as she finished the letter. Lady Juliana looked petrified. Then recollecting that this was the first intimation her mother had received of such an event being even in contemplation, she made haste to exculpate her aunt at her own expense, by informing her of the truth. But nothing could be more unpalatable than the truth; and poor Mary's short-lived joy was soon turned into the bitterest sorrow at the reproaches that were showered upon her by the incensed Lady Juliana. But for her these people never would have thought of coming to Bath; or if they did, she should have had no connection with them. She had been most excessively ill-used by Mr Douglas's family, and had long since resolved to have no further intercourse with them—they were nothing to her, &c. &c. The whole concluding with a positive prohibition against Mary's taking any notice of her aunt.

" From all that has been said, Mary," said Lady Emily, gravely, " there can be no doubt but that you are the origin of Lady Juliana's unfortunate connection with the family of Douglas."

"Undoubtedly," said her ladyship.

"But for you, it appears that she would not have known—certainly never would have acknowledged—that her husband had an aunt?"

"Certainly not," said Lady Juliana, warmly.

"It is a most admirable plan," continued Lady Emily, in the same manner, "and I shall certainly adopt it. When I have children I am determined they shall be answerable for my making a foolish marriage; and it shall be entirely their fault if my husband has a mother—*En attendant*, I am determined to patronize Edward's relations to the last degree; and therefore, unless Mary is permitted to visit her aunt as often as she pleases, I shall make a point of bringing the dear aunt Grizzy here. Yes," putting her hand to the bell, "I shall order my carriage this instant, and set off. To-morrow, you know, we give a grand dinner in honour of Adelaide's marriage—Aunt Grizzy shall be queen of the feast."

Lady Juliana was almost suffocated with passion; but she knew her niece too well to doubt her putting her threat in execution, and there was distraction in the idea of the vulgar obscure Grizzy Douglas being presented to a fashionable party as her aunt. After a violent altercation, in which Mary took no part, an ungracious permission was at length extorted, which Mary eagerly availed herself of; and, charged with kind messages from Lady Emily, set off in quest of aunt Grizzy, and the green door.

After much trouble, and many unsuccessful attacks upon green doors and balconies, she was going to give up the search in despair, when her eye was attracted by the figure of aunt Grizzy herself at full length, stationed at a window, in an old-fashioned riding-habit, and spectacles. The carriage was stopped; and in an instant Mary was in the arms of her aunt, all agitation, as Lochmarlie flashed on her fancy, at again hearing its native accents uttered by the voice familiar to her from infancy. Yet the truth must be owned. Mary's taste was somewhat startled, even while her heart warmed at the sight of the good old aunt. Association and affection still retained their magic influence over her; but absence had dispelled the blest illusions of habitual intercourse; and, for the first time, she beheld her aunt freed from its softening spell. Still her heart clung to her as to one known and loved from infancy; and she soon rose superior to the weakness she felt was besetting her, in the slight sensation of shame as she contrasted her awkward manner and uncouth accent with the graceful refinement of those with whom she associated.

Far different were the sensations with which the good spinster regarded her niece. She could not often enough declare her admiration of the improvements that had taken place. Mary was grown taller, and stouter, and fairer, and fatter, and her back was as straight as an arrow, and her carriage would even surprise Miss M'Gowk herself. It was quite astonishing to see her, for she had always understood Scotland was the place for beauty, and that nobody ever came to anything in England. Even Sir Sampson and Lady Maclaughlan were forgot as she stood rivetted in admiration, and Mary was the first to recall her recollection to them. Sir Sampson, indeed, might well have been overlooked by a more accurate observer, for, as Grizzy observed, he was worn away to nothing, and the little that remained seemed as if it might have gone too without being any loss. He was now deaf, paralytic, and childish, and the only symptoms of life he showed was an increased restlessness and peevish-

ness.   His lady sat by him calmly pursuing her work,
and, without relaxing from it, merely held up her face
to salute Mary as she approached her.

" So, I'm glad you are no worse than you was, dear
child," surveying her from head to foot ; " that's more
than *we* can say.   You see these poor creatures,"
pointing to Sir Sampson and aunt Grizzy : " They
are much about it now.   Well, we know what
we are, but who knows what we shall be —
humph ! "

Sir Sampson showed no signs of recognising her, but
seemed pleased when Grizzy resumed her station beside
him ; and began, for the five hundredth time, to tell
him why he was not in Lochmarlie Castle, and why
he was in Bath.

Mary now saw that there are situations in which a
weak capacity has its uses, and that the most foolish
chat may sometimes impart greater pleasure than all the
wisdom of the schools even when proceeding from a
benevolent heart.

Sir Sampson and Grizzy were so much upon a par
in intellect, that they were reciprocally happy in each
other.   This the strong sense of Lady Maclaughlan
had long perceived, and was the principal reason of her
selecting so weak a woman as her companion ; though,
at the same time, in justice to her ladyship's heart, as
well as head, she had that partiality for her friend, for
which no other reason can be assigned than that given
by Montaigne : " *Je l'amais parceque c'étoit* elle, *parceque
c'étoit moi.*"

With exemplary patience Mary devoted the whole
morning to her aunt, and even then was with difficulty
allowed to depart.   She, however, fixed an early day
on which to return for the purpose of accompanying
Miss Grizzy on a round of visits, in which she was to
deliver sundry letters of introduction she had received

from her Highland friends to certain distinguished individuals in Bath, and which had not been left to the
chances of the carrier and the snow.

———o———

Chapter IX.

Here, wrapt in the arms of Quiet let me lie,
Quiet companion of Obscurity !
Here let my life with as much silence slide,
As time that measures it does glide.

COWLEY.

ALTHOUGH, on her return, Mary read her
mother's displeasure in her looks, and was
grieved at again having incurred it, she yet
felt it a duty towards her father to persevere in her
attentions to his aunt.   She was old, poor, and unknown—plain in her person—weak in her intellects—
vulgar in her manners ; but she was related to her by
ties more binding than the laws of fashion or the rules
of taste.   Even these disadvantages, which, to a worldly
mind, would have served as excuses for neglecting her,
to Mary's generous nature were so many incentives to
treat her with kindness and attention.

As Lady Emily was too fearless and independent to
be deterred by the world's dread laugh from doing what
she thought right, she declared her intention of accompanying Mary in her next visit to her aunt, and also of
inviting the whole party to spend a day at Beech Park.
Lord Courtland approved of the proposal, as he never
took any trouble with his guests, and was rather amused
at the thoughts of seeing such oddities as he had heard
described.   Lady Juliana, finding remonstrance was
vain, resolved upon keeping her apartment, rather than
submit to the mortification of such an exhibition.

On the day appointed the cousins set off for Pultney Street, where they found aunt Grizzy *sola ;* Sir Sampson having been so uncommonly fretful, she said, that Lady Maclaughlan had been obliged to take him to the Pumpwell to please him. For the first time in her life, Miss Grizzy (to use a Scotch phrase) looked really *wise-like,* for she had been equipped by her friend in a handsome cloak and bonnet ; and in these and her letters of introduction, she was so wrapped up in the bewilderment of self - importance, that she sat quite silent and abstracted. It may be questioned whether the old woman of famous memory, whose garments were so unmercifully curtailed during her slumbers, doubted more as to her own identity, than did Grizzy, as her eye in a fine frenzy rolled—now from an upward glance at the Chantilly " fall " * which embellished the front of her bonnet, to the ample folds of satin which gave unwonted magnitude to the meagre outline of her form. Lady Emily was therefore agreeably surprised with the first *coup d'œil,* though greatly disappointed in the amusement she had expected from the *naïveté* of her character. Like wayward children who always make a point of behaving worst when they are most earnestly wished to do their best, Grizzy was acting not less by contraries. By the quietness of her deportment, and the unwonted reserve of her manners, she put Mary's account of her to open shame, and made it appear as though she had completely *travestied* her good aunt. Under this impression, therefore, Lady Emily took leave and set forth on a shopping expedition on foot, attended by a servant, as she insisted on her friends making use of the carriage for their visits.

---

* For the information of single gentlemen, it may be necessary to mention that a fall in the milliner's vocabulary does not signify a fall either moral or physical, but merely a piece of lace which *depends* from the front of the bonnet as a demi-veil.

After much delay and many small difficulties, such as usually occur in the outset of elderly ladies from the country, all was at last adjusted, and Mary and her aunt were fairly seated; but some time elapsed before the latter could be satisfied that her pocket-handkerchief was in her reticule, and that her reticule was on her arm, that her money was in her purse, and that her purse was in her pocket, that her cards were in her card case, and her card case was in one hand, and her gloves and her letters of introduction were in the other.

All these facts and several more of the same kind having been clearly demonstrated, the carriage was at length in motion, and then the floodgates of Grizzy's eloquence were opened.

"Oh, Mary, my dear," said she, "this has been a most extraordinary day! I declare I never knew the like of it; and I am sure I hardly know what I'm about—and no wonder. Such a cloak and bonnet! Only feel that satin, Mary! I'm sure the cloak could stand itself!" half rising as she spoke—"and have you seen my bonnet?" turning her head round as if on a pivot. I declare anybody might go to court in this cloak and bonnet!—And such a fall! I'm sure it will be a fall in our family for generations to come; there can be no doubt about that!"

Mary expressed her admiration of the cloak and bonnet with due energy, and in such unqualified terms as she trusted would leave nothing more to be said on that subject. But not so.

"Well, as you say, Mary, nothing can be more handsome of their kind—everybody must allow that! but I'm just afraid that——I'm sure I hope to goodness nobody will think them *too* handsome. And to think of Lady Maclaughlan going about in her old pelisse and bonnet! I declare I don't know what

people may think when they see me set up like a
princess! But she said, what is certainly very true,
that anybody that sat still and did not speak, in a handsome satin cloak and fine Chantilly fall, would be sure
to be much respected; there can be no doubt about
that! So I hope you'll explain that to Lady Emily;
for I'm sure if she doesn't know the reason, she must
think me very stupid!"

Mary cordially acquiesced in this worldly-wise policy
of Lady Maclaughlan's; but she could scarcely repress
a smile as her ready fancy rendered it into her ladyship's own peculiar phraseology, which she guessed
might run thus—"My dear child, you're a great simpleton; but a simpleton in black satin and fine lace is
one thing, a simpleton in printed cotton and coarse
muslin is another; so you must be well dressed if you
would not be despised: hold your tongue, and let your
clothes speak for you.—Humph!"

Having satisfied her good aunt's scruples as to what
she thought the unbefitting magnificence of her own
appearance, Mary then opened another valve for her
ideas by an inquiry concerning the letters she held in
her hand.

"Oh, Mary, do you not know?—did I not
tell you? But indeed it's no wonder I'm confused,
considering!—but that letter is entirely on your account, and I hope to goodness you will profit by it,
for it would be very provoking, after all the trouble
your aunt Jacky took about it, if it was to be thrown
away,"—and she grasped it firmly with both hands as
if to prevent the possibility of such a thing literally
taking place.

"I trust my dear aunt's kindness will never be quite
thrown away upon me," said Mary, "though it may
not be in my power always to profit by it."

"That's very true, Mary; and unless I had been

with you it couldn't have been expected that you
would have gone by yourself; but since you have me
with you, it must be your own fault if you don't profit
by it,—there can be no doubt about that; for it's a
great thing for you, and, indeed, for me too (for, as
your aunt Jacky says, we are never too old to learn),
to have got a letter of introduction to an authoress."

"I was not aware," said Mary, as she glanced at
the superscription on the letter, "that Mrs Blanque
laid claim to that title."

"Oh, as to that, Miss M'Turk says there can be
no doubt about it; she says, to her certain knowledge
she has written I can't tell you how many different
books, but I've forgot what they're all about; and,
indeed, I never read any of them, for there are some
excellent books, well worth reading, we have never
read yet."

"But she has never put her name to any"——

"Oh, but Miss M'Turk says that doesn't signify,
for that she should just do as other people do, and put
her name to her books at once: there can be no doubt
about that!"

"She may surely be allowed to please herself in
that particular," said Mary, with a smile; "but I am
not so sure that, as strangers, we are at liberty to
intrude"——

"Oh, as to that, I'm sure she will be delighted to
see us; for, though she never receives strangers, she
won't reckon *us* strangers; for you know *we* are
always happy to see strangers."

"Who is the letter from?" inquired Mary, not
quite convinced by her aunt's reasoning.

"I'm not quite certain; but I know it's from a
lady who is not acquainted with her herself, but she
has a niece who is married to a relation of Miss
M'Turk's, and I promised that I would make a point

of seeing her, and giving her the letter myself, for servants are very careless, especially when a person's quite blind and very deaf, which they say Mrs Blanque is; and her memory gone too!"

"In that case we shall not gain much by the introduction," said Mary; "and"——

"Mary, my dear, you are too young yet to be a judge. We are all of opinion it would be of the *greatest* advantage for you to be introduced to an authoress: there can be no doubt about that! And we expect you will do great credit to us all when you go back, and be able to tell all about her: and, indeed, as Miss M'Turk said, and we all thought it an excellent plan, you should make a point of writing down every thing she says; for there's no knowing but what it may come to be printed yet, for it's all the fashion now to print what people say, it doesn't signify what it is. So I hope to goodness you will take great care what you say before her, for it never would do for you to have your words printed: you are a great deal too young for that yet!"

Mary readily assented to this profound aphorism of Grizzy's, while she smiled at the confusion of her ideas as to the *morale* of mental intercourse. She had heard of the lady in question as of one who, in the decline of life and in delicate health, loved retirement and the society of dear relatives and familiar friends, but whom bodily. languor unfitted for the fatiguing intercourse and ceremonious observances of mere acquaintances or utter strangers. But Grizzy, like many other people, thought that any one who had written a book, or even been suspected of such a thing, was from henceforth and for evermore to be looked upon as a *spectacle*, ready to be shown up at all times to all men, women, and children who might choose to flock to the exhibition; and so firmly was this idea entwined, or rather entangled, in her brains, that it would have been a work of no small difficulty and danger to have disengaged it. In short, aunt Grizzy's sentiments differed widely from those of Cowley on that, as probably on most other subjects; but, that the reader may have the benefit of both, we shall subjoin a few passages from his excellent essay on that much dreaded, much despised, much detested thing, " Obscurity; " premising, that we do not mean thereby the obscurity of low birth, abject poverty, personal insignificance, mental inferiority, or utter uselessness,—but simply the obscurity of not being conspicuous.

" For my part," says Cowley, " I think the pleasantest condition of life is in *incognito*. If we engage in a large acquaintance and various familiarities, we set open our gates to the invaders of most of our time; we expose our life to a quotidian ague of frigid impertinences, which would make a wise man tremble to think of. Now, as for being much known by sight and pointed at, I cannot comprehend the honour that lies in that. . . . . The common story of Demosthenes's confession, that he had taken great pleasure in hearing a tanker-woman say, as he passed, 'this is that Demosthenes,' is wonderfully ridiculous for so solid an orator. Democritus relates (and in such a manner as if he gloried in the good fortune and commodity of it), that when he came to Athens, nobody there did so much as take notice of him; and Epicurus lived there very well, that is, lay hid many years in his garden (so famous since that time), with his friend Metrodorus; after whose death, making in one of his letters a kind commemoration of the happiness they had enjoyed together, he adds, at last, that he thought it no disparagement to those kind felicities of their life, that, in the midst of the most talked-of and talking country in the world, they had lived so long, not

only without fame, but almost without being heard
of."

*   *   *   *   *   *   *

Yet " I love and commend a true good fame, because
it is the shadow of virtue; not that it doth any good
to the body which it accompanies, but it is an efficacious
shadow, and, like that of St. Peter, cures the diseases
of others.   The best kind of glory, no doubt, is that
which is reflected from honesty, as was the glory of
Cato and Aristides; but it was hurtful to them both,
and is seldom beneficial to any man whilst he lives:
what it is to him after his death, I cannot say, because
I love not philosophy merely notional and conjectural;
and no man who has made the experiment has been so
kind as to come back to inform us.

> "To him alas! to him I fear
> The face of death will terrible appear,
> Who, in his life flattering his senseless pride
> By being known to all the world beside,
> Does not himself, when he is dying, know
> Nor what he is, nor whither he's to go."

———o———

Chapter lrl.

Tie up the knocker; say I'm sick—I'm dead.
POPE.

MEANWHILE Grizzy continued to babble on
till the carriage stopped at the door of the
mansion, where, as Mary had anticipated, they
were not to be admitted—the lady was engaged.   This
was a phrase quite unheard-of by native Highland ears
of those days, and was consequently altogether unac-
ceptable.   In vain Mary endeavoured to explain to her
aunt, that it simply implied the lady was either not at

leisure or not disposed to receive company, and besought her to leave the letter and her card. Grizzy
would do no such thing, but repeated again and again,
" Engaged! engaged!—I declare I never heard the
like of it, and I can't understand it! There's none of
us ever engaged, although there's so many of us!
Engaged! I never heard of anybody being engaged,
unless they were engaged to be married, or engaged
out to dinner—I declare I don't know what to do!"

"There seems nothing to be done but to leave the
letter and your card," said Mary, endeavouring to take
them gently from her, but Grizzy resisted the attempt
most pertinaciously.

"Just let me alone, Mary, my dear, for I must
know a great deal better than you, you know, what to
do; there can be no doubt about that." Then beckoning to the servant of the house, who still stood at the
open door, but now advanced to the carriage, she thus
began :—

" My niece and I are two ladies from the Highlands
who are just come up—at least, I came only last Tuesday with Sir Sampson and Lady Maclaughlan—and
my niece has been staying all winter at her uncle
Lord Courtland's for her health; and this is a letter I
have brought to your mistress, and I am sure—there
can be no doubt of it—she would be very much
disappointed if she was not to see us, for we are
strangers."

" My missis is engaged, ma'am."

" Engaged!—hem—is she engaged out to dinner?
for it's too early, we thought "——

Here Mary made an attempt to arrest her progress;
but Grizzy had become almost rabid in her eagerness,
and she turned upon her with one of Jacky's worn-out
rebukes—

" Mary, my dear! you shouldn't interrupt me when

you see me speaking, for you may be sure I know what
I'm saying better than you can do." Then turning to
the servant,—

"Perhaps your lady is going to have company at
dinner, and there's no doubt that makes a great confusion in a house—but we wouldn't stay long, for
we "——

"There is no company expected, ma'am."

"Then I'm certain if your lady knew we were here,
and had a letter for her, and who we are, she would be
quite delighted to see us, there can be no doubt about
that! She wouldn't be 'engaged' to us, I am quite
certain of that!"

"Who shall I say, ma'am?" inquired the servant,
somewhat staggered by the confident tone in which this
was pronounced. Grizzy was about to enter upon a
most elaborate account of herself, when Mary contrived
to extract one of her cards, which she gave to the
servant: the letter itself was unattainable.

"There can be no doubt of our getting in now,
when she knows who we are," said Grizzy. "Am I
all right, Mary?" As she began to settle the preliminaries of her appearance, presently the servant returned.—Mrs Blanque was very sorry, and so forth;
but she had got a bad headach.

"A bad headach! Oh, that accounts for it!—I
was certain she wouldn't be 'engaged' to us if she
could help it—but I hope that she's not subject to
headachs, though headachs are going very much about,
and this is just the season for headachs. I hear the
healthiest people complaining of headachs."

"I will send Mrs Blanque's maid, ma'am," said the
servant, hastening away to answer another summons;
and Mary, in speechless woe, beheld the maid presently
take her station by the carriage, and heard her aunt
resume her colloquy:—

"I'm very sorry, and so is my niece, to hear that your lady has got a headach—is she subject to them?"

"Occasionally, mem."

"I know a great many cures for them. There's leeches on the soles of the feet, Lady Maclaughlan has the highest opinion of; and a blister on the crown of the head is a charming thing! I hope your lady has had her head shaved, for there's nothing worse than a quantity of hair for headachs. You know, Mary, you had your head shaved after an illness, when it was coming off; and it grew on ten times thicker than ever. So nobody need be afraid of having their head shaved; will you tell Mrs Blanque that?"

"Certainly, mem."

"And I hope her deafness is not affected by her headachs?—though there's a great connexion between the head and the ears"——

"Mem?"

"Is your lady very deaf?" raising her own voice, as people usually do when deafness is even alluded to.

"La, mem, not in the least!"

"Well, I'm sure that's a great blessing; but if she *had* been deaf, Sir Sampson Maclaughlan has a trumpet"——

"My dear aunt!" whispered Mary, "do let us be gone."

"Stop a little, my dear; you are always in a hurry. —Well, it's a great comfort not to be deaf"—(Mary sighed!) "And since your lady's not deaf, I'm sure I hope to goodness she's not blind either?"

"Oh, no, mem."

"That's very lucky! for I assure you the eyes have a great deal to do with the head—but I hope her eyes are quite strong?"

"No, mem, very weak."

"That's a great pity; at the same time it's a great

thing that she sees at all, for there is such a report going about—but I hope there's no appearance of ophthalmia about her eyes?"

"Not in the least, mem."

"Well, I assure you that's a great blessing, considering how our poor troops suffered from ophthalmia when they were in Egypt—I'm sure Buonaparte had much to answer for! and, indeed, many people who have not been in the army at all suffer very much from ophthalmia now, I am told; so your lady may be thankful she has escaped!"

"Ma-a-m?"

Mary felt as though her whole face had the ophthalmia; and again she attempted to get possession of the fatal letter with "My dear aunt! do let me"—but again Grizzy turned upon her; for Grizzy, arrayed in robes of satin, with a Chantilly fall on her head, and the sceptre of state in the form of the letter in her hand, seated in a coroneted carriage, primed with the oft-repeated injunctions of Misses M'Turk and Jacky, was altogether a different creature from the simple home-clad spinster sitting under the dominion of Jacky's supreme authority in the little grim parlour at Glenfern.

"Now, Mary, my dear, just hold your tongue, and let me alone, for it's all for your good I'm taking this trouble—not that I think it any trouble; so just be quiet, my dear." Then addressing the servant,—"I'm really very sorry, and so is my niece, to hear that your lady suffers so much from her eyes—but I hope she does not work much by candle-light?"

"Oh, no, mem, never."

"Well, that shows her good sense,—indeed she's famous for her sense,—she's not like many ladies, that are always working by candle-light: and I hope she does not read too much, for that's just as bad, especially small print; there can be no doubt about that."

"I believe not, mem."

"Well, that says a great deal for her, for some people never give over reading; and I'm sure, I declare, I don't know what it's about, — indeed, there's no end to reading with some people: and I hope she doesn't write much, for that's just as bad, and there can be no use for it now there are so many excellent books already, — nobody can dispute that."

"Very little indeed, mem."

"That's very right; and I hope she uses the golden ointment, for that's a delightful thing for the eyes; it makes them smart, and does them a great deal of good."

"No, mem, Mrs Blanque does not use anything for them."

"Then she's very wrong to neglect them, considering what valuable things eyes are; and Lady Maclaughlan has the highest opinion of the golden ointment, I know that; and *we* all use it, and our eyes are wonderful, considering, though we are all very subject to sore eyes, from our grandmother; and, indeed, my poor brother's were almost gone before he died, and I'm sure if it wasn't for the golden ointment I don't think we would have an eye in our heads."

"Sure, mem!"

"But I dare say your lady wears spectacles?"

"No, mem."

"Well, I'm surprised to hear that, for I thought every body had worn glasses now—at least, every body that ought to do it,—and, indeed, a great many people have them, both ladies and gentlemen, and perfect children, too, for they're quite the fashion; so I'm sure nobody need be ashamed to wear glasses now.

Lady Maclaughlan saw a little girl of five years old
with spectacles at the Pumpwell one day; and they
have them of all colours now—blue, and green, and
yellow, and black, and every colour you can think of;
so I hope to goodness Mrs Blanque will get a pair of
green spectacles and the golden ointment directly,—
you'll be sure to tell her that?"

"Certainly, mem."

Mary flattered herself aunt Grizzy had now reached
her climax,—but not so.

"And I hope your lady hears well?" raising her
own voice, as people usually do when deafness is even
alluded to.

"Perfectly well, mem."

"I'm sure that's a great blessing, and I daresay she's
very thankful for it; for many deaf people suffer very
much from headachs,—indeed, deaf headachs are become very common now. I hear they are going very
much about, and this is just the season for them, so
people ought really to be upon their guard"——

At that moment Mary descried Lady Emily on the
opposite side of the street, and, beckoning to her, she
immediately crossed, and was soon made to comprehend,
in some degree, the awkward predicament in which her
friend was placed; upon which, stepping into the carriage, she, by a graceful *legerdemain*, instantly trans-
ferred the letter from the hand of the astonished Grizzy
to that of the maid, and gave orders to drive on. But,
while the horses were making some preliminary curvets,
she rallied sufficiently to reiterate her message with redoubled emphasis. "And you'll be sure to remember
the green spectacles and golden ointment, with my
compliments and my niece's?"

"I shall be very particular, mem; gold spectacles and
green ointment; you may depend upon me, mem," replied
the Abigail, with an obeisance, as she closed the door.

Although Lady Emily could not but smile at her dismay, she sought to comfort her under her disappointment, by assuring her she would have been greatly disappointed by an introduction to Mrs Blanque, who was very cold and reserved in her manners, and devoid of conversational talent. "Of her," said she, addressing Mary, "it may truly be said (using a slight transposition), '*qu'elle avait* moins *que personne l'ésprit qu'a tout le monde ;*' and the consciousness of this has doubtless added to the embarrassment of the position in which she finds herself placed, and makes her often appear haughty and uncourteous to strangers; and this no one can feel or condemn more bitterly than she does herself. There are, no doubt, many who can and do sustain the part of an authoress to admiration; but it must be at some cost of time, and ease, and comfort. Indeed, for my own part, I should think it such a very tiresome thing to be authorised, and lionised, and newspaperised, and annualised, and albumised, that I am sure it would not lead to my ever being canonised : truly it would require the patience of Job and the strength of Sampson to bear with it. How insupportable to have one's daily path beset by a great Birmingham Fame, with her blowzy cheeks and her squeaking trumpet, flapping her wings in one's face, and making a dust wherever one stirred."

"I have heard of one," said Mary, "who, from a different motive, was equally averse to the *éclat* of authorship; one who, with a high reverence for the standard of Christian excellence, was so conscious of her deficiency in Christian attainments, as to shrink from undue exaltation on account of any mere natural gift or endowment which had not been devoted to the service of God."

"That sounds very like humility," replied Lady Emily, "but I suspect pride is at the root of the matter in that case, as in almost every other. *True* humility, I take it, would care so little about mere human applause, that it would neither shrink from nor court it. I was reading Pascal yesterday, so I am just off the irons upon that subject; but, however, your friend's *may* be what the doctors might call a compound case—such, perhaps, as may some day be my own,—when a sense of better things may make what at present I call my perception of the ridiculous, and *gaité de cœur*, look ugly as satire and levity; and still I may indulge the imps even while I hate them.—But where are we going? I have done my part, and must now leave you to proceed on what Dr Redgill would call your *tower* of visits; when that is accomplished, you will pick me up at Selby's." She stopped the carriage, and, having spoken a few kind words to aunt Grizzy, who still sat in mute bewilderment, took leave, and left the aunt and the niece to complete their progress.

———o———

Chapter lxij.

This sort of person is skilled to assume the appearance of all virtues, and all good qualities; but their favourite mask is universal benevolence. And the reason why they prefer this disguise to all others, is, that it tends to conceal its opposite, which is, indeed, their true character—an universal selfishness. —KNOX's *Essays.*

GRIZZY'S ambitious projects for the advancement of learning had sustained a downfall, from which her mind required some time to recover, and for a few minutes Mary was left to a state of blissful tranquillity. But Grizzy's was not a genius to lie long prostrate; so she soon rallied her forces, and began anew. "Well, Mary, this has been a sad

disappointment to me, but especially to you, there can
be no doubt about that! But I hope you will keep
up your spirits, for I dare say you'll see somebody
that has written a book, yet; you may be sure I'll
make a point of that before you go back, and at any rate
this letter will be a great thing for you. I got it from
Mrs Menzies, whose friend, Mrs Campbell's half-
sister, Miss Grant, is a great friend of Mrs Fox's,
and she says she is a most charming woman. Of
course, she is no friend to the great Fox; or, you
know, it would have been very odd in me, with Sir
Sampson's principles, and my poor brother's principles,
and all our own principles, to have visited her. But
she's quite of a different family of Foxes: she's a
Fox of Pickwell, it seems a very old family, and a
most amiable woman, very rich and prodigiously charitable. I am sure we have been most fortunate in
getting a letter to such a woman!" And, with this
heartfelt ejaculation, they found themselves at Mrs
Fox's. There the door was at once thrown open,
and free admittance seemed the order of the house.

Every thing corresponded with the account of this
lady's wealth and consequence; the mansion was
spacious, and handsomely furnished, with its due proportion of livery servants; and they were ushered into
a sitting-room, which was filled with all the wonders
of nature and art. Indian shells—inlaid cabinets—
ivory boxes—stuffed birds—old china—Chinese mandarins—stood disclosed in all their charms. The lady
of the mansion was seated at a table covered with
works of a different description: it exhibited the
various arts of woman, in regular gradation, from the
painted card-rack and gilded fire-screen to the humble
thread-paper and shirt-button. Mrs Fox was a fine,
fashionable-looking woman, with a smooth countenance, and still smoother address. She received her

visitors with that overstrained complaisance which, to Mary's nicer tact, at once discovered that all was hollow; but poor Miss Grizzy was scarcely seated before she was already transfixed with admiration at Mrs Fox's politeness, and felt as if her whole life would be too short to repay such kindness. Compliments over—the weather, &c. discussed, Mrs Fox began:

"You must be surprised, ladies, to see me in the midst of such a litter, but you find me busy arranging the works of some poor *protégées* of mine. A most unfortunate family!—I have given them what little instruction I could in these little female works; and you see," putting a gaudy work-basket into Grizzy's hands, "it is astonishing what progress they have made. My friends have been most liberal in their purchases of these trifles, but I own I am a wretched beggar: they are in bad hands when they are in mine, poor souls! The fact is, I can give, but I *cannot* beg. I tell them they really must find somebody else to dispose of their little labours—somebody who has more of what I call the gift of begging than I am blest with."

Tears of admiration stood in Grizzy's eyes—her hand was in her pocket. She looked to Mary, but Mary's hands and eyes betrayed no corresponding emotions; she felt only disgust at the meanness and indelicacy of the mistress of such a mansion levying contributions from the stranger within her door.

Mrs Fox proceeded: "That most benevolent woman, Miss Gull, was here this morning, and bought no less than seven of these sweet little pin-cushions. I would fain have dissuaded her from taking so many —it really seemed such a stretch of virtue; but she said, 'My dear Mrs Fox, how can one possibly spend their money better than in doing a good action, and at the same time enriching themselves?'"

Grizzy's purse was in her hand.   " I declare that's
very true.   I never thought of that before; and I'm
certain Lady Maclaughlan will say the very same ; and
I'm sure she will be delighted—I've no doubt of that
—to take a pin-cushion; and each of my sisters, I'm
certain, will take one, though we have all plenty of pin-
cushions ; and I'll take one to myself, though I have
three, I'm sure, that I've never used yet."

" My dear Miss Douglas, you really are, I could
almost say, *too* good.   Two and two's four, and one's
five—five half-crowns ! My poor *protégées* ! You will
really be the making of their fortune ! "

Grizzy, with trembling hands, and a face flushed
with conscious virtue, drew forth the money from her
little hoard.

But Mrs Fox did not quit her prey so easily.   " If
any of your friends are in want of shirt-buttons, I
would fain recommend those to them.   They are made
by a poor woman in whom I take some interest, and
are far superior to any that are to be had from the
shops.   They are made from the very best materials.
Indeed, I take care of that, as " (in a modest whisper)
" I furnish her with the materials myself ; but the
generality of those you get to purchase are made from
old materials.   I've ascertained that, and it's a fact you
may rely upon."

Poor Grizzy's hair stood on end, to hear of such de-
pravity in a sphere where she had never even suspected
it ; but, for the honour of her country, she flattered
herself such practices were there unknown ; and she
was entering upon a warm vindication of the integrity
of Scotch shirt-buttons, when Mrs Fox coolly observed,—

" Indeed, our friend Miss Grant was so conscious of
the great superiority of these buttons over any others,
that she bespoke thirty-six dozen of them to take to

Scotland with her. In fact, they are the real good old-fashioned shirt-buttons, such as I have heard my mother talk of; and for all that, I make a point of my poor woman selling them a penny a dozen below the shop price; so that in taking twelve dozen, which is the common quantity, there is a shilling saved at once."

Grizzy felt as if she would be the saving of the family by the purchase of these incomparable shirt-buttons, and, putting down her five shillings, became the happy possessor of twelve dozen of them.

Fresh expressions of gratitude and admiration ensued, till Grizzy's brain began to whirl, even more rapidly than usual, at the thought of the deeds she had done.

"And now," said Mrs Fox, observing her eyes in a fine frenzy rolling from her lapful of pin-cushions and shirt-buttons, to a mandarin nearly as large as life, "perhaps, my dear Miss Douglas, you will do me the favour to take a look of my little collection."

"Favour!" thought Grizzy; "what politeness!" and she protested there was nothing she liked so much as to look at everything, and that it would be the greatest favour to show her anything. The mandarin was made to shake his head—a musical snuff-box played its part—and a variety of other expensive toys were also exhibited.

Mary's disgust increased. "And this woman," thought she, "professes to be charitable, amidst all this display of selfish extravagance! Probably the price of one of these costly baubles would have provided for the whole of these poor people, for whom she affects so much compassion, without subjecting her to the meanness of turning her house into a beggar's repository." And she walked away to the other end of the room, to examine some fine scriptural paintings.

"Here," said Mrs Fox to her victim, as she un-locked a superb cabinet, "is what I value more than my whole collection put together. It is my specimens of Scotch pebbles; and I owe them solely to the generosity and good-will of my Scotch friends. I assure you, that is a proud reflection to me. I am a perfect enthusiast in Scotch pebbles, and, I may say, in Scotch people. In fact, I am an enthusiast in whatever I am interested in; and at present, I must own, my heart is set upon making a complete collection of Scotch pebbles."

Grizzy began to feel a sort of tightness at her throat, at which was affixed a very fine pebble brooch pertain-ing to Nicky, but lent to Grizzy to enable her to make a more distinguished figure in the gay world. "Oh!" thought she, "what a pity this brooch is Nicky's, and not mine; I would have given it to this charming Mrs Fox. Indeed, I don't see how I can be off giving it to her, even although it is Nicky's."

"And, by the by," exclaimed Mrs Fox, as if suddenly struck with the sight of the brooch, "that seems a very fine stone of yours. I wonder I did not observe it sooner; but, indeed, pebbles are thrown away in dress. May I beg a nearer view of it?"

Grizzy's brain was now all on fire. On the one hand, there was the glory of presenting the brooch to such a polite, charitable, charming woman; on the other, there was the fear of Nicky's indignation. But then it was quite thrown away upon Nicky—she had no cabinet, and Mrs Fox had declared that pebbles were quite lost anywhere but in cabinets, and it was a thousand pities that Nicky's brooch should be lost. All these thoughts Grizzy revolved with her usual clearness, as she unclasped the brooch and gave it into the hand of the collector.

"Bless me, my dear Miss Douglas, this is really a

very fine stone! I had no conception of it when I saw it at your throat. It looks quite a different thing in the hand. It is a species I am really not acquainted with. I have nothing at all similar to it in my poor collection. Pray, can you tell me the name of it, and where it is found, that I may at least endeavour to procure a piece of it?"

"I'm sure, I wish to goodness my sister Nicky was here—I'm certain she would—though, to be sure, she has a great regard for it—for it was found on the Glenfern estate, the very day my grandfather won his plea against Drimsydie; and we always called it the lucky stone from that."

"The 'lucky stone!' what a delightful name! I shall never think myself in luck till I can procure a piece of your lucky stone. I protest I could almost go to Scotland on purpose. Oh, you dear lucky stone!" kissing it with rapture.

"I'm sure—I'm almost certain—indeed I'm convinced, if my sister Nicky was here, she would be delighted to offer—it would certainly be doing my sister Nicky the greatest favour, since you think it would be seen to so much greater advantage in your cabinet, which, for my own part, I have not the least doubt of, as certainly my sister Nicky very seldom wears it for fear of losing it, and it will be a thousand pities if it was lost; and, to be sure, it will be much safer locked up—nobody can dispute that—so I am sure it's by far the best thing my sister Nicky can do—for certainly a pebble brooch is quite lost as a brooch."

"My dear Miss Douglas! I am really quite ashamed! This is a perfect robbery, I protest! But I must insist upon your accepting some little token of my regard for Miss Nicky in return." Going to her charity-table, and returning with a set of painted thread-papers, " I must request the favour of you to present these to Miss Nicky, with my kind regards, and assure her I shall consider her lucky stone as the most precious jewel in my possession."

The whole of this scene had been performed with such rapidity, that poor Grizzy was not prepared for the sudden metamorphose of Nicky's pebble brooch into a set of painted thread-papers, and some vague alarms began to float through her brain.

Mary now advanced, quite unconscious of what had been going on ; and, having whispered her aunt to take leave, they departed. They returned in silence. Grizzy was so occupied in examining her pin-cushions, and counting her buttons, that she never looked up till the carriage stopped in Milsom Street.

Mary accompanied her in. Grizzy was all impatience to display her treasures ; and, as she hastily unfolded them, began to relate her achievements. Lady Maclauchlan heard her in silence, and a deep groan was all that she uttered ; but Grizzy was too well accustomed to be groaned at, to be at all appalled, and went on, " But all that's nothing to the shirt-buttons, made of Mrs Fox's own linen, and only five shillings the twelve dozen ; and, considering what tricks are played with shirt - buttons now — I assure you people require to be on their guard with shirt-buttons now."

" Pray, my dear, did you ever read the Vicar of Wakefield ? "

" The Vicar of Wakefield ? I—I think always I must have read it ;—at any rate, I'm certain I've heard of it."

" Moses and his green spectacles was as one of the acts of Solomon compared to you and your shirt-buttons. Pray, which of you is it that wears shirts ? "

" I declare that's very true—I wonder I did not

think of that sooner: to be sure, none of us wear shirts since my poor brother died."

"And what's become of her brooch?" turning to Mary, who for the first time observed the departure of Nicky's crown-jewel.

"Oh, as to the brooch," cried Grizzy, "I'm certain you'll all think that well bestowed, and certainly it has been the saving of it." Upon which she commenced a most entangled narrative, from which the truth was at length extracted.

"Well," said Lady Maclauchlan, "there are two things I pray I may never become; an *amateur* in charity, and a collector of curiosities. No Christian can be either—both are pickpockets. I wouldn't keep company with my own mother were she either one or other. As for your fancy-mongers, I know nothing about them—humph!"

Mary was grieved at the loss of the brooch; but Grizzy seemed more than ever satisfied with the exchange, as Sir Sampson had taken a fancy for the thread-papers, and it would amuse him for the rest of the day to be told every two minutes what they were intended for. Mary, therefore, left her quite happy, and returned to Beech Park.

———o———

Chapter lxiij.

He either fears his fate too much,
  Or his deserts are small,
Who dares not put it to the touch,
  To gain or lose it all.
  MARQUIS OF MONTROSE.

TIME rolled on, but no event occurred in Grizzy's life worthy of being commemorated. Lady Juliana began to recover from the shock of her arrival, and at length was even prevailed upon to pay

her a visit, and actually spent five minutes in the same
room with her.   All her ladyship's plans seemed now
on the point of becoming accomplished.   Mr Downe
Wright was now Lord Glenallan, with an additional
fifteen thousand per annum, and, by wiser heads than
hers, would have been thought an exceptionable match
for any young woman.   Leaving his mother to settle
his affairs in Scotland, to which she was much more *au
fait* than himself, he hastened to Beech Park to claim
Mary's promised hand.

But neither wealth nor grandeur possessed any sway
over Mary's well-regulated mind, and she turned from
that species of happiness which she felt would be insufficient to satisfy the best affections of her heart.
" No," thought she, " it is not in splendour and distinction that I shall find happiness ; it is in the cultivation of the domestic virtues—the peaceful joys of a
happy home, and a loved companion, that my felicity
must consist.   Without these, I feel that I should still
be poor, were I mistress of millions : " and she took
the first opportunity of acquainting Lord Glenallan
with the nature of her sentiments.

He received the communication with painful surprise ;
but as he was one of those who do not easily divest
themselves of an idea that has once taken possession of
their brain, he seemed resolved to persevere in his quiet,
though pointed, attentions.

Lady Juliana's anger at the discovery of her daughter's refusal, it is needless to describe—it may easily be
imagined ; and poor Mary was almost heart-broken by
the violence and duration of it.   Sometimes she wavered
in her ideas as to whether she was doing right in thus
resisting her mother's wishes ; and, in the utmost distress, she mentioned her scruples to Lady Emily.

" As to Lady Juliana's wishes," said her cousin,
" they are mere soap-bubbles ; but as to your own

views—why, really, you are somewhat of a riddle to me. I rather think, were I such a quiet, civil, well-disposed person as you, I could have married Lord Glenallan well enough. He is handsome, good-natured, and rich; and though 'he is but a lord, and nothing but a lord,' still there is a dash and bustle in twenty thousand a-year that takes off from the *ennui* of a dull companion. With five hundred a-year, I grant you, he would be execrable."

"Then I shall never marry a man with twenty thousand a-year, whom I would not have with five hundred."

"In short, you are to marry for love—that's the old story, which, with all your wisdom, you wise, well-educated girls always end in. Where shall I find a hero upon five hundred a-year for you? Of course, he must be virtuous, noble, dignified, handsome, brave, witty. What would you think of Charles Lennox?"

Mary coloured. "After what passed, I would not marry Colonel Lennox—no," affecting to smile, "not if he were to ask me, which is certainly the most unlikely of all things."

"Ah! true, I had forgot that scrape. No, that won't do—it certainly would be most pitiful in you, after what passed.—Well, I don't know what's to be done with you: there's nothing for it but that you should take Lord Glenallan, with all his imperfections on his head; and, after all, I really see nothing that he wants but a little more brain, and, as you'll have the managing of him, you can easily supply that deficiency."

"Indeed," answered Mary, "I find I have quite little enough for myself, and I have no genius whatever for managing. I shall therefore never marry, unless I marry a man on whose judgment I could rely for advice and assistance, and for whom I could feel a

certain deference that I consider due from a wife to
her husband."

"I see what you would be at," said Lady Emily;
"you mean to model yourself upon the behaviour of
Mrs Tooley, who has such a deference for the judgment of her better half, that she consults him even
about the tying of her shoes, and would not presume to
give her child a few grains of magnesia without his full
and unqualified approbation. Now, I flatter myself,
my husband and I shall have a more equitable division;
for, though a man is a reasonable being, he shall know
and own that woman is so too—sometimes. All things
that men ought to know better, I shall yield: whatever
may belong to either sex, I either seize upon as my
prerogative, or scrupulously divide; for which reason,
I should like the profession of my husband to be something in which I could not possibly interfere. How
difficult must it be for a woman in the lower ranks of
life to avoid teaching her husband how to sew, if he is
a tailor; or how to bake, if he is a baker, &c.

"Nature seems to have provided for this tendency of
both sexes, by making your sensible men—that is, men
who think themselves sensible, and wish every body
else to think the same—incline to foolish women. I
can detect one of these sensible husbands at a glance,
by the pomp and formality visible in every word, look,
or action: men whose 'visages do cream and mantle
like a standing pond;' who are perfect Joves in their
own houses—who speak their will by a nod, and lay
down the law by the motion of their eye-brow—and
who attach prodigious ideas of dignity to frightening
their children, and being worshipped by their wives till
you see one of these wiseacres looking as if he thought
himself and his obsequious helpmate were exact personifications of Adam and Eve—'he for God only, she
for God in him.' Now, I am much afraid, Mary,

with all your sanctity, you are in some danger of becoming one of these idolatresses."

"I hope not," replied Mary, laughing; "but if I should, that seems scarcely so bad as the sect of Independents in the married state: for example, there is Mrs Boston, who by all strangers is taken for a widow, such emphasis does she lay upon the personal pronoun —with her, 'tis always, *I* do this, or *I* do that, without the slightest reference to her husband; and she talks of *my* house, *my* gardens, *my* carriage, *my* children, as if there were no copartnery in the case."

"Ah! she is very odious," cried Lady Emily; "she is both master and mistress, and more, if possible. She makes her husband look like her footman, but she is a fool, as every woman must needs be who thinks she can raise herself by lowering her husband. Then, there is the sect of the Wranglers, whose marriage is only one continued dispute. But, in short, I see it is reserved for me to set a perfect example to my sex in the married state. But I'm more reasonable than you, I suspect, for I don't insist upon having a bright genius for my mate."

"I confess, I should like that my husband's genius was at least as bright as my own," said Mary, "and I can't think there is anything unreasonable in that; or, rather, I should say, were I a genius myself, I could better dispense with a certain portion of intellect in my husband; as it has been generally remarked, that those who are largely endowed themselves, can easier dispense with talents in their companions than others of more moderate endowments can do; but virtue and talents on the one side, virtue and tenderness on the other, I look upon as the principal ingredients in a happy union."

"Well, I intend to be excessively happy, though I don't think Edward will ever set the Thames on fire;

and as for my tenderness—humph!—as your Lady
Maclauchlan says. But as for you, I rather think
you're in some danger of turning into an aunt Grizzy,
with a long waist and large pockets, peppermint drops,
and powdered curls. But, whatever you do, for
mercy's sake let us have no more human sacrifices! if
you do, I shall certainly appear at your wedding in
sackcloth and ashes." And this was all of comfort or
advice that her ladyship could bestow.

As Lady Emily was not a person who concealed
either her own secrets or those of others, Colonel
Lennox was not long of hearing from her what had
passed, and of being made thoroughly acquainted with
Mary's sentiments on love and marriage. "Such a
heart must be worth winning," thought he; but he
sighed to think that he had less chance for the prize
than another. Independent of his narrow fortune,
which, he was aware, would be an insuperable bar to
obtaining Lady Juliana's consent, Mary's coldness and
reserve towards him seemed to increase rather than
diminish. Or, if she sometimes gave way to the
natural frankness and gaiety of her disposition before
him, a word or look expressive of admiration on his
part instantly recalled to her those painful ideas which
had been for a moment forgot, and seemed to throw
him at a greater distance than ever.

Colonel Lennox was too noble-minded himself to
suppose for an instant that Mary actually felt dislike
towards him because, at the commencement of their
acquaintance, he had not done justice to her merits;
but he was also aware, that, until he had explained to
her the nature of his sentiments, she must naturally regard his attentions with suspicion, and consider them
rather as acts of duty towards his mother, than as the
spontaneous expression of his own attachment. He
therefore, in the most simple and candid manner, laid

open to her the secret of his heart, and, in all the eloquence of real passion, poured forth those feelings of love and admiration with which she had unconsciously inspired him.

For a moment, Mary's distrust was overcome by the ardour of his address, and the open manly manner in which he had avowed the rise and progress of his attachment, and she yielded herself up to the delightful conviction of loving and being beloved.

But soon that gave way to the mortifying reflection that rushed over her mind. " He *has* tried to love me ! " thought she ; " but it is in obedience to his mother's wish, and he thinks he has succeeded. No, no ; I cannot be the dupe of his delusion—I will not give myself to one who has been solicited to love me ! " And again wounded delicacy and woman's pride resumed their empire over her, and she rejected the idea of *ever* receiving Colonel Lennox as a lover. He heard her determination with the deepest anguish, and used every argument and entreaty to soften her resolution ; but Mary had wrought herself up to a pitch of heroism—she had rejected the man she loved —the only man she ever *could* love—that done, to persist in the sacrifice seemed easy ; and they parted with increased attachments in their hearts, even though those hearts seemed severed for ever.

Soon after, he set off to join his regiment ; and it was only in saying farewell ! that Mary felt how deeply her happiness was involved in the fate of the man she had for ever renounced. To no one did she impart what had passed ; and Lady Emily was too dull herself, for some days after the departure of her friend, to take any notice of Mary's dejection.

———o———

Chapter lxib.

What taught the parrot to cry, hail?
What taught the chattering pie his tale?
Hunger; that sharpener of the wits,
Which gives e'en fools some thinking fits.
                              DRUMMOND's *Persius.*

MARY found herself bereft of both her lovers
nearly at the same time. Lord Glenallan,
after formally renewing his suit, at length took
a final leave, and returned to Scotland. Lady Juliana's
indignation could only be equalled by Dr Redgill's
upon the occasion. He had planned a snug retreat for
himself during the game season at Glenallan Castle;
where, from the good-nature and easy temper of both
master and mistress, he had no doubt but that he should
in time come to *rule the roast,* and be lord paramount
over kitchen and larder. His disappointment was
therefore great at finding all the solid joys of red deer
and moor-game, kippered salmon and mutton hams,
"vanish like the baseless fabric of a vision," leaving
not a wreck behind.

"Refused Lord Glenallan!" exclaimed he to Lady
Emily, upon first hearing of it. "The thing's in-
credible — absolutely impossible. I won't believe
it!"

"That's right, doctor: who is it that says, 'and
still believe the story false that *ought* not to be true?'
I admire your candour, and wish I could imitate
it."

"Then your ladyship really believes it? 'Pon my
honour, I—I—it's really a very vexatious affair. I
feel for Lady Juliana, poor woman! No wonder she's
hysterical—five-and-twenty thousand a-year refused!—
What is it she would have? The finest deer-park in

Scotland! Every sort of game upon the estate! A salmon-fishing at the very door!—I should just like to know what *is* the meaning of it?"

"Cannot you guess, doctor?" asked Lady Emily.

"Guess! No—'pon my soul! I defy any man to guess what could tempt a woman to refuse five-and-twenty thousand a-year, unless, indeed, she has something higher in view, and even then she should be pretty sure of her mark. But I suppose, because Miss Adelaide has got a duke, she thinks she must have one too. I suppose that's the story; but I can tell her, dukes are not so plenty, and she's by no means so fine a woman as her sister; and her market's spoilt, or I'm much mistaken. What man in his senses would ever ask a woman who had been such an idiot as to refuse five-and-twenty thousand a-year?"

"I see, doctor, you are quite a novice in the tender passion. Cannot you make allowance for a young lady's not being in love?"

"In what?" demanded the doctor.

"In love," repeated Lady Emily.

"Love! Bah—nonsense—no mortal in their senses ever thinks of such stuff now."

"Then you think love and madness are one and the same thing, it seems?"

"I think the man or woman who could let their love stand in the way of five-and-twenty thousand a-year is the next thing to being mad," said the doctor warmly; "and in this case I can see no difference."

"But you'll allow there are some sorts of love that may be indulged without casting any shade upon the understanding?"

"I really can't tell what your ladyship means," said the doctor, impatiently.

"I mean, for example, the love one may feel towards a turtle, such as we had lately."

"That's quite a different thing," interrupted the doctor.

"Pardon me, but, whatever the consequence may be, the effects in both cases were very similar, as exemplified in yourself. Pray what difference did it make to your friends, who were deprived of your society, whether you spent your time in walking with 'even step and musing gait' before your dulcinea's window, or the turtle's cistern?—whether you were engrossed in composing a sonnet to your mistress's eyebrow, or in contriving a new method of heightening the enjoyments of *calipash?*—whether you expatiated with greater rapture on the charms of a white skin, or green fat?—whether you were most devoted to a languishing or a lively beauty?—whether "——

"'Pon my honour, Lady Emily, I really—I—I—can't conceive what it is you mean! There's a time for every thing; and I'm sure nobody but yourself would ever have thought of bringing in a turtle to a conversation upon marriage."

"On the contrary, doctor, I thought it had been upon love; and I was endeavouring to convince you, that even the wisest of men may be susceptible of certain tender emotions towards a beloved object."

"You'll never convince me that any but a fool can be what you call in love," cried the doctor, his visage assuming a darker purple as the argument advanced.

"Then you must rank Lord Glenallan, with his five-and-twenty thousand a-year, amongst the number; for he is desperately in love, I assure you."

"As to that, Lord Glenallan, or any man with his fortune, may be whatever he chooses. He has a right to be in love: he can afford to be in love."

"I have heard much of the torments of love," said Lady Emily; "but I never heard it rated as a luxury before. I hope there is no chance of your being made premier, otherwise I fear we should have a tax upon love marriages immediately."

"It would be greatly for the advantage of the nation, as well as the comfort of individuals, if there was," returned the doctor. "Many a pleasant fellow has been lost to society, by what you call a love-marriage. I speak from experience: I was obliged to drop the oldest friend I had, upon his making one of your love marriages."

"What! were you afraid of the effects of evil example?" asked Lady Emily.

"No, it was not for that; but he asked me to take a family dinner with him one day, and I, without knowing anything of the character of the woman he had married, was weak enough to go. I found a very so-so table-cloth, and a shoulder of mutton, which ended our acquaintance. I never entered his door after it. In fact, no man's happiness is proof against dirty table-cloths and bad dinners; and you may take my word for it, Lady Emily, these are the invariable accompaniments of your love marriages."

"Pshaw! that is only amongst the *bourgeois*," said Lady Emily, affectedly; "that is not the sort of *ménage* I mean to have. Here is to be the style of my domestic establishment;" and she repeated Shenstone's beautiful pastoral—

"My banks they are furnished with bees," &c.

till she came to—

"I have found out a gift for my fair,
I have found where the wood-pigeons breed."

"There's some sense in that," cried the doctor, who had been listening with great weariness. "You may have a good pigeon-pie, or *un sauté de pigeons au sang*, which is still better when well-dressed."

"Shocking!" exclaimed Lady Emily; "to mention pigeon-pies in the same breath with nightingales and roses!"

"I'll tell you what, Lady Emily, it's just these sort of nonsensical descriptions that do all the mischief amongst you young ladies. It's these idiotical poets that turn all your heads, and make you think you have nothing to do after you are married, but sit beside fountains and grottos, and divert yourself with birds and flowers, instead of looking after your servants, and paying your butcher's bills: and, after all, what is the substance of that trash you have just been reading, but to say that the man was a substantial farmer and grazier, and had bees; though I never heard of any man in his senses going to sleep amongst his bee-hives before. 'Pon my soul! if I had my will, I would burn every line of poetry that ever was written. A good recipe for a pudding is worth all that your Shenstones, and the whole set of them, ever wrote; and there's more good sense and useful information in this book," rapping his knuckles against a volume he held in his hand, "than in all your poets, ancient and modern."

Lady Emily took it out of his hand, and opened it.

"And some very poetical description, too, doctor; although you affect to despise it so much. Here is an eulogium on the partridge; I doubt much if St. Preux ever made a finer on his adorable Julie:" and she read as follows:—

"*La Perdrix tient le premier rang après la Bécasse, dans la catégorie des gibiers à plumes. C'est, lorsqu'elle est rouge, l'un des plus honorables et des meilleurs rôtis qui puissent être étalés sur une table gourmande. Sa forme appétissante, sa taille élégante et svelte, quoiqu' arrondie, son embonpoint modéré, ses jambes d'écarlate; enfin, son fumet divin et ses qualités restaurantes, tout concourt à la faire rechercher des vrais amateurs. D'autres gibiers sont plus rares, plus chers, mieux acceuillis par la vanité, le préjuge, et la mode ; la Perdrix rouge, belle de sa propre beauté, dont les qualités sont indépendantes de la fantaisie, qui réunit en sa personne tout ce qui peut charmer les yeux, délecter le palais, stimuler l'appétit, et ranimer les forces, plaira dans tous les temps, et concourra à l'honneur de tous les festins, sous quelque forme qu'elle y paroisse."* *

The doctor sighed. "That's nothing to what he says of the woodcock; "—and with trembling hands he turned over the leaves, till he found the place. "Here it is," said he, "page 88. chap. xvi. Just be so good as read that, Lady Emily, and say whether it is not infamous that Monsieur Grillade has never even attempted to make it."

With an air of melancholy enthusiasm she read—
" Dans les pays où les Bécasses sont communes, on obtient, de leurs carcasses pilées dans un mortier, une purée sur laquelle on dresse diverses entrées, telles que de petites côtelettes de mouton, &c. Cette purée est l'une des plus delicieuses choses qui puisse être introduite dans le palais d'un gourmand, et l'on peut assurer que quiconque n'en a point mangé n'a point connu les joies du paradis terrestre. Une purée de Bécasse, bien faite, est le ne plus ultrà des jouissances humaines. Il faut mourir après l'avoir goutée, car toutes les autres alors ne paroîtront plus qu'insipides."

"And these *bécasses*, these woodcocks, perfectly swarm on the Glenallan estate in the season," cried the doctor; "and to think that such a man should have been refused!—but Miss Mary will repent this the longest day she lives. I had a cook in my eye for them, too—one who is quite up to the making of this *purée*. 'Pon my soul! she deserves to live upon sheep's head and haggis for the rest of her life; and if I was Lady Juliana, I would try the effect of bread and water."

* Manuel des Amphitryons.

" She certainly does not aspire to such joys as are here portrayed in this *your* book of life," said Lady Emily ; " for I suspect she could endure existence even upon roast mutton, with the man she loves."

" That's nothing to the purpose, unless the man she loves, as you call it, loves to live upon roast mutton too. Take my word for it, unless she gives her husband good dinners, he'll not care twopence for her in a week's time. I look upon bad dinners to be the source of much of the misery we hear of in the married life. Women are much mistaken if they think it's by dressing themselves they are to please their husbands.

" Pardon me, doctor, we must be the best judges there, and I have the authority of all ages and sages in my favour. The beauty and the charms of women have been the favourite theme, time immemorial ; now, no one ever heard of a fair one being celebrated for her skill in cookery."

" There I beg leave to differ from you," said the doctor, with an air of exultation, again referring to his *text-book ;* " here is the great Madame Pompadour, celebrated for a single dish : ' *Les tendrons d'agneau au soleil et à la Pompadour, sont sortis de l'imagination de cette dame célèbre, pour entrer dans la bouche d'un roi.'* "

" But it was Love that inspired her—it was Love that kindled the fire in her imagination. In short, you must acknowledge that

    'Love rules the court, the camp, the grove.' "

" I'll acknowledge no such thing ! " cried the doctor, with indignation. " Love rule the camp, indeed ! A very likely story ! Don't I know that all our first generals carry off the best cooks—that there's no such living anywhere as in camp — that their *aides-de-camp* are quite ruined by it — that in time of war they live at the rate of twenty thousand a-year, and when they come home they can't get a dinner they can eat ? As for the court, I don't pretend to know much about it ; but I suspect there are more cooks than Cupids to be seen about it. And for the groves, I shall only say I never heard of any of your *fêtes champêtre*, or *picnics*, where all the pleasure didn't seem to consist in the eating and drinking."

" Ah, doctor ! I perceive you have taken all your ideas on that subject from Werter, who certainly was a sort of a sentimental *gourmand*, he seems to have enjoyed so much drinking his coffee under the shade of the lime-trees, and going to the kitchen to make his own pease-soup ; and then he breaks out into such raptures at the idea of the illustrious lovers of Penelope killing and dressing their own meat — butchers and cooks in one ! only conceive them with their great knives and blue aprons, or their spits and white nightcaps ! Poor Penelope ! no wonder she preferred making webs to marrying one of these creatures — faugh ! I must have an ounce of civet to sweeten my imagination." And she flew off, leaving the doctor to con over the *Manuel des Amphitryons*, and sigh at the mention of joys, sweet, yet mournful to his soul.

——o——

Chapter lxb.

The ample proposition that hope makes
In all designs begun on earth below,
Fails in the promised largeness.

SHAKSPEARE.

THERE is no saying whether the doctor's system might not have been resorted to, had not Lady Juliana's wrath been for the present suspended by an invitation to Altamont House. True, nothing

could be colder than the terms in which it was couched;
but to that her ladyship was insensible, and would have
been equally indifferent had she known that, such as it
was, she owed it more to the obstinacy of her son-in-
law than the affection of her daughter.   The Duke of
Altamont was one of those who attach great ideas of
dignity to always carrying their point ; and though he
might sometimes be obliged to suspend his plans, he
never had been known to relinquish them.   Had he
settled in his own mind to tie his neckcloth in a particular way, not all the eloquence of Cicero, or the
tears of O'Neil, would have induced him to alter it ;
and Adelaide, the haughty self-willed Adelaide, soon
found, that of all yokes the most insupportable is the
yoke of an obstinate fool.   In the thousand trifling
occurrences of domestic life (for his grace was interested in all the minutiæ of his establishment), where
good sense and good humour on either side would have
gracefully yielded to the other, there was a perpetual
contest for dominion, which invariably ended in
Adelaide's defeat.   The duke, indeed, never disputed, or reasoned, or even replied ; but the thing
was done : till, at the end of six weeks, the Duchess
of Altamont most heartily hated and despised the man
she had so lately vowed to love and obey.   On the
present occasion, his grace certainly appeared in the
most amiable light, in wishing to have Lady Juliana
invited to his house ; but, in fact, it proceeded entirely
from his besetting sin, obstinacy.   He had proposed
her accompanying her daughter at the time of her
marriage, and been overruled ; but, with all the per-
tinacity of a little mind, he had kept fast hold of the
idea, merely because it was his own, and he was now
determined to have it put in execution.   In a postscript to the letter, and in the same cordial style, the
duchess said something of a hope, that *if* her mother

did come to town, Mary should accompany her; but this her ladyship, to Mary's great relief, declared should not be, although she certainly was very much at a loss how to dispose of her. Mary timidly expressed her wish to be permitted to return to Lochmarlie, and mentioned that her uncle and aunt had repeatedly offered to come to Bath for her, if she might be allowed to accompany them home; but to this her mother also gave a decided negative, adding that she never should see Lochmarlie again if she could help it. In short, she must remain where she was, till something could be fixed as to her future destination. "It was most excessively tiresome to be clogged with a great unmarried daughter," her ladyship observed, as she sprang into the carriage with a train of dogs, and drove off to dear delightful London.

But, alas! the insecurity of even the best-laid schemes of human foresight! Lady Juliana was in the midst of arrangements for endless pleasures, when she received accounts of the death of her now almost forgotten husband! He had died from the gradual effects of the climate, and that was all that remained to be told of the unfortunate Henry Douglas! If his heartless wife shed some natural tears, she wiped them soon; but the wounds of disappointment and vanity were not so speedily effaced, as she contrasted the brilliant court-dress with the unbecoming widow's cap. Oh! she so detested black things—it was so hateful to wear mourning—she never could feel happy or comfortable in black! and, at such a time, how particularly unfortunate! Poor Douglas! she was very, very sorry! —And so ended the holiest and most indissoluble of human ties!

The duchess did not think it incumbent upon her to be affected by the death of a person she had never seen; but she put on mourning, put off her presenta-

tion at court for a week, and staid away one night from
the opera.

On Mary's warm and unpolluted heart the tidings
of her father's death produced a very different effect.
Though she had never known, in their fullest extent,
those feelings of filial affection whose source begins
with our being, and over which memory loves to
linger as at the hallowed fount of the purest of earthly
joys, she had yet been taught to cherish a fond remembrance of him to whom she owed her being. She
had been brought up in the land of his birth—his
image was associated in her mind with many of the
scenes most dear to her—his name and his memory
were familiar to those amongst whom she dwelt; and
thus her feelings of natural affection had been preserved in all their genuine warmth and tenderness.
Many a letter, and many a token of her love, she had,
from her earliest years, been accustomed to send him;
and she had ever fondly cherished the hope of her
father's return, and that she would yet know the
happiness of being blest in a parent's love. But now
all these hopes were extinguished; and, while she
wept over them in bitterness of heart, she yet bowed
with pious resignation to the decree of heaven.

———o———

Chapter lxbj.

——— Shall we grieve their hovering shades,
Which wait the revolution in our hearts?
Shall we disdain their silent, soft address;
Their posthumous advice, and pious prayer?
                                        YOUNG.

FOR some months all was peaceful seclusion in
     Mary's life, and the only varieties she knew
     were occasional visits to aunt Grizzy's, and now
and then spending some days with Mrs Lennox. She

saw, with sorrow, the declining health of her venerable friend, whose wasted form and delicate features had now assumed an almost ethereal aspect. Yet she never complained, and it was only from her languor and weakness that Mary guessed she suffered. When urged to have recourse to medical advice, she only smiled and shook her head; yet, ever gentle and complying to the wishes of others, she was at length prevailed upon to receive the visits of a medical attendant, and her own feelings were but too faithfully confirmed by his opinion. Being an old friend of the family, he took upon himself to communicate the intelligence to her son, then abroad with his regiment; and in the meantime Mary took up her residence at Rose Hall, and devoted herself unceasingly to the beloved friend she felt she was so soon to lose. In these tender and pious offices, Mary found herself strengthened and assisted by the frequent visits of the excellent clergyman of the parish. He was a man most gentle and persuasive—earnest and sincere—in whom the beauty and the excellency of Christianity were felt in their practical effects, and the affections were engaged while the understanding was enlightened. This was the "spirit of love," as well as of "a sound mind," which

> ———"Shed round him in the common strife
> Or mild concerns of ordinary life
> A constant influence, a peculiar grace"———

Even the influence and the grace which ever accompanies the teaching of him who is himself taught of the Spirit of God.

Many and precious were the communings the good man held with the soul which now hovered on the brink of eternity—but whose human affections still clung with fond tenacity to the dear objects of her earthly love.

" Ah! Mary," she would sometimes say, "God forgive me! but my heart is not yet weaned from worldly wishes. Even now, when I feel all the vanity of human happiness, I think how it would have soothed my last moments could I have but seen you my son's before I left the world! Yet, alas! our time here is so short, that it seems little whether it be spent in joy or sorrow, provided it be spent in Christian faith and love. Mine has been a long life compared to many; but when I look back upon it, what a span it seems! And it is not the remembrance of its brightest days that are now a solace to my heart. Dearest Mary, if you live long, you will live to think of the hours you have given to me, as the fairest, perhaps, of many a happy day that, I trust, Heaven has yet in store for you. Surely, you were sent to be the comfort and support of my latter days; and in fulfilling that merciful purpose you *will* be blessed—it may not be in the way that I would have chosen; but He who best knows what is for our good has willed it otherwise, and His will be done!"

Mary listened to the half-breathed wishes of her venerable friend with painful feelings.

"Charles Lennox loved me," thought she, "truly, fondly loved me; I know he did! and had I but repaid his noble frankness—had I suffered him to read my heart when he laid open his own to me, we might now have been what I never shall be—happy in mutual affection. I might now have gladdened the last days of his dear mother. I might now have proudly avowed the attachment I must for ever meanly conceal.—Oh pride! pride! what a cruel sacrifice you require of me!" and tears of regret—of self-reproach—almost of despair, forced their way in spite of her firmest resolves.

So passed several weeks, during which Mrs Lennox's health and strength visibly and rapidly declined, till at length she almost ceased to be susceptible of emotions, either of pleasure or pain. Her son had hastened to her the instant he could procure leave of absence, without compromising his honour; but even the intelligence of his arrival had scarcely power to rouse her from the insensibility into which she had then fallen. In Colonel Lennox's heart every other feeling was at first absorbed in grief, at finding his mother in a condition so mournful and, humanly speaking, so hopeless. But as that subsided, and his attention was directed to Mary, she could not but feel that the agitation he betrayed in addressing her, indicated the reality and the depth of his unabated attachment. Yet still the humiliating recollection would arise to check the genial current of her heart in return, and she would turn with averted eyes from witnessing his tender solicitude, and unwearying cares for his mother, even while she almost envied the object of such devoted affection.

A short time after his arrival, his leave of absence was abruptly recalled, and he was summoned to repair to headquarters with all possible expedition. The army was on the move, and a battle was expected to be fought. At such a time hesitation or delay, under any circumstances, would have been inevitable disgrace; and, dreadful as was the alternative, Colonel Lennox wavered not an instant in his resolution. With a look of anguish, but without uttering a syllable, he put the letter into Mary's hands as she sat by his mother's bedside, and then left the room to order preparations to be made for his instant departure. On his return, Mary witnessed the painful conflict of his feelings in his extreme agitation, as he approached his mother, to look, for the last time, on those features, already moulded into more than mortal beauty. A bright ray of the setting sun streamed full upon that face, now reposing in the awful but hallowed calm which is sometimes dif-

fused round the bed of death. The sacred stillness was
only broken by the evening song of the blackbird, the
bleating of the sheep, and the distant lowing of the
cattle—sounds which had often brought pleasure to that
heart, now, as it seemed, insensible to all human emotion. All nature shone forth in smiles and beauty, but
the eye and the ear were alike closed against all earthly
objects. Yet who can tell the brightness of those
visions with which the parting soul may be visited?
Sounds and sights, alike unheard, unknown to mortal
sense, may then hold divine communion with the
soaring spirit, and inspire it with bliss inconceivable,
ineffable!

Colonel Lennox gazed upon the countenance of his
mother. Again and again he pressed with his lips the
pale tranquil brow, and bedewed with tears the almost
lifeless hands he held in his own as loth to relinquish
the last look—the last touch of one so dear—as loth to
resign, even to his God, the author of his earthly being.
"My mother!" was all he could utter; but it seemed
as if the well-known voice had reached the departing
spirit and stayed its course. The darkened eyes were
half opened—the feeble hand essayed to stretch itself
forth, and a faint murmur indicated a wish there wanted
energy to express. Colonel Lennox gave one look to
Mary—both had felt the silent appeal, and as they knelt
by the bed of death, he placed her hand in his mother's,
and said, "May a mother's blessing be on both her
children!"

A faint smile shed its radiance over the face of the
dying, and the lips for a moment moved as if in prayer,
though no sound escaped them; but the sweetness of
Christian love and holy joy lingered there like a beam
of heaven's own light, long after the spirit had forsook
its dwelling of clay, and entered on its bright and
never-ending existence.

Chapter lxvij.

Cette liaison n'est ni passion ni amitié pure: elle fait une classe à part.—LA BRUYERE.

IT was long before Mary could believe in the reality of what had passed. It appeared to her as a beautiful, yet awful dream. Could it be, that she had plighted her faith by the bed of death; that the last look of her departed friend had hallowed the vow now registered in heaven; that Charles Lennox had claimed her as his own, even in the agony of tearing himself from all he loved; and that she had only felt how dear she was to him at the very moment when she had parted from him, perhaps for ever! But Mary strove to banish these overwhelming thoughts from her mind, as she devoted herself to the performance of the last duties to her departed friend. These paid, she again returned to Beech Park.

Lady Emily had been a daily visitor at Rose Hall during Mrs Lennox's illness, and had taken a lively interest in the situation of the family; but, notwithstanding, it was some time before Mary could so far subdue her feelings as to speak with composure of what had passed. She felt, too, how impossible it was, by words, to convey to her any idea of that excitement of mind, where a whole life of ordinary feeling seems concentrated in one sudden but ineffable emotion. All that had passed might be imagined, but could not be told; and she shrunk from the task of pourtraying those deep and sacred feelings, which language never could impart to the breast of another.

Yet she felt it was using her cousin unkindly to keep her in ignorance of what she was certain would give her pleasure to hear, and summoning her resolution, she at length disclosed to her all that had taken place. Her

own embarrassment was too great to allow her to remark Lady Emily's changing colour, as she listened
to her communication; and after it was ended, she
remained silent for some minutes, evidently struggling
with her emotions.

At length she exclaimed, indignantly—" And so it
seems Colonel Lennox and you have all this time been
playing the dying lover, and the cruel mistress, to each
other? How I detest such duplicity! and duplicity
with me! My heart was ever open to you, to him, to
the whole world; while yours—nay, your very faces
—were masked to me!"

Mary was too much confounded by her cousin's
reproaches to be able to reply to them for some
time; and when she did attempt to vindicate herself,
she found it was in vain. Lady Emily refused to
listen to her, and, in haughty displeasure, quitted the
room, leaving poor Mary overwhelmed with sorrow
and amazement.

There was a simplicity of heart, a singleness of
idea in herself, that prevented her from ever attaching
suspicion to others. But a sort of vague undefined apprehension floated through her brain as she revolved the
extraordinary behaviour of her cousin. Yet it was that
sort of feeling to which she could not give either a local
habitation or a name; and she continued for some time
in that most bewildering state of trying, yet not daring
to think. Some time elapsed, and Mary's confusion of
ideas was increasing rather than diminishing, when
Lady Emily slowly entered the room, and stood some
moments before her without speaking.

At length, making an effort, she abruptly said—
" Pray, Mary, tell me what you think of me?"
Mary looked at her with surprise.

" I think of you, my dear cousin, as I have always
done."

" That is no answer to my question. What do you think of my behaviour just now ? "

" I think," said Mary, gently, " that you have misunderstood me ; that, open and candid yourself, almost to a fault, you readily resent the remotest appearance of duplicity in others. But you are too generous not to do me justice——"

" Ah, Mary ! how little do I appear in my own eyes at this moment ; and how little, with all my boasting, have I known my own heart ! No ! It was not because I am open and candid that I resented your engagement with Colonel Lennox ; it was because I was—because—cannot you guess ? "

Mary's colour rose, as she cast down her eyes, and exclaimed, with agitation, " No—no, indeed ! "

Lady Emily threw her arms around her :—" Dear Mary, you are perhaps the only person upon earth I would make such a confession to—it was because I, who had plighted my faith to another—I, who piqued myself upon my openness and fidelity—I—how it chokes me to utter it ! I was beginning to love him myself !—only beginning, observe, for it is already over —I needed but to be aware of my danger to overcome it. Colonel Lennox is now no more to me than your lover, and Edward is again all that he ever was to me ; but I —— what am I — faithless and self-deceived ! " and a few tears dropped from her eyes.

Mary, too much affected to speak, could only press her in silence to her heart.

" These are tears of shame, of penitence, though I must own they look very like those of regret and mortification. What a mercy it is that ' the chemist's magic art ' cannot ' crystallise these sacred treasures ! ' " said she, with a smile, as she shook a tear-drop from her hand ; " they are gems I am really not at all fond of appearing in."

"And yet you never appeared to greater advantage," said Mary, as she regarded her with admiration.

"Ah! so you say; but there is, perhaps, a little womanish feeling lurking there.   And now you doubt-less expect—no, *you* don't, but another would—that I should begin a sentimental description of the rise and progress of this ill-fated attachment, as I suppose it would be styled in the language of romamce; but, in truth, I can tell you nothing at all about it."

"Perhaps Colonel Lennox"—said Mary, blushing, and hesitating to name her suspicion.

"No, no—Colonel Lennox was not to blame. There was no false play on either side; he is as much above the meanness of coquetry, as—I must say it—as I am.   His thoughts were all along taken up with you, even while he talked, and laughed, and quarrelled with me.   While I, so strong in the belief that worlds could not shake my allegiance to Edward, could have challenged all mankind to win my love; and this wicked, wayward, faithless heart kept silent till you spoke, and then it uttered such a fearful sound!   And yet I don't think it was love, neither—'*l'on n'aime bien qu'une seule fois; c'est la première;*'—it was rather a sort of an idle, childish, engrossing sentiment, that *might* have grown to something stronger, but 'tis past now.   I have shown you all the weaknesss of my heart—despise me if you will."

"Dearest Lady Emily, had I the same skill to show the sentiments of mine, you would there see what I cannot express—how I admire this noble candour, this generous self-abasement——"

"Oh, as to meanly hiding my faults, that is what I scorn to do.   I may be ignorant of them myself, and in ignorance I may cherish them; but, once convinced of them, I give them to the winds, and all who choose may pick them up.   Violent and unjust, and self-deceived, I have been, and may be again; but deceitful I never was, and never will be."

"My dear cousin, what might you not be, if you chose!"

"Ah! I know what you mean, and I begin to think you are in the right; by and by, I believe, I shall come to be of your way of thinking, (if ever I have a daughter she certainly shall,) but not just at present, the reformation would be too sudden. All that I can promise for at present is, that 'henceforth I will chide no breather in the world but myself,' against whom I know most faults; and now, from this day, from this moment, I vow——"

"No, I will do it for you," said Mary, with a smile, as she threw her arms around her neck; "henceforth—

> "The golden laws of love shall be
>   Upon this pillar hung;
> A simple heart, a single eye,
>   A true and constant tongue.

> "Let no man for more love pretend
>   Than he has hearts in store;
> True love begun shall never end:
>   Love one, and love no more." *

But much as Mary loved and admired her cousin, she could not be blind to the defects of her character, and she feared they might yet be productive of great unhappiness to herself. Her mind was open to the reception of every image that brought pleasure along with it; while, in the same spirit, she turned from every thing that wore an air of seriousness or self-restraint; and even the best affections of a naturally warm and generous heart were borne away by the ardour of her feelings, and the impetuosity of her temper. Mary

* Marquis of Montrose.

grieved to see the graces of a noble mind thus running wild for want of early culture; and she sought by every means, save those of lecture and admonition, to lead her to more fixed habits of reflection and self-examination.

But it required all her strength of mind to turn her thoughts, at this time, from herself to another. She, the betrothed of one who was now in the midst of danger, of whose existence she was even uncertain, but on whose fate she felt her own suspended.

"Oh!" thought she, with bitterness of heart, "how dangerous it is to yield too much even to our best affections! I, with so many objects to share in mine, have yet pledged my happiness on a being perishable as myself!" And her soul sickened at the ills her fancy drew. But she strove to repress this strength of attachment, which she felt would otherwise become too powerful for her reason to control; and if she did not entirely succeed, at least the efforts she made, and the continual exercise of mind, enabled her, in some degree, to counteract the baleful effects of morbid anxiety, and overweening attachment. At length her apprehensions were relieved for a time, by a letter from Colonel Lennox. An engagement with the enemy had taken place, but he had escaped unhurt. He repeated his vows of unalterable affection, and Mary felt that she was justified in receiving them. She had made Lady Juliana and Mrs Douglas both acquainted with her situation; the former had taken no notice of the communication, but the latter had expressed her approval, in all the warmth and tenderness of gratified affection.

—— o ——

Chapter lxviij.

Preach as I please, I doubt our curious men
Will choose a pheasant still before a hen.

HORACE.

AMONGST the various occupations to which
Mary devoted herself, there was none which
merits to be recorded as a greater act of im-
molation, than her unremitting attentions to aunt
Grizzy. It was not merely the sacrifice of time and
talents that was required for carrying on this intercourse: these, it is to be hoped, even the most selfish
can occasionally sacrifice to the *bienseances* of society;
but it was, as it were, a total surrender of her whole
being. To a mind of any reflection, no situation can
ever be very irksome, in which we can enjoy the
privileges of sitting still and keeping silent; but, as the
companion of Miss Grizzy, quiet and reflection were
alike unattainable. When not engaged in *radotage*
with Sir Sampson, her life was spent in losing her
scissars, mislaying her spectacles, wondering what had
become of her thimble, and speculating on the dis-
appearance of a needle—all of which losses daily and
hourly recurring, subjected Mary to an unceasing annoyance, for she could not be five minutes in her
aunt's company without being at least as many times
disturbed, with—"Mary, my dear, will you get up—
I think my spectacles must be about you"—or,
"Mary, my dear, your eyes are younger than mine,
will you look if you can see my needle on the carpet?"
—or, "Are you sure, Mary, that's not my thimble
you have got? it's very like it; and I'm sure I can't
conceive what's become of mine, if that's not it,"
&c. &c. &c. But her idleness was, if possible, still
more irritating than her industry. When she betook

herself to the window, it was one incessant cry of—
" Whose coach is that, Mary, with the green and
orange liveries? Come and look at this lady and
gentleman, Mary; I'm sure I wonder who they are?
Here's something, I declare I'm sure I don't know
what you call it—come here, Mary, and see what it
is "—and so on, *ad infinitum.* Walking was still
worse. Grizzy not only stood to examine every
article in the shop windows, but actually turned round
to observe every striking figure that passed. In short,
Mary could not conceal from herself that weak vulgar
relations are an evil to those whose taste and ideas are
refined by superior intercourse. But even this discovery she did not deem sufficient to authorise her
casting off or neglecting poor Miss Grizzy, and she
in no degree relaxed in her patient attention towards
her.

Even the affection of her aunt, which she possessed
in the highest possible degree, far from being an
alleviation, was only an additional torment. Every
meeting began with " My dear Mary, how did you
sleep last night? Did you make a good breakfast this
morning? I declare I think you look a little pale.
I'm sure I wish to goodness you mayn't have got cold
—colds are going very much about just now—one of
the maids in this house has a very bad cold—I hope
you will remember to bathe your feet, and take some
water-gruel to-night, and do every thing that Dr
Redgill desires you, honest man ! " If Mary absented
herself for a day, her salutation was, " My dear
Mary, what became of you yesterday? I assure you
I was quite miserable about you all day, thinking,
which was quite natural, that something was the matter
with you; and I declare I never closed my eyes all
night, for thinking about you. I assure you, if it had
not been that I couldn't leave Sir Sampson, I would

have taken a hackney coach, although I know what impositions they are, and have gone to Beech Park to see what had come over you."

Yet all this Mary bore with the patience of a martyr, to the admiration of Lady Maclaughlan, and the amazement of Lady Emily, who declared she could only submit to be bored as long as she was amused.

On going to Milsom Street one morning, Mary found her aunt in high delight at two invitations she had just received for herself and her niece.

" The one," said she, " is to dinner at Mrs Pullens's. You can't remember her mother, Mrs Macfuss, I dare say, Mary—she was a most excellent woman, I assure you, and got all her daughters married. And I remember Mrs Pullens when she was Flora Macfuss; she was always thought very like her mother ; and Mr Pullens is a most worthy man, and very rich ; and it was thought at the time a great marriage for Flora Macfuss, for she had no money of her own, but her mother was a very clever woman, and a most excellent manager ; and I dare say so is Mrs Pullens, for the Macfusses are all famous for their management—so it will be a great thing for you, you know, Mary, to be acquainted with Mrs Pullens."

Mary was obliged to break in upon the eulogium on Mrs Pullens, by noticing the other card.—This was a subject for still greater gratulation.

" This," said she, " is from Mrs Bluemits, and it is for the same day with Mrs Pullens, only it is to tea, not to dinner.—To be sure it will be a great pity to leave Mrs Pullens so soon ; but then it would be a great pity not to go to Mrs Bluemits' ; for I've never seen her, and her aunt, Miss Shaw, would think it very odd if I was to go back to the Highlands without seeing Nancy Shaw, now Mrs Bluemits ; and, at any rate, I assure you we may think much of being asked, for she is a

very clever woman, and makes it a point never to ask
any but clever people to her house ; so it's a very great
honour to be asked."

It was an honour Mary would fain have dispensed
with. At another time she might have anticipated
some amusement from such parties, but at present her
heart was not tuned to the ridiculous, and she attempted
to decline the invitations, and get her aunt to do the
same ; but she gave up the point when she saw how
deeply Grizzy's happiness, for the time being, was
involved in these invitations, and she even consented to
accompany her, conscious, as Lady Maclaughlan said,
that the poor creature required a leading-string, and was
not fit to go alone. The appointed day arrived, and
Mary found herself in company with aunt Grizzy, at
the mansion of Mr Pullens, the fortunate husband of
the *ci-devant* Miss Flora Macfuss ; but as Grizzy is
not the best of biographers, we must take the liberty of
introducing this lady to the acquaintance of our reader.

The domestic economy of Mrs Pullens was her own
theme, and the theme of all her friends ; and such was
her zeal in promulgating her doctrines, and her anxiety
to see them carried into effect, that she had endeavoured
to pass it into a law, that no preserves could be eatable
but those preserved in her method ; no hams could be
good but those cured according to her receipt ; no
liquors drinkable but such as were made from the
results of her experience ; neither was it possible that
any linens could be white, or any flannels soft, or any
muslins clear, unless done up after the manner practised
in her laundry. By her own account, she was the
slave of every servant within her door, for her life
seemed to be one unceasing labour to get every thing
done in her own way, to the very blacking of Mr
Pullens' shoes, and the brushing of Mr Pullens' coat.
But then these heroic acts of duty were more than

repaid by the noble consciousness of a life well spent. In her own estimation, she was one of the greatest characters that had ever lived; for, to use her own words, she passed nothing over—she saw every thing done herself—she trusted nothing to servants, &c. &c. &c.

From the contemplation of these her virtues, her face had acquired an expression of complacency foreign to her natural temper; for, after having scolded and slaved in the kitchen, she sat down to taste the fruits of her labours with far more elevated feelings of conscious virtue than ever warmed the breast of a Hampden or a Howard; and when she helped Mr Pullens to pie, made, not by the cook, but by herself, it was with an air of self-approbation that might have vied with that of the celebrated Jack Horner upon a similar occasion. In many cases there might have been merit in Mrs Pullens' doings—a narrow income, the capricious taste of a sick or a cross husband, may exalt the meanest offices which woman can render into acts of virtue, and even diffuse a dignity around them: but Mr Pullens was rich and good-natured, and would have been happy had his cook been allowed to dress his dinner, and his barber his wig, quietly in their own way. Mrs Pullens, therefore, only sought the indulgence of her own low inclinations, in thus interfering in every menial department; while, at the same time, she expected all the gratitude and admiration that would have been due to the sacrifice of the most refined taste and elegant pursuits.

But "envy does merit as its shade pursue," as Mrs Pullens experienced; for she found herself assailed by a host of housekeepers, who attempted to throw discredit on her various arts. At the head of this association was Mrs Jekyll, whose arrangements were on a quite contrary plan. The great branch of science on

which Mrs Pullens mainly relied for fame, was her
unrivalled art in keeping things long beyond the date
assigned by nature; and one of her master-strokes was,
in the middle of summer, to surprise a whole company
with gooseberry tarts made of gooseberries of the preceding year; and her triumph was complete, when any
of them were so polite as to assert that they might have
passed upon them for the fruits of the present season.
Another art in which she flattered herself she was unrivalled, was that of making things pass for what they
were not; thus, she gave pork for lamb—common fowls
for turkey poults—currant wine for champagne—whisky
with peach leaves for noyau; but all these deceptions
Mrs Jekyll piqued herself in immediately detecting, and
never failed to point out the difference; and, in the
politest manner, to hint her preference of the real over
the spurious.   Many were the wonderful morsels with
which poor Mr Pullens was regaled; but he had now
ceased to be surprised at anything that appeared on his
own table; and he had so often heard the merit of his
wife's housekeeping extolled by herself, that, contrary
to his natural conviction, he now began to think it must
be true; or if he had occasionally any little private
misgivings when he thought of the good dinners he
used to have in his bachelor days, he comforted himself
by thinking that his lot was the lot of all married men
who are blessed with active, managing, economical
wives.   Such were Mr and Mrs Pullens; and the
appearance of the house offered no adequate idea of
the mistress.   The furniture was incongruous, and every
thing was ill-matched—for Mrs Pullens was a fre-
quenter of sales, and, like many other liberal-minded
ladies, never allowed a bargain to pass, whether she
required the articles or not.   Her dress was the same:
there was always something to wonder at; caps that
had been bought for nothing, because they were a little

soiled, but by being taken down and washed, and new trimmed, turned out to be just as good as new; gowns that had been dyed, turned, cleaned, washed, &c.; and the great triumph was when nobody could tell the old breadth from the new.

The dinner was of course bad, the company stupid, and the conversation turned solely upon Mrs Pullens' exploits, with occasional attempts of Mrs Jekyll to depreciate the merits of some of her discoveries. At length the hour of departure arrived, to Mary's great relief, as she thought any change must be for the better. Not so Grizzy, who was charmed and confounded by all she had seen, and heard, and tasted, and all of whose preconceived ideas on the subjects of washing, preserving, &c. had sustained a total *bouleversement*, upon hearing of the superior methods practised by Mrs Pullens.

"Well, certainly, Mary, you must allow Mrs Pullens is an astonishing clever woman! Indeed, I think nobody can dispute that! Only think of her never using a bit of soap in her house—everything is washed by steam! To be sure, as Mrs Jekyll said, the table-linen was remarkably ill-coloured—nobody could deny that; but no wonder, considering. It must be a great saving, I'm sure—and she always stands and sees it done herself, for there's no trusting these things to servants. Once when she trusted it to them, they burned a dozen of Mr Pullens' new shirts, just from carelessness, which I'm sure was very provoking. To be sure, as Mrs Jekyll said, if she had used soap, like other people, that wouldn't have happened; and then it is wonderful how well she contrives to keep things. I declare I can't think enough of these green peas that we had at dinner to-day, having been kept since summer was a year! To be sure, as Mrs Jekyll said, they certainly were hard—nobody could dispute that; but then, you know, anything would be hard that had been kept since summer was a year; and I'm sure I thought they ate wonderfully well, considering. And these red currants, too—I'm afraid you didn't taste them—I wish to goodness you had tasted them, Mary. They were sour and dry, certainly, as Mrs Jekyll said; but no wonder; for you know anything would be sour and dry that had been kept in bottles for three years—there can be no doubt about that!"

Grizzy was now obliged to change the current of her ideas, for the carriage had stopped at Mrs Bluemits'.

———o———

Chapter lxix.

It is certain, great knowledge, if it be without vanity, is the most severe bridle of the tongue. For so have I heard, that all the noises and prating of the pool, the croaking of frogs and toads, is hushed and appeased upon the instant of bringing upon them the light of a candle or torch. Every beam of reason, and ray of knowledge, checks the dissolutions of the tongue.—JEREMY TAYLOR.

THEY were received by Mrs Bluemits with that air of condescension which great souls practise towards ordinary mortals, and which is intended, at one and the same time, to encourage and to repel; to show the extent of their goodness, even while they make, or try to make, their *protégé* feel the immeasurable distance which nature or fortune has placed between them.

It was with this air of patronising grandeur that Mrs Bluemits took her guests by the hand, and introduced them to the circle of ladies already assembled.

Mrs Bluemits was not an authoress; but she was a professed critic, a superior woman, a well-informed woman, a woman of great conversational powers, &c.,

and, to use her own phrase, nothing but conversation was spoke in her house. Her guests were therefore always expected to be distinguished, either for some literary production, or for their taste in the *belles lettres.* Two ladies from Scotland, the land of poetry and romance, were consequently hailed as new stars in Mrs Bluemits' horizon. No sooner were they seated, than Mrs Bluemits began :

" As I am a friend to ease in literary society, we shall, without ceremony, resume our conversation ; for, as Seneca observes, the ' comfort of life depends upon conversation.' "

" I think," said Miss Graves, " it is Rochefoucault who says, ' the great art of conversation is to hear patiently and answer precisely.' "

" A very poor definition for so profound a philosopher," remarked Mrs Apsley.

" The amiable author of what the gigantic Johnson styles the melancholy and angry Night Thoughts, gives a nobler, a more elevated, and, in my humble opinion, a juster explication of the intercourse of mind," said Miss Parkins : and she repeated the following lines with pompous enthusiasm :—

> " Speech ventilates our intellectual fire,
> Speech burnishes our mental magazine,
> Brightens for ornament, and whets for use.
> What numbers, sheath'd in erudition, lie,
> Plung'd to the hilts in venerable tomes,
> And rusted in, who might have borne an edge,
> And play'd a sprightly beam, if born to speech —
> If born blest heirs of half their mother's tongue ! "

Mrs Bluemits proceeded :—

> " 'Tis thought's exchange, which, like the alternate push
> Of waves conflicting, breaks the learned scum,
> And defecates the student's standing pool."

" The sensitive poet of Olney, if I mistake not,"

said Mrs Dalton, " steers a middle course, betwixt the
somewhat bald maxim of the Parisian philosopher, and
the mournful pruriency of the Bard of Night, when he
says,

> " Conversation, in its better part,
> May be esteem'd a gift and not an art."

Mary had been accustomed to read, and to reflect
upon what she read, and to apply it to the purpose for
which it is valuable, viz. in enlarging her mind and
cultivating her taste ; but she had never been accustomed
to prate, or quote, or sit down for the express purpose
of displaying her acquirements ; and she began to
tremble at hearing authors' names " familiar in their
mouths as household words ; " but Grizzy, strong in
ignorance, was nowise daunted. True, she heard what
she could not comprehend, but she thought she would
soon make things clear ; and she therefore turned to
her neighbour on her right hand, and accosted her with
—" My niece and I are just come from dining at Mrs
Pullens'—I dare say you have heard of her—she was
Miss Flora Macfuss ; her father, Dr Macfuss, was a
most excellent preacher, and she is a remarkable clever
woman—nobody can dispute that ! "

" Pray, ma'am, has she come out, or is she simply
bel esprit ? " inquired the lady.

Grizzy was rather at a loss ; and, indeed, to answer
a question put in an unknown language, would puzzle
wiser brains than hers ; but Grizzy was accustomed to
converse, without being able to comprehend, and she
therefore went on.

" Her mother, Mrs Macfuss—but she is dead—was
a very clever woman too ; I'm sure, I declare, I don't
know whether the doctor or she was the cleverest ; but
many people, I know, think Mrs Pullens beats them
both."

" Indeed! may I ask in what department she chiefly excels?"

" Oh, I really think in everything. For one thing, everything in her house is done by steam; and then she can keep everything, I can't tell how long, just in paper bags and bottles; and she is going to publish a book with all her receipts in it. I'm sure it will be very interesting—there can be no doubt about that!"

" I beg ten thousand pardons for the interruption," cried Mrs Bluemits from the opposite side of the room; "but my ear was smote with the sounds of *publish*, and *interesting*—words which never fail to awaken a responsive chord in my bosom. Pray," addressing Grizzy, and bringing her into the full blaze of observation, " may I ask, was it of *the* Campbell these electric words were spoken? To you, madam, I am sure I need not apologise for my enthusiasm—you who claim the proud distinction of being a countrywoman, need I ask—an acquaintance?"

All that poor Grizzy could comprehend of this harangue, was, that it was reckoned a great honour to be acquainted with a Campbell; and chuckling with delight at the idea of her own consequence, she briskly replied—

" Oh, I know plenty of Campbells; there's the Campbells of Auchnagruan, relations of ours; and there's the Campbells of Ballachnayoil, married into our family; and there's the Campbells of Castleclanoch Windlestrae Glen, are not very distant by my mother's side, and there's——"

Mary felt as if perforated by bullets in all directions, as she encountered the eyes of the company, turned alternately upon her aunt and her; but they were on opposite sides of the room; therefore to interpose between Grizzy and her assailants was impossible.

" Possibly," suggested Mrs Dalton, " Miss Douglas

prefers the loftier strains of the mighty Minstrel of the Mountains, to the more polished periods of the Poet of the Transatlantic Plain."

"Or perhaps," said Miss Crick, "Miss Douglas prefers nature in its simplest, homeliest form; pray, ma'am," turning full upon the now bewildered Grizzy, "are you an admirer of Crabbe's Tales?"

"Crabs' tails!" repeated Grizzy, in astonishment, "I don't think ever I tasted them—Indeed, I don't think our crabs have tails; but I'm very fond of crabs' claws when there's anything in them." Fortunately, the confusion of tongues was at this moment so great, that Grizzy's *lapsus* passed unnoticed by all but Mary, whose ears tingled at every word she uttered.

"Without either a possibility or a perhaps," said Mrs Apsley, "the probability is, Miss Douglas prefers the author of The Giaour to all the rest of her poetical countrymen. Where, in either Walter Scott or Thomas Campbell, will you find such lines as these?

'Wet with their own best blood, shall drip
    Thy gnashing tooth and haggard lip!'"

"Pardon me, madam," said Miss Parkins; "but I am of opinion you have scarcely given a fair specimen of the powers of the Noble Bard in question. The image here presented is a familiar one; 'the gnashing tooth,' and 'haggard lip,' we have all witnessed, perhaps some of us may even have experienced. There is consequently little merit in presenting it to the mind's eye: it is easy, comparatively speaking, to pourtray the feelings and passions of our own kind. We have only, as Dryden expresses it,

'To descend into ourselves to find
    The secret imperfections of our mind.'

It is, therefore, in his portraiture of the canine race,

that the illustrious author has so far excelled all his
contemporaries : in fact, he has given quite a dramatic
cast to his dogs : " and she repeated with an air of
triumph—

" And he saw the lean dogs beneath the wall,
    Hold o'er the dead their carnival ;
    Gorging and growling o'er carcase and limb,
    They were too busy to bark at him !
    From a Tartar's skull they had stripped the flesh,
    As ye peel the fig when its fruit is fresh ;
    And their white tusks crunched o'er the whiter skull,
    As it slipped through their jaws when their edge grew dull ;
    As they lazily mumbled the bones of the dead,
    When they scarce could rise from the spot where they fed."

" Now, to enter into the conceptions of a dog—to
embody one's self, as it were, in the person of an
animal—to sympathise in its feelings—to make its propensities our own—to 'lazily mumble the bones of the
dead,' with our own individual 'white tusks !' Pardon
me, madam, but with all due deference to the genius
of a Scott, it is a thing he has not dared to attempt.
Only the greatest mind in the universe was capable of
taking so bold a flight. Scott's dogs, madam, are
tame, domestic animals—mere human dogs, if I may
say so. Byron's dogs——— But let them speak for
themselves !

    ' The scalps were in the wild dog's maw,
        The hair was tangled round his jaw.'

Show me, if you can, such an image in Scott?"
    " Very fine, certainly ! " was here uttered by five
novices, who were only there as probationers, consequently not privileged to go beyond a response.
    " Is it the dancing dogs they are speaking about?"
asked Grizzy. But looks of silent contempt were the
only replies she received.
    " I trust I shall not be esteemed presumptuous," said

Miss Entick, "or supposed capable of entertaining views of detracting from the merits of the Noble Author at present under discussion, if I humbly, but firmly, enter my caveat against the word 'crunch,' as constituting an innovation in our language, the purity of which cannot be too strictly preserved, or pointedly enforced. I am aware that by some I may be deemed unnecessarily fastidious; and possibly Christina, Queen of Sweden, might have applied to me the celebrated observation, said to have been elicited from her by the famed work of the laborious French Lexicographer, viz. that he was the most troublesome person in the world, for he required of every word to produce its passport, and to declare whence it came, and whither it it was going. I confess, I too, for the sake of my country, would wish that every word we utter might be compelled to show its passport, attested by our great lawgiver, Dr Samuel Johnson."

"Unquestionably," said Mrs Bluemits, "purity of language ought to be preserved inviolate at any price; and it is more especially incumbent upon those who exercise a sway over our minds—those who are, as it were, the moulds in which our young imaginations are formed, to be the watchful guardians of our language. But I lament to say, that in fact it is not so; and that the aberrations of our vernacular tongue have proceeded solely from the licentious use made of it by those whom we are taught to reverence as the fathers of the Sock and Lyre."

"Yet, in familiar colloquy, I do not greatly object to the use of a word occasionally, even although unsanctioned by the authority of our mighty Lexicographer," said a new speaker.

"For my part," said Miss Parkins, "a genius fettered by rules, always reminds me of Gulliver in the hairy bonds of the Lilliputians; and the sentiment of the elegant and enlightened bard of Twickenham is also mine :

> ' Great wits sometimes may gloriously offend,
> And rise to faults true critics dare not mend;
> From vulgar bounds with brave disorder part,
> And snatch a grace beyond the reach of art.'

So it is with the subject of our argument; a tamer genius than the illustrious Byron would not have dared to ' crunch ' the bone.   But where, in the whole compass of the English language, will you find a word capable of conveying the same idea ? ''

" Pick," modestly suggested one of the novices in a low key, hoping to gain some celebrity by this her first effort ; but this dawn of intellect passed unnoticed.

The argument was now beginning to run high; parties were evidently forming of crunchers and anti-crunchers, and etymology was beginning to be called for, when a thundering knock at the door caused a cessation of hostilities.

" That, I flatter myself, is my friend, Miss Griffon," said Mrs Bluemits, with an air of additional importance ; and the name was whispered round the circle, coupled with " Celebrated Authoress—Fevers of the Heart—Thoughts of the Moment," &c. &c.

" Is she a *real* authoress that is coming ? " asked Miss Grizzy of the lady next her.   And her delight was great at receiving an answer in the affirmative ; for Grizzy thought to be in company with an authoress was the next thing to being an authoress herself ; and, like some other people, she had a sort of vague mysterious reverence for every one whose words had been printed in a book.

" Ten thousand thousand pardons, dearest Mrs Bluemits ! " exclaimed Miss Griffon, as she entered.   " I fear a world of intellect is lost to me by this cruel delay."   Then in an audible whisper—" But I was

detained by my publisher : he quite persecutes me to
write. My 'Fevers of the Heart' has had a prodigious run ; and even my 'Thoughts,' which, in fact,
cost me no thought, are amazingly *recherché*. And I
actually had to force my way to you to-night through
a legion of printer's devils, who were lying in wait for
me with each a sheet of my 'Billows of Love.'"

"The title is most musical, most melancholy," said
Mrs Bluemits, "and conveys a perfect idea of what
Dryden terms 'the sweeping deluge of the soul ;' but
I flatter myself we shall have something more than a
name from Miss Griffon's genius. The Aonian Graces,
'tis well known, always follow in her train."

"They have made a great hole in it, then," said
Grizzy, officiously displaying a fracture in the train of
Miss Griffon's gown, and from thence taking occasion
to deliver her sentiments on the propriety of people who
tore gowns always being obliged to mend them.

After suitable entreaties had been used, Miss Griffon
was at last prevailed upon to favour the company with
some specimens of the "Billows of Love" (of which
we were unable to procure copies), and the following
sonnet, the production of a friend :

"Hast thou no note for joy, thou weeping lyre ?
   Doth yew and willow ever shade thy string,
   And melancholy sable banners fling,
Warring 'midst hosts of elegant desire ?
How vain the strife—how vain the warlike gloom !
   Love's arms are grief—his arrows sighs and tears
   And every moan thou mak'st, an altar rears,
To which his worshippers devoutly come.
Then rather, lyre, I pray thee, try thy skill,
   In varied measure, on a sprightlier key :
   Perchance thy gayer tones' light minstrelsy,
May heal the poison that thy plaints distil.
But much I fear that joy is danger still ;
And joy, like woe, love's triumph must fulfil."   C.

This called forth unanimous applause—"delicate

imagery "—" smooth versification "—" classical ideas "
—" Petrarchian sweetness," &c. &c. resounded from
all quarters.

"And now," said Mrs Bluemits, with an air of
ineffable importance, " ' here is a pearl richer than all
its tribe,' even a letter, which I had this morning the
happiness to receive from one whom I shall simply
designate as the empress of letter writers, since otherwise to designate her would be superfluous in a circle
such as now surrounds me. This matchless composition
may, in my opinion, be looked upon as a perfect gem in
criticism ; "—and with a portentous hem Mrs Bluemits
commenced reading as follows :

"Ditchmont Cottage, August 21st, 18—.

"Ah, madam, I have lately been enriched by my
friend the good, the great, the excellent, the eloquent
Dr Parr, with a priceless copy of that undying epic
'The Death of Cock Robin!' Though possessing
neither Shaksperian sublimity nor Miltonic majesty, yet
must the soul-harrowing horrors of this Homeric poem
thrill the heart and suffuse the eyes of every lover of the
Aonian Graces. Often have my orbs been deluged by
the soft descending stream of pity for the sad, the
sudden, the ever-to-be-deplored fate of the red-bosomed
chorister : that fate which still remains wrapt in the
darkest, the most profound, the most inscrutable mystery, for of the *motive* which prompted to the sanguinary deed we are left to wander in the endless
mazes of conjecture. Yet august from its noble abrupt-
ness is the commencement of this heart-grappling
epic !—

'Who killed Cock Robin?'

There is no cold cautious exordium to put Feeling on
her guard—no flat and formal introduction to chill the

powers of fancy : the terrible is here brought before us
by the all-powerful hands of Truth and Justice. Truth
proclaims the deed—Justice calls for the destroyer !
How matchless the daring reply of the murderer :—

> 'I, said the sparrow,
> With my bow and arrow,
> And I killed Cock Robin ! "

How tame, how spiritless, appears Macbeth's

> 'I have done the deed ! '

in comparison with this :—

> 'Who saw him die ?
> I, said the fly,
> With my little eye,
> And I saw him die.'

"Here the word *little* may possibly be objected to as
being merely a make-weight epithet, since, in point of
fact, there could exist no reasonable doubt as to the
smallness of the eye of the fly ; but we have the sanction of the immortal bard of Avon in support of its
usage. Imogene says,

> 'Thou shouldst have made him as *little* as a crow ; '

and amongst the moderns we find in a Peteronian
Pindaric ode the following coincidence :—

> 'And now thy *little* drunken eyes unclose,
> And now thou feelest for thy *little* nose.'

"There is rather a falling off in the following stanza,
which is deficient both in dignity and in discrimination :—

> 'Who catched his blood ?
> I, said the fish,
> With my little dish,
> And I catched his blood.'

" There is something almost ludicrous in the image here suggested of a fish holding a dish, and surely nothing calculated to call forth a smile ought to mingle with the awe-inspiring investigation in which, by the consummate skill of the author, we find ourselves parties in this dread-inspiring drama.

" Moreover, the particular species of fish ought unquestionably to have been specified, since incalculable are the varieties of the finny tribe, from the humble herring to the huge leviathan. I have endeavoured to obviate the endless cavils, the ever-enduring disputes to which I perceive this unaccountable omission will give birth, by lending a local name to this blood-thirsty creature :—

> ' I, said the whale,
>   Had a rich regale,
>   For he ate like a quail,
> And I suck'd his blood.'

This satisfies to luxury the whole soul of my imagination.

" In the following exquisite personifications we find a remarkable coincidence with the ever-to-be-admired Greyonian Elegy in a Churchyard :—

> ' Who made his shroud?
>   I, said the beetle,
>   With my little needle,
> And I made his shroud.'

" In the second stanza of the exquisite elegy we find

> ' Save where yon beetle wheels his droning flight,
>   And leaves the world to darkness and to me ! '

> ' Who will dig his grave?
>   I, said the owl,
>   With my spade and show'l,
> And I will dig his grave.'

'Save that from yonder ivy-mantled tower,
   The moping owl does to the moon complain.'

"Mark, madam, I entreat you, the striking coincidence between the 'moping moon-struck owl' and the solemn bird of night with his 'spade and show'l!'

"This is too glaring to be similarity: it speaks imitation, if not positive plagiarism, almost equal to that I have elsewhere pointed out from the ancient Scottish ballad of 'Thou'rt gane awa frae me, Mary,' to Cooper's address to his venerable Mary—that is, it appears but too evident there were two owls and two Marys in the world who had each their admirers in the Aonian train.

"But I have digressed from my subject, and must hereafter resume my strictures on this inimitable Cockonian epic. It is then my purpose to enter upon a calm, careful, and critical examination of the 'Courtship and Marriage' of the enamoured chorister, together with the 'Sickness and Death of Jenny Wren.' Of these rare and invaluable works I have, by the kind assistance of a literary friend, been enabled to procure authentic copies; and I confess it appears to me that considerable light may be elicited from their graphic pages upon the dark and sanguinary catastrophe of these ill-starred nuptials. Strange that works of such paramount interest should hitherto have escaped the notice of our critics, commentators, and annotators! Hail, and farewell!"

But even intellectual joys have their termination, and carriages and servants began to be announced in rapid succession.

"Fly not yet, 'tis just the hour," said Mrs Bluemits to the first of her departing guests, as the clock struck ten.

"It is gone, with its thorns and its roses," replied her friend with a sigh, and a farewell pressure of the hand.

Another now advanced—"Wilt thou be gone?—it is not yet near day."

"I have less will to go than care to stay," was the reply.

"*Parto ti lascio adio,*" warbled Miss Parkins.

" I vanish," said Mrs Apsley, snatching up her tippet, reticule, &c.; " and, like the baseless fabric of a vision, leave not a rack behind."

" Fare-thee-well at once—Adieu, adieu, adieu, remember me!" cried the last of the band, as she slowly retreated.

Mrs Bluemits waved her hand with a look of tender reproach, as she repeated—

> " An adieu should in utterance die,
>   Or if written should faintly appear—
> Should be heard in the sob of a sigh,
>   Or be seen in the blot of a tear."

" I'm sure, Mary," said Grizzy, when they were in the carriage, " I expected, when all the ladies were repeating, that you would have repeated something too. You used to have all Watts' Hymns by heart, when you was little, and when they were speaking so much about dogs, I wonder you didn't think of repeating that one—

> ' Let dogs delight to bark and bite—'

and there's that beautiful thing the Hermit, which I know our girls can say; for I really thought Becky would have cried herself blind before she learnt it, so I'm sure I'll never forget it—

> ' Far in a wild exposed to public view—

A—I—A—I'm sure it's very stupid in me, but I always compare it with something that's very like it, but it's not it—

> ' There was an old woman that lived in a shoe,
> And she had so many children she didn't know what to do;'

but that couldn't be the Hermit, you know; but that doesn't signify—it's nothing for me to forget, but it's a thousand pities that you didn't think of it in time; for I declare, I was quite affronted to see you sitting like a stick, and not saying a word, when all the ladies were speaking, and turning up their eyes, and moving their hands so prettily; but I hope next time you go to Mrs Bluemits', you will take care to learn something by heart before you go. I'm sure I haven't a very good memory, but I remember some things; and I was very near going to repeat ' Farewell to Lochaber' myself, as we were coming away; and I wish to goodness I had done it; but I suppose it wouldn't do to go back now; and, at any rate, all the ladies are away, and I dare say the candles will be out by this time."

Mary felt it a relief to have done with this surfeit of soul, and was of opinion, that learning, like religion, ought never to be forced into conversation; and that people, who only read to talk of their reading, might as well let it alone. Next morning she gave so ludicrous an account of her entertainment, that Lady Emily was quite charmed.

"Now I begin to have hopes of you," said she, "since I see you can laugh at your friends as well as me."

"Not at my friends, I hope," answered Mary; "only at folly."

"Call it what you will: I only wish I had been there. I should certainly have started a controversy upon the respective merits of Tom Thumb and Puss in Boots, and so have called them off Lord Byron. Their pretending to measure the genius of a Scott or a Byron, must have been something like a fly attempting to take the altitude of Mount Blanc. How I detest those ' idle disquisitions about the colour of a goat's beard, or the blood of an oyster! ' "

Mary had seen, in Mrs Douglas, the effects of a highly-cultivated understanding shedding its mild radiance on the path of domestic life, heightening its charms, and softening its asperities, with the benign spirit of Christianity. Her charity was not like that of Mrs Fox; she did not indulge herself in the purchase of elegant ornaments, and then, seated in the easy-chair of her drawing-room, extort from her visitors money to satisfy the wants of those who had claims on her own bounty. No: she gave a large portion of her time, her thoughts, her fortune, to the most sacred of all duties—charity in its most comprehensive meaning. Neither did her knowledge, like that of Mrs Bluemits, evaporate in pedantic discussion or idle declamation, but showed itself in the tenor of a well-spent life, and in the graceful discharge of those duties which belonged to her sex and station. Next to goodness, Mary most ardently admired talents. She knew there were many of her own sex who were justly entitled to the distinction of literary fame. Her introduction to the circle at Mrs Bluemits' had disappointed her; but they were mere pretenders to the name. How different from those described by one no less amiable and enlightened herself!—" Let such women as are disposed to be vain of their comparatively petty attainments, look up with admiration to those contemporary shining examples, the venerable Elizabeth Carter, and the blooming Elizabeth Smith. In them let our young ladies contemplate profound and various learning, chastised by true Christian humility. In them let them venerate acquirements, which would have been distinguished in an university, meekly softened and beautifully shaded by the exertion of every domestic virtue, the unaffected exercise of every feminine employment." *

* Hannah More

Chapter lxx.

The gods, to curse Pamela with her pray'rs,
Gave the gilt coach and dappled Flanders mares;
The shining robes, rich jewels, beds of state,
And, to complete her bliss, a fool for mate.
She glares in balls, front boxes, and the ring—
A vain, unquiet, glitt'ring, wretched thing!
Pride, pomp, and state, but reach her outward part;
She sighs, and is no duchess at her heart.

POPE.

FOR many months, Mary was doomed to experience all the vicissitudes of hope and fear, as she heard of battles and sieges, in which her lover had a part. He omitted no opportunity of writing to her; but scarcely had she received the assurance of his safety from himself, when her apprehensions were again excited by rumours of fresh dangers he would have to encounter; and it required all her pious confidence and strength of mind to save her from yielding to the despondency of a naturally sensitive heart. But in administering to the happiness of others, she found the surest alleviation to the misfortune that threatened herself; and she often forgot her own cares in her benevolent exertions for the poor, the sick, and the desolate. It was then she felt all the tenderness of that divine precept, which enjoins love of the Creator as the engrossing principle of the soul. For, oh! the unutterable anguish that heart must endure which lavishes all its best affections on a creature mutable and perishable as itself, from whom a thousand accidents may separate or estrange it, and from whom death must one day divide it! Yet there is something so amiable, so exalting, in the fervour of a pure and generous attachment, that few have been able to resist its overwhelming influence; and it is only time and suffering that can teach us to comprehend the miseries that wait

on the excess, even of our virtuous inclinations, where
these virtues aspire not beyond this transitory
scene.

Mary seldom heard from her mother or sister.
Their time was too precious to be wasted on dull
country correspondents; but she saw their names
frequently mentioned in the newspapers, and she
flattered herself, from the *éclat* with which the
duchess seemed to be attended, that she had found
happiness in those pleasures where she had been
taught to expect it. The duchess was, indeed, surrounded with all that rank, wealth, and fashion could
bestow. She had the finest house, jewels, and equipages in London, but she was not happy. She felt the
draught bitter, even though the goblet that held it was
of gold. It is novelty only that can lend charms to
things in themselves valueless; and when that wears
off, the disenchanted baubles appear in all their native
worthlessness. There is even a satiety in the free indulgence of wealth, when that indulgence centres solely
in self, and brings no generous self-approving reflections along with it. So it was with the Duchess of
Altamont. She sought, in the gratification of every
expensive whim, to stimulate the languid sense of joy;
and, by loading herself with jewels, she strove to still
the restless inquietude of a dissatisfied heart. But it is
only the vulgar mind which can long find enjoyment in
the mere attributes of wealth—in the contemplation of
silk hangings, and gilded chairs, and splendid dresses,
and showy equipages. Amidst all these, the mind of
any taste or refinement, "distrusting, asks if this be
joy." And Adelaide possessed both taste and refinement, though her ideas had been perverted, and her
heart corrupted, by the false maxims early instilled into
her. Yet selfish and unfeeling as she was, she sickened
at the eternal recurrence of self-indulged caprices; and

the bauble that had been hailed with delight the one
day as a charmed amulet to dispel her *ennui*, was the
next beheld with disgust or indifference. She believed,
indeed, that she had real sources of vexation in the
self-will and obstinacy of her husband, and that, had
he been otherwise than he was, she should then have
been completely happy. She would not acknowledge,
even to herself, that she had done wrong in marrying a
man whose person was disagreeable to her, and whose
understanding she despised, while her preference was
decidedly in favour of another. Even her style of life
was, in some respects, distasteful to her; yet she was
obliged to conform to it. The duke retained exactly
the same notions of things as had taken possession of
his brain thirty years before; consequently, everything
in his establishment was conducted with a regularity
and uniformity unknown to those whose habits are
formed on the more eccentric models of the present
day; or rather, who have no models, save those of
their own capricious tastes and inclinations. He had
an antipathy to balls, concerts, and masquerades; for
he did not dance, knew nothing of music, and still less
of *badinage*. But he liked great dull dinners, for there
the conversation was generally adapted to his capacity;
and it was a pleasure to him to arrange the party—to
look over the bill of fare—to see all the family plate
displayed—and to read an account of the grand dinner
at the Duke of Altamont's, in the Morning Post of
the following day. All this sounds very vulgar for the
pastimes of a duke; but there are vulgar-minded dukes,
as there are gifted ploughmen, or any other anomalies.
The former duchess, a woman of high birth, similar
years, and kindred spirit of his own in all matters of
form and *etiquette*, was his standard of female propriety; and she would have deemed it highly
derogatory to her dignity to have patronised any

other species of entertainment than grand dinners and dull assemblies.

Adelaide had attempted, with a high hand, at once to overturn the whole system of Altamont House, and had failed. She had declared her detestation of dinners, and been heard in silence. She had kept her room thrice when they were given, but without success. She had insisted upon giving a ball, but the duke, with the most perfect composure, had peremptorily declared it must be an assembly. Thus baffled in all her plans of domestic happiness, the duchess would have sought her pleasures elsewhere. She would have lived anywhere but in her own house—associated with everybody but her own husband—and done everything but what she had vowed to do. But even in this she was thwarted. The duke had the same precise formal notions of a lady's conduct abroad, as well as her appearance at home ; and the very places she would have most wished to go to, were those she was expressly prohibited from ever appearing at.

Even all that she could have easily settled to her own satisfaction, by the simple apparatus of a separate establishment, carried on in the same house ; but here, too, she was foiled, for his Grace had stubborn notions on that score also, and plainly hinted, that any separation must be final and decided ; and Adelaide could not yet resolve upon taking so formidable a step in the first year of her marriage. She was, therefore, compelled to drag the chain by which, with her own will, she had bound herself for life to one she already despised and detested. And bound she was, in the strict sense of the metaphor ; for, though the duke had not the smallest pleasure in the society of his wife, he yet attached great ideas of propriety to their being always seen together, side by side. Like his sister, Lady Matilda, he had a high reverence for appearances, though he had not her *finesse* in giving them effect. He had merely been accustomed to do what he thought looked well, and gave him an air of additional dignity. He had married Adelaide, because he thought she had a fine presence, and would look well as Duchess of Altamont; and, for the same reason, now that she was his wedded wife, he thought it looked well to be seen always together. He therefore made a point of having no separate engagements; and even carried his sense of propriety so far, that as regularly as the duchess's carriage came to the door, the duke was prepared to hand her in, in due form, and take his station by her side. This alone would have been sufficient to have embittered Adelaide's existence, and she had tried every expedient, but in vain, to rid herself of this public display of conjugal duty: she had opened her landaulet in cold weather, and shut it, even to the glasses, in a scorching sun; but the duke was insensible to heat and cold: he was most provokingly healthy; and she had not even the respite which an attack of rheumatism, or tooth-ache, would have afforded. As his Grace was not a person of keen sensation, this continual effort to keep up appearances cost him little or nothing; but to the duchess's nicer tact, it was martyrdom to be compelled to submit to the semblance of affection where there was no reality. Ah, nothing but a sense of duty, early instilled, and practically enforced, can reconcile a refined mind to the painful task of bearing, with meekness and gentleness, the ill-temper, adverse will, and opposite sentiments, of those with whom we can acknowledge no feeling in common.

But Adelaide possessed no sense of duty, and was a stranger to self-command; and, though she boasted refinement of mind, yet it was of that spurious sort, which, far from elevating and purifying the heart, tends only to corrupt and debase the soul, while it sheds a false and dazzling lustre upon those perishable graces which captivate the senses.

It may easily be imagined, the good sense of the mother did not tend to soothe the irritated feelings of the daughter. Lady Juliana was, indeed, quite as much exasperated as the duchess, at these obstacles thrown in the way of her pleasures, and the more so as she could not quite clearly comprehend them. The good-nature of her husband, and the easy indolence of her brother, even *her* folly had enabled her, on many occasions, to get the better of; but the obstinacy of her son-in-law was invincible to all her arts—she could, therefore, only wonder to the duchess, how she could not manage to get the better of the duke's prejudices against balls, and concerts, and masquerades: It was so excessively ridiculous, so perfectly foolish, not to do as other people did; and there was the Duchess of Ryston gave Sunday concerts, and Lady Oakham saw masks, and even old ugly Lady Loddon had a ball, and the prince at it! How vastly provoking! how unreasonable in a man of the duke's years, to expect a girl like Adelaide to conform to all his old-fashioned notions! And then she would wisely appeal to Lord Lindore, whether it was not too absurd in the duke to interfere with the duchess's arrangements.

Lord Lindore was a frequent visitor at Altamont House; for the Duke, satisfied with his having been once refused, was nowise jealous of him; and Lord Lindore was too quiet and refined in his attentions to excite the attention of any one so stupid and obtuse. It was not the least of the duchess's mortifications, to be constantly contrasting her former lover—elegant, captivating, and *spirituel*—with her husband, awkward, insipid, and dull, as the " fat weed that rots on Lethe's shore." Lord Lindore was, indeed, the most admired man in London, celebrated for his conquests, his horses, his elegance, manner, dress; in short, in everything he gave the tone. But he had too much taste to carry anything to extreme; and, in the midst of incense, and adulation, and imitation, he still retained that simple, unostentatious elegance, that marks the man of real fashion—the man who feels his own consequence, independent of all extraneous modes, or fleeting fashions.

There is, perhaps, nothing so imposing, nothing that carries a greater sway over a mind of any refinement, than simplicity, when we feel assured that it springs from a genuine contempt of show and ostentation.   Lord Lindore was aware of this, and he did not attempt to vie with the Duke of Altamont, in the splendour of his equipage, the richness of his liveries, the number of his attendants, or any of those obvious attractions: on the contrary, every thing belonging to him was of the plainest description; and, except in the beauty of his horses, he seemed to scorn every species of extravagance. But then, he rode with so much elegance, he drove his curricle with such graceful ease, as formed a striking contrast to the formal duke, sitting bolt upright in his state-chariot, *chapeau bras,* and star; and the duchess often quitted the Park, where Lord Lindore was the admired of all admirers, mortified and ashamed at being seen in the same carriage with the man she had chosen for her husband.   Ambition had led her to marry the duke, and that same passion now heightened her attachment for Lord Lindore; for, as some one has remarked, ambition is not always the desire for that which is in itself excellent, but for that which is most prized by others; and the handsome Lord Lindore was courted and caressed in circles, where the dull, precise Duke of Altamont was wholly overlooked.   Months passed in this manner, and every day added something to Adelaide's feelings of chagrin and disappointment.

But it was still worse when she found herself settled for a long season at Norwood Abbey—a dull, magnificent residence, with a vast unvaried park, a profusion of sombre trees, and a sheet of still water, decorated with leaden deities. Within doors everything was in the same style of vapid, tasteless grandeur, and the society was not such as to dispel the *ennui* these images served to create. Lady Matilda Sufton, her satellite Mrs Finch, General Carver, and a few stupid, elderly lords, and their well-bred ladies, comprised the family circle; and the duchess experienced, with bitterness of spirit, that "rest of heart, and pleasures felt at home," are blessings wealth cannot purchase, nor greatness command; while she sickened at the stupid, the almost *vulgar* magnificence of her lot.

At this period Lord Lindore arrived on a visit, and the daily, hourly contrast that occurred between the elegant, impassioned lover, and the dull, phlegmatic husband, could not fail of producing the usual effects on an unprincipled mind. Rousseau and Goëthe were studied, French and German sentiments were exchanged, till criminal passion was exalted into the purest of all earthly emotions. It were tedious to dwell upon the minute, the almost imperceptible occurrences, that tended to heighten the illusion of passion, and throw an air of false dignity around the degrading spells of vice; but so it was, that in something less than a year from the time of her marriage, this victim of self-indulgence again sought her happiness in the gratification of her own headstrong passions, and eloped with Lord Lindore, vainly hoping to find peace and joy amid guilt and infamy.

———o———

Chapter lxxj.

On n'est guères obligé aux gens qui ne nous viennent voir que pour nous quereller, qui pendant toute eune visite ne nous disent pas une seule parole obligeante, et qui se font un plaisir malin, d'attaquer notre conduite, et de nous faire entrevoir nos défauts.—L'ABBE DE BELLEGARDE.

THE duke, although not possessed of the most delicate feelings, it may he supposed, was not insensible to his dishonour. He immediately set about taking the legal measures for avenging it; and damages were awarded, which would have the effect of rendering Lord Lindore for ever an alien to his country. Lady Juliana raved, and had hysterics, and seemed to consider herself as the only sufferer by her daughter's misconduct. At one time, Adelaide's ingratitude was all her theme: at another, it was Lord Lindore's treachery, and poor Adelaide was everything that was amiable and injured: then it was the duke's obstinacy; for, had Adelaide got leave to do as she liked, this never would have happened; had she only got leave to give balls, and to go to masquerades, she would have made the best wife in the world, &c. &c. &c.

All this was warmly resented by Lady Matilda, supported by Mrs Finch and General Carver, till open hostilities were declared between the ladies, and Lady Juliana was compelled to quit the house she had looked upon as next to her own, and became once more a denizen of Beech Park.

Mary's grief and horror at her sister's misconduct was proportioned to the nature of the offence. She considered it not as how it might affect herself, or would be viewed by the world, but as a crime committed against the law of God; yet, while she the more deeply deplored it on that account, no bitter words of condemnation passed her lips. She thought, with humility, of the superior advantages she had enjoyed, in having principles of religion early and deeply engrafted in her soul; and that but for these, such as her sister's fate was, hers might have been.

She felt for her mother, undeserving as she was of commiseration, and strove, by every means in her power, to promote her comfort and happiness. But that was no easy task; Lady Juliana's notions of comfort and happiness differed as widely from those of her daughter as reason and folly could possibly do. She was, indeed, "than folly more a fool—a melancholy fool without her bells." She still clung to low earth-born vanities, with as much avidity as though she had never experienced their insecurity; still rung the same changes on the joys of wealth and grandeur, as if she had had actual proof of their unfading felicity. Then she recurred to the duke's obstinacy, and Lord Lindore's artifices, till, after having exhausted herself in invective against them, she concluded by comforting herself with the hope that Lord Lindore and Adelaide would marry; and although it would be a prodigious degradation to her, and she could not be received at court, she might yet get into very good society in town: there were many women of high rank exactly in the same situation, who had been driven to elope from their husbands, and who married the men they liked, and made the best wives in the world.

Mary heard all this in shame and silence; but Lady Emily, wearied and provoked by her folly and want of principle, was often led to express her indignation and contempt, in terms which drew tears from her cousin's eyes. Mary was, indeed, the only person in the world who felt her sister's dereliction with the keenest feelings of shame and sorrow. All Adelaide's coldness and unkindness had not been able to eradicate from her heart those deep-rooted sentiments of affection which seem to have been entwined with our existence, and which, with some generous natures, end but with their being. Yes! there are ties that bind together those of one family, stronger than those of taste, or choice, or friendship, or reason; for they enable us to love, even in opposition to them all.

It was understood the fugitives had gone to Germany; and after wonder and scandal were exhausted, and a divorce obtained, the Duchess of Altamont, except to her own family, was as though she had never been. Such is the transition from grandeur to guilt— from guilt to insignificance!

Amongst the numerous visitors who flocked to Beech Park, whether from sympathy, or curiosity, or exultation, was Mrs Downe Wright. None of these motives, singly, had brought that lady there, for her purpose was that of giving what she genteelly termed some *good hits* to the Douglases' pride; a delicate mode of warfare, in which, it must be owned, the female sex greatly excel.

Mrs Downe Wright had not forgiven the indignity of her son having been refused by Mary, which she imputed entirely to Lady Emily's influence, and had, from that moment, predicted the downfall of the whole pack, as she styled the family; at the same time always expressing her wish that she might be mistaken, as she wished them well—she bore them no ill will, &c. She entered the drawing-room at Beech Park with a countenance cast to a totally different expression from that with which she had greeted Lady Matilda Sufton's widowhood. Melancholy would there have been appropriate—here it was insulting; and, accordingly, with downcast eyes, and silent pressures of the hand, she saluted every member of the family, and inquired after their healths with that air of anxious solicitude, which implied, that if they were all well, it was what they ought not to be. Lady Emily's quick tact was presently aware of her design, and she prepared to take the field against her.

"I had some difficulty in getting admittance to you," said Mrs Downe Wright. "The servant would fain have denied you; but at such a time, I knew the visit of a friend could not fail of being acceptable, so I made good my way in spite of him."

"I had given orders to admit friends only," returned Lady Emily, with marked emphasis, "as there is no end to the inroads of acquaintances."

"And poor Lady Juliana," said Mrs Downe Wright, in a tone of affected sympathy, "I hope she is able to see her friends?"

"Did you not meet her?" asked Lady Emily, carelessly: "She is just gone to Bath, for the purpose of securing a box during the term of Kean's engagement; she would not trust to *l'eloquence du billet* upon such an occasion."

"I'm vastly happy to hear she is able for anything of the kind," in a tone of vehement and overstrained joy, rather unsuitable to the occasion.

A well-feigned look of surprise from Lady Emily made her fear she had overshot her mark; she therefore, as if from delicacy, changed the conversation to her own affairs. She soon contrived to let it be known, that her son was going to be married to a Scotch earl's daughter; that she was to reside with them; and that she had merely come to Bath for the purpose of letting her house, breaking up her establishment, packing up her plate — and, in short, making all those magnificent arrangements which wealthy dowagers usually have to perform on a change of residence. At the end of this triumphant declaration, she added—

"I fain would have the young people live by themselves, and let me just go on in my own way; but neither my son, nor Lady Grace, would hear of that, although her family are my son's nearest neighbours, and most sensible, agreeable people they are. Indeed, as I said to Lord Glenallan, a man's happiness depends fully as much upon his wife's family as upon herself."

Mary was too noble-minded to suspect that Mrs Downe Wright could intend to level *inuendos*, but the allusion struck her : she felt herself blush; and, fearful Mrs Downe Wright would attribute it to a wrong motive, she hastened to join in the eulogium on the Benmavis family in general, and Lady Grace in particular.

"Lady Benmavis is, indeed, a sensible well-principled woman, and her daughters have been all well brought up."

Again Mary coloured at the emphasis which marked the sensible, well-principled mother, and the well-brought-up daughters; and, in some confusion, she said something about Lady Grace's beauty.

"She certainly is a very pretty woman," said Mrs Downe Wright, with affected carelessness ; "but what is better, she is out of a good nest. For my own part, I place little value upon beauty now; commend me to principles. If a woman is without principles, the less beauty she has the better."

"If a woman has no principles," said Lady Emily, "I don't think it signifies a straw whether she has beauty or not — ugliness can never add to one's virtue."

"I beg your pardon, Lady Emily ; a plain woman will never make herself so conspicuous in the world as one of your beauties."

"Then you are of opinion, wickedness lies all in the

eye of the world, not in the depths of the heart? Now, I think the person who cherishes—no matter how secretly—pride, envy, hatred, malice, or any other besetting sin, must be quite as criminal in the sight of God, as those who openly indulge their evil propensity."

"I go very much by outward actions," said Mrs Downe Wright; "they are all we have to judge by."

"But I thought we were forbidden to judge one another?"

"There's no shutting people's mouths, Lady Emily."

"No; all that is required, I believe, is that we should shut our own."

Mary thought the conversation was getting rather too *piquante* to be pleasant, and tried to soften the tone of it, by asking that most innocent question, Whether there was any news?

"Nothing but about battles and fightings, I suppose," answered Mrs Downe Wright. "I'm sure they are to be pitied who have friends or relations either in army or navy at present. I have reason to be thankful my son is in neither. He was very much set upon going into one or other, but I was always averse to it; for, independent of the danger, they are professions that spoil a man for domestic life, they lead to such expensive, dissipated habits, as quite ruin them for family men. I never knew a military man but what must have his bottle of port every day; with sailors, indeed, it's still worse;—grog and tobacco soon destroy them. I'm sure, if I had a daughter, it would make me miserable if she was to take a fancy to a naval or military man; but," as if suddenly recollecting herself, "after all, perhaps it's a mere prejudice of mine."

"By no means," said Lady Emily, "there is no prejudice in the matter; what you say is very true.

They are to be envied who can contrive to fall in love with a stupid, idle man : *they* never can experience any anxiety : *their* fate is fixed ; 'the waveless calm, the slumber of the dead,' is theirs ; as long as they can contrive to slumber on, or at least to keep their eyes shut, 'tis very well ; they are in no danger of stumbling till they come to open them ; and if they are sufficiently stupid themselves, there is no danger of their doing even that. They have only to copy the owl, and they are safe."

" I quite agree with your ladyship," said Mrs Downe Wright, with a well *got-up*, good-humoured laugh. "A woman has only not to be a wit or a genius, and there is no fear of her : not that *I* have that antipathy to a clever woman that many people have, and especially the gentlemen. I almost quarrelled with Mr Headley, the great author, t'other day, for saying that he would rather encounter a nest of wasps than a clever woman."

" I should most cordially have agreed with him," said Lady Emily, with equal *naïveté*.—" There is nothing more insupportable than one of your clever women, so called. They are generally under-bred, consequently vulgar ; they pique themselves upon saying good things *coûte qu'il coûte*. There is something, in short, quite professional about them ; and they wouldn't condescend to chat nonsense, as you and I are doing at this moment—oh ! not for worlds ! Now, I think one of the great charms of life consists in talking nonsense. Good nonsense is an exquisite thing ; and 'tis an exquisite thing to be stupid sometimes, and to say nothing at all. But these enjoyments the clever woman must forego ; clever she is, and clever she must be. Her life must be a greater drudgery than that of any actress. *She* merely frets her hour upon the stage : the curtain dropped, she may become as dull as she chooses; but the clever woman must always stage it, even at her own fireside."

"Lady Emily is certainly the last person from whom I should have expected to hear a panegyric on stupidity," said Mrs Downe Wright, with some bitterness.

"Stupidity!—Oh, heavens! my blood curdles at the thought of real, genuine, downright stupidity. No! I should always like to have the command of intellect, as well as of money, though my taste, or my indolence, or my whim, perhaps, never would incline me to be always sparkling, whether in wit or in diamonds. 'Twas only when I was in the nursery that I envied the good girl who spoke rubies and pearls. Now, it seems to me only just better than not spitting toads and vipers;" and she warbled a sprightly French *ariette* to a tame bullfinch that perched upon her hand.

There was an airy high-bred elegance in Lady Emily's impertinence, that seemed to throw Mrs Downe Wright's coarse sarcasms to an immeasurable distance, and that lady was beginning to despair, but she was determined not to give in while she could possibly stand out. She accordingly rallied her forces, and turned to Mary—"So you have lost your neighbour, Mrs Lennox, since I was here? I think she was an acquaintance of yours. Poor woman, her death must have been a happy release to herself and her friends. She has left no family, I believe?" quite aware of the report of Mary's engagement with Colonel Lennox.

"Only one son," said Mary, with a little emotion.

"Oh! very true. He's in the law, I think?"

"In the army," answered Mary, faintly.

"That's a poor trade," said Mrs Downe Wright, "and I doubt he'll not have much to mend it. Rose Hall's but a poor property. I've heard they might have had a good estate in Scotland if it hadn't been for the pride of the general, that wouldn't let him change his name for it. He thought it grander to be a poor Lennox than a rich Macnaughton, or some such name. It's to be hoped the son's of the same mind."

"I have no doubt of it," said Lady Emily: "'tis a noble name—quite a legacy in itself."

"It's one that, I am afraid, will not be easily turned into bank-notes, however," returned Mrs Downe Wright, with a *real* hearty laugh: and then, delighted to get off with what she called flying colours, she hastily rose with an exclamation at the lateness of the hour, and a remark how quickly time passed in pleasant company; and, with friendly shakes of the hand, withdrew.

"How very insupportable is such a woman," said Lady Emily to Mary, "who, to gratify her own malice, says the most cutting things to her neighbours, and, at the same time, feels self-approbation in the belief that she is doing good. And yet, hateful as she is, I blush to say I have sometimes been amused by her ill-nature, when it was directed against people I hated still more. Lady Matilda Sufton, for example—there she certainly shone,—for hypocrisy is always fair game; and yet the people who love to hunt it are never amiable. You smile, as much as to say, here is Satan preaching a sermon on holiness. But, however satirical and intolerant you may think me, you must own that I take no delight in the discovery of other people's faults; if I want the meekness of a Christian, at least I don't possess the malice of a Jew. I quite agree with one of your old divines, who says, 'He that falls into sin is a man; that grieves at it, may be a saint; that rejoices in it, must be a devil.' Now, Mrs Downe Wright has a real heartfelt satisfaction in saying malicious things, and in thrusting herself into company, where she must know she is unwelcome, for the sole purpose of saying them. Yet many people are blessed with such blunt perceptions, that they are not at all aware of her real character, and only wonder, when she has left them, what made them feel so uncomfortable when she was present. But she has put me in such a bad humour, that I must go out of doors, and apostrophise the sun, like Lucifer. Do come, Mary, you will help to dispel my chagrin. I feel as if my heart had been in a lime-kiln, all its kindly feelings are so burnt up by the malignant influences of Mrs Downe Wright; while you," continued she, as they strolled into the gardens, "are as cool, and as sweet, and as sorrowful as these violets," — gathering some still wet with an April shower. "How delicious, after such a mental *sirocco*, to feel the pure air, and hear the birds sing, and look upon the flowers and blossoms, and sit here, and bask in the sun from laziness to walk into the shade. You must needs acknowledge, Mary, that spring in England is a much more amiable season than in your ungentle clime."

This was the second spring Mary had seen set in, in England; but the first had been wayward and backward as the seasons of her native climate. The present was such a one as poets love to paint. Nature was in all her first freshness and beauty—the ground was covered with flowers—the luxuriant hedge-rows were white with blossoms—the air was filled with the odours of the gardens and orchards. Still Mary sighed as she thought of Lochmarlie; its wild tangled woods, with here and there a bunch of primroses peeping forth from amidst moss and withered fern—its gurgling rills, blue lakes, rocks and mountains, all rose to view; and she felt that, even amid fairer scenes, and beneath brighter suns, her heart would still turn with fond regret to the land of her birth.

Chapter lxxij.

Wondrous it is to see in diverse mindes
How diversely Love doth his pageants play
And shows his power in variable kinds.
                                    SPENSER.

BUT even the charms of spring were overlooked
by Lady Emily in the superior delight she experienced at hearing that the ship in which
Edward Douglas was, had arrived at Portsmouth; and
the intelligence was soon followed by his own arrival at
Beech Park. He was received by her with rapture,
and by Mary with the tenderest emotion. Lord Courtland was always glad of an addition to the family party;
and even Lady Juliana experienced something like emotion, as she beheld her son, now the exact image of
what his father had been twenty years before.

Edward Douglas was, indeed, a perfect model of
youthful beauty, and possessed of all the high spirits
and happy *insouciance*, which can only charm at that
early period. He loved his profession, and had already
distinguished himself in it. He was handsome, brave,
good-hearted, and good-humoured, but he was not
clever; and Mary felt some solicitude as to the permanency of Lady Emily's attachment to him. But
Lady Emily, quick-sighted to the defects of the whole
world, seemed happily blind to those of her lover; and,
when even Mary's spirits were almost exhausted by his
noisy rattle, Lady Emily, charmed and exhilarated,
entered into all his practical jokes and boyish frolics,
with the greatest delight.

She soon perceived what was passing in Mary's
mind.

" I see perfectly well what you think of my *penchant*
for Edward," said she one day; " I can tell you

exactly what was passing in your thoughts just now. You were thinking how strange, how passing strange it is, that I, who am (false modesty avaunt) certainly cleverer than Edward, should yet be so partial to him, and that my lynx eyes should have failed to discover in him faults, which, with a single glance, I should have detected in others. Now, can't you guess what renders even these very faults so attractive to me?"

"The old story, I suppose?" said Mary. "Love."

"Not at all. Love might blind me to his faults altogether, and then my case would be, indeed, hopeless, were I living in the belief that I was loving a piece of perfection—a sort of Apollo Belvidere in mind, as well as in person. Now, so far from that, I could reckon you up a whole catalogue of his faults; and nevertheless, I love him with my whole heart, faults and all. In the first place, they are the faults with which I have been familiar from infancy; and therefore they possess a charm (to my shame be it said!) greater than other people's virtues would have to me. They come over my fancy like some snatch of an old nursery song, which one loves to hear in defiance of taste and reason, merely because it is something that carries us back to those days which, whatever they were in reality, always look bright and sunny in retrospection. 'Thus,' (as your favourite Wordsworth says) 'from my first dawn of childhood, didst thou intertwine for me the passions that build up a human soul.' In the second place, his faults are real, genuine, natural faults; and, in this age of affectation, how refreshing it is to meet with even a natural fault! I grant you, Edward talks absurdly, and asks questions, *à faire dresser les cheveux*, of a Mrs Bluemits. But that amuses me; for his ignorance is not the ignorance of vulgarity or stupidity, but the ignorance of a light head and a merry heart—of one, in short, whose understanding has been at sea when other people's were at school. His *bon mots* certainly would not do to be printed; but then they make me laugh a great deal more than if they were better, for he is always *naif* and original, and I prefer an indifferent original any day to a good copy. How it shocks me to hear people recommending to their children to copy such a person's manners! A copied manner, how insupportable! The servile imitator of a set pattern, how despicable! No! I would rather have Edward in all the freshness of his own faults, than in the faded semblance of another person's proprieties."

Mary agreed to the truth of her cousin's observations in some respects, though she could not help thinking, that love had as much to say in her case as in most others; for if it did not blind her to her lover's faults, it certainly made her much more tolerant of them.

Edward was, in truth, at times, almost provokingly boyish and unthinking, and possessed a flow of animal spirits as inexhaustible as they were sometimes overpowering; but she flattered herself time would subdue them to a more rational tone: and she longed for his having the advantages of Colonel Lennox's society—not by way of pattern, as Lady Emily expressed it, but that he might be gradually led to something of more refinement, from holding intercourse with a superior mind. And she obtained her wish sooner than she had dared to hope for it. That battle was fought which decided the fate of Europe, and turned so many swords into plough-shares; and Mary seemed now touching the pinnacle of happiness, when she saw her lover restored to her. He had gained additional renown in the bloody field of Waterloo; and, more fortunate than others, his military career had terminated both gloriously and happily.

If Mary had ever distrusted the reality of his affection, all her doubts were now at an end. She saw she was beloved with all the truth and ardour of a noble ingenuous mind, too upright to deceive others, too enlightened to deceive itself. All reserve between them was now at an end; and, secure in mutual affection, nothing seemed to oppose itself to their happiness.

Colonel Lennox's fortune was small; but, such as it was, it seemed sufficient for all the purposes of rational enjoyment. Both were aware that wealth is a relative thing, and that the positively rich are not those who have the largest possessions, but those who have the fewest vain or selfish desires to gratify. From these they were happily exempt. Both possessed too many resources in their own minds to require the stimulus of spending money to rouse them into enjoyment, or give them additional importance in the eyes of the world: and, above all, both were too thoroughly Christian in their principles, to murmur at any sacrifices or privations they might have to endure in the course of their earthly pilgrimage.

But Lady Juliana's weak worldly mind saw things in a very different light; and when Colonel Lennox, as a matter of form, applied to her for her consent to their union, he received a positive and angry refusal. She declared she never would consent to any daughter of hers making so foolish, so very unsuitable a marriage. And then sending for Mary, she charged her, in the most peremptory manner, to break off all intercourse with Colonel Lennox.

Poor Mary was overwhelmed with grief and amazement at this new display of her mother's tyranny and injustice, and used all the powers of reasoning and entreaty to alter her sentiments; but in vain. Since Adelaide's elopement, Lady Juliana had been much in want of some subject to occupy her mind—something to excite a sensation, and give her something to complain of and talk about, and put her in a bustle, and make her angry, and alarmed, and ill-used, and, in short, all the things which a fool is fond of being.

Although Mary had little hopes of being able to prevail by any efforts of reason, she yet tried to make her mother comprehend the nature of her engagement with Colonel Lennox as of a sacred nature, and too binding ever to be dissolved. But Lady Juliana's wrath blazed forth with redoubled violence at the very mention of an engagement. She had never heard of anything so improper. Colonel Lennox must be a most unprincipled man to lead her daughter into an engagement unsanctioned by her; and she had acted in the most improper manner in allowing herself to form an attachment without the consent of those who had the best title to dispose of her. The person who could act thus was not fit to be trusted, and in future it would be necessary for her to have her constantly under her own eye.

Mary found her candour had therefore only reduced her to the alternative of either openly rebelling, or of submitting to be talked at, and watched, and guarded, as if she had been detected in carrying on some improper clandestine intercourse. But she submitted to all the restrictions that were imposed, and the torments that were inflicted, if not with the heroism of a martyr, at least with the meekness of one; for no murmur escaped her lips. She was only anxious to conceal from others the extent of her mother's folly and injustice, and took every opportunity of entreating Colonel Lennox's silence and forbearance. It required, indeed, all her influence, to induce him to submit patiently to the treatment he experienced. Lady Juliana had so often repeated to Mary that it was the greatest presumption in Colonel Lennox to aspire to a daughter of hers, that she had fairly talked herself into the belief that he was all she asserted him to be—a man of neither birth nor fortune—certainly a Scotsman, from his name—consequently having thousands of poor cousins, and vulgar relations of every description. And she was determined that no daughter of hers should ever marry a man whose family connections she knew nothing about. She had suffered a great deal too much from her (Mary's) father's low relations, ever to run the risk of anything of the same kind happening again. In short, she at length made it out clearly to her own satisfaction, that Colonel Lennox was scarcely a gentleman ; and she therefore considered it as her duty to treat him, on every occasion, with the most marked rudeness. Colonel Lennox pitied her folly too much to be hurt by her ill-breeding and malevolence ; but he could scarcely reconcile it to his notions of duty, that Mary's superior mind should submit to the thraldom of one who evidently knew not good from evil.

Lady Emily was so much engrossed by her own affairs, that for some time all this went on unnoticed by her. At length, she was struck with Mary's dejection, and observed that Colonel Lennox seemed also dispirited ; but, imputing it to a lover's quarrel, she laughingly taxed them with it. Although Mary could suppress the cause of her uneasiness, she was too ingenuous to deny it ; and, being pressed by her cousin, she at length disclosed to her the cause of her sorrow.

"Colonel Lennox and you have behaved like two fools," said she, at the end of her cousin's communication. "What could possibly instigate you to so absurd an act as that of asking Lady Juliana's consent ? You surely might have known, that the person who is never consulted about anything, will invariably start difficulties to everything ; and that people, who are never accustomed to be even listened to, get quite unmanageable when appealed to.   Lady Juliana gave an immediate assent to Lord Glenallan's proposals, because she was the first person consulted about them ; and, besides, she had a sort of an instinctive knowledge that it would create a sensation, and make her of consequence.   In short, she was to act in a sort of triple capacity, as parent, lover, and bride.   Here, on the contrary, she was aware that her consent would stand as a mere cypher, and, once given, would never be more heard of.   Liberty of opinion is a latitude many people quite lose themselves in.   When once they attempt to think, it makes confusion worse confounded ; so it is much better to take that labour off their hands, and settle the matter for them.   It would have been quite time enough to have asked Lady Juliana's consent after the thing was over, or, at any rate, the minute before it was to take place.   I would not even have allowed her time for a flood of tears, or a fit of hysterics.   And now, that your duty has brought you to this, even my genius is at a loss how to extricate you.   Gretna Green might have been advisable, and that would have accorded with your notions of duty ; that would have been following your mamma's own footsteps ; but it is become too vulgar an exploit.   I read of a hatter's apprentice having carried off a grocer's heiress t'other day—What do you purpose doing yourself ? "

" To try the effect of patience and submission," said Mary, " rather than openly set at defiance one of the most sacred duties—the obedience of a child to a parent.   Besides, I could not possibly be happy were I to marry under such circumstances."

" You have much too nice a conscience," said Lady Emily, " and yet I could scarcely wish you otherwise than you are.   What an angel you are, to behave as

you do to such a mother, with such sweetness, and
gentleness, and even respect! Ah! they know little
of human nature who think that, to perform great
actions, one must necessarily be a great character. So
far from that, I now see there may be much more real
greatness of mind displayed in the quiet tenor of a
woman's life, than in the most brilliant exploits that
ever were performed by man. Methinks, I myself
could help to storm a city; but to rule my own spirit
is a task beyond me. What a pity it is you and I
cannot change places! Here am I, languishing for a
little opposition to my love. My marriage will be
quite an insipid, every-day affair. I yawn already to
think of it! Can anything be more disheartening to a
young couple, anxious to signalise their attachment in
the face of the whole world, than to be allowed to take
their own way? Conceive my vexation at being told
by papa this morning, that he had not the least objection to Edward and me marrying whenever we pleased,
although he thought we might both have done better;
but that was our own affair—not his: that he thought
Edward a fine good-humoured fellow—excessively
amusing — hoped he would get a ship some day,
although he had no interest whatever in the Admiralty
—was sorry he could not give us any money, but hoped
we should remain at Beech Park as long as we liked.
I really feel quite flat with all those dull affirmations."

"What! you had rather have been locked up in a
tower, wringing your hands at the height of the windows,
the thickness of the walls, and so forth?" said Mary.

"No; I should never have done anything so like a
washerwoman as to wring my hands, though I might,
like some heroines, have fallen to work in a regular
blacksmith way, by examining the lock of the door, and,
perhaps, have succeeded in picking it; but, alas! I live
in degenerate days. Oh! that I had been born the

persecuted daughter of some ancient baron bold, instead of the spoiled child of a good-natured modern earl!—Heavens! to think that I must tamely, abjectly submit to be married in the presence of all my family, even in the very parish-church! Oh! what detractions from the brilliancy of my star!"

In spite of her levity, Lady Emily was seriously interested in her cousin's affairs, and tried every means of obtaining Lady Juliana's consent; but Lady Juliana was become more unmanageable than ever. Her temper, always bad, was now soured by chagrin and disappointment into something, if possible, still worse, and Lady Emily's authority had no longer any control over her; even the threat of producing aunt Grizzy to a brilliant assembly had now lost its effect. Dr Redgill was the only auxiliary she possessed in the family, and he most cordially joined her in condemning Miss Mary's obstinacy and infatuation. What could she see in a man with such an insignificant bit of property, a mere nest for blackbirds and linnets and such sort of vermin? —not a morsel of any sort of game on his grounds; while at Glenallan, he had been credibly informed, such was the abundance, that the deer had been seen stalking, and the blackcock flying, past the very door! But the doctor's indignation was suddenly suspended by a fit of apoplexy, from which, however, he rallied, and passed it off for the present as a sort of vertigo, in consequence of the shock he had received at hearing of Miss Mary's misconduct.

At length, even Colonel Lennox's forbearance was exhausted, and Mary's health and spirits were sinking beneath the conflict she had to maintain, when a sudden revolution in Lady Juliana's plans caused also a revolution in her sentiments. This was occasioned by a letter from Adelaide, now Lady Lindore. It was evidently written under the influence of melancholy and discontent; and, as Lady Emily said, nothing could be a stronger proof of poor Adelaide's wretchedness than her expressing a wish that her mother should join her in the south of France, where she was going on account of her health.

Adelaide was, indeeed, one of the many melancholy proofs of the effects of headstrong passions and perverted principles. Lord Lindore had married her from a point of honour; and although he possessed too much refinement to treat her ill, yet his indifference was not the less cutting to a spirit haughty as hers. Like many others, she had vainly imagined, that, in renouncing virtue itself for the man she loved, she was for ever insuring his boundless gratitude and adoration; and she only awoke from her delusive dream to find herself friendless in a foreign land—an outcast from society—an object of indifference, even to him for whom she had abandoned all.

But Lady Juliana would see nothing of all this: she was charmed at what she termed this proof of her daughter's affection in wishing to have her with her, and the prospect of going abroad seemed like a vision of paradise to her. Instant preparations were made for her departure, and, in the bustle attendant on them, Mary and her affairs sunk into utter insignificance. Indeed, she seemed rather anxious to get her disposed of in any way that might prevent her interfering with her own plans; and a consent to her marriage, such as it was, was easily obtained.

"Marry whom you please," said she; "only remember I am not responsible for the consequences. I have always told you what a wretched thing a love-marriage is, therefore you are not to blame me for your future misery."

Mary readily subscribed to the conditions; but, as she embraced her mother at parting, she timidly whis-

pered a hope that she would ever consider her house as
her home.   A smile of contempt was the only reply
she received, and they parted never more to meet.
Lady Juliana found foreign manners and principles too
congenial to her taste ever to return to Britain.

———o———

Chapter lrriij.

O most gentle Jupiter! what tedious homily of love have
you wearied your parishioners withal, and never cried, *Have
patience, good people!—As You Like It.*

THE only obstacle to her union thus removed,
Mary thought she might now venture to let her
aunt Grizzy into the secret; and accordingly,
with some little embarrassment, she made the disclosure
of the mutual attachment subsisting between Colonel
Lennox and herself.   Grizzy received the communication with all the astonishment which ladies usually
experience upon being made acquainted with a marriage
which they had not the prescience to foresee and foretell
—or even one which they had; for, common and
natural as the event seems to be, it is one which, perhaps, in no instance, ever took place without occasioning
the greatest amazement to some one individual or
another; and it will also be generally found, that either
the good or the bad fortune of one or other of the
parties is the subject of universal wonder.   In short,
a marriage which excites no surprise, pity, or indignation, must be something that has never yet been
witnessed on the face of this round world.   It is
greatly to be feared none of my readers will sympathise
in the feelings of the good spinster on this occasion, as
she poured them forth in the following *extempore* or
improvisatorial strain :—

" Well, Mary, I declare I am perfectly confounded
with all you have been telling me! I'm sure I never
heard the like of it! It seems but t'other day since
you began your sampler; and it looks just like yesterday since your father and mother were married. And
such a work as there was at your nursing! I'm sure
your poor grandfather was out of all patience about it.
And now to think that you are going to be married!
not but what it's a thing we all expected, for there's
no doubt England's the place for young women to get
husbands—we always said that, you know; not but
what I dare say you might have been married if you
had staid in the Highlands, and to a real Highlander,
too, which, of course, would have been still better for
us all; for it will be a sad thing if you are obliged to
stay in England, Mary; but I hope there's no chance
of that: you know Colonel Lennox can easily sell his
place, and buy an estate in the Highlands. There's a
charming property, I know, to be sold just now, that
marches with Glenfern. To be sure it's on the wrong
side of the hill—there's no denying that; but then,
there's I can't tell you how many thousand acres of
fine muir for shooting, and I dare say Colonel Lennox
is a keen sportsman; and they say a great deal of it
might be very much improved. We must really inquire
after it, Mary, and you must speak to Colonel Lennox
about it, for you know such a property as that may be
snapped up in a minute."

Mary assented to all that was said, and Grizzy proceeded,—

"I wonder you never brought Colonel Lennox to
see us, Mary: I'm sure he must think it very odd.
To be sure, Sir Sampson's situation is some excuse;
but, at any rate, I wonder you never spoke about him.
We all found out your aunt Bella's attachment from
the very first, just from her constantly speaking about

Major M'Tavish and the militia; and we had a good
guess of Betsy's too, from the day her face turned so
red after giving Captain M'Nab for her toast; but you
have really kept yours very close, for, I declare, I never
once suspected such a thing. I wonder if that was
Colonel Lennox that I saw you part with at the door
one day; tall, and with brown hair and a blue coat. I
asked Lady Maclaughlan if she knew who it was, and
she said it was Admiral Benbow; but I think she must
have been mistaken, for I dare say, now, it was just
Colonel Lennox. Lennox—I'm sure I should be able
to remember something about somebody of that name;
but my memory's not so good as it used to be, for I
have so many things, you know, to think about, with
Sir Sampson, that, I declare, sometimes my head is
quite confused; yet I think always there's something
about them. I wish to goodness Lady Maclaughlan
was come from the dentist's, that I might consult her
about it; for, of course, Mary, you'll do nothing without consulting all your friends: I know you've too
much sense for that. And here's Sir Sampson coming;
it will be a fine piece of news to tell him."

Sir Sampson having now been wheeled in by the
still active Philistine, and properly arranged, with the
assistance of Miss Grizzy, she took her usual station
by the side of his easy-chair, and began to shout into
his ear—

"Here's my niece Mary, Sir Sampson! you remember her when she was little, I dare say?—you
know, you used to call her the fairy of Lochmarlie;
and I'm sure we all thought for long she would have
been a perfect fairy, she was so little; but she's tall
enough now, you see, and she's going to be married to
a fine young man—none of us know him yet, but I
think I must have seen him; and, at any rate, I'm to
see him to-morrow, and you'll see him too, Sir Samp-

son, for Mary is to bring him to call here, and he'll
tell you all about the battle of Waterloo and the Highlanders; for he's half a Highlander too; and I'm certain
he'll buy the Dhuanbog estate; and then when my niece
Mary marries Colonel Lennox "——

"Lennox!" repeated Sir Sampson, his little dim
eyes kindling at the name—"Who talks of Lennox?
—I—I won't suffer it.—Where's my lady?—Lennox!
—he's a scoundrel!—you shan't marry a Lennox!"—
Turning to Grizzy, "Call Murdoch and my lady!"
And his agitation was so great, that even Grizzy,
although accustomed for forty years to witness similiar
ebullitions, became alarmed.

"You see it's all for fear of my marrying," whispered she to Mary: "I'm sure such a disinterested
attachment, it's impossible for me ever to repay it!"

Then turning to Sir Sampson, she sought to soothe
his perturbation by oft-repeated assurances that it was
not her, but her niece Mary, that was going to be
married to Colonel Lennox: but in vain. Sir Sampson quivered, and panted, and muttered; and the louder
Grizzy screamed out the truth, the more his irritation
increased. Recourse was now had to Murdoch; and
Mary, thoroughly ashamed of the *éclat* attending the
disclosure of her secret, and finding she could be of no
use, stole away in the midst of Miss Grizzy's endless
verbiage; but, as she descended the stairs, she still
heard the same assurance resounding—"I can assure
you, Sir Sampson, it's not me, but my niece Mary
that's going to be married to Colonel Lennox," &c.

On returning to Beech Park, she said nothing of
what had passed either to Lady Emily or Colonel
Lennox—aware of the amusement it would furnish to
both; and she felt that her aunt required all the dignity
with which she could invest her, before presenting her
to her future nephew. The only delay to her marriage

now rested with herself; but she was desirous it should take place under the roof which had sheltered her infancy, and sanctioned by the presence of those whom she had ever regarded as her parents. Lady Emily, Colonel Lennox, and her brother, had all endeavoured to combat this resolution, but in vain; and it was therefore settled, that she should remain to witness the union of her brother and her cousin, and then return to Lochmarlie. But all Mary's preconceived plans were threatened with a downfall, by the receipt of the following letter from Miss Jacky:—

" *Glenfern Castle*, ——*shire*,
June 19. 18—.

" It *is* impossible for *language* to express to *you* the *shame*, grief, amazement, and *indignation*, with *which* we are *all* filled at the distressing, the *ignominious* disclosure that has *just* taken *place* concerning you, *through* our most *excellent* friend Miss P. M'Pry. Oh, Mary, *how* have you *deceived* us all ! ! ! What a *dagger* have *you* plunged into *all* our hearts ! Your *poor* aunt *Grizzy !* how my *heart* bleeds *for* her ! What a difficult part *has* she to act ! and at her *time* of life ! with her acute *feelings !* with her devoted *attachment* to the *house* of Maclaughlan ! What a *blow !* and a *blow* from your *hand !* Oh, Mary, I *must* again repeat, how *have* you deceived us *all ! ! !* Yet *do* not imagine I mean to *reproach* you ! Much, much of the blame is *doubtless* imputable to the errors of *your* education ! At the *same* time, even these *offer* no justification of your *conduct* upon the present occasion ! You are now (I lament to say it) *come* to that time of *life* when *you* ought to know *what* is right ; or, where you entertain *any* doubts, you ought *most* unquestionably to *apply* to those *who*, you *may* be certain, *are* well qualified to direct you. *But*, instead *of* that, you have *pursued* a diametrically opposite *plan:* a plan which *might* have *ended* in your destruction! Oh, Mary, *I* cannot too *often* repeat, how have *you* deceived us all!!! From no *lips* but those of Miss M'Pry *would* I have believed *what* I have heard, videlicet, that you (oh, Mary!) have, for many, many months *past*, been carrying on a clandestine *correspondence* with a *young* man, unknown, unsuspected by *all* your friends here! and that *young* man, the very *last* man on the face of the *earth* whom you, or any of *us*, ought to have given our countenance *to!* The very man, in *short*, whom we were all *bound*, by every *principle* of duty, gratitude, and esteem, to have shunned, and who you are *bound*, from this *moment*, to renounce for ever. How you ever *came* to be acquainted *with* Colonel Charles Lennox of Rose Hall, is a mystery none of us can fathom; but surely the person, *whoever* it was that *brought* it about, has much, *much* to answer for! Mrs Douglas (to whom I *thought* it proper to *make* an immediate *communication* on the subject) pretends to *have* been well-informed of all that has *been* going on, and even insists that *your* acquaintance *with* the Lennox family *took* place through Lady Maclaughlan! *But* that we *all* know to be *morally* impossible. Lady Maclaughlan is the *very* last person in the *world* who would have *introduced* you, or any *young* creature for whom she had the *slightest* regard, to a Lennox, the *mortal enemy of the Maclaughlan race!* I most *sincerely* trust she is spared the *shock* we have all experienced at this painful *disclosure.* With her *high* principles, and *great* regard for us, I tremble to think *what* might be the consequences! And dear Sir Sampson, in his delicate state, how *would* he ever be able to *stand* such a blow! and a blow, too, from your *hand*, Mary! you, who he *was* always *like* a father to! *Many* a time, I am sure, *have* you sat upon his *knee;* and you certainly *cannot* have forgot the *elegant* Shetland pony he presented you *with* the day you was five *years* old ! and *what* a return for such favours !

" But I fondly trust it *is* not yet too late. You have *only* to give up this unworthy attachment, and all *will* be forgotten and *forgiven ;* and we will all receive you as if *nothing* had happened. Oh, Mary ! I must, for the last *time*, repeat, how have you deceived us *all ! !*

" I am your *distressed* aunt,   JOAN DOUGLAS.

" P.S.—I conclude abruptly, in *order* to leave *room* for your aunt Nicky to *state* her sentiments also on this *most* afflicting subject."

Nicky's appendix was as follows :—

" DEAR MARY,

" Jacky has read her letter to us. It is most excellent. We are all much affected by it. Not a word but deserves to be printed. I can add nothing. You see, if you marry Colonel L. none of us can be at your marriage. How could we ? I hope you will think twice about it. Second thoughts are best. What's done cannot be undone.

" Yours,   N. D."

Mary felt somewhat in the situation of the sleeper awakened, as she perused these mysterious anathemas ; and rubbed her eyes more than once, in hopes of dispelling the mist that she thought must needs be upon them. But in vain : it seemed only to increase with every effort she made to remove it. Not a single ray of light fell on the palpable obscure of Miss Jacky's composition, that could enable her to penetrate the dark profound that encompassed her. She was aware, indeed, that when her aunt meant to be pathetic or

energetic, she always had recourse to the longest and
the strongest words she could possibly lay her hands
upon ; and Mary had been well accustomed to hear her
childish faults and juvenile indiscretions denounced, in
the most awful terms, as crimes of the deepest dye.
Many an exordium she had listened to, on the tearing
of her frock, or the losing of her glove, that might
have served as a preface to the Newgate Calendar,
Colquhoun on the Police, or any other register of
crimes. Still she had always been able to detect some
clew to her own misdeeds ; but here even conjecture
was baffled, and in vain she sought for some resting-
place for her imagination, in the probable misdemeanour
of her lover. But, even allowing all possible latitude
for Jacky's pen, she was forced to acknowledge there
must be some ground for her aunt to build upon.
Superficial as her structures generally were, like children's card-houses, they had always something to rest
upon ; though (unlike them) her creations were invariably upon a gigantic scale.

Mary had often reflected with surprise, that, although
Lady Maclaughlan had been the person to introduce
her to Mrs Lennox, no intercourse had taken place
between the families themselves ; and when she had
mentioned them to each other, Mrs Lennox had only
sighed, and Lady Maclaughlan had humphed. She
despaired of arriving at the knowledge of the truth
from her aunts. Grizzy's brain was a mere wisp of
contradictions ; and Jacky's mind was of that violent
hue that cast its own shade upon every object that came
in contact with it. To mention the matter to Colonel
Lennox was only to make her relations ridiculous ;
and, in short, although it was a formidable step, the
result of her deliberation was to go to Lady Maclaughlan, and request a solution of her aunt's dark
sayings. She therefore departed for Milsom Street,

and, upon entering the drawing-room, found Grizzy
alone, and evidently in even more than usual perturbation.

"Oh, Mary!" cried she, as her niece entered,
"I'm sure, I'm thankful you're come. I was just
wishing for you. You can't think how much mischief your yesterday's visit has done. It's a thousand
pities, I declare, that ever you said a word about your
marriage to Sir Sampson. But, of course, I don't
mean to blame you, Mary. You know you couldn't
help it; so don't vex yourself, for you know that will
not make the thing any better now. Only if Sir
Sampson should die—to be sure I must always think
it was you that killed him; and I'm sure that will soon
kill me too—such a friend—Oh, Mary!" Here a
burst of grief choked poor Miss Grizzy's utterance.

"My dear aunt," said Mary, "you certainly must
be mistaken. Sir Sampson seems to retain no recollection of me. It is therefore impossible that I could
cause him any pain or agitation."

"Oh, certainly!" said Grizzy. "There's no
doubt Sir Sampson has quite forgot you, Mary—and
no wonder—with your being so long away; but I dare
say he'll come to know you yet. But I'm sure, I hope
to goodness he'll never know you as Mrs Lennox,
Mary. That would break his heart altogether; for
you know the Lennoxes have always been the greatest
enemies of the Maclaughlans,—and, of course, Sir
Sampson can't bear anybody of the name, which is
quite natural. And it was very thoughtless in me to
have forgot that, till Philistine put me in mind of it,
and poor Sir Sampson has had a very bad night; so
I'm sure, I hope, Mary, you'll never think any more
about Colonel Lennox: and, take my word for it,
you'll get plenty of husbands yet. Now, since there's
a peace, there will be plenty of fine young officers

coming home. There's young Balquhadan, a captain, I know, in some regiment; and there's Dhalahulish, and Lochgrunason, and "——— But Miss Grizzy's ideas here shot out into so many ramifications upon the different branches of the county tree, that it would be in vain for any but a true Celt to attempt to follow her.

Mary again tried to lead her back to the subject of the Lennoxes, in hopes of being able to extract some spark of knowledge from the dark chaos of her brain.

" Oh, I'm sure, Mary, if you want to hear about that, I can tell you plenty about the Lennoxes, or, at any rate, about the Maclaughlans, which is the same thing. But I must first find my huswife."

To save Miss Grizzy's reminiscences, a few words will suffice to clear up the mystery. A family feud, of remote origin, had long subsisted between the families of Lennox and Maclaughlan, which had been carefully transmitted from father to son, till the hereditary brand had been deposited in the breast of Sir Sampson. By the death of many intervening heirs, General Lennox, then a youth, was next in succession to the Maclaughlan estates; but the power of alienating it was vested in Sir Sampson, as the last remaining heir of the entail. By the mistaken zeal of their friends, both were, at an early period, placed in the same regiment, in the hope that constant association together would quickly destroy their mutual prejudices, and produce a reconciliation. But the inequalities were too great ever to assimilate. Sir Sampson possessed a large fortune, a deformed person, and a weak, vain, irritable mind. General (then Ensign) Lennox had no other patrimony than his sword, a handsome person, high spirit, and dauntless courage. With these tempers, it may easily be conceived that a thousand trifling events occurred to keep alive the hereditary animosity.

Sir Sampson's vain narrow mind expected from his
poor kinsman a degree of deference and respect which
the other, so far from rendering, rather sought oppor-
tunities of showing his contempt for, and of thwarting
and ridiculing him upon every occasion, till Sir Sampson
was obliged to quit the regiment. From that time it
was understood, that all bearing the name of Lennox
were for ever excluded from the succession to the
Maclaughlan estates; and it was deemed a sort of
petty treason even to name the name of a Lennox
in presence of this dignified chieftain.

Many years had worn away, and Sir Sampson had
passed through the various modifications of human
nature, from the "mewling infant" to "mere
oblivion," without having become either wiser or
better. His mind remained the same—irascible and
vindictive to the last. Lady Maclaughlan had too
much sense to attempt to reason or argue him out of
his prejudices, but she contrived to prevent him from
ever executing a new entail. She had known and
esteemed both General and Mrs Lennox before her
marriage with Sir Sampson, and she was too firm aud
decided in her predilections ever to abandon them;
and, while she had the credit of sharing in all her
husband's animosity, she was silently protecting the
lawful rights of those who had long ceased to consider
them as such. General Lennox had always understood that he and his family were under Sir Sampson's
ban, and he possessed too high a spirit ever to express
a regret, or even allude to the circumstances. It
had, therefore, made a very faint impression on the
minds of any of his family; and, in the long lapse of
years, had been almost forgot by Mrs Lennox, till
recalled by Lady Maclaughlan's letter. But she had
been silent on the subject to Mary, for she could not
conceal from herself that her husband had been to

blame—that the heat and violence of his temper had
often led him to provoke and exasperate, where mild-
ness and forbearance would have soothed and conciliated
without detracting from his dignity ; but her gentle
heart shrank from the task of unnecessarily disclosing
the faults of the man she had loved ; and when she
heard Mary talk with rapture of the wild beauties of
Lochmarlie, she had only sighed to think that the
pride and prejudice of others had alienated the inheritance of her son.

But all this Mary was still in ignorance of, for Miss
Grizzy had gone completely astray in the attempt to
trace the rise and progress of the Lennox and Maclaughlan feud. Happily, Lady Maclaughlan's entrance
extricated her from her labyrinth, as it was the signal
for her to repair to Sir Sampson. Mary, in some little
confusion was beginning to express to her ladyship her
regret at hearing that Sir Sampson had been so unwell,
when she was stopped—

" My dear child, don't learn to tell lies. You don't
care twopence for Sir Sampson. I know all. You are
going to be married to Charles Lennox—I am glad of
it—I wished you to marry him. Whether you'll
thank me for that twenty years hence, *I* can't tell—*you*
can't tell—*he* can't tell—God knows—humph ! Your
aunts will tell you he is Beelzebub, because his father
said he could make a Sir Sampson out of a mouldy
lemon. Perhaps he could. I don't know—but your
aunts are fools. You know what fools are, and so do
I.   There are plenty of fools in the world ; but if
they had not been sent for some wise purpose, they
wouldn't have been here ; and since they are here, they
have as good a right to have elbow-room in the world
as the wisest. Sir Sampson hated General Lennox
because he laughed at him ; and if Sir Sampson had
lived a hundred years ago, his hatred might have been

a fine thing to talk about now.   It is the same passion that makes heroes of your De Montforts, and your Manuels, and your Corsairs, and all the rest of them ; but *they* wore cloaks and daggers, and these are the supporters of hatred.   Everybody laughs at the hatred of a little old man in a cocked hat.   You may laugh too.   So now, God bless you !   Continue as you are, and marry the man you like, though the world should set its teeth against you.   'Tis not every woman can be trusted to do that—Farewell ! "   And with a cordial salute they parted.

Mary was too well accustomed to Lady Maclaughlan's style, not to comprehend that her marriage with Colonel Lennox was an event she had long wished for, and now most warmly sanctioned ; and she hastened home to convey the glad tidings in a letter to her aunts, though doubtful if the truth itself would be able to pierce its way through their prejudices.

Another stroke of palsy soon rendered Sir Sampson unconscious even to the charms of Miss Grizzy's conversation ; and as she was no longer of use to him, and was evidently at a loss how to employ herself, Mary proposed that she should accompany her back to Lochmarlie, to which she yielded a joyful assent.   Once convinced of Lady Maclaughlan's approbation of her niece's marriage, she could think and talk of nothing else.

Some wise individuals have thought, that most people act from the inspiration of either a good or an evil power : to which class Miss Grizzy belonged, would have puzzled the most profound metaphysician to determine.   She was, in fact, a Maclaughlanite ; but to find the *root* of Maclaughlan is another difficulty —thought is lost.

Colonel Lennox, although a little startled at his first introduction to his future aunt, soon came to understand the *naïveté* of her character ; and his enlarged mind, and good temper, made such ample allowance for her weaknesses, that she protested, with tears in her eyes, she never knew the like of him—she never could think enough of him. She wished to goodness Sir Sampson was himself again, and could only see him, she was sure he would think just as she did, &c. &c. &c.

The day of Lady Emily's marriage arrived, and found her in a more serious mood than she had hitherto appeared in, though it seemed doubtful whether it was most occasioned by her own prospects, or the thoughts of parting with Mary, who, with aunt Grizzy, was to set off for Lochmarlie immediately after witnessing the ceremony. Edward and his bride would fain have followed; but Lord Courtland was too much accustomed to his daughter, and amused by his nephew, to bear so long an absence, and they therefore yielded the point, though with reluctance.

"This is all for want of a little opposition to have braced my nerves," said Lady Emily, as she dropped a few tears. "I verily believe I should have wept outright, had I not happily descried Dr Redgill shrugging his shoulders at me; that has given a fillip to my spirits. After all, 'tis perhaps a foolish action I've committed. The icy bonds of matrimony are upon me already: I feel myself turning into a fond, faithful, rational, humble, meek-spirited wife! Alas! I must now turn my head into a museum, and hang up all my smart sayings inside my brain, there to petrify, as warnings to all pert misses. Dear Mary! if ever I am good for anything, as I trust I shall yet be, it will be to you I owe it!"

"My dear sister!" said Mary, as she tenderly embraced her, "I feel assured that one day we shall be united in faith as we now are in love."

Lady Emily was too much affected to reply; but again she pressed Mary to her heart, then gave her hand to Colonel Lennox, who led her to the carriage, and she and her gay merry-hearted bridegroom were soon whirled out of sight. Mary and her aunt next took their departure, but in a different direction; to be followed in a few days by Colonel Lennox.

"Good bye, Mary," said Lord Courtland, as he pressed the tips of her fingers. "You are going to follow Emily's example, I hear?"

"I wish you a pleasant journey, Miss Mary," cried Redgill. "The game season is coming on, and "—— But the carriage drove off, and the rest of the sentence was dispersed by the wind; and all that could be collected was, "grouse always acceptable—friends at a distance—roe-buck stuffed with heather carries well at all times," &c. &c.

To one less practised in her ways, and less gifted with patience, the eternal babbling of aunt Grizzy, as a travelling companion, would have occasioned considerable *ennui*, if not spleen. There are, perhaps, few greater trials of temper, than that of travelling with a person who thinks it necessary to be *actively pleasant*, without a moment's intermission, from the rising till the setting sun. Grizzy was upon this fatal plan, the rock of thousands! Silence she thought synonymous with low spirits, and she talked, and wondered, and exclaimed incessantly, and assured Mary she need not be uneasy, she was certain Colonel Lennox would follow very soon; she had not the least doubt of that. She would not be surprised if he was to be at Lochmarlie almost as soon as themselves; at any rate, very soon after them.

But even these little torments were forgot by Mary when she found herself again in her native land. The hills, the air, the waters, the people, even the *peat-stacks*, had a charm that touched her heart, and brought tears into her eyes as they pictured home, and her heart responded to the well-known lines,——

> " Land of brown heath and shaggy wood !
> Land of the mountain and the flood !
> Land of my sires ! what mortal hand
> Can e'er untie the filial band
> That knits me to thy rugged strand ? "

But her feelings arose to rapture when Lochmarlie burst upon her view, in all the grandeur, beauty, and repose of a setting sun, shedding its farewell rays of gold and purple, and tints of such matchless hue as no pencil e'er can imitate—no poet's pen describe. Rocks, woods, hills, and waters, all shone with a radiance that seemed of more than earthly beauty. "Oh! there are moments in life, keen, blissful, never to be forgotten!" and such was the moment to Mary when the carriage stopped, and she again heard the melody of that voice familiar from infancy—and looked on a face known with her being—and was pressed to that heart where glowed a parent's love !

When Mary recovered from the first overflowing transports of joy, she marked with delight the increased animation and cheerfulness visible in Mrs Douglas. All the livelier feelings of her warm heart had, indeed, been excited, and brought into action, by the spirit and playfulness of her little boy, and the increased happiness of her husband ; while all her uneasiness respecting her former lover was now at an end. She had heard from himself that he had married, and was happy. Without being guilty of inconstancy, such are the effects of time upon mutable human nature !

Colonel Lennox lost no time in arriving to claim his promised bride ; and Mary's happiness was complete, when she found her own choice so warmly approved of by the friends she loved.

The three aunts, and their unmarried nieces, now the sole inhabitants of Glenfern Castle, were not quite decided in their opinions at first. Miss Jacky looked with a suspicious eye upon the *mortal enemy of the*

Maclaughlan race ; but, upon better acquaintance, his gaiety and good-humour contrived to charm asleep even her good sense and prejudices, and she pronounced him to be a pleasant, well-informed young man, who gave himself no airs, although he certainly had rather a high look.

Nicky doubted, from his appearance, that he would be nice, and she had no patience with nice men ; but Nicky's fears vanished when she saw, as she expressed it, "how pleasantly he ate the sheep's-head, although he had never seen one in his life before."

The younger ladies thought Captain M'Nab had a finer complexion, and wondered whether Colonel Lennox (like him) would be dressed in full regimentals at his marriage.

But, alas ! " all earthly good still blends itself with harm ; " for on the day of Mary's marriage—a day consecrated to mirth, and bridecake, and wedding favours, and marriage presents, and good cheer, and reels, and revelry, and bagpipes—on that very day, when the marriage ceremony was scarcely over, arrived the accounts of the death of Sir Sampson Maclaughlan ! But, on this joyous day, even Grizzy's tears did not flow so freely as they would have done at another time ; and she declared, that although it was impossible anybody could feel more than she did, yet certainly it would not be using Colonel and Mrs Lennox well, to be very distressed upon such an occasion ; and there was no doubt but she would have plenty of time to be sorry about it yet, when they were all sitting quietly by themselves, with nothing else in their heads ; though, to be sure, they must always think what a blessing it was that Colonel Lennox was to succeed.

" I wish he may ever fill Sir Sampson's shoes ! " said Miss Nicky, with a sigh.

" Colonel Lennox cannot propose a better model to himself than Sir Sampson Maclaughlan," said Miss

Jacky: "he has left him a noble example of propriety, frugality, hospitality, and respectability; and, above all, of forgiveness of his mortal enemies."

"Oh, Mary!" exclaimed Miss Grizzy, as they were about to part with their niece; "what a lucky creature you are! Never, I am sure, did any young person set out in life with such advantages. To think of your succeeding to Lady Maclaughlan's laboratory, all so nicely fitted up with every kind of thing, and especially plenty of the most charming bark, which, I am sure, will do Colonel Lennox the greatest good, as you know all officers are much the better of bark. I know it was the saving of young Ballingall's life, when he came home in an ague from some place; and I'm certain Lady Maclaughlan will leave you every thing that is there, you was always such a favourite. Not but what I must always think that you had a hand in dear Sir Sampson's death,—indeed, I have no doubt of it. Yet, at the same time, I don't mean to blame you in the least; for I'm certain, if Sir Sampson had been spared, he would have been delighted, as we all are, at your marriage."

Colonel and Mrs Lennox agreed in making choice of Lochmarlie for their future residence; and, in a virtuous attachment, they found as much happiness as earth's pilgrims ever possess, whose greatest felicity must spring from a higher source. The extensive influence which generally attends upon virtue joined to prosperity, was used by them for its best purposes. It was not confined either to rich or poor, to caste or sect—but all shared in their benevolence whom that benevolence could benefit. And the poor, the sick, and the desolate united in blessing what Heaven had already blessed—this happy Marriage.

THE END.

The first Virago Modern Classic was published in London in 1978, launching a list dedicated to the celebration of women writers and to the rediscovery and reprinting of their works. While the series is called "Modern Classics" it is not true that these works of fiction are universally and equally considered "great," although that is often the case. Published with new critical and biographical introductions, books appear in the series for different reasons: sometimes for their importance in literary history; sometimes because they illuminate particular aspects of women's lives, both personal and public. They may be classics of comedy or storytelling; their interest can be historical, feminist, political, or literary. In any case, in their variety and richness they promise to confuse forever the question of what women's fiction is about, while at the same time affirming a true female tradition in literature.

Initially, the Virago Modern Classics concentrated on English novels and short stories published in the early decades of the century. As the series has grown, it has broadened to include works of fiction from different centuries and from different countries, cultures, and literary traditions; there are books written by black women, by Catholic and Jewish women, by women of almost every English-speaking country, and there are several relevant novels by men.

Nearly 200 Virago Modern Classics will have been published in England by the end of 1985. During that same year, Penguin Books began to publish Virago Modern Classics in the United States, with the expectation of having some 40 titles from the series available by the end of 1986. Some of the earlier books in the series were published in the United States by The Dial Press.

Other PENGUIN/VIRAGO MODERN CLASSICS

CATHERINE CARSWELL
Open the Door!

MARY CHOLMONDELEY
Red Pottage

DOROTHY EDWARDS
Rhapsody
Winter Sonata

GEORGE ELIOT
The Lifted Veil

M. J. FARRELL
Devoted Ladies
Mad Puppetstown
The Rising Tide
Two Days in Aragon

SUSAN FERRIER
Marriage

MARY AND JANE
FINDLATER
Crossriggs

RADCLYFFE HALL
Adam's Breed

WINIFRED HOLTBY
Poor Caroline

STORM JAMESON
Company Parade
Women Against Men

MARGARET KENNEDY
Troy Chimneys

BETTY MILLER
On the Side of the Angels

KATE O'BRIEN
Mary Lavelle
That Lady

MRS. OLIPHANT
Hester

MOLLIE
PANTER-DOWNES
One Fine Day

VITA SACKVILLE-WEST
No Signposts in the Sea

LAURA TALBOT
The Gentlewomen

ELIZABETH TAYLOR
The Devastating Boys
Palladian
The Wedding Group

E. H. YOUNG
The Curate's Wife
Jenny Wren

MRS. HUMPHRY WARD
Marcella

MARTHA GELLHORN
A Stricken Field

ELSA TRIOLET
A Fine of 200 Francs